VOWS OF THE HEART ARE *NEVER* MEANT TO BE BROKEN...

LOVE...

The minute beautiful but angry Dana Roberts burst into the genteel restaurant, preppy Jason Halloran was hooked—first a left, then a right. But Jason vowed the final bell would toll for two!

HONOR...

Kevin Halloran was stunned! After years of loving, his wife, Lacey Grainger Halloran, left him, claiming they'd grown apart. Pride kept Kevin from chasing after her, until a crisis reminded him that with love went honor.

CHERISH...!

World War II had abruptly come between Brandon Halloran and the girl of his dreams, Elizabeth Forsythe. Could the love of a lifetime be rekindled two separate lifetimes later?

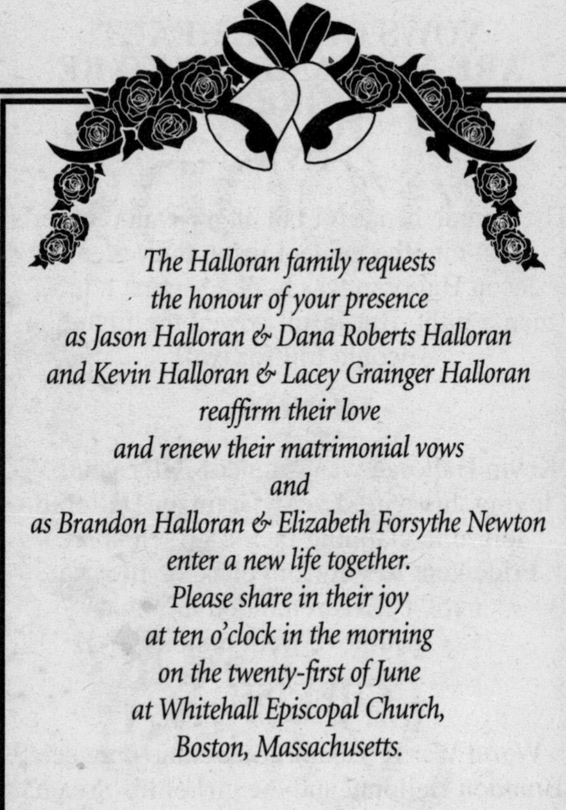

The Halloran family requests
the honour of your presence
as Jason Halloran & Dana Roberts Halloran
and Kevin Halloran & Lacey Grainger Halloran
reaffirm their love
and renew their matrimonial vows
and
as Brandon Halloran & Elizabeth Forsythe Newton
enter a new life together.
Please share in their joy
at ten o'clock in the morning
on the twenty-first of June
at Whitehall Episcopal Church,
Boston, Massachusetts.

SHERRYL WOODS

LOVE, HONOR & CHERISH

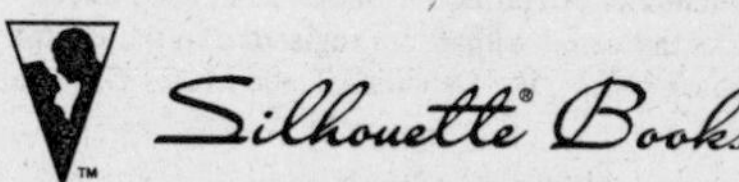

Published by Silhouette Books
America's Publisher of Contemporary Romance

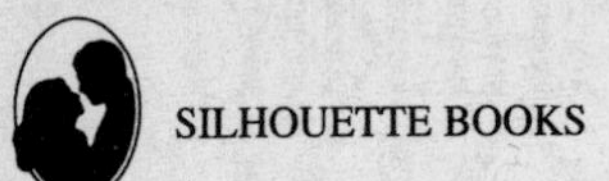

ISBN 0-373-20174-5

by Request

LOVE, HONOR & CHERISH

This edition published by arrangement with Harlequin Books S.A.

Visit Silhouette at www.eHarlequin.com

Printed in U.S.A.

CONTENTS

Dear Reader,

One day while watching a television talk show on which several couples were renewing their wedding vows, I began to think about all the various reasons why two people might choose to do this. To express their love once again in front of friends and family, to strengthen a bond that might have been broken—the possibilities were endless. Out of that came the first three books in the VOWS series.

I chose three generations of men in the same family for this series—the Hallorans of Boston. *Love* is the traditional romance of the youngest Halloran. *Honor* is the story of his parents, whose marriage has faltered, but who find new strength because of the struggles. And finally, in *Cherish* I focus on the grandfather, who after years of a rock-solid marriage, finds himself a widower and sets out in search of the woman he had loved before a war intervened. In that tender and emotional story, he finds far more than he bargained for.

I hope as you read these three favorites of mine that you'll think about the vows in your own life, whether to a mate, a child or a friend, and make your own renewed commitment to love, honor and cherish the people you care about.

With all good wishes,

Sherryl Woods

LOVE

Prologue

Sunlight streamed through the stained-glass windows of Boston's Whitehall Episcopal Church early on the morning of June 21, as three glowing brides walked down the aisle—one of them very pregnant.

Jason Halloran stood next to his father and grandfather in front of the altar and watched the three generations of women come toward them. He was every bit as nervous today as he had been a year ago, when he'd waited alone. Today, however, Jason was worried that his wife might not make it through the renewal of their vows without going into labor. Dana had a habit of bucking tradition.

As she had done on their original wedding day, Dana caught his eye and winked. The unexpected audacity in the midst of the solemn occasion brought an immediate smile to his lips. His wife was as uniquely irreverent as ever, and he was as enchanted with her now as he had been then.

He glanced over at his grandfather and saw that Brandon's normally fierce expression had gentled as he regarded his wife-to-be. Jason knew this day was one his grandfather had dreamed about for close to fifty years. It had been suggested by Brandon and his beloved Elizabeth that all three generations of the Halloran family use the occasion as a chance to give thanks for the blessings of their marriages.

Brandon's voice held steady, but there was a sheen of tears in his eyes as he gazed at Elizabeth Forsythe Newton, whose adoring eyes never once left his.

"I, Brandon, take thee, Elizabeth, a woman I loved and lost and have been blessed to find again, to be my wedded wife. I promise to cherish thee all the rest of my days."

Next the minister turned to Jason's parents. Kevin Halloran looked shaken as he kept his gaze fastened on the lovely, gentle lady who'd been his wife for nearly thirty years. They had met as children, fought for the same causes in the turbulent sixties and loved each other with equal passion and exuberance. Later they'd found themselves changing. Jason knew the road had not been easy for his parents, but they had survived. Today was their chance to tell the world and each other that time and change had not destroyed the foundation of their marriage.

Jason saw his mother's hand tremble before his father enfolded it in his own.

"I, Kevin, take thee, Lacey, a woman who has stood by me through hard times and good, who has provided love and understanding, I take thee again to be my wedded wife. For the blessing of your undying love,

I thank God. For the joy of our family, I thank you. And I promise to honor you and all that you have meant to me all the rest of my days.''

Jason heard the heartfelt commitment in his father's voice and knew that it mirrored his own deep feelings of commitment for his wife. The last year with Dana had been filled with joy and laughter, with unpredictability and unstinting love. She was a woman who had learned in childhood to reach undaunted for the elusive brass ring and to hold on tight. She faced each new day with optimism and determination, and she had given him the same joyous—if occasionally unorthodox—outlook.

When their turn came, Dana handed her bouquet of spring's brightest wildflowers to Jason's mother, then placed her hands in his. Her eyes shimmered with tears, but there was no mistaking the strength of purpose in their sapphire depths. Her generous mouth curved into a smile that radiated warmth.

His voice suddenly choked with emotion, Jason began slowly, ''I, Jason, take thee, Dana, to be my wedded wife all over again.''

He felt the reassuring squeeze of her hands, and his voice steadied. ''I thank you for a wonderful year filled with the unexpected. As we await the birth of our first child, I pray that he or she will be blessed with your imagination and your generous heart and guided by your sense of loyalty and your love of family. And today as all of us reaffirm our vows before God and our friends, I promise to love you and care for you and our children all the rest of our days.''

As he said the special vows he'd labored to put into

words, Jason thought back to that incredible winter day when Dana Roberts had come bursting into his dull, predictable life and changed everything.

Chapter One

Boring. Predictable. Tedious. As he crossed Boston Commons, Jason Halloran ran through an entire list of adjectives describing the way he felt about his so-called charmed life. He might have blamed his mood on the heavy, overcast skies that promised snow by nightfall, but he'd been feeling this way for weeks now. He knew his state of mind was one of the reasons for this lunch today with his grandfather. Brandon Halloran had lost patience. Jason had been ordered to appear at Washington's Tavern at noon on a Saturday for what would no doubt be a stern lecture intended to snap him out of his doldrums. Jason didn't hold out much hope that it would work.

At the corner Jason paced impatiently, waiting for his tall, distinguished grandfather to stride through the weekend throng. The blustery winds cut right through his topcoat made of Halloran Industries' finest cashmere-and-wool blend. Shivering, he glanced at his watch and realized that he was early. Brandon Halloran was a creature of habit. He would not appear until precisely noon and it was now barely 11:30, another indication of the boredom of Jason's days. After picking up the new VCR he'd ordered earlier in the week, Jason had then rushed to get to the one engagement on his calendar that held any promise of challenge.

The VCR weighed a ton and there was no point in freezing to death while he waited, he decided after several more minutes. So he headed for the restaurant. Inside the overheated tavern with its elegant antique mahogany bar, gleaming brass fixtures and private, well-cushioned booths, Jason shrugged out of his overcoat and slid into the booth that was reserved daily for his grandfather's use. A waiter placed a Scotch and water on the table mere seconds later.

"Shall I bring you something more while you wait?" the dour-faced man inquired. He'd looked exactly the same since the first day Jason had come here with his grandfather nearly twenty-two years before. Jason had been six at the time and had been dressed in his best suit in honor of the occasion.

"Another one of these," Jason said, finishing the first drink in two gulps.

"As you wish, sir."

Jason caught the faint sniff of disapproval as the waiter retreated. It would be just like old Giles to feel duty-bound to cut him off. Jason's gaze followed the elderly man as he crossed to the bar, his back ramrod stiff as he placed the order. Once assured that the drink would be forthcoming, Jason surveyed the other occupants of the tavern—the handful of people who'd sought refuge from the cold even though it wasn't quite lunchtime.

The usual stuffy crowd. Even on weekends everyone had an uptight, button-down look about them, he'd decided until his glance fell on the woman at the end of the bar. For the first time in ages he felt a stirring of interest. Among those dressed in Brooks Brothers basic black pinstripe and those sporting academic tweeds, she stood out like a vibrant wildflower in a field of grass.

Her boots caught his attention first. They weren't the elegant Italian leather boots favored by the style-conscious women in his crowd, but heavy black boots suitable for riding a Harley-Davidson. Even so, they couldn't disguise the long shapely legs they covered to midcalf. Black jeans, faded nearly to gray, kept his attention as they hugged slender, boyish hips. The jeans nipped in at an impossibly tiny waist, where a bright orange sweater with a jagged thunderbolt of purple was tucked in. A black leather jacket completed the ensemble. Again the style was more suited to motorcycles than a Rolls-Royce.

Jason was both appalled and fascinated, even before his gaze reached her incredible, heart-stopping face. Her skin was pale as cream, her features delicate. Full, sensuous lips looked as if they'd just been kissed to a rosy pink. Short blond hair stood up in spikes, not from some outrageous styling, he guessed, but from a nervous habit of running her fingers through it. The result was part pixie, part biker.

The look in her eyes was definitely streetwise and every bit of her attention seemed to be as riveted on him as his was on her. Though he couldn't explain the attraction, he was jolted by the first genuine excitement he'd felt in weeks.

Forgetting all about the second Scotch, forgetting the boredom, forgetting just about everything, he slid out of the booth and crossed the tavern's wide plank floor. At twenty-seven Jason knew all about seduction, all about provocative charm. It was the one thing at which he was very successful. His walk was deliberately slow, paced to increase the mounting tension already sizzling between them. He kept his gaze locked with hers and felt another shock of pure adrenaline when she didn't blink, didn't look away. That serious, hard stare remained boldly fastened on him.

Jason was two steps away from her, poised to introduce himself, when she came off the barstool in one fluid, graceful motion—and slammed a fist into his jaw. Before he could recover from the shock of that, she was all over him, pummeling him with more fury than skill, landing just enough blows to assure him she was deadly serious. Her colorful curses turned the bar's genteel air blue while an expectant hush fell over the room.

If the respected Halloran image hadn't been deeply ingrained in him since birth, Jason might have laughed with sheer exhilaration at the unexpectedness of the attack. As it was, he knew if his grandfather caught him brawling with a woman in public, Siberia wouldn't be far enough away for him to run.

Jason hadn't boxed at Yale for nothing, though even that hadn't quite prepared him for the unprovoked fury of this tall, lanky stranger. He dodged her next well-aimed blow, which had obviously been intended to do serious harm to his masculinity. He grabbed one of her arms and pinned it behind her, then latched on to her other wrist. Pressed tight against her and all too aware of every inch of invigorating contact, he looked straight into wide eyes that had turned an exciting, stormy shade of blue. Amusement tugged at his lips as he murmured, "Have we met?"

Apparently she was in no mood for his dry humor. Muttering another string of curses, she hauled off and kicked him. When Jason gasped and reached down to rub his injured shin, she twisted free and came at him again. Obviously she wasn't nearly as familiar with the Marquis of Queensberry rules of fighting as he was. She got in two or three more solid shots before he wrapped his arms around her from behind and held her still, his blood pumping like crazy.

The bartender hovered nearby, obviously in shock. The tavern probably hadn't seen this much action since the Revolutionary War. "Should I call the police, Mr. Halloran?" he inquired with an obvious air of dread at the stir that would cause.

Jason felt the woman stiffen in his arms. "I don't think that will be necessary," he said, then added more softly for her ears alone, "Will it?"

Her shoulders sagged in defeat. "No."

Jason had learned the hard way not to trust her docility. "If I let you go, will you come with me quietly so we can talk about whatever's on your mind?"

When she failed to answer, Jason chuckled. "So, you can't bring yourself to lie. That's good. It's a basis for trust."

Eyes flashing, she glared at him. "I wouldn't trust you if you were the last man on earth."

"I wonder why, since to the best of my recollection I've never had occasion to lie to you."

"You're worse than a liar. You're scum. You're evil."

Her voice rose with each charge, which seemed to fascinate the rapidly growing crowd of onlookers. The words cut far more than the flying fists. Hallorans were rarely humiliated in public. Jason could just imagine how the gossips would enjoy the news, which he had no doubt would spread like wildfire by evening. It would probably make the Sunday papers as well. The faint amusement and exhilaration he'd felt vanished, replaced by a sense of growing outrage. Who the hell was this woman and where did she get off calling him scum? he wondered indignantly.

To his growing fury, it sounded as if she was just getting started. In fact, she might have gone on berating him, but Jason decided enough was enough. He ended the tirade by clamping a hand over her mouth and nudging her firmly across the room and into the booth. She gasped as her knees buckled, but she sat. Just to be sure she stayed until he could wrestle some answers from her, Jason wedged himself in beside her.

"Start talking," he commanded in a low voice.

"I have *nothing* to say to you."

"Amazing. Not more than sixty seconds ago, you couldn't shut up." He rubbed his aching jaw and wished for the first time in his life for a little anonymity. Too many people seemed as interested as he was in her answers. She disappointed them all by remaining stonily silent.

Jason had plenty of experience in social graces, but this situation defied the conventions. To the best of his recollection no one had ever defined the etiquette for chit-chat following an unprovoked attack by a woman he'd never seen before in his life. It she'd been a man, he could have slugged her back and felt avenged. As it was, he felt a little like Perry Mason stuck with a reluctant witness.

"Dammit, you owe me an explanation," he said, sensing as soon as the words were out of his mouth that they were wasted.

"I owe you nothing." The spark of fury in her eyes hadn't dimmed a bit.

Jason sighed. Something told him right then and there to send her packing, but he couldn't bring himself to do it without satisfying his curiosity. "Okay, let's try this another way. How about a drink?"

"Not from you." Patches of color on her cheeks emphasized her indignation.

"Fine. You can pay for it."

"With what? Sammy gave you every dime I had saved."

Jason stared at her, startled by the depth of her anger and the unwarranted accusation behind it. Despite his own conviction that it was time to cut his losses, he was undeniably intrigued by the puzzle she represented. The women he knew did not enjoy scenes, much less creating them. This woman appeared totally unfazed by the stir she'd caused. If anything, she was itching for another round, still righteous in her fury. At least in that they had something in common—he was charged up enough to do a full bout with her.

"Who the devil is Sammy and why would you think he gave me your money?"

Apparently startled by his blank response, she studied him thoughtfully, then shook her head. "Nice act. You're really good. For a minute there, I almost believed you."

The sarcasm had a nasty sting to it. Even considering the source—a wacko woman he'd never met before in his life—Jason was offended by the attack on his honor. "I'm not acting, dammit. I'm losing patience. Who is this Sammy?"

She shot him a look of pure disgust. "I told you I'm not buying it. You know perfectly well who Sammy is."

With a sense that he was in over his head for the very first time in his smooth, well-ordered life, Jason tried a little deductive reasoning. "Is Sammy your husband?"

She shook her head.

The response cheered him in a way that probably didn't bear close examination. "You're too young to have a son who's stealing cash from the cookie jar," he decided.

"I'm not as young as I look."

"Sorry. Of course not. You're probably ancient—maybe even twenty-five."

"Twenty-three."

"Like I said, ancient. So what's the story with Sammy?"

She huddled in the corner of the booth, as far from him as it was possible to get in the confined space. Her expression settled into a mutinous glare. Whatever her problem with him was, apparently she hadn't thought much beyond beating the daylights out of him.

"Hungry?" Jason inquired politely, hoping to catch her off guard by trying a different tack. She ignored him.

"No problem," he said then. "I've got all afternoon." To prove it he settled more comfortably in the booth and took a sip of his drink.

Her eyes widened at that. "You can't keep me here all afternoon."

"Oh, but I can," he said mildly. "You can talk to me or you can talk to the police. I'd say we have enough witnesses to make an assault charge stick."

"I'll swear you were coming on to me."

"I was coming *over* to you. There's a big difference."

"Where'd you get your law degree? In jail?"

"No law degree. No jail."

There was a faint glint of curiosity in her eyes before she banked it and fell silent again.

"I'm waiting," he reminded her.

"Sammy's my brother," she said finally. "He's only sixteen, which makes what you did particularly reprehensible."

It was a start, but the woman definitely had an attitude. She clearly intended to be stingy with her information. "So your sixteen-year-old brother stole your money?" he prodded.

"Every cent I'd saved for the past three months," she confirmed wearily. Her fingers swept through her hair, leaving more spikes.

Jason was filled with the sudden and astonishing urge to find this Sammy and pummel some sense into him. "Haven't you ever heard of banks?" he asked instead, astounded by the notion of someone leaving large amounts of cash lying around the house.

She gave him a scathing look. "It was in a bank. Well, it *was* in a cookie jar actually."

"Which means when Sammy turned larcenous—or hungered for chocolate chip cookies—all he had to do was lift the lid."

"Okay, it was stupid," she admitted, abandoning

her hair to fiddle with a napkin. Little strips piled up in front of her. Her gaze rose to clash with his. ''It didn't seem to make much sense to go to all the bother of opening an account for a couple hundred bucks. I have a checking account to pay the bills, but this was just savings. If I'd put the money in the checking account, I'd have used it to pay the rent or the electric or something.''

Jason didn't like the picture he was getting of a woman struggling to make ends meet, only to be taken advantage of by her no-good kid brother. Where were her parents? Why weren't they disciplining the brat? He barely resisted the urge to reach in his pocket and replace the missing money. But he figured that was the surest way he knew to get another punch in the mouth.

''Where do I fit in?'' he asked. ''What makes you think Sammy gave me your money?''

''I found this VCR in his room. He told me he bought it.''

''From a store?''

She regarded him accusingly again. ''No, from some man he met on the streets. He was supposed to see the guy again today. The guy offered him a deal on all sorts of fancy things—stereos, computers, who knows what else—if Sammy would go in with him.''

Incredulous, Jason was beginning to get the whole ugly picture. ''What the hell are you suggesting?'' he demanded indignantly. ''Surely you didn't think I was dealing in stolen property and recruiting your brother to help?''

He could see from her expression that that was exactly what she'd thought. It was the last straw.

He leaned in close and lowered his voice. ''You've

made a mistake, okay? If you leave quietly, right now, we'll forget this ever happened."

"I have no intention of staying quiet about this, mister. You won't get away with it. Men like you are a blight on society, a disgrace to decent people."

"Men like me?" Jason repeated. Now his voice was climbing to the fishmonger level of hers. "*Men like me!* What the hell would you know about me?"

"I know that you were willing to use my brother, that you played on a kid hungry for a little money and attention."

Jason raked his hand through his hair and tried to control his temper. Another five minutes of listening to this woman's outrageous accusations and he might forget all the rules of propriety and...and what? Hit her? Hardly. Give her a stern talking to? That would certainly terrify her. He faced the fact that he was stymied, unless he could get to the bottom of this story.

"Maybe we should start at the beginning," he said very slowly. He was gritting his teeth. "Why did you assume that I knew your brother?"

"You were right where Sammy said you'd be," she said defensively. "You stood on the corner down the block, right under the old clock. You had another one of those VCRs. The exact same model. It said so on the box. It was obvious you were waiting for someone, so don't even bother trying to deny it."

Jason prayed for patience. "I bought that VCR less than an hour ago. I can show you the sales slip." He got it out of his pocket and waved it under her nose. She didn't look impressed.

"And I was waiting for someone—my grandfather. We're meeting at noon for lunch and I was early. I thought about waiting outside, but it was too damned cold.'' He shook his head at the ridiculousness of her mistake. ''Can I give you a bit of advice? Next time be sure of your facts before you attack some stranger in a bar. Otherwise, you're likely to land yourself in jail or worse.''

She regarded him defiantly. ''What makes you think I'm not sure of my facts now?''

Jason realized that she was absolutely serious. He hadn't convinced her of a thing. On a day when he'd decided nothing would ever surprise him again, the idea of being considered shady and dangerous held a certain insane appeal. ''You honestly think I'm a thief?''

She shrugged. ''You could be. Just because you're wearing fancy clothes and talk smooth doesn't mean you're honest. Some of the biggest crooks I know spend a bundle on clothes.''

''And the sales slip?''

''If you're any good as a thief, you can probably forge that.''

''You're very cynical.''

''I've had to be.''

To his utter astonishment, Jason found that he wanted to ask why. He wanted to spend the next twelve hours talking to this woman, finding out what made her tick, explaining that a kid who'd knowingly bought a stolen VCR probably couldn't be counted on to lead her to the thief. He wanted to discover the source of all that fierce determination and protectiveness, because one thing was perfectly clear—she didn't blame Sammy for his crime. She blamed the man who'd lured him into it. He wondered if anyone stood up for her the way she stood up for her brother. He wondered about parents and lovers. He wondered a lot about lovers and cursed the notion that there might be one.

He dragged a hand through his hair. It was obvious he was every bit as nuts as she was.

She was sitting perfectly still beside him, as alert as a predatory jungle creature waiting for a chance to spring on some unsuspecting prey. Jason looked up and then caught sight of his grandfather striding across the tavern. Even though his hair had gone silver and his shoulders were slightly stooped, at sixty-eight he was an impressive man. No one could mistake Brandon Halloran for anything less than the distinguished, *legitimate* businessman he was.

Hallorans had been held in high esteem in Boston since the first one had made his way over in the 1800s. Brandon had done his part to see that the image of respectability remained intact. As he stopped to talk with one of his cronies, Jason could just imagine the wild tale he was hearing about his grandson's latest escapade.

"Okay, whatever game you've been playing, it's over now," he said with finality. "I want you to leave before my grandfather gets over here. And if I hear the slightest hint that you've continued to spread these lies about me, I'll slap you with a slander suit that will make your head spin. Is that clear?"

He moved out of the booth to let her pass. She slid across the seat and stood up. Instead of going, though, she stood toe-to-toe with him, undaunted. Her chin jutted up a defiant notch and her hands went to her hips.

"I'll leave," she said. "But don't think for one minute that I'm intimidated by the likes of you. And as long as we're issuing warnings and threats, you might remember this—if you come near my brother again with one of your shady deals, I'll turn you over to the cops. Is *that* clear?"

With his grandfather approaching, Jason didn't have the option of telling her exactly what he thought of a woman who managed to get her facts so incredibly screwed up, then tossed around slanderous charges.

"Oh, I think we understand each other," he muttered.

She nodded. "I'm sure we do."

She cast one final glare in his direction, then whirled around and stalked off, leaving both Jason and his grandfather staring after her.

"Who the devil was that?" Brandon demanded.

"Some lunatic."

Brandon's gaze narrowed speculatively. "What'd she do to get your dander up?"

"Nothing." Jason slid into the booth and gulped down the remainder of his Scotch.

"Oh, really? Last time a woman got me that hot and bothered, I asked her to marry me."

Jason's horrified gaze shot to his grandfather. "I don't even *know* that woman."

Brandon shrugged, his expression pure innocence. "Maybe you should get to know her. Mind you, I don't know the whole story, but judging by what I've heard in the last five minutes, she'd give you one hell of a run for your money. Seems to me you could use the challenge."

"Granddad, if I ever need the skills of a matchmaker, remind me not to come to you for advice. That woman would would drive a saint to drink."

Brandon eyed the empty glass in front of Jason and

nodded complacently. "Yes, indeed. A regular hellion. You could do worse."

"Frankly, I don't see how," Jason said. "With any luck, I'll never see her again."

Sammy Roberts was sprawled on the frayed living room sofa watching television when Dana got home. He spared her an all-too-familiar sullen, hostile glance then returned his attention to the thirteen-inch screen where black-and-white images flickered weakly. At least she knew that set hadn't been stolen. She'd bought it herself. Sammy would have gone for color.

Still shaken by her encounter in the bar and worried sick by what was happening to her brother these days, she crossed the room in three quick strides and snapped off the TV. "We need to talk."

"Again? I got nothin' more to say."

Filled with determination and furious that she might actually have made a complete fool of herself earlier, she pulled up a chair in front of him and sat on the edge. "Well, I do. I want you to tell me again about this man who sold you the hot VCR."

Sammy sighed heavily and stared at the ceiling. A hank of limp hair hung down in his eyes. Dana barely resisted the desire to brush it off his face. She supposed he was just being a teenager, but he'd grown increasingly resentful of any suggestions she made about his clothes or appearance. It had nearly killed her when he'd shaved one side of his head to crew cut length and left the other side long, but she'd bitten her tongue and chalked it up to his need for self-expression. She'd seen at least a half dozen other boys in the neighborhood sporting equally horrifying hairstyles.

"Dammit, Sammy, I want you to talk to me."

"He's just a guy."

"How old? How tall? What's his name?"

"I figured you'd know all that by now. Didn't you find him and turn him over to the cops?"

"No, I did not," she answered truthfully.

There was no mistaking the relief in Sammy's eyes. He'd been scared when she'd stormed out of the apartment earlier, not for her, but for himself. He'd obviously feared retaliation, but he'd been wise enough to know there was no way he could stop her.

"Sammy, the man belongs in jail. What he did—what you did—was wrong."

"So turn me in," he said with the sort of smug bravado that made her want to shake him. He knew she wouldn't do it, knew that she was a soft touch where he was concerned.

It had been seven years since she'd taken on the responsibility for raising Sammy. He'd been nine and she had just turned sixteen when their ne'er-do-well father had vanished for the last time. Their mother had died two months later, of a broken heart as near as Dana had been able to tell. Dana had been more concerned with survival than with a medical diagnosis that was too late to do anybody any good.

It had taken every ounce of ingenuity Dana had possessed to keep herself and Sammy two steps ahead of the social workers and out of the legal system. She'd conned one of her mother's friends into posing as a legal guardian, whenever the need arose. She'd even trumped up some very official-looking documents to make it all appear legal. Since Rosie hated authority and had always wanted to be an actress, she'd been more than willing to step in occasionally and present herself as the responsible adult in the household. Overworked school officials had been easy enough to fool.

The scheme had turned out just fine. Dana had worked hard, taking any job she could get, from waiting tables to mowing lawns. Sammy had helped out after school and she'd even managed to take night courses until she'd passed her high school equivalency exam. Right now Sammy had only two more years until graduation. The Roberts kids had done okay so far.

It was only in the past year that Sammy had begun rebelling, wanting more than she could give, more than he could earn. He was a good kid, but he'd done without for a long time. She couldn't really blame him for wanting all the fancy things his friends took for granted. Yet that didn't mean she was about to condone his buying stolen property.

"What does this man look like?" she repeated. Though she wasn't entirely convinced that the man she'd accosted in Washington's Tavern was innocent, she wanted to be certain. As she'd told him, she wasn't impressed by his clothes, his smooth talk or that sales slip he'd waved under her nose. The seemingly refined grandfather had made her pause, but she supposed it was possible the whole family was involved in a well-paying life of crime.

Still, she hadn't expected a thief to have eyes that could melt stone, gentle gray-blue eyes that had at least momentarily filled with compassion once he'd gotten over the shock of that reasonably accurate left hook to his jaw. She would really hate to think she owed the guy an apology. In fact, she would hate like heck to have to see him again at all. He'd made her nervous in a way no man ever had before, a way that guaranteed trouble even for a woman who considered herself an expert at dodging it.

"I didn't pay that much attention," Sammy said evasively.

"Then how did you expect to meet up with him again? Was he supposed to find you?" She couldn't keep the sarcasm out of her voice.

Sammy squirmed uncomfortably. "Yeah. No. I don't know. Come on, sis, gimme a break."

Dana sighed. This was getting her nowhere. "Was he tall? About six-one?"

Sammy shrugged.

She thought of the man's wind-tousled golden hair and deliberately asked, "Dark hair?"

"Yeah, I guess."

She studied Sammy's pale face, but couldn't for the life of her tell if he was lying or telling the truth. What difference did it make? She wasn't going to turn the guy in, not when she was still so uncertain of his identity. She might as well let it go for now. She cupped her hand around Sammy's chin and forced him to meet her gaze.

"If one thing comes into this house without a proper sales slip from a regular store, I will personally turn you over to the police and let them deal with you. Got it?"

He didn't look nearly as intimidated as she might have liked, but he mumbled an affirmative response. Dana nodded. "Okay. I've got a design presentation to do this weekend, if I'm going to have a prayer of getting that ad agency job."

Dana took twenty dollars from her purse. She didn't want Sammy to get the idea she was rewarding him for his dishonesty, but she really needed the peace and quiet. "Why don't you call one of your friends, maybe take in a movie? Stop at the store on the way home and buy something for dinner, maybe spaghetti. I'll make homemade sauce."

For the first time since their fight over the VCR she'd discovered in his room that morning, Sammy's expression brightened. He wrapped skinny arms around her for a quick hug. "You're okay, sis."

Dana sighed. "You're pretty okay yourself. Don't forget the onions and green peppers and be back here by six-thirty."

"You got it."

As soon as he left, Dana pushed aside all her doubts and worries. The only way to deal with Sammy—with any teenage boy, from what she'd seen in the neighborhood—was to take each day as it came. She couldn't panic over each and every failure. If she did, it would mean conceding that she had done the wrong thing by trying to raise him by herself. No matter how bad things got, she refused to believe that they would have been better off separated and placed in a couple of loveless foster homes.

With a sigh she got out her art supplies and set up her drawing board in front of the living room window. The light was terrible in the dreary apartment, but at least she had a view. It was better than the cubbyhole she'd been assigned to in the back room at the printing company. It was there that she proofread type and, if she was lucky, designed an occasional cheap flyer for the dry cleaners down the block or the bookstore two streets over.

On Friday she'd applied for a better job in the graphics department at an advertising agency. Despite an impressive portfolio, they had required that she do an actual assignment before offering her the job. She pulled out the materials she'd been given by the art director and began to read about the textile manufacturing company that was looking for a new corporate logo to jazz up its staid image.

By the time she'd read the first half dozen pages of the company's annual report, she suspected that their idea of a more modern image would be a nudge into the twentieth century, not a daring leap into the twenty-first. It was the sort of assignment she'd hated in her night school design classes. It required little imagination and even less skill to create a bland logo, which would be barely distinguishable from the old one that had satisfied for the past hundred years.

Dana flipped through the rest of the report. She had just turned to the last page when she felt her heart screech to a halt, then begin to hammer.

"Oh, hell," she muttered under her breath as she stared at the page of photos of the company's corporate executives. Unmistakably, right in the middle and listed as the head of marketing was the man she'd accused just a few short hours ago of being a thief: Jason Halloran—as in Halloran Industries.

Oh, God, why hadn't the name registered when the bartender had mentioned it earlier? Why hadn't she made the connection in time to retract her stupid charges?

With a sense of urgency she flipped to the front of the report and took another look at the letter from the chairman of the board. She'd skipped over it before, not even glancing at the accompanying postage-stamp-sized photo. The only difference between this distinguished-looking older man and the one she'd brushed past this noon was the fierce expression on his face. This morning he'd merely looked stunned.

''Oh, hell,'' she repeated as weariness and a sense of doom spread through her. Leave it to her to ruin a perfectly good job opportunity.

Chapter Two

Dana stood outside the glass doors of the small but prestigious Lansing Agency for the better part of a half hour Monday morning, trying to work up the courage to submit her work. She knew the logo designs were good. She wanted the job more than almost anything she could ever remember wanting, except maybe a real home complete with fireplaces and window seats and ceilings tall enough for a storybook-style ten-foot Christmas tree.

But more than any other time in her life, she was gut-deep scared. Scared she would get the job and fail, equally terrified that she would have to meet Jason Halloran again and be fired on the spot.

She had spent the entire weekend alternately working on the presentation and staring at his picture, reminding herself that he hadn't called the cops on her, remembering that brief instant of compassion she'd seen in his eyes as she told him all about Sammy and the stolen VCR. Though he wasn't all that old, Jason Halloran struck her as a man who'd known some pain, who'd learned the value of forgiveness. It was there in his eyes, showing up when he was trying his best to appear stern and unyielding.

Obviously he'd been embarrassed, but that was hardly terminal. And anger faded…eventually. Maybe he wouldn't hold what happened in Washington's Tavern against her. If he was as chauvinistic as most men, he'd probably already chalked her crazy accusations up to some female idiosyncrasy and dismissed her as a flake.

Dana sighed. That might get her off the hook with him, but it sure wouldn't land her this job. Her designs would have to do that.

Ultimately her confidence in those designs had given her the courage to show up at the agency this morning. That and the realization that a lowly design person was unlikely ever to meet with the client. For all she knew this logo assignment had been a fake, nothing more than a way to test her skills. It was possible that lots of companies did that. She'd never gotten this far in the interview process before.

Bundled up against the snowy day, but shivering just the same, Dana opened the door to a blast of warm air and low music. Inside she quickly removed her leather jacket. It looked thoroughly out of place with her brand-new spike heels and her one decent, professional-looking outfit. After half a dozen unsuccessful interviews, she'd finally realized it was her unorthodox appearance, rather than her designs that were her downfall. She'd found a sedate skirt and sweater on sale the previous weekend. So far they'd brought her luck, in the form of this second interview, which probably proved a point about appearances meaning every bit as much as talent in this business.

Glancing into a mirror, she decided she looked boring but presentable, except for her windblown hair. She tried taming it with her fingers, but the cropped style refused to be tamed. Shrugging, she gave up and walked across the lobby's thick gray carpeting to the reception desk. Wobbling a little on the unfamiliar heels, she couldn't resist glancing back to see if she'd left footprints in the thick pile.

On Friday she'd been too nervous to note the contrast between the reception area, with its subdued lighting, modern furniture and pricey artwork, and the brightly lit chaos closed away from public view by glass bricks and a curved wall painted a muted shade of peach. Today as she was directed to John Lansing's office, she took in each detail, trying to imagine herself a part of the cheerful confusion and resulting creativity.

Seated in John Lansing's office, she waited nervously for him to return from a conference with his art director. She tried to tell herself that this job wasn't the only chance she'd ever have. She reminded herself that just last week her boss at the printing shop had told her she could expand her duties and take on more special jobs for local stores, if she wanted. They would split the extra income. He'd get seventy-five percent, for overhead he'd explained, and she'd get the rest. She hadn't laughed in his face—she couldn't afford to. But she hadn't said yes, either.

John Lansing and Lesley Bates rushed in finally, amid a flurry of apologies. Lansing, a devilishly handsome man in his mid-forties, and Bates, a sleek, stylish woman in a severely cut suit and discreet but obviously expensive gold jewelry, stared at her expectantly. They were both so polished, so sophisticated that Dana had to fight the urge to check for runs in her hose. She noted every detail of the art director's attire for the time when she could afford to dress that way.

"What do you have for us?" the agency founder asked, giving her an encouraging smile.

Dana opened her portfolio and pulled out a half dozen designs. As she started to spread them on Lansing's desk, the art director shook her head. "Let's hear about them one at a time. Tell us the reasoning behind each one. You might as well get used to making a presentation."

Swallowing hard, Dana nodded and picked up the first design, a subtle alteration of the present logo. "From everything I read about the company, it seemed likely that they're not looking for a drastic change," she said, managing to sound confident even though she was quaking inside. She detailed the reasons behind her color changes, the minimal updating of the design itself.

Though their expressions were impassive, she took heart. She ran through four more alternatives, each bolder and more creative than the one before. The last, in which the company's name would be embossed across an artistic swatch of fabric from its latest collection, had the substance, fluidity and style that she was convinced was both an exciting and impressive change from the current outdated design. The embossing would give it a texture she thought suitable for an internationally prominent manufacturer of rich textiles.

She caught the subtle exchange of glances between Lansing and his art director. "I love it," Lesley Bates said finally.

"So do I," Lansing agreed, taking a closer look at the final proposal. "You've captured exactly the look they need. But you're right about Halloran Industries. The old man is not looking to do something this drastic. He'd be happier with the first one."

"I'm not so sure about that," Lesley countered. "I've always had the feeling that Jason's the conservative one. Brandon didn't get where he is by avoiding risks."

"What about Jason, then? Since you can't go over his head, do you think you can convince him?" Lansing asked the art director.

Lesley Bates shook her head. "I honestly don't know. For one thing, he's not all that interested in anything going on over there these days. From what I hear, he's bored and making no pretense about it. I doubt he'll be the least bit interested in rocking the boat. He's certainly not going to put his faith in someone with little formal training and no experience."

Nor was he likely to put his faith in a woman who'd labeled him a liar and a thief, Dana thought with a sinking sensation in the pit of her stomach. She listened to the arguments pro and con on her designs, trying desperately to hear something that would indicate for certain that she would get the job even if Jason Halloran turned down her designs. She didn't like having her fate linked to the whims of a man she'd publicly insulted.

Unwilling to leave the decision to chance, she decided she had to do something and do it fast to convince them she was the sort of bold, assertive designer they owed it to themselves to hire.

"Let me talk to him," she said impulsively. Of all the limbs she'd ever climbed out on, this was by far the most dangerous. It was also a mark of her desperation. "If I sell him, I get the job."

John Lansing smiled. "I like your attitude, but you're taking a big risk and an unnecessary one at that. It's up to us to convince the client."

Dana fought to hide a grim smile. He had no idea how big a risk she was offering to take, both professionally and, in some way she couldn't quite define, to her own emotions. She took a deep breath. "It's worth it. This could be the break I've been praying for. I believe in these ideas. If I could sell you, don't you think I could convince him?"

"Could you give us a moment?" the art director asked. "Leave the designs and wait just outside."

Dana nodded. Outside the office she paced and paced some more, wishing she dared to kick off the uncomfortable heels. Though they'd sounded enthusiastic about her work, she wasn't sure that they were equally excited about hiring her. She'd sensed the unspoken reservations. The art director had come right out and said she was an amateur. Her ideas, though, were bold and new. Even they couldn't deny that.

Still, she sensed that a lot more was at stake for the Lansing Agency than she'd realized. Maybe she'd put them into an untenable position by suggesting that they send a mere novice over to Halloran Industries. It didn't matter, though. Her audacity was just about all she'd had going for her her whole life. She wanted this job so badly she ached, even more so now that she'd had the small taste of real professional approval of her ideas.

It was another ten minutes before they called her back in. "It's a deal," John Lansing told her. "But Lesley will go with you as a backup. Okay?"

The request was hardly unreasonable. Even so, the possibility that the art director would learn the whole story about her previous encounter with Jason Halloran made Dana almost as nervous as the prospect of making her first presentation to a man who had little reason to give her a break. Because she had little choice, she nodded. "Okay."

"I'll call you when we have the appointment scheduled," Lesley Bates told her.

John Lansing handed her portfolio back to her and walked her to the door. "You have a bright future, Ms. Roberts. I hope we'll be working together soon."

"I hope so, too."

Outside, Dana clutched her portfolio and made one more thoroughly impulsive decision. Too much was at stake to leave anything about this meeting with Jason Halloran to chance. Drawing in a deep breath of icy air, she straightened her shoulders, walked halfway down the block and caught the next bus to the Halloran Industries building on the outskirts of town.

Inside the lobby she consulted the directory, located the administrative offices and took the elevator to the top floor. She was halfway down the hall when Brandon Halloran stepped into the corridor. Dana's breath caught in her throat as a look of recognition spread across the older man's face.

"Hello, there," he said, a surprising twinkle in his eyes.

Dana regarded him warily. Why wasn't he throwing

her out? Hadn't he heard about what had happened on Saturday between her and his grandson?

"Are you here to see Jason?"

"As a matter of fact, I am."

He nodded in satisfaction. "Splendid. Before you do that, though, why don't you and I have a little talk?"

Before she could blink, he'd tucked her arm through his and steered her into a lavish corner office with an incredible view of the Boston skyline in the distance. The view was the only thing impressive about it, however. The large space was thoroughly cluttered. Whatever furniture there was was buried under piles of fabric. Swatches of silk tumbled across the desk in a rainbow of colors. Bolts of wool littered a sofa. Drapes of printed cotton hung over the backs of every chair.

Dana had never seen more beautiful fabrics in her life. Intrigued, she circled the room and impulsively ran her fingers over the material, awed by the various textures. She was more certain than ever that her most innovative logo design was right.

She looked up and realized Brandon Halloran was watching her closely, an expression of approval on his face.

"I can see you appreciate fine quality fabrics," he said.

"They're beautiful. I've never owned anything like them."

"Perhaps one day you will," he said. He swept the bolts of cloth from the sofa and motioned for her to sit down. "What's your name, young lady? My grandson didn't take the time to introduce us properly on Saturday. You seemed to be in a bit of a hurry."

Dana winced. "Actually he didn't know my name."

"Really? How fascinating. I could have sworn the two of you were having a pretty heated argument, too heated for a couple of strangers."

"It was a stupid mistake on my part. I thought he was someone else. When I realized how wrong I was, I came to apologize."

"Carrying a portfolio?"

Dana tried to evade that penetrating gleam in his eyes, but it was unavoidable. Before she could consider the consequences, she was spilling the whole story.

"So you can see why he'd be furious with me. This is the first time I've even come close to getting a job like this. I couldn't risk having him tell the Lansing Agency people what I'd done. I planned on throwing myself at his mercy."

"An interesting tactic, but I have a better idea. Let me take a look at those designs. If they're as innovative as you suggest, Jason will hate them. Then I'll have to overrule him and he'll have even more reason to resent you."

Though this comment echoed what John Lansing and Lesley Bates had suggested earlier, about which man was a risk taker, Dana was puzzled why Brandon Halloran seemed to so eager to help her. "Why would you care if he resents me?"

"Let's just say I'm concerned with the future of Halloran Industries and leave it at that, shall we?"

Dana didn't have the vaguest idea what she had to do with the future of this man's company, but she was more than willing to show him the designs. The expression of delight that spread across his face when he saw the final concept was better than any verbal praise, but he said all the right words, too.

"This is perfect. Perfect! Young lady, you are very talented. Why hasn't someone snapped you up long before now?"

"I'm just getting started. To be honest, I was a little unorthodox for some of the companies I applied to."

He grinned. "I can just imagine. Well, you're not too unorthodox for Halloran Industries. Shall I call John Lansing right now?"

"No!" she said hurriedly. She swallowed hard. "I mean, I wish you wouldn't. I just interviewed with him. He doesn't know I'm here with you. It wouldn't look good."

"I see," he said nodding slowly. "You may have a point. Let's let John and Lesley go ahead and schedule that meeting, then. This conversation will be our secret."

"What about your grandson?"

"You just leave Jason to me."

That worrisome twinkle was back in his eyes when he said it, but Dana was far too grateful about having Brandon Halloran in her corner to question his motives. She realized much later that not finding out about his motives was probably the second major mistake she'd made with the Halloran men.

Jason swiveled his chair around to face the window and stared out at the bleak gray landscape. The snow that had fallen over the weekend had turned to slush, and a new batch of thick clouds kept the Tuesday-morning sky a dull gunmetal shade.

What was wrong with him? Why couldn't he seem to get his life into focus? He needed a goal, a purpose, but he was damned if he could find one. Despite his talk with his grandfather on Saturday, nothing had really changed. Only the unexpected, volatile encounter with the outrageously feisty woman in the bar had shaken the depressing status quo, and that was hardly an experience he cared to repeat.

In fact, he had tried to dismiss the entire incident, but that was easier said than done. Too many people at the symphony gala on Saturday night had heard about it and wanted to know the fascinating details. To his irritation Jason found himself quelling rumors that he was secretly involved with the outrageous woman and that the scene had been a very public lovers' quarrel. Unfortunately his own date had been one of those who'd taken that particular rumor as fact. Marcy Wellington had lifted her aristocratic nose in the air, told him in no uncertain terms what she thought of him and had taken a cab home. He'd been astonishingly unmoved by her departure.

He glanced at his calendar and saw that his secretary had noted a meeting in the boardroom for ten o'clock. He buzzed the outer office.

"Harriet, what's this meeting all about?"

"Your grandfather scheduled it late yesterday afternoon. He said it was essential you be there. He mentioned something about the Lansing Agency and those logo designs you ordered." As if she'd anticipated his next question, she added, "John Lansing had tried to reach you earlier, but you'd already left for the day. I transferred him to your grandfather."

Jason pretended not to notice the censure in her voice. Harriet had very rigid ideas about the length of the workday. He rarely met her standards or those set by his workaholic father and his dedicated grandfather. As near as Jason could tell, he didn't have enough to do to justify sitting in his office for more than the bare minimum of hours it took to complete the few real tasks assigned to him.

"There's not a problem, is there? I didn't see any conflict on your calendar," she said. The latter was meant as a subtle dig about his habit of scheduling things without telling her.

"No, there's no problem." No matter how it got scheduled, at least a ten o'clock meeting would break up the morning's endless tedium.

Jason wasn't surprised to find that he was the first to arrive. His grandfather, a stickler for most things, thought meetings were generally a waste of time. Harriet usually had to track him down in the mill and remind him that he was late. Then he breezed in, ran through whatever was on the agenda and raced back to his beloved fabrics.

Jason paced the boardroom anticipating John Lansing's arrival. He was anxious to see what the agency had come up with based on the suggestions he'd given them. He turned when the door opened. With any luck perhaps he and his grandfather would agree for once.

"Sir, Dana Roberts is here," Harriet said.

The faint note of disapproval in her voice intrigued him. "Does she have an appointment?"

"She's the designer the Lansing people used. Should I send her in or have her wait for the others?"

"By all means, send her in."

The door opened bit by bit. At his first glimpse of the woman framed in the doorway, Jason felt his stomach knot. It couldn't be! Surely fate couldn't be that unkind. Though she'd chosen a more sedate attire—a pencil-slim skirt in disgracefully cheap black wool and a rose-colored sweater that was equally ordinary—there was no mistaking the hellion who'd attacked him on Saturday. For one thing, her hair had been worried into spikes again. For another, his blood was already racing just a little faster. Anger? Sex appeal? He wasn't sure he could tell the difference where she was concerned. From the start she had aroused all sorts of contradictory feelings in him.

He scowled at her. "*You* work for the Lansing Agency?" he queried, not bothering to keep the note of incredulity from his voice.

"Not yet," she said, looking almost as desperate as he felt. She swallowed nervously. "Where is everyone?"

"You're the first."

She slid into the room, careful to keep her distance. She put her portfolio on the floor, then on a chair, then on the table, then back on the floor again. By the time she was done, Jason was tempted to take it and toss it through a window.

"Am I making you nervous?" he asked instead, taking a certain amount of grim satisfaction in the thought.

"Yes," she said, perching on the edge of a chair as if she were prepared to run at the first sign of trouble.

He nodded and took a seat opposite her, training an unflinching gaze on her. If he'd hoped to further disconcert her, however, the attempt failed miserably. She drew in a deep breath and returned his gaze evenly, then said, "Maybe we should talk about it."

"Oh, no," he said softly, a warning note in his voice. "Believe me, I am in no mood to hear anything you have to say unless it has to do with those designs you brought."

The silence that fell after that was nerve-racking. After another ten minutes of strained quiet, he jumped to his feet, opened the door and shouted down the hall. "Harriet, what the hell is keeping my grandfather?"

At his shout Harriet came running, an expression of alarm on her normally passive face. "He just called, sir. He had an emergency, out of the building. He said you should go ahead without him."

"Out of the building?" His voice again rose to a level he would never have considered using before Saturday. Just being around this Roberts woman seemed to shatter every bit of self-control he had. He lowered his voice. "What kind of emergency would take him away from here?"

"I don't know, sir. He didn't say."

"How about Lansing?"

"Actually his office called, too. He said you and Ms. Roberts should be able to reach a decision without him."

Desperation curled inside him. He did not want to go back into that room with Dana Roberts. He might very well strangle her.

He reminded himself that he was a civilized, sophisticated man. Surely he could contain his anger long enough to look at her designs objectively, then get her out of here. He would never have to see her again, especially if the designs were awful. The prospect of turning them down cheered him considerably.

"Shall I reschedule?" Harriet asked.

"No. As long as Ms. Roberts is here with the designs, we'll go ahead. Tell my grandfather I want him to join us the minute he gets back."

"Of course."

When he walked back into the room, wide blue eyes met his. "If this isn't a good time..." she began.

"No," he said impatiently. "Let's get this over with. Show me what you've brought."

"But your grandfather..."

"Isn't coming."

"But he..." Her voice trailed off in confusion. She cast a panicked glance in the direction of the door and looked as if she'd like to make a run for it.

Jason regarded her oddly. "He what?"

"Nothing." With an expression of grim determination in her eyes, she opened her portfolio. She looked at the stretch of table between them and inched closer. She seemed to be assessing her odds for survival.

Finally she drew in a deep breath. "I can't get into this without at least apologizing first. What I said on Saturday, it was a terrible mistake."

"Yes," he said curtly, "it was." He gestured toward the designs. "Get on with it."

For a minute she looked as if she wanted to say more, but finally she shrugged and began describing her work.

She had just started when Jason interrupted, "You enjoyed slugging me, didn't you?" The words popped out before he could stop them.

Pink stole into her cheeks. "No, really. I mean, if you'd been a thief, I would have enjoyed it, but you're not. Look, I really didn't realize who you are."

"I did try to tell you."

She shrugged. "I wasn't in the mood to listen. It's a bad habit I have. I make up my mind about something or someone and that's it. No second chances."

"Yet you're here, expecting me to forget all about what happened. Why should I?"

"Because I'm genuinely sorry and I really need this break."

"Lucky for you, then, that I'm able to separate my personal feelings from my business decisions." He tried to make it sound noble, but it came out smug. He only hoped it was true. Right this second he wanted very badly to hate her designs. He wanted to tell her she was incompetent. He wanted to make her feel as lousy and humiliated as he'd felt on Saturday.

Unfortunately the logo designs were impossible to dislike. He had to admit he was impressed, his eye immediately drawn to one that was simple and conservative. Elegant. He could see it on some nice gray stationery. Or maybe cream-colored. It would be very businesslike.

"I like this one," he said, quickly settling the matter. "I'll call John."

Dana immediately began shaking her head, no longer the least bit meek or shy. "That one's old-fashioned," she said emphatically.

"We're an old-fashioned company."

"No. Don't you see, the fabrics you create are rich and bold. They're exciting. You need a logo that reflects that. This one," she said, pointing to the one he'd instinctively disliked as being too brash, too much like Dana herself.

Unfortunately he had a hunch Brandon would agree with her. His grandfather was far more daring than he was. His father would only care how much it was going to cost to implement.

"Too expensive," he countered, mouthing what he was certain would be his father's objection.

"Actually, I don't think so. I've costed it out," she said and shoved a piece of paper toward him.

"What do you know about costing out something like this?"

"I work for a printer. We do jobs like this all the time. I figured in all the different ways you'd be likely to use a logo and what it would cost to get a new one implemented."

Disconcerted by her thoroughness, Jason looked over the figures. They looked reasonably accurate. He caught the hopeful glint in her eyes and cursed the day he'd ever met her. She was going to win, though he wasn't about to concede victory too easily. He stood and began to pace, trying to figure out his tactics.

"Okay," he began finally, "if it were up to me alone, I'd consider this one, but..."

Suddenly he found himself enveloped in an impulsive hug. Whisper-soft wool caressed his cheek. The scent of spring flowers teased his senses. Every muscle in his body responded to the lightning-quick roar of his blood.

"Oh, thank you," she said. "Your grandfather said..."

The words had the effect of dashing icy water over him. Jason stepped carefully away from her. His gaze narrowed. "That's the second time you've mentioned my grandfather. When exactly did you speak to him?"

She looked miserable. And guilty. Damn the pair of them, he thought.

"Well, I..." she began.

"Never mind," he said, cutting her off before she could offer him lies. "It's clear that this entire meeting was a set-up. I'm sure the two of you will be very pleased to know that I will go along with your choice. Now, if you don't mind, I have things to do."

Before he could make his exit, the door swung open

and his grandfather rushed in, looking harried. ‘‘Sorry I’m late. Are you two finished? Jason, what did you think?’’

‘‘I think you two are in cahoots,’’ he said bluntly. He glared at his grandfather, then let his furious gaze settle on Dana. ‘‘I still don’t know how you did it, but let me warn you. Stay the hell out of my way from here on out.’’

Chapter Three

Stunned by the depth of anger behind Jason Halloran's softly-spoken warning, Dana stared after him as he slammed the boardroom door behind him. Her heart pounded wildly as her own temper rose to match his. Of all the arrogant, condescending jerks! She hadn't arranged this meeting. She hadn't conspired with anyone. Didn't he realize that she'd simply been told to show up, just as he had been? Couldn't he see that she'd been every bit as shocked as he at finding them alone?

When her pulse finally slowed, she glanced at Brandon Halloran to see how he was taking his grandson's outburst. Obviously he was the one who'd set them both up, but there wasn't a hint of remorse in his expression. If anything, he looked downright smug.

"I thought it went rather well, didn't you?" he said, sounding pleased.

Dana regarded him as if he were several cards shy of a full deck. "*Well?* You think it went well?" She shook her head. "Where was Lesley Bates? And where were you anyway? You promised to be here."

"No," he corrected. "I promised to take care of Jason. And I told Lesley not to come."

"And what do you think you accomplished?"

He leaned back in his chair and beamed. "What I wanted to, and quite well, as a matter of fact. Jason almost never loses his temper."

"Oh, really? Well, I have a news flash for you. He seems to make a habit of it around me."

"Exactly," Brandon said.

"Not that I blame him entirely," Dana said before the full impact of Brandon Halloran's comment registered. "You wanted him to lose his temper? Why?"

"The man's bored. He needs a challenge."

Suddenly Dana began to catch on. She didn't like the implication one bit. "Oh, no," she said, shoving designs into her portfolio with little regard to neatness. "Forget it. I'm not hiring on as entertainment for your grandson."

"Of course not," he soothed. "You're an excellent graphic artist. John Lansing will be lucky to have you on staff."

Suddenly the job at the printing company began to look better and better. She could stay on, do a few odd design jobs. Eventually she would find another agency job, one that wouldn't put her into contact with one man who seemed to enjoy yelling at her and another who thought such behavior was tantamount to a mating ritual.

"I'll be in touch," the old man said as she grabbed her purse and headed for the door.

"No, really. Please let it go." There was an edge of desperation in her voice. "If you want the designs, they're yours. I'll leave them at the Lansing Agency. You make whatever arrangements you want with them."

"You don't want the job?"

Dana thought of what it would mean to her to be hired by the small, prestigious agency. She compared that to one more second in the presence of the disconcerting, manipulating Halloran men. "No," she said firmly. "I do not want the job, not if it means seeing that man again." She glared in the direction Jason had gone in case there was any doubt about which man she'd meant.

Even that seemed to bring a smile to Brandon Halloran's lips. Why did she have this terrible feeling in the pit of her stomach that he was likely to have the last word?

"Ms. Roberts? John Lansing. Congratulations!"

Dana sank down on the stool in front of her design table. "Congratulations," she repeated weakly. "For what?"

"Halloran Industries wants the logo design. The job is yours."

Where was the sense of elation? The satisfaction? All she felt was panic.

"I don't think so," she said, forcing herself not to think about the opportunity she was giving up. The future. The money. Was she every bit as crazy as Brandon Halloran and his grandson?

Her response was greeted by silence, then, "I don't understand. You don't want the job? Is it the salary? Have you had a better offer? I'm sure I can come up with a deal that will match anything anyone else in town is likely to give you.''

''It's not the money,'' she said, practically choking on the words.

''What then?''

''I just don't think I'm cut out for that sort of work,'' she lied.

''Of course you are. I can't tell you how impressed Brandon Halloran is with you.''

''I'm sure,'' she muttered.

''I hate to pressure you, Ms. Roberts, but the truth of the matter is, Brandon wants you on this account very badly,'' he said. Then he added the clincher: ''If you don't agree to join the Lansing Agency, we could lose Halloran Industries.''

Dana gasped as she recognized Brandon Halloran's trump card. The man intended to lay a monumental guilt trip on her. ''That's ridiculous,'' she said. ''You've had that account forever.''

''It's a cutthroat business and it all turns on the quality of the campaign. Brandon Halloran insists he'll take his business to whichever agency you *do* join. It's as simple as that.''

''The man is nuts,'' she said with feeling. ''He is certifiably nuts. A fruitcake! Loony tunes!''

''He's one of the smartest businessmen I've ever met and he drives one helluva bargain. He wants you on this account. *I* want you on this account.''

''Why me?'' she said, but she already knew the answer and it had nothing to do with her designs. Brandon Halloran had handpicked her for that ill-tempered grandson of his. She was sure he hadn't told John Lansing that.

''Maybe I could talk him out of it,'' she said. Thinking of the stubborn, determined glint she'd seen in his eyes, though, she doubted he'd listen to reason.

"Wouldn't it just be simpler to accept my offer?" Lansing suggested.

Simpler, maybe, Dana agreed. Then images of Jason Halloran popped up. Disconcerting images, the kind that made a woman's pulse race even against her own will. Sure it would be simpler to say yes, but wiser? No way. She and Jason Halloran were like oil and water—they just weren't destined to mix. One or the other of them was always likely to be clinging to a last shred of sanity.

"It's the chance of a lifetime," Lansing reminded her.

Dana sighed. "I'll think about it," she promised as a compromise when she couldn't seem to manage a flat-out no a second time.

"I'll call you tomorrow," he responded. "I'm looking forward to your decision," he said, suddenly sounding every bit as confident as Brandon Halloran that things were going to go his way.

Dana wasted nearly half an hour trying to finish the design she was doing for the next event at the bookstore. Unfortunately all of the children she drew surrounding a storyteller looked like pint-sized versions of Jason Halloran.

He was the crux of the problem, she admitted, not his grandfather. Brandon might be a manipulating, conniving sneak, but her relationship with Jason was the real issue. They'd gotten off on the wrong foot and things had gone from bad to worse.

Leaving Brandon's scheming aside, maybe if she went to Jason, told him how important this job was to her, maybe they could find some way to get along.

Barring that, maybe they could simply agree to avoid each other. That was, after all, what he'd said he wanted—rather emphatically, as she recalled. Although it was beyond her imagination to come up with a way for a designer to stay out of the path of the head of marketing, she was desperate enough to try anything at this point. At least she could almost guarantee that their paths would never cross outside the office.

She looked up the number for Halloran Industries and called before she could change her mind.

"I'm sorry, Mr. Halloran has left for the day," his secretary said.

Dana glanced at her watch. "At four-thirty?"

"Yes," she said, her disapproval evident. "May I tell him who called?"

"It's Dana Roberts. I don't suppose you know where I could find him?"

"You might try Washington's Tavern."

Dana nearly groaned. The bartender would probably run her off on sight. "Thanks. I'll try to catch up with him there," she said.

Why did she have this terrible feeling that returning to the scene of their original encounter did not bode well for putting their relationship on an improved footing?

Jason was on his third Scotch. It had clarified his thinking considerably. He had to get out of Halloran Industries before he went stark raving mad. He had a degree in marketing, but it was obvious any important decisions were still being made by his grandfather. In fact, judging from the way today had gone, Brandon had every intention of planning every last detail of his life. Trying to hook him up with Dana Roberts was the clincher. Just the thought of what life would be with that brash, impetuous woman made him shudder.

''Mr. Halloran?''

The familiar feminine voice punctured his Scotch-induced serenity. ''No,'' he said firmly without looking up. ''Go away.''

A knee bumped his as Dana Roberts ignored his plea and slid into the booth. Awareness rocketed through him.

''We need to talk,'' she said.

Jason groaned. ''I thought I told you...''

''I know what you told me. Believe me, if there were any other way, I wouldn't be here, but something has to be done to stop your grandfather.''

He glanced up and met her determined gaze. ''Now there's something we can agree on. What's the old man done to you?''

''He has some crazy idea that you...that you and I...''

She sounded so thoroughly embarrassed that for once Jason couldn't help a rueful chuckle. ''Yeah, I know what you mean.''

''He has to be stopped. Now he's told John Lansing that if I don't take this job, he'll take the Halloran Industries account away from them and follow me wherever I go.''

Jason blinked and stared. ''He what?''

''You heard me. John Lansing shouldn't lose an account just because your grandfather's gotten it into his head to throw us together. Now either you talk him out of that or you and I have to find some other way to put our differences behind us and work together.''

''Not damned likely!'' At her hurt expression, he

mumbled, "Sorry, but you know yourself it would never work."

"We could try."

To his amazement she sounded almost wistful. He would have thought that the one thing they were never likely to agree on was staying out of each other's way. He squinted at her across the table and saw something vulnerable in her expression. He realized then just how much she wanted this job. She looked like a kid who'd awakened on Christmas morning to discover a longed-for doll under the tree, only to realize it was meant for someone else. It made his usually impervious heart flip over. As crazy as it seemed, he was almost envious of her eagerness.

"This job really means a lot to you, doesn't it?" Jason said, wondering what it would be like to be embarking on a career that hadn't been preordained by generations of tradition.

Had he ever felt that kind of excitement and anticipation? He vaguely recalled feeling that way the first time he'd toured Halloran Industries perched on his grandfather's shoulders, listening for the first time to the company's rich history. But that had been long ago. For too long now his job had seemed nothing more than an obligation and a misguided one at that. He had only himself to blame, however, for allowing it to go on so long, for permitting his talent and allegiance to be taken for granted. All of that was about to change, though. He was about to take charge of his own fate. Maybe if he got a grip on his life, he'd feel a little of that energy that seemed to drive Dana Roberts.

"I can't begin to tell you how much I would give

to work for a man like John Lansing,'' Dana admitted with that candor he found so disconcerting.

None of Jason's friends would have dared to be so open with their excitement about a mere job. Many, like him, had had their futures cast in stone from birth. All subscribed to the never-let-them-see-you-sweat school of ambition. By hiding any real feelings, they could protect themselves against the humiliation of rejection. Dana had exposed all of her hopes, trusting him with her vulnerability. For some reason Jason couldn't quite explain, it made him want to do anything to prove himself deserving of her trust. Maybe they could find some way of reaching a truce.

''How about some dinner? Have you eaten?'' If they could actually get through an entire meal without arguing, he would consider it a good omen.

''No.''

''Then I recommend the clam chowder.''

Neither of them seemed quite sure what to do next. They waited in silence for the chowder. When it arrived, Dana ate hers with enthusiasm, but Jason didn't want to touch it.

Under her watchful gaze, he made a pretense of eating, dipping up a spoonful of the chowder. But before he could taste it, he pursued all the answers that had eluded him the last time they'd talked. Maybe if he understood her, she wouldn't get under his skin so. Maybe she wouldn't torment his dreams the way she had the past few nights.

''Why are you so anxious about this particular job? You're good,'' he conceded grudgingly. ''Any agency would be lucky to have you.''

''When I was a kid, the place I lived wasn't so terrific,'' she said in what sounded like it might be a massive understatement. "I'll never forget the first time I went to a museum. All those colors. So much beauty and imagination. After that there weren't enough colors in my box of crayons to satisfy me. Unfortunately my portraits never quite looked like the people I painted and my landscapes were never as good as what I saw in my mind's eye. By the time I was a teenager I'd accepted the fact that I wasn't going to be an artist. I did have an eye for design, though, so I traded in my watercolors and oils for stacks of magazines. I'd clip and paste and create whole new ads."

"Then you went to design school, right?"

She shook her head. "Nope. No money and no time. I took a class or two. I even had an instructor who encouraged me, helped me put together a portfolio, but I couldn't manage any more than that. Since then I've tried to study on my own. I've done a lot of reading. My boss at the print shop has let me build a little side business doing small jobs for his customers, but he takes most of the money I bring in."

Something that felt a lot like guilt crept over Jason. "This job with Lansing would be your first real break, then?"

She nodded. "But I can't take it if it means battling with you every step of the way. We'd both have ulcers inside of a month. No job's worth that."

Jason was surprised by the comment. He'd expected Dana to relish an occasional brawl. She'd struck him as the kind of woman who thrived on doing battle. After all she'd taken him on when she'd perceived him as a threat to her brother.

"You puzzle me," he said finally. "Looking at you, I get the impression of someone with a lot of street smarts, someone who doesn't ever walk away from a fight."

"It's the leather jacket," she said.

"It's true that no one I know would dare to wear one and none of them could carry it off the way you do, but it's more than that. It's an attitude. My guess is that you picked that jacket and the other clothes you were wearing when we met—the boots and jeans—on purpose as a way to defy the world, a way to define who you are, a way to cover up just how sensitive you really are."

"You can tell all that from a jacket?" she said dryly. "Actually, Dr. Freud, I picked the jacket because it was warm and would last through more then one season. It was on special at one of those out-of-season sales at a discount store."

"Right. Would you have picked a cashmere coat if you'd been able to afford it?"

She reached over and touched the topcoat he'd left hanging from a rack at the end of the booth. An expression of near reverence crossed her face. "Is that what this is?"

He nodded.

"It's very soft."

"But would you wear it?"

She stroked it again, the gesture so sensual that Jason could practically feel her touch his flesh. His pulse hammered as her fingers caressed the wool, and his breath seemed to lodge in his throat. If he got this overheated watching her touch a piece of material, what would happen if she ever caressed him with the same level of intense curiosity?

"It doesn't have a lot of flair," she finally admitted.

"Exactly."

"If you hate it so much, why do you wear it?"

"The material comes from Halloran Industries. It would be tacky if the owners of the company didn't wear clothes made from our own fabrics. According to Grandfather, we're all walking advertisements for the company. He keeps a tailor on staff, just to do custom work for us."

"So convention means a lot to you?"

Jason thought about the question. The answer wasn't nearly as simple as it should have been. In his world convention meant everything—and nothing. He tried to explain, as much for his own benefit as hers.

"I've been brought up to believe that the world operates according to certain rules. Some of those rules may seem silly and outdated to me, but I can't deny that they're pretty deeply ingrained. It's only been in the past few weeks that I've ever thought of even questioning them, much less rebelling."

She propped her chin on her hand and regarded him with evident fascination. "And what would a man like you consider rebellious? Trading cashmere for leather? Having dinner with the hired help?"

Jason couldn't miss the edge of cynicism in her voice, even though there was a glimmer of surprisingly tolerant amusement in her eyes. "It's funny," he observed, "I can't tell if it's me you're putting down or yourself."

"Whether I'm dressed like this or in jeans, I know who I am," Dana retorted. "Doesn't sound to me as if you can say the same."

Jason didn't like the fact that this woman seemed capable of reading him so easily. "I suppose there's no denying that. I've been questioning a lot of things about my life lately."

"Why? You have everything a man could want."

"On the surface I suppose that's the way it seems. But don't make the mistake of thinking that just because I'm a Halloran things automatically run smoothly in my life. It's not true. Haven't you ever heard the expression money can't buy happiness?"

"I've heard it. I just never believed it. Having money sure beats what's second best. I'm an expert at that."

Because she'd opened the door and because he didn't want to delve too deeply into his own admittedly sour attitude, Jason dared to probe. "How much trouble are you in financially?" he said, thinking of her reaction to the loss of the few hundred dollars Sammy had stolen.

"I'm not in trouble. I'm not even in debt." She gave him a wry little smile. "I pay as I go. I learned long ago that credit is a dangerous business. When my father walked out, he left us with a stack of bills that my mother couldn't have paid if she'd worked nonstop until she was eighty. As it was, she just died right then instead. I paid what I could."

Jason felt something constrict in his chest. "How old were you?"

"Sixteen."

He couldn't hide his dismay. "What on earth does a sixteen-year-old do to pay off her father's debts?"

Dana's expression darkened at something in his tone. "I didn't do it on my back, if that's what you're wondering about," she said with ice in her voice. "I've never been *that* desperate."

The angry retort stunned him. Her fury was awfully close to the surface. Why, he wondered. Had too many men assumed she'd be grateful for a little help in exchange for a closer relationship? His own tone softened. "You're very quick to jump to conclusions, aren't you? I never for a moment thought that you did anything like that."

"Not even for a split second?" she countered, her disbelief plain. "I mean what else can some uneducated woman who needs money do, right? Maybe you should tell your grandfather your suspicions. That certainly ought to discourage him."

He leveled a look straight into her eyes. "I have a feeling a woman as determined and remarkable as you are could do a lot besides trade sex for money," he said quietly. "How did you survive?"

Apparently his tone calmed her down. She shrugged. "As a matter of fact there were days when I thought it was going to come to...what we were talking about, but I had Sammy to think about. I didn't want him growing up with a twisted view of what it took to get ahead."

"Is this the same Sammy who stole your savings?" he said wryly.

She nodded, her expression pained at the implied failure. "I've tried so hard with him. He's just going through a rough time right now, like all teenagers," she said with more hope than conviction. "He'll be okay."

"How old was Sammy when all this first happened?"

"Nine."

Jason was appalled. And impressed. This hellion with the fierce pride and the fiery temper had gumption. He'd give her that. It made his own complaints seem petty. Obviously Dana had never been daunted by the task she'd set out to accomplish. Nor did she seem the least bit resentful of the circumstances which had heaped such a burden on her slender young shoulders. She had simply coped. Would any of the women he'd known before have done as well? For all of their strengths and charm, he suspected many of them would have floundered without wealthy daddies to turn to, without deep pockets to finance their fancy colleges and designer wardrobes or to provide seed money for their first businesses. His respect for Dana grew enormously.

"Why didn't you ask for help?" he said. "There are social programs, legal aid, food stamps."

"Sure. And the minute they discovered that we had no adult supervision, they would have split Sammy and me up. I couldn't let that happen. We may not have much of an example, but family counts," she said fiercely. "I wanted Sammy to know that."

"Where did you live? How did you make ends meet?"

"At first I found a rooming house that would take us. This friend of my mom's got us in. Nobody paid much attention to who lived there. I worked two jobs most of the time. I had to lie about my age, which wasn't all that difficult since I was always tall for my age. At the kind of places I worked, no one looked that closely, anyway. They were more interested in whether you'd steal from the cash register. I never touched a dime, I showed up on time and I didn't spill coffee on the customers. Those were the only credentials they seemed to care about."

As if she'd just realized how revealing the conversation was becoming, she began to withdraw. Jason could see the mask shift into place, the struggle to regain the distance she normally kept between herself and the outside world. She took a deliberate drink of her coffee, then another spoonful of soup. Jason waited, wondering whether she'd say more about herself or hide behind a wall of defensiveness.

Again, Jason was struck by the combination of childlike enthusiasm and innocence counterpointed by the tough exterior. He noticed for the first time that the fingers clutching the spoon were short, the nails blunt and unpolished. There were scratches on her knuckles, testimony to her attack on him, perhaps. They were a girl's hands. Yet earlier, as she'd caressed his cashmere topcoat, the gesture had been all woman.

How many other new things could he bring into Dana's life to inspire that same balance of innocent wonder and womanly sensuality? Something told him that sharing those experiences with her would banish his jaded mood. He needed desperately to recapture the sense of awe, the sense of unlimited possibilities that remained unshaken in Dana despite her struggles. Perhaps she could show him the way.

Wide blue eyes, filled with uncertainty, met his gaze at last. ''I'm sorry. You didn't come here to listen to my life story.''

''No, it's okay. I think I can see now why you jumped all over me on Saturday. If I had been the man who tried to get your brother involved in selling stolen property, I would have deserved it. Have you found out who was responsible?''

''Not yet,'' she said with a glint of determination in her eyes. ''But I haven't given up. Sooner or later, I'll find him.''

''Why not just turn what you know over to the police?'' He guessed the answer even before she could speak. ''Never mind. You don't want to involve your brother, right? Maybe you should. Maybe he should get a taste of the kind of tough questions they ask criminals, the kind of future in store for him if he gets in any deeper with this guy."

"I will not turn my brother in to the police," she said with fierce protectiveness. "We seem to have gotten off the track here. Can you forgive me for what happened on Saturday? Can we try to work together?"

For an instant he actually considered saying yes. Then he saw a future filled with conflict. They were too different. Opposites, in fact. They would clash over everything. And, despite what his grandfather thought, she was all wrong for Halloran Industries and for him.

"Have you ever planned a marketing campaign?" he asked mildly.

"No, but..."

"Do you know anything about advertising?"

"Not exactly, but..."

"Can you buy TV time, magazine space, newspaper ads?"

"That isn't..."

"Tell me, what demographics should Halloran Industries be appealing to?"

Her face was flushed by now and the sparks in her eyes could have started a blaze. He had a hunch she was about to tell him off in no uncertain terms, but he forestalled all of her arguments by saying, "Sorry. I think it's pretty obvious that it just wouldn't work."

She blinked furiously against the tears welling up in her eyes. Jason felt like a heel. He knew that half of those questions he'd thrown at her weren't things she needed to know. An experienced graphic artist might have known the answers, but it was hardly a requirement for doing skillful designs. That's why agency staffs included copy writers, researchers and all the other experts needed to plan a successful marketing strategy.

"I'll help you find something else, though," he promised in a rush of guilt. "I'll even recommend that Lansing take you on and assign you to other accounts."

"I really wouldn't want you to put yourself out," Dana said stiffly, stubborn pride written all over her face. "I'd better be going. I can see this was a mistake."

She scrambled out of the booth, grabbing her jacket and ran from the restaurant. An odd, empty feeling came over Jason when she'd gone.

"It was the only thing to do," he muttered under his breath.

"Sir?" Giles said, his expression concerned as he gathered up the dishes from the table. "Is everything okay?"

"No," Jason said. "Everything is definitely not okay. Bring me another Scotch, will you? In fact, bring me the whole damned bottle."

Chapter Four

All the way home on the bus, through a sleepless night and on into the next day day Dana tried to dismiss the trembly feeling in the pit of her stomach as nothing more than the pitch of acid. Jason Halloran had infuriated her. He'd led her on, hinted that perhaps they could find some means to coexist. Then he'd shot her down. No wonder her stomach was churning.

As angry as she was, though, she sensed she had made a very narrow escape. The unexpected effect of those few brief moments of Jason Halloran's warm attention had just about stolen her breath away. No man had ever, *ever* looked at her quite that way, had ever listened so intently, as if she were special and not just another conquest. The guys in the neighborhood had made their crude passes, but she'd fended them off easily enough and forgotten about them in a heartbeat.

None of them had made her tingle inside, though. None of them had stirred the kind of waking, temptation-filled dreams Jason Halloran stirred without even trying. A woman could land in a lot of trouble if she took his kindness seriously. Those warm feelings he inspired had turned to ashes.

Luckily her work at the print shop was piled high. It kept her from remembering the way his gaze had lingered, the way his fingers had curled reassuringly around hers for just an instant, the way his lips had curved into an unforgettable smile.

No, dammit! She would not remember. She had plans and those plans did not include making big mistakes, not when it came to her heart. Besides, she couldn't afford to allow herself to become distracted by a man, especially one as unsuitable as Jason Halloran. With his stuffy, conservative way of thinking, he was the kind of man who could easily turn into a white knight. He would want to do things for her, make her life better. Just look how he'd offered to help her find a job, if only to get himself off the hook. Before she knew it, she would be counting on those little snatches of generosity. She would become weak. And when he lost interest in helping, as everyone who'd ever mattered to her had, this time she might not have the strength to fight back.

Who was she kidding? Jason Halloran didn't want any part of her. He'd made that clear. The last thing she had to worry about was becoming dependent on him in any way. He'd see to that.

"Dana!"

Filled with guilt, she jerked around to meet the impatient gaze of her boss, Henry Keane. "I thought you told me if I gave you yesterday morning off so you could go to your meeting, you'd make up for it today. I don't see that stack of proofreading shrinking."

"Sorry. I'm just a little distracted. Did I have any calls while I was taking those flyers over to Mr. Webster?" she asked, thinking that John Lansing was likely to call at any moment to hear her decision. She was going to force a no past her lips, even if it killed her.

"You were expecting that brother of yours to check in? Is he in trouble again?"

"No, Mr. Keane," she replied dutifully.

"A boyfriend, then?"

His sarcastic tone was meant to remind her about his edict that she not receive or make personal calls except on her break. It meant that Sammy spent too many unsupervised hours after school, but she had little choice in the matter. She doubted a few five-minute phone calls were likely to keep him out of trouble, anyway. The truth of the matter was that he'd been a latchkey kid from the beginning, except on those rare occasions when Rosie had looked after him in her haphazard way.

"No, not a boyfriend, either," she said. "Never mind. I'll catch up on all this by the end of the day. I promise."

He stood behind her until he was apparently reassured that she meant what she'd said. Finally she heard his small, satisfied huff, then the shuffle of his feet as he went back to his own office.

As irritating as she found the man, she knew she owed him. He'd offered her the latitude to expand her duties, to develop a small design business. Even though he took the money, she'd gained in experience. Her portfolio was crammed with top quality flyers and brochures she'd been able to create on shoestring budgets.

Maybe she could even convince him to improve the terms of the last deal he'd offered her. As cranky as he often was, deep down he was fair. She'd pull together some statistics to show him that his own printing business had improved since having her on board to do occasional designs.

There was a timid tap on her door and she looked up to see Mrs. Finch, who owned the neighborhood bookstore, hovering in the doorway. "Dana, honey? Do you have a minute? I could come back."

Dana smiled. "For you, I always have time. Come in. What's up?"

"I hate to impose, but I wondered if those flyers for the storytelling session are ready. I hate to rush you when I know how busy you are."

Mrs. Finch was a sweet old lady, who'd given Dana a break more than once on books she needed for her classes. Dana liked helping her out now and then by doing the posters for her special events. She also endured the woman's tendency to meddle in her life.

"I have the flyers right here," Dana said, handing her the bundle of bright yellow paper.

"Oh, thank you, dear." She looked at the design and beamed. "They're lovely as usual. By the way, did you apply for that job, like you planned?" Mrs. Finch asked, practically on cue. She hefted her round body up on a stool next to Dana, clearly ready for a nice long chat.

"Yes."

"You'll get it," the old woman said loyally. "Is that Mr. Lansing an attractive man?"

"Very."

''Married?''

''I don't know.''

Mrs. Finch sighed with obvious disappointment. ''Dana, it's time you started looking for a nice young man. You can't ignore opportunities that come your way.''

''I don't have time for a relationship,'' she said for probably the hundredth time this month alone. Her social life—or lack of one—was Mrs. Finch's favorite topic. She used inquiries about Dana's job hunting only as an introduction to the more important subject of the men she'd met on the interviews.

''You have to make the time.'' At Dana's glowering expression, she held up her hands. ''Okay. I can see you're busy. You can't talk about this now. You just remember what I said.''

''I'll remember,'' Dana said as dutifully as always. It was no surprise that this time an image of Jason Halloran crept into her mind. There was a predatory gleam in his eyes that would have made Mrs. Finch's romantic fantasies turn downright steamy. Dana tried to banish the image, but Jason's face lingered with the pesky persistence of a man on a mission. She didn't dare to think what that mission might be.

She was still considering the possibilities when the phone rang.

''Dana, it's John Lansing. Can you get over to my office this afternoon?''

She sighed. She could turn him down now or wait and turn him down in person. Waiting could be risky, especially once she saw the inside of that office again and felt those stirrings of creative energy.

''Actually I've reached a decision. I don't think it

will be necessary for me to come by. I'm afraid I can't accept your offer."

"Because of the Halloran situation, right?"

She doubted if they were referring to exactly the same *Halloran situation,* but he was close enough. "Right."

"I think I've found a solution. Can you get over here to discuss it?"

All those dreams she'd had about a career in graphic design combined to overcome her doubts. "I can't get there before five-thirty."

"Then I'll see you at five-thirty."

For the rest of the afternoon and all during the bus ride across town, Dana was torn between anticipation and dread. What sort of solution could he possibly have found? Had he found some way of getting Brandon Halloran to change his mind about taking his business away from the Lansing Agency if he didn't get his way? Brandon didn't strike her as the sort of man to surrender so easily. Besides, would John Lansing even want to hire her if it weren't for Brandon's enthusiasm?

At the agency she was ushered into John Lansing's office immediately. He stood up and held out his hand.

"Congratulations!" he said warmly. "You've got yourself a job and your first account. Jason Halloran has loosened up a bit. He's very anxious to work with you."

She stared at him blankly. "That can't be."

"Excuse me?"

"I spoke with him last night. He said..." She shook her head, trying to clear it. "I'm afraid I don't understand. He wants to work with me directly? You actually spoke to him and he said that?"

Lansing regarded her oddly. "I'll admit I never thought he'd go for those designs, but why does that surprise you so? Your work is good."

"It's a long story," she muttered, not at all sure how she felt about this turn of events. Maybe Jason had simply decided he could put up with her temporarily. Later he would find some way to shift the account to another artist. That way everyone would be happy. Everyone except Dana. She couldn't imagine working with a man who'd made it abundantly clear he couldn't stand the sight of her.

"Tell me something, Mr. Lansing. Is it unusual for a beginner like me to be assigned to an account the size of Halloran Industries?"

John Lansing didn't bat an eye at the question or its implication. "Unusual, yes. Unheard of, no. When an artist is as talented as you are, sometimes career moves happen very quickly."

"But you were surprised by Mr. Halloran's request," she persisted.

"Surprised? Perhaps a little, but not displeased, Ms. Roberts. My goal is always to keep the client satisfied. Clearly Mr. Halloran is more than satisfied by what he's seen so far, as is his grandfather. But you already knew that."

"Yes. So you said," Dana muttered.

"I beg your pardon?"

"Nothing. Shouldn't someone with more experience supervise this account? Lesley, perhaps? I'd be happy to work on smaller jobs at first."

"Absolutely not. As long as the Hallorans are happy with your work, that's all that matters. You will be able to start right away, won't you?"

Dana had no idea what was going on, but she had

to take a risk that things would work out. ‘‘I’ll have to give notice at my current job, but I could begin doing a few things for you in my spare time for the next two weeks if that would be helpful.’’

‘‘I’ll let you work your schedule out directly with Mr. Halloran. I got the impression he wants to work closely with you on this campaign and he wants to get started as soon as possible.’’

Dana bit back another sarcastic comment. The minute she’d agreed to a starting date and said goodbye, she went straight to the nearest pay phone and called Halloran Industries. Though it was past four o’clock closing time by Jason Halloran’s standards, she wasn’t surprised to discover that he was still in his office. No doubt he’d been waiting for her to call and bless him for this gift he’d bestowed on her.

‘‘Listen,’’ she said abruptly when he picked up. ‘‘I can’t begin to understand what made you change your mind, but I think there are one or two things you and I need to get clear.’’

‘‘What the devil are you talking about now?’’

‘‘One, I will do the very best job on the Halloran Industries account that I can.’’

‘‘What?’’

She was too busy warming up to pay much attention to the stunned tone in his voice. ‘‘I’m not through. Two, I don’t want you to think for one minute that I am so grateful that I will fall into your bed. If I sense even the tiniest hint that you have anything in mind besides business, I will quit and slap you with a harassment suit that will make your head spin. Have I made myself clear?’’

‘‘Have you lost your mind?’’

''Not yet, but I'm a little concerned that a few weeks around you and I just might.''

''Are you finished?'' he asked quietly. ''I'd like to say something.''

''I don't think so,'' she said, her blood pumping fast and furiously with righteous outrage. ''I'm afraid if I stay on this phone for another second I will tell you what I really think of a man who uses his position and power to control other people's lives, to jerk them around like puppets. I'm not a puppet, Mr. Halloran. Remember that!''

She heard his muttered exclamation just as she slammed the receiver into place. If Jason Halloran thought for one second he was going to play games with her life, he was very sadly mistaken.

With her anger vented, she took a deep breath and allowed herself to think about the fact that she had gotten a job that would be coveted by any design school graduate. Not even Jason Halloran's odd change of heart and questionable motives could take away the pure rush of satisfaction.

''Hot damn!'' she said, spinning around in the middle of the sidewalk, oblivious to the smiles of those passing by. For the first time in her life, she really believed that things were going her way.

That notion crashed the minute she got home. She found Sammy in the bathroom trying frantically to disguise the fact that his eyes were black and blue and his jaw bloodied.

''Oh, Sammy,'' she murmured, gingerly touching the swelling. ''What happened to you?''

''I bumped into a door,'' he muttered, shoving her hand away.

''Did this door have a name?'' she asked wryly.

''Stay out of it, sis.''

''Did this have anything to do with the VCR? Is that man still bothering you?''

With a glare in her direction, he pushed past her and headed for the front door.

''Sammy!''

''It's nothing, okay. I can handle it.''

''Is this your idea of handling it? What about next time?''

For just an instant he looked like a scared kid, then the bravado was back in place. It reminded her all too clearly of her own tendency to mask her fears with false courage.

''I don't think they'll mess with me anymore,'' he said, sounding hopeful.

''But what if they do?'' she asked. ''They have to be stopped now, before you wind up really hurt.''

He whirled on her furiously. ''You know what'll really hurt me? Having my big sister let everyone know that she thinks I'm still a baby, that's what. No wonder these guys think they can push me around. You treat me like a kid.''

Dana swallowed the desire to remind him that he was just a kid. Obviously his pride had been almost as battered as his face. He didn't need her to deliver the final blow.

''I'm sorry,'' she said gently. ''It's just that I worry about you. If anything every happened to you, I really don't know what I'd do.''

Sammy's tough facade crumpled the instant he detected the tears welling up in her eyes. ''Aw, sis. Don't cry,'' he pleaded.

''How can I help it?'' she said, swiping at the tears. ''Seeing you like this scares me. Sammy, if you don't stop hanging around with guys like these you'll end up in more trouble than I can ever bail you out of."

"I can take care of myself," he reminded her.

Dana sighed. She couldn't win this argument. No matter how badly she wanted to protect him, no matter how hard she tried to steer him on the right course, it was clear that there were some lessons Sammy was just going to have to learn for himself. Letting go, though, was absolute hell.

She drew in another deep breath and forced a smile. "How about pizza for dinner? We can celebrate my new job."

Sammy's responding smile was far more natural than hers. "You got it? I thought you said you weren't gonna take it, that those Halloran guys were nuts."

"I still think that, but I start in two weeks, anyway. The opportunity is too good to pass up. I'll find a way to get along with them."

Sammy's arms came around her waist and he hoisted her into the air, twirling her around until they were both giddy with laughter.

"I knew it!" he whooped. "You've got it made now. Are they payin' you big bucks?"

Dana's laughter faltered. "Oh, my gosh. I never even asked."

Sammy groaned. "Sis, you really gotta toughen up. Want me to go in and negotiate for you?"

Grinning at his change in mood, she said, "No, I really think I can handle this on my own, but thanks for offering. Now how about that pizza? A large one."

"Pepperoni, onions and mushrooms?"

"The works," she countered. "Everything except anchovies."

"You got it. I'll be back in a flash."

It wasn't until Sammy was out the door and thundering down the stairs that she stopped to wonder where he'd gotten enough money to pay for the pizza.

Chapter Five

The impossible woman was going to disrupt his life after all! Jason could have sworn they'd reached a total understanding about steering clear of each other the night before. Now Dana was accusing him of who knew what and seemed to have some crazy notion that the two of them were going to work together despite that agreement. He couldn't allow that to happen. Sooner or later he was likely to abandon all common sense and either kiss her or kill her. He didn't want to lay odds on which it would be.

It had taken a lot of very fast talking, but he had finally convinced John Lansing to give him Dana's home address. She would not have the last word, not this time. The woman had an infuriating knack for jumping to the wrong conclusions, at least where he was concerned. His jaw still ached from the first incident. Once again he didn't know what the hell she was talking about. That phone call of hers was yet more evidence that she was way too impulsive. So was her decision to slam the phone down in his ear. It had set his teeth on edge, tipping the scales more toward murder than seduction.

He had to admit, though, that for one brief flash he had found it exhilarating to battle wits with a woman who wasn't afraid to offend him. Ironically Dana had more to lose than most women, yet she'd blasted him with both barrels just now on the phone. What she'd said might have irritated him with its unfairness, but the plain speaking had made his blood fairly sizzle with excitement. As Jason drove across town, he realized he could hardly wait to see her. He couldn't help wondering what would happen when all that misguided fury turned to passion.

Now that he was actually in her neighborhood, however, he was so appalled by what he saw that this latest argument faded in importance. Used to Boston's finest old sections, Jason was unprepared for the general air of poverty and neglect he found in this cramped, worn-down area. The buildings were in a sad state of disrepair, some of them clearly deserted. Most worrisome, though, were the young thugs hanging around on street corners obviously looking for trouble.

In some measure the neighborhood explained Dana's fearless nature. But there was no doubt in Jason's mind that a young woman as beautiful and guileless as Dana was in danger here, no matter how hardened she thought she was. A surprising and overwhelming desire to protect her swept through him. Despite her tough exterior, despite the strength he'd seen in her, he'd sensed an underlying vulnerability that aroused all sorts of unexpected and unfamiliar white knight fantasies in him. Dana would probably laugh in his face if he suggested such a thing.

Maybe he should try to talk her into moving, though. He'd find her something safer himself. He'd insist that Lansing pay her a decent salary. Then he could fire her from the Halloran account with a clear conscience, satisfied that her life was in order—or at least in as much order as the life of anyone like Dana was ever likely to be. He would have done his duty, as Hallorans always did.

Despite the evidence all around him, Jason actually hoped to find something nicer once he reached Dana's address. Instead, her building was no better than the rest on the block. He parked his flashy sports car with great reluctance, wondering if it would still be there when he returned. There was a trio of rough-looking characters eyeing it with evident fascination when he set the alarm. He figured they could override the expensive system in less than twenty seconds if they dared to try. No wonder Sammy had developed a larcenous streak, if guys like these had been his playmates.

The downstairs windows in Dana's building were covered with bars. The linoleum in the foyer was yellowed and peeling, though he noticed that someone had recently scrubbed it and the air was scented with a light, flowery fragrance. He climbed the stairs to the third floor and knocked.

He heard footsteps, the cautious rattle of chains, then "Who is it?"

"Jason."

The silence grew thick before she finally said flatly, "We have nothing to discuss."

The stubborn tone was exactly what he'd expected.

"I think we do. I can say what I have to say from out here or you can let me in. Which is it?"

The chained door across the hall opened a discreet crack. Curious eyes watched him. Dana's door remained solidly closed, testimony to her fondness for scenes. Apparently she was just itching for another one.

"Okay, we'll do it your way," he said, unbuttoning his coat and leaning casually against the doorjamb. Fortunately he doubted anyone in this neighborhood had ever heard of the Hallorans. "You seem to have gotten some crazy idea that I want you on the Halloran account, after all. Believe me, nothing could be farther from the truth."

There was a long pause while she apparently wrestled with reality, something that obviously eluded her most of the time. Finally she countered, "John Lansing told me point-blank that you wanted to work with me. He said you'd insisted on it."

"I have not spoken to John Lansing in days. Are you absolutely certain he said this was my idea?"

"He said...he implied..." She groaned. "Your grandfather," she said wearily. "Why didn't I think of that? It must have been your grandfather."

Jason rolled his eyes. Now *that* made perfect sense. He should have detected the fine touch of Brandon Halloran himself. "That would be my guess," he agreed.

"Doesn't that man ever take no for an answer?"

"Not that I've noticed."

The door crept open. "I suppose you'd better come in, so we can figure something out."

She sounded resigned. The door across the hall inched open another fraction. Now that he understood what had happened, Jason began to relax. This was a mix-up they could fix. Yet her attitude irked him just a little. Getting involved with him, as his grandfather wanted her to do, was hardly the awful sacrifice she'd painted it to be. Some of Boston's wealthiest, most sophisticated women considered him quite a catch.

"Sure you trust me?" he taunted in a deliberately lazy, seductive tone. A real streak of mischief seemed to creep over him.

The gap in both doorways widened. Dana saw what was happening across the hall and motioned him inside. "Get in here."

"You don't have to let the dude in," a male voice said from behind her. The adolescent tone traveled over several octaves, but it was heavy with animosity. "You want him outta here, I'll take care of it."

Jason caught sight of the skinny young boy with blond hair and blue eyes that matched Dana's. Sammy, no doubt. Jason took an instinctive and immediate dislike to him. If Dana puzzled and disturbed him, this boy was like an alien creature. The kid was in serious need of a decent barber. His expression was filled with hostility and his stance was brotherly protective. On one level Jason admired the attitude; on another he began to realize just exactly what Dana was up against with the little punk.

Dana sighed. "It's okay, Sammy. I can handle Mr. Halloran."

Jason's eyebrows lifted a fraction.

She ignored the implied skepticism. "Do you want some coffee or something? We have a couple slices of pizza left."

Sammy scowled at the invitation. Clearly he would have preferred to slug Jason or, at the very least, escort him forcefully from the apartment. It made him wonder exactly what Dana had told her brother about him. Or if the boy was simply savvy enough to understand the odd chemistry at work between Jason and his sister, a chemistry he didn't begin to understand himself. Now that he was here, he realized he'd been drawn by more than a need to settle some crazy mix-up about a job.

"Coffee would be nice," Jason said.

Sammy took a step closer to his sister. "Sis, you want me to hang around?"

Dana shook her head slowly as if she were reluctant to let him leave, but unwilling to admit to the weakness. "No," she said finally. "It's okay. Mr. Halloran and I need to resolve some business matters."

"I'll be at Joey's if you need me." He glared at Jason. "It's just downstairs."

Jason nodded seriously. "I'll keep that in mind."

When Sammy had gone, Jason observed, "Looks like he's picked up your protective streak."

"We learned a long time ago to stick together."

There was a note of defiance in her voice, a warning that Jason couldn't miss. How many times had Dana put herself on the line to bail out her troublesome brother? He'd figured it for a one-sided avenue, but seeing Sammy just now he realized that the guardian angel activities worked both ways.

"He looks a little the worse for wear. Did he run into a door?"

"So he claims," she said ruefully.

"What happened to the VCR?" he asked, wondering how she'd handled that after she'd foolishly risked her neck to go after the thief who'd sold it to her brother.

"I made him give it to the church down the block." She grinned. "I was hoping maybe it would make him go down there a little more often, instead of hanging out with those creeps he seems to like so much."

"Has it worked?"

"Not so far, as you can probably tell from the black eyes, but I'm still hopeful."

Dana started to lead the way into the apartment's kitchen. Jason tossed his coat on a chair, then looked around as he followed her. He was hoping for clues that would help him to understand this woman whose personality clashed so with his.

The cracked walls had been painted a shade as bright as whitewashed adobe. A tall basket held paper flowers in poppy red, vibrant orange and sunshine yellow. Throw pillows in similar colors had been tossed on the faded beige sofa that looked uncomfortably lumpy. Clay pots of plants lined the windowsill with shades of green. Despite the frayed condition of the furniture, the room had a cheerful, homey air about it, all achieved on a shoestring. Books were stacked helter-skelter, worn copies of everything from business texts to art books, from history to philosophy. He doubted they were Sammy's.

"You read a lot?" he said. When the question drew her back into the room, he gestured toward the well-dusted, obviously well-used collection.

"Buying books is cheaper than taking classes," she said from the archway leading to the kitchen.

"Looks like some pretty heavy stuff. What made you pick it?"

"I got my hands on the reading lists for some of the courses at Boston College," she admitted with a shrug, as if the act had been no big deal. Once again, though, Jason was impressed by her tenacious desire to improve her lot in life. He had taken so much in his life for granted. Dana would probably have made much better use of a college education than he had thus far.

"You amaze me," he said quietly.

Dana's gaze met his, lingered for a heartbeat, then skittered nervously away. Her cheeks turned pink and she hurriedly took the remaining steps into the kitchen. Jason went after her.

The kitchen held a tiny table for two. The red Formica top was decades old and the chairs didn't match. The stove and refrigerator were so ancient Jason wondered that they worked at all.

Dana was silent as she made the coffee. Jason sat down and watched, surprisingly content for the first time since she'd slammed the phone in his ear an hour earlier.

Odd how little time he'd ever spent in a kitchen, he thought. His mother had been a haphazard cook at best, too busy with her causes to bake cookies or stir homemade soup, though he had a vague recollection of a time when that hadn't been so. On those rare days when a housekeeper hadn't left something warming in the oven for their dinner and his father had stayed late at the office, they had ordered pizza or brought home Chinese take-out. Once in a while they'd even gorged themselves on fast-food hamburgers and fries. Always, though, they'd eaten at the huge mahogany table in the dining room. That table could have seated every Pilgrim at the first Thanksgiving. Jason had always hated it.

Now he discovered there was something cozy and intimate about sitting here while Dana bustled around, putting home-baked cookies on a plate and pouring coffee for the two of them. Another knot of tension eased.

She was dressed as she had been when he'd first seen her, in snug-fitting jeans and a sweater that skimmed past her slender hips. This one was as orange as those fake flowers in the living room and featured an abstract design in electric blue. It took everything in him to refrain from the impulse to trace the design from the V-neckline over the swell of her breasts and on to a waistline he was sure he could span with his hands. Instead he forced his gaze on, focusing finally on her feet. Despite the chill in the air, she was wearing only a pair of orange socks. There was something unexpectedly sexy about the sight.

Face it, he told himself. There was something just plain sexy about Dana. He'd fought it, but there was no denying he'd felt it each time he was around her. His body responded forcefully to the slightest touch, the most fleeting glance. Working with her would be sheer torture. The most exquisite sort of torture, but painful none the less.

"Thank you," he said when she finally sat down opposite him. "I take it you've decided to declare a truce."

"For the moment," she acknowledged. "It's your grandfather I should have yelled at."

"I'll give you the number," he offered with a grin. "In fact, I'll even dial it for you."

"What are we going to do?"

After seeing the way she lived, how badly she needed the money, Jason knew he had no choice. He drew in a deep breath. "You're going to take the job."

Troubled eyes met his. ''Are you sure? I know it's not what you want.''

''I'm sure I'll survive.''

''Could you manage to sound at least a little bit enthusiastic about it?''

''Don't expect miracles overnight.''

She nodded, but she no longer met his gaze. ''Okay, so where do we go from here?''

Jason followed her cue. ''I suppose you should come by the plant. I think it would be helpful if you could see what we're all about. It may give you some ideas. Then I'd like to go over the timetable I have in mind for the entire campaign, see if it works for you. I don't want you to feel pressured to meet an unreasonable deadline just to prove yourself. Once we're certain everything's in place, then we'll arrange a meeting with my father and grandfather.''

''I think the less I see of your grandfather the better.''

''You may have a point, but there's no escaping it. Granddad likes to be involved in everything. His father founded Halloran Industries and handed it down to him. Of course, at the rate Granddad is going, my father and I won't get our turns until sometime in the next century.''

''He doesn't want to retire?''

''He tosses the idea around every once in a while, then some new project comes along and he can't bring himself to let go.''

Jason couldn't keep the bitterness out of his voice. He loved his grandfather dearly, but Brandon's tight grip on the company's entire operation was keeping both him and his father from any real sense of ownership. No wonder he was bored. He hadn't made a significant decision since he'd joined the firm, at least not without his grandfather looking over his shoulder.

"When can you start?" he asked.

"It'll be a couple of weeks before I can work full-time, but if you need me for something specific before that, I'll try to work it out."

"How about tomorrow?"

"I'll be working."

"Come over on your lunch hour. I'll show you around. I'll order in lunch."

"It takes a half-hour each way on the bus. That hardly leaves time for lunch and a tour."

"You don't have a car?"

"No."

"Then I'll send one for you. Better yet, why don't you let me finance one through our company credit union? You'll need it if you're going to be running back and forth between Halloran Industries and the Lansing offices. Or would you prefer to have me set up an office over at Halloran? I'm sure John would agree."

Once Jason had accepted the fact that there was no way around working with Dana, he'd actually begun warming to the idea. If his grandfather was so enchanted with Dana, perhaps this was Jason's opportunity to actually impress him with the marketing campaign he'd been trying to implement for months now.

However, Dana's expression grew increasingly distressed as Jason's whirlwind enthusiasm mounted. She held up a hand.

"Whoa! Wait a minute!"

"What?"

"I do not want a car of my own. I can't afford it and you know how I feel about credit. As for any running back and forth, I'll manage. I've been taking public transportation around Boston for years.'' She ticked off the points on her fingers. ''Finally if I am going to be working for the Lansing Agency then I should be based at the Lansing Agency. You're just one account. John may have other work for me.''

''Not right away,'' Jason argued. ''I'll need you full-time until we get this off the ground.''

''Then John can bill you for the travel time. I'm staying at the agency.''

Jason recognized the stubborn finality and decided it was time to slow down and stop pressuring her. He wasn't entirely sure himself why his mood had shifted from reluctance to excitement. They could both use a little time to analyze this new relationship and all of its implications.

''We'll try it your way,'' he conceded. ''At the end of a month we'll take a look at it and see how it's working out. Fair enough?''

''Fair enough,'' she agreed, but without much enthusiasm.

Just then the living room door slammed shut and seconds later Sammy loomed in the doorway. ''You're still here?'' he said, an accusatory note in his voice. The rudeness immediately made Jason's hackles rise.

''Mr. Halloran and I are just finishing up,'' Dana told him.

Looking none to pleased, but staying silent, Sammy grabbed a handful of cookies, then went to the refrigerator and poured himself a glass of milk. All the while his distrustful gaze never left Jason.

Jason tried to remember all those lessons in humanity his father had preached for years during his social consciousness phase, but Sammy grated on his nerves.

The kid had trouble written all over his face and an attitude that needed changing. That didn't mean Jason couldn't be polite to him, though. He fished around for a neutral topic.

"Dana tells me you're a junior this year," he said. "I remember what that was like."

"Sure," Sammy said skeptically. "At some prep school, right?"

Jason sensed the resentment and countered. "No, as a matter of fact, I went to school right here in the city. What classes are you taking?"

"English, history, the usual stuff."

"Doing okay?"

Sammy looked disgusted by the whole line of questioning. Dana jumped in. "He makes good grades. Mostly Bs."

Sammy shrugged.

"Thinking of college?" Jason asked.

"You've gotta be kiddin'. Where am I gonna get the money for college?"

"There are scholarships. You've still got plenty of time to apply."

"My grades aren't that good and I ain't no athlete superstar."

"Don't say that," Dana said. "You're on the swim team."

"Big deal. I don't see anybody offering big bucks to people because they can swim the length of a pool."

"Plenty of colleges have swim teams and they do offer scholarships," Jason contradicted. Too many years of liberal dinner table conversations prompted him to offer, "Want me to look into it for you?"

Sammy regarded him with blatant suspicion. "Why

would you do that? You figure if you get rid of me, you can get my sister into bed?''

Dana turned pale. Infuriated at the kid's insulting audacity, Jason was halfway out of his chair when Dana shot him a quelling look. She leveled a furious gaze on her brother and said quietly, ''I think it's time you did your studying.''

Sammy looked ready to argue, but Dana's expression stopped him. Finally he shrugged and left the room without a goodbye.

''He owes you an apology,'' Jason said, keeping a tight rein on his temper. ''For that matter, he owes me one, too. Or maybe you should just wash his mouth out with soap.''

Dana regarded him levelly. ''That's a little outdated, isn't it?''

''It may be old-fashioned, but it's effective when garbage comes out of a kid's mouth.''

''Look, he didn't mean anything by it. He's probably just feeling threatened. I don't usually have men coming around. He doesn't understand that this is just business.''

Her expression dared him to contradict her. Jason ran his fingers through his hair in a gesture of pure frustration. By now his hair was probably every bit as mussed as hers. He was beginning to see how her style had evolved. Sammy seemed to have that effect on everyone.

''Dana, you can't make excuses for a kid that age. He needs to learn that there are consequences for stepping out of line. Did you punish him when he stole the VCR? I mean did you do something more than make him give it to the church?''

Her hands were shaking when she finally looked at him. "This is none of your business."

"It is when he makes an ugly remark about our relationship."

"Since we don't *have* a relationship, I don't think we need to worry about any more remarks."

"One was too many."

"And I'm telling you it won't happen again. I can handle Sammy."

Dana's tone didn't allow for any more interference from him. Jason bit back the desire to tell her that he'd seen kids like Sammy before. Even in his circle of friends, there had been born troublemakers, kids destined to give their families a rough time. If Sammy wasn't taken in hand now, he was going to cross too far over the line between adolescent pranks and serious criminal activity. He may have already. The VCR deal proved that.

Clearly Sammy was already more troublesome than a caring woman like Dana deserved, Jason thought. Sooner or later she wouldn't be able to bail him out just by running interference for him. He needed firm discipline and he needed it now. Dana, however, would have to reach that conclusion on her own.

Jason sighed. "Just promise that you'll ask if you need some help with him. All boys that age are a handful. I was a terror myself, according to my parents. They like to remind me of that periodically."

"I won't need any help," she said flatly.

Reluctant to leave things on that note, but aware that they'd only end up arguing if he stayed, Jason stood up. "I'll send a car for you tomorrow at noon."

"I told you..."

"I know what you told me, but I need you to look

things over as soon as possible. Until you're available full-time, I'll try to make our meetings as convenient for you as possible. Okay?''

Reluctance clearly warred with practicality. ''Okay,'' Dana agreed finally and gave him the address of the print shop where she'd been working.

At the door, Jason's gaze met hers. Confusion filled her eyes.

''I am sorry about Sammy,'' she said. ''What he said was inexcusable.''

He touched a fingertip to her lips. ''You're not the one who needs to apologize.''

She looked so lost that something inside him twisted. Before he could think about what he was doing, Jason leaned down and brushed a gentle kiss across her forehead. As innocent as the kiss was, Dana's breath caught in her throat. Something that might have been panic leaped into her eyes. Jason knew exactly how she felt. He felt as if he'd been slam-dunked by one of the Celtics and was still tangled in the net.

''I'm glad we're going to be working together,'' he told her, his fingers lingering to caress her cheek. The gentle touch was meant to soothe and tame. ''See you tomorrow.''

After one last glance, he left hurriedly, before she could see that he was only a scant hairbreadth away from pulling her into his arms and kissing her the way a man kissed a desirable woman who made his senses spin. Who was he kidding? He wasn't running to spare Dana. He was running because in the last five seconds he'd realized he was in water way over his head and sinking fast.

* * *

All morning Dana tried to think of some way to avoid going out to Halloran Industries on her lunch hour. She wasn't blind to her own foibles; she recognized that Jason represented a temptation that she couldn't afford in her life. It was getting harder and harder to resist his kisses, more and more difficult to recall why he was all wrong for her, why they were all wrong for each other.

She was not looking for complications, she reminded herself sternly. She was looking to put her foot on the first rung up a tall, professional ladder. Money represented power and, after years of feeling powerless, she wanted that sense of control. She wanted to earn it, though, to know it belonged to her no matter what. Getting involved with Jason would sidetrack that plan. She'd waited too long to lose more time by heading down a dead-end road.

The door to her cramped little office opened. "There's some fellow here for you," Mr. Keane said. "He said you'd be expecting him."

Dana sighed. Obviously she'd hesitated too long to call off Jason's plans. She had a feeling that spoke volumes about her determination to steer as clear of him as was humanly possible under the circumstances.

"You'll be back?" her boss asked, his expression worried. He'd been wearing that same expression since she'd told him this morning that she'd be leaving in two weeks. Though he'd wished her well, he was clearly at a loss about how he'd find anyone to replace her who would do as many extra jobs as she'd done for the same paltry salary. He wanted her fully productive until the last possible second.

"I'll be back," she reassured him. "I'm just going

to a lunch meeting with the client I'll be working with when I start my new job.''

''Must be some client if he can afford to send a fancy car for you.''

''Yeah,'' she said ruefully. ''It's some client.''

Chapter Six

Maybe it had been wishful thinking on her part, but Dana had actually expected to find some hired driver waiting for her on the curb outside. She should have known better.

Instead it was Jason himself, his posture relaxed, his golden hair windblown, a smile spreading across his face when she walked out the door. He surveyed the boots, jeans and leather jacket she'd worn in an apparently wasted gesture of defiance and nodded appreciatively, his smile growing. Something about the warmth and approval of that smile heated her insides. Once Jason Halloran decided to make the best of things, obviously he threw over all traces of resentment. She supposed she should have felt grateful. Instead she felt terrified.

No man should have the right to have such a potent effect on a woman, she thought wistfully. Especially on a woman who was trying hard to keep her wits about her.

Jason swept open the door of a low-slung red sports car that was exactly what she would have expected a man like him to drive. It was expensive, impractical and very, very sexy. She barely resisted the urge to run her fingers over the gleaming finish.

Inside she sank into a luxurious bucket seat. She touched the smooth, cream-colored upholstery. The leather was soft as butter. Suddenly she felt as if she were Cinderella on her way to the ball and midnight was still several tantalizing hours away.

"What happened?" she asked, when he was settled behind the wheel. "Couldn't you find a taxi to send for me at this hour?"

"I had an appointment on this side of town, anyway. It was no trouble at all for me to swing by, myself. I figured it would give us longer to talk."

"Very practical," she said. "Why don't I believe you?"

"Because you have this habit of distrusting me?" he suggested without the slightest hint of irritation in his tone. "It's like Pavlov's reflex. I speak, you distrust. Since we've just met, the response can't possibly have anything to do with me. Maybe somebody who looked like me cheated on you in a previous life."

Dana chuckled despite herself and felt a little of her wariness slide away. "I honestly don't recall any cads in my past."

"It's hard to say how many past lives back we're talking about. Can you recall what you were doing in the Middle Ages?"

"Afraid not."

"Any recollections of the French Revolution? The Boston Tea Party? The Civil War?"

"Not a one."

"There, you see? Whatever happened between you and this louse in the past was so awful it's buried in your subconscious. Maybe you ought to see some shrink and dredge it up. Once you've dealt with it, we can get on with things here in the present." He glanced over and grinned at her. "What do you think?"

"I think some of your brain cells froze on the drive over. Did you have the top down?"

"Nope. This is just my lighthearted, accepting-the-inevitable personality."

Dana felt herself responding to Jason's unexpected mood in a way that made her very nervous. It was easy to keep her distance from a man who was stuffy and rigid. This new, relaxed Jason Halloran was devastating. Her defenses were vanishing, even though she didn't trust his declared intentions one bit. She tried to analyze why she distrusted a man she barely knew, but all of a sudden she couldn't think of a single reason more logical than the absurd past-life theory he'd suggested. Which meant there was no reason at all, unless she was willing to admit to the sensual spell he threatened to cast over her.

Maybe she owed the man a chance. If they were going to work together, she really would have to learn to relax just as he had. She couldn't go on questioning his motives for every little action. Then again, if she let down her guard, who knew where things could lead. She bit back the urge to sigh. Her uncomplicated, very focused life suddenly seemed fraught with confusion.

"Tell me about Halloran Industries," she said, hoping to remind both of them that their attention was supposed to be strictly on business. "I know what was in the annual report, but that didn't give me a real feel for the company's history. I think maybe that's what you should be capitalizing on. What do you think?"

To her relief a rare excitement immediately sparked in his light blue eyes. "You mean exploit the fact that this is a family business, that it's been around for four generations, ever since my great-grandfather came over from England at the end of the last century?"

"Exactly. It'll give it a more human image, especially in this age of impersonal conglomerates. Think of a slogan. Four generations of dedication to quality, that sort of thing."

Before Dana realized what he intended, Jason swerved the car to the curb and cut the engine. His hands cupped her cheeks and he kissed her—a quick, impulsive brush of his lips across hers.

Gratitude. That's all it was, she told herself sternly. Like last night's startling goodbye kiss, this one was over almost before the sensation registered. *Almost.* Its swiftness didn't prevent the rise of heat, the lightning flash of desire, but both vanished in a heartbeat, leaving Dana all too readily with the illusion of safety.

"You're fantastic!" he declared, his fingers still warm against her cheeks. "For once Granddad's instincts may have been right. Maybe you will work out. That's the ideal slogan. Everyone will love it, especially my grandfather. Tradition is the only thing that really matters to him."

Dana couldn't help being caught up in his enthusiasm, though a part of her was surprised that he'd embraced the phrase so readily, that he apparently didn't intend to throw up roadblocks at every opportunity. "Are you sure? I mean it was just a suggestion off the top of my head."

"Sometimes the first instincts are the best."

At the exact same instant they both seemed to realize that his hands now rested on her shoulders, that they were still just inches apart.

Talk about first instincts! Suddenly hers had nothing to do with discovering more about textiles. Heat and desire spun through her again, gathering intensity. He was so close that his breath fanned her skin. The exuberant kiss just moments earlier was nothing more than a prelude to this, she realized now. Innocence had been lost to this sparkling awareness. An increasingly familiar, increasingly demanding tension throbbed between them. The lure was irresistible.

"Dana?" It was a soft, questioning plea that matched the confusion in his eyes.

Dana merely sighed, her heart hammering in her chest. Heaven help her, she wanted his mouth to close over hers. She wanted their breath to mingle. She wanted to know the taste of him, the texture of his skin. She could deny it from now until doomsday, but it would be a lie. She wanted to be in his arms. Just for a kiss. Just for this brief moment of discovery.

When she couldn't make herself utter the protest that would have stopped him, he leaned closer, still hesitant, still giving her time to say no. But she couldn't bring herself to do it. With each second that passed, her desire grew. She wanted his lips to caress hers, wanted him to linger long enough for her to savor the unfamiliar sensations that were already exploding inside her.

The first touch was velvet soft and cool. But as if

a fire had been lit somewhere deep inside, the kiss heated. She was aware of the gentle caress of his fingers, of the growing hunger as his mouth claimed hers. With the motor off, the air in the car turned chilly, but Dana felt every bit as hot as if it had been a sunny ninety-five degrees. When the touch of his tongue urged her lips apart, need ripped through her, shaking her with its unexpected intensity.

Why hadn't she known a mere kiss could be like this, that it could awaken astonishing, aching needs? Why did every kiss she'd shared in the past seem as immature and unimportant as those in some silly adolescent game? This one held promise and comfort and danger in an intoxicating blend.

When Jason finally moved away, they were both breathing hard. If she looked half as shaken as she felt, he would know in an instant that he had a power over her that went far beyond his influence with the Lansing Agency. She hoped desperately that he couldn't see that, that the look of triumph and satisfaction on his face had something to do with that crazy slogan she'd come up with and not the few breath-stealing seconds she'd spent in his embrace.

Deep down she knew better, knew that their relationship had shifted onto what for her was uncharted ground. She had gone this far with men before, but never farther. Never had she felt the consuming desire to see where a few kisses might lead.

"I think we ought to be going, don't you?" she said, irritated by the breathless quality of her voice. She knew it would be a waste of what little breath she had to protest that the kiss had been a mistake. They both knew that. She recognized it with dismaying certainty. Jason, for all of his impetuous claiming of her lips, had to know it as well. If anything, he was probably having more second thoughts than she was. It hadn't seemed to matter. That kiss had been as inevitable as a sunrise or the pull of the tides.

"I'm perfectly content to stay right here," he said, his voice low, his gaze lingering in a way that kept her pulse scrambling frantically.

"Jason," she warned, sensing that she was going to have to try those probably futile protests after all.

"Okay, we're going," he said, starting the engine. "But that's not the end of this—not by a long shot."

"It has to be," she retorted quietly.

Serious eyes met hers. "Why?"

"I think that's obvious."

"Not to me."

"Because you're used to getting what you want."

He nodded. "Remember that."

"I don't think I'm likely to forget it," she murmured, grateful that the Halloran Industries building was just ahead.

How was she going to protect herself enough to keep from getting hurt when he remembered that they were all wrong for each other? He was pushy and demanding and powerful. She was struggling to carve a niche in the world. She wouldn't have it handed to her. Power given as a gift could be taken away. How did she make him see that? How did she abstain from the temptation of those potent kisses, the gentle, alluring caresses?

Those questions taunted her as they toured the facility. She was fascinated with everything from the raw wool to the vats of dye, from the giant looms to the finished bolts of cloth. Though it was barely winter, they were already in production on summer fabrics: fine cottons being hand printed with wooden blocks that were centuries old and imported from France. She could have lingered for hours, absorbed by the magic of colorless threads being transformed into rainbows of prints.

Despite her fascination, however, not once could Dana seem to forget that Jason was beside her. One instant his hand was on her back as he guided her through a maze of machinery. Another moment his touch grazed her hand as he held out cloth for her to caress. Nothing, not the coolness of the silks, the soft shimmer of the satins or the richness of the wool blends, could compare with the impact of those seconds when Jason's innocent touch skimmed over her flesh.

By the time they went into his office, Dana felt as if she'd spent six months in the Garden of Eden avoiding the first sinful bite of apple. Her nerves were raw. Desire simmered just below the surface, slamming into her consciousness with the slightest contact.

"How about a glass of wine?" Jason said, forcing her to meet his gaze.

"Wine?"

"With lunch."

Wine was the last thing she needed. She was already too warm, too giddy, deep inside where such reactions were dangerous. Inhibitions flickered too weakly, then disappeared altogether. She mustered one last bit of resolve.

"Just a cup of coffee," she said. "I really should be getting back."

"Not until you've had something to eat. Harriet ordered for us."

Resolved or not, Dana had gone without on too

many occasions to be able to leave food untouched. Reluctantly she sat down at the small table that had been set up by the window in Jason's office. Outside the sun had broken through for the first time in days. It gave the city a silvery cast as it bounced off the windows of the skyscrapers in the distance.

Despite her feelings of guilt over the waste, she found herself merely picking at the lobster salad. She broke off chunks of a croissant and popped them into her mouth without really tasting the delicate, buttery flakiness. The only sensation she was truly aware of was the heat that flared deep inside her each time she met Jason's intense gaze. She tried her best to avoid looking into the blue-gray depths, but again and again her gaze was drawn back.

It irritated the daylights out of her that the man made her so nervous. She'd been on countless dates. Goodness knows, she knew how to carry on a conversation. Most of the time she couldn't seem to shut up. Now, just because she was alone with someone with a little bit of high-class polish, she felt all tongue-tied. No, she corrected. It had nothing to do with Jason's class. The blame belonged on the responses he stirred in her.

Jason was just a man, Dana reminded herself.

Yeah, but what a man! countered a dreamy, feminine voice she'd never heard before.

Oh, grow up, Dana shot right back.

That's the problem, honey. You've just grown up.

Dana was not at all pleased with the way this mental conversation was going. She wasn't much happier with the fascinated expression on Jason's face. He looked as if he could hear every word and was thoroughly enjoying his role in the unexpected awakening of her libido.

"Don't even think about it," she muttered, partly to him, partly to herself.

A knowing grin spread across Jason's face. "Think about what?"

Dana threw down her napkin. "I have to get back to work. Would you call a cab for me?"

"You're running," he observed.

"Will you call the cab or should I do it myself?"

"I'll take you back to work."

When he made no move to get up, she said, "Now."

"As soon as you've eaten your dessert. It's cherry cobbler."

Dana nearly groaned in frustration. How had Jason guessed that cobbler was her favorite? Had he done a background check? He was just the type to leave nothing to chance. Even so, that kind of attention to detail could too easily become addictive. When was the last time anyone had paid attention to what she wanted or needed? Sammy, who knew her better than anyone, couldn't even remember her birthday.

Before Dana could protest that she was full—a blatant lie he'd see through in an instant, anyway—Jason was setting a warm bowl of the rich dessert in front of her. Ice cream melted over the pastry crust, just the way he knew she liked it. He looked so damned pleased with himself, so anxious to please her.

"You don't leave anything to chance, do you?" She didn't mean it as a compliment, but the resentment got lost somewhere between her brain and her voice. Jason heard nothing more than her reluctant gratitude.

"I try my best to please."

''Why?''

''This is your first day with Halloran Industries, after all.''

His tone was quietly serious. It was a logical explanation, but she heard the unspoken undercurrents. She put down her spoon and leveled a look at him. ''So, Sammy was right. You are aiming to get me into your bed. Or are you trying to scare me off, Mr. Halloran?''

''For some reason, I don't think you scare that easily.''

''No, I don't.''

He didn't look nearly as embarrassed as she had hoped at having his motives questioned. There was definitely no sign of a quick retreat, just an infuriating, lip-curving hint of amusement.

''I think I liked it better when you were snapping my head off. I don't trust this new act one bit,'' she said.

''Funny. I would have guessed it was yourself you no longer trusted.''

Jason sat back and watched in satisfaction as the full meaning of his remark slowly registered. A blush stole into Dana's cheeks, and the wariness in her eyes increased tenfold. She raked her fingers through her hair.

''Jason, we can't work together if you're going to try to turn this into some sort of seduction every time we have a meeting.''

''If you'll recall, I didn't bring it up. You did.''

''No, I just...''

''Asked if I wanted to sleep with you.''

If anything, Dana looked even more flustered than she had in the car when she had realized that she had kissed him back with every bit as much fervor as he'd displayed. Obviously there was one area in which they could reach an agreement—they both enjoyed playing with fire.

"Okay, you're right. I did say that," she said. "It's best if we get this out in the open and face the fact that it wouldn't work between us."

"I agree," he said, clearly surprising her. "On the other hand, there's something at work here that we can't very well ignore or it will drive us both crazy."

"No, there's not," she denied.

Jason merely regarded her skeptically.

"Okay, so maybe there is this…something. I never expected…"

Jason seized the opening. "What? To get along with me? To want me?"

Dana looked as if she might be grinding her teeth. Finally she said, "I do not want you."

"I could prove just what a liar you are."

Her chin lifted. "How?"

"Don't tempt me."

"How?" she repeated evenly. The dare in her voice belied the doubt in her eyes.

Without allowing himself so much as an instant to consider what he was doing, Jason was around to her side of the table before she could blink. Hands firmly on her waist, he lifted her to her feet and dragged her against him. He looked into the worried blue depths of her eyes and said softly, "Like this."

Then his lips claimed hers, tasting the faint sweetness of cherries, the creaminess of ice cream, the flavor that was uniquely hers. This time Jason abandoned gentle persuasiveness in favor of raw hunger. He had to rid himself of this need that had sprung up seemingly overnight. Those kisses had been like drink for an alcoholic, intoxicating and addictive. It was clear he would never be satisfied until he'd made love to her. Perhaps then he could get back to thinking rationally, the way he always did. This wouldn't be the first time in his life he'd given in to a foolish impulse.

Dana didn't even pretend to fight the kiss. There was the faintest hint of an astonished gasp, and then she was kissing him back, fitting her body to his with an instinctive need every bit as hot and urgent as his own. He could feel the scrambling of her pulse as his fingers curved around her neck. His own heart pounded, the strength of its beat an affirmation of the passion he knew existed between them. Her skin, soft as silk beneath the hem of her sweater, went from shivery cool to searing hot at his touch.

She was still trembling in his arms, her fingers laced together behind his neck, her lips soft and sweet and yielding beneath his, when the door to his office banged open.

''What the devil?'' His grandfather's startled reaction was quickly followed by a tolerant chuckle. ''Maybe this is a bad time.''

''It is,'' Jason confirmed, holding an obviously embarrassed Dana tight against him. ''Go away.''

Brandon wasn't about to be turned away so easily. ''Not before I say hello to this young woman again,'' he insisted, striding across the room.

''Save the charm, Granddad. We're both on to you.''

Undaunted, Brandon just shrugged. ''Just looking out for the company's interests.'' He grinned at Dana. His gaze lingered on her sweater, a crazy quilt of hot pink, lime green and lemon yellow. His eyes narrowed.

"Interesting," he muttered finally. "Where did you get it?"

Dana was regarding him as if he'd lost his mind. "Get what, sir?"

"The sweater, girl. Cheap yarn, but the design's good. Bold. I like it."

She seemed more confused than offended by the criticism of the wool's quality. "You like it?"

Brandon chuckled. "Sorry. Occupational hazard. Can't resist seeing what the competition's up to."

"I'm afraid I'm not much competition. You have nothing to worry about. It's a very limited edition."

"You designed it?" he said, sounding no more surprised than Jason was himself. Jason regarded the sweater more closely and began to wonder about all the others he'd seen her wear. Had she designed those as well?

"Designed and knit it. I'm afraid you're right about the yarn, but it's the dimestore's best."

She stepped away from Jason. He dragged her back and leaned down to whisper, "Remember, we're in this together."

She glared at him, then tried to stare Brandon Halloran down. "Just for the record, sir, I'm not *dating* your grandson. I don't even *like* your grandson."

Brandon chuckled. "I see. Too bad. Seems to me he could use a woman with a little spunk in his life. The boy doesn't have anyone around to keep him on his toes. Needs to have a little fun."

Dana regarded him with an expression that was both disbelieving and irritated. "Love is a responsibility. It's not some game you play."

''That's true enough,'' Brandon told her with a gentleness and sensitivity Jason wouldn't have believed his grandfather capable of. Apparently the old man had detected Dana's insecurities and intended to rid her of them.

He went on, ''I have a few years on you, young lady, and I'm here to tell you, a relationship works a whole lot better if you can pack a little fun and a lot of sparks into it. Now, you two get back to whatever it was you were—'' he hesitated, a twinkle in his eyes ''—discussing. Oh, and Jason, I'd like to see you in my office whenever you're free… No rush,'' he added slyly as he closed the door firmly behind him.

Dana immediately spun out of Jason's arms. ''Now, see what you've done! He's going to think because he caught us…''

''Kissing,'' Jason supplied.

''He's going to think he's winning.''

Jason drew her to him. ''Well, we'll have the last laugh, won't we?''

She jerked away from him. He sat on the edge of his desk and watched her pace, her agitation mounting with each step. She stopped in front of him.

''I don't think you're taking this seriously.''

''Believe me, when it comes to my future, I take everything seriously.''

''Well then?'' she demanded. ''How are you going to convince him he can't manipulate us?''

''Would you suggest I take him out and give him a stern talking to?''

''It wouldn't hurt,'' she grumbled.

''It wouldn't help, believe me. Granddad's as stubborn as they come.''

Her fingers plowed nervously through her hair, setting it on end as she began pacing again. ''You're awfully calm about this.''

''Dana, he can't make us do anything we don't want to do.''

''I'm not so sure about that.''

''Well, I am. Relax.''

Apparently Dana did not appreciate his matter-of-fact attitude about his grandfather. She looked as if she'd like to strangle the pair of them.

''Jason, what happened just now...''

''And earlier and last night,'' he reminded her.

She scowled at him. ''It is not going to happen again. Ever! We are working together, that's all. If you can't accept that, then I'll arrange to have someone else assigned to your account.'' She grabbed her jacket and purse from the sofa where she'd dropped them and stormed through the door.

Jason figured it would take about ten seconds for her to realize that she was stranded unless she asked him to arrange for a ride back to her office. He counted on another sixty seconds for her to cool down enough to ask for a lift.

When three minutes had passed without her return, he realized she had every intention of getting back to the print shop on her own. He snatched his coat off the coatrack and took off after her.

''Mr. Halloran,'' Harriet called after him, ''where are you going?''

''I'll be back in an hour.''

''But...''

''Take messages, Harriet.''

''Your grandfather...''

''He'll understand.''

He found Dana halfway to the bus stop. He pulled

his car alongside of her. She didn't even look his way. He used the power button to roll down the window.

"Get in."

"Go to hell." She tripped over a mound of icy slush and nearly fell facedown. She grabbed the hood of the car to steady herself.

Teeth clenched, Jason said again, "Get in. I'll take you back to work."

Stubbornly, Dana marched on. There were half a dozen people at the bus stop. Jason wedged his car into the curb, cut the engine and got out.

"Dana, for heaven's sake, don't be an idiot. Let me give you a lift."

She stood behind the other riders and stoically ignored him. He clambered through the slush until he stood face-to-face with her—Italian loafer toe-to-toe with her motorcycle boot.

"Are you more upset over the kiss, or my grandfather catching us or over the fact that you didn't want to be interrupted any more than I did?"

Six faces turned toward the two of them. It was impossible to mistake the amused interest. With the wind whipping down the street, Jason was sure their intimate conversation provided some much-needed heat. How the hell did he wind up in the middle of some scene every time he was with this woman?

"Jason," Dana protested weakly.

"Well, which is it?"

"Do we have to discuss this here?" she demanded in an undertone.

He shook his head. "No. We could discuss it in my car."

She sighed. "Okay, you win." She slogged through the slush and got into the car, leaving the observers thoroughly disappointed. One of the men gave Jason a thumbs-up sign.

"Hey, man, good luck. I have a hunch you're going to need it."

Jason grinned. "I have a hunch you're right," he said, just as a handful of filthy snow landed squarely in the middle of his face. Stunned by her daring, he slowly wiped it away as he rounded the car to the driver's side. As he slid in, he shot Dana a meaningful look.

"You will pay for that, sweetheart," he said quietly.

"Hey, it was your grandfather who said you needed me to bring a little fun into your life. I see what he means. You can't take a joke."

As the remnants of the snowball melted and dripped down his face, Jason found himself chuckling. "I'm not sure this was exactly the fun he had in mind."

"Oh?" she said innocently. "Trust me, *sweetheart,* it's the only kind you and I are likely to have."

"I guess we'll see about that, won't we?" Actually he had discovered in the past twenty-four hours that he could hardly wait for the games to begin.

Dear Lord, he really was losing his mind.

Chapter Seven

Jason pulled his car into the first space he could find along the crowded street near the print shop. Before he could cut the engine, Dana had the door open. She swung her long legs out, stepped onto the curb and practically raced down the sidewalk without a backward glance. Jason sat for about sixty seconds admiring the sway of those slender hips, then slowly climbed out to follow. As if she sensed him behind her and actually thought she could elude him, she picked up her pace.

He assumed that sooner or later she would cool off, but for the moment her temper was still steaming mad and her determination to hold him at arm's length was rock solid. It would be fascinating to see how long she could hold out once he launched his full-fledged assault on her senses.

Jason was so busy imagining Dana's eventual passionate capitulation that he nearly missed the fact that she'd paused in her impatient rush back to work. Standing in the middle of the sidewalk, she leaned down to talk to a tiny, white-haired woman, who was bundled up from head to toe in the wildest combination of colors Jason had ever seen besides one of Dana's sweaters. Bright blue sweatpants were topped by a garish green jacket. A plaid scarf in bold squares of bumble bee black and yellow had been wound around her neck. A perky red cap sat jauntily on her head. She looked like a delightful gnome.

Jason was even more enchanted when he overheard her ask in a conspiratorial whisper that carried on the winter wind, "Was that him? Was that handsome man who picked you up earlier your new boss? I couldn't believe that fancy car of his. It must have cost a fortune. You don't suppose he'd take me for a ride in it one of these days, do you?"

Jason couldn't quite hear Dana's murmured response, but it was impossible to miss the sudden stain of color in her cheeks.

The woman patted Dana's hand. "Dear, mind what I say now. You really mustn't let him get away. He looks like the kind of man who would know how to treat a woman like you the way she deserves to be treated."

Dana was almost as red as the woman's cap by the time Jason reached her side. The old woman squinted up at him through lenses as thick as bottle glass.

"Oh my, yes," she murmured without the slightest hint of embarrassment at being overheard. Once she'd examined him thoroughly from head to toe with blatant curiosity, she declared, "I was right. You are a handsome one."

Jason grinned and introduced himself since Dana seemed to be both speechless and mortified.

"And I'm Mrs. Finch," the little woman replied. "I own a small bookstore in the neighborhood. Stop in sometime and I'll give you a cup of tea. We can have a nice long chat." Catching sight of Dana's glare, she added, "About books."

"I'd like that," Jason said.

"Mrs. Finch's favorites are romances," Dana muttered, her expression sour.

Jason grinned. "There's absolutely nothing I'd rather talk about. Maybe you'd like to go for a spin in my car. I've always preferred driving with an appreciative passenger." He glanced pointedly at Dana.

"I have to go to work," Dana said, turning her back on the two of them.

With a final conspiratorial wink at Mrs. Finch and a promise to visit her shop soon, Jason followed Dana inside. She had her jacket off and was seated at a desk piled high with galleys by the time he got to her. Her brow was furrowed in concentration as she stared at the top sheet of type. He might have believed her absorption, if the page hadn't been upside down. He righted it.

She scowled up at him. "Jason, go away. I have work to do. I'm not on your payroll yet."

"Actually, you are. John started billing me for your time as of today."

"I trust you'll let him charge you for the lunch you insisted I eat."

He leaned closer to look over her shoulder, bracing his hands on either side of her. His voice dropped to a seductive purr. "Nope. The lunch and the kiss were definitely not business."

Jason caught the quick, undeniable flare of heat in her eyes at the mention of that kiss. Dana could protest from now until doomsday that there was nothing between them, but her eyes would always give her away. Instead she shook her head and sighed as if she'd grown tired of fighting with him.

"Less than twenty-four hours ago you acted as if you couldn't stand the sight of me. What happened to change your mind?"

"I caved in to my baser instincts."

She gave him a disgusted look. "Is that supposed to make me feel better?"

"Actually I do have a smoother technique. Should I try it out?"

"Can't you give it a rest?"

"I don't think so. Not until you agree to see me again."

"I will see you again," she said, too quickly. "We're going to be working together."

"Not good enough."

"It has to be."

Just then her rotund, balding boss huffed up with a harried expression on his face. "You're back, finally!" he said, his tone more worried than accusing, though Dana seemed to hear only an accusation.

"I'm sorry, Mr. Keane," she apologized at once, her tone uncharacteristically meek. "My lunch hour took longer than I'd planned. I'll stay late to make up the work."

He waved off the offer. "No, no, forget the work. You had a call—emergency, they said."

Dana's face went pale. "Sammy?"

Jason put his arm around her and felt her whole body trembling. When he took her icy hands in his, she instinctively clung to him. He doubted she was even aware of the contact. She was totally focused on her boss, her expression anxious.

''His school,'' Mr. Keane confirmed, ''again. They want you there right away. I told them I couldn't reach you and that I would send you as soon as you got back.''

''Is he sick?'' she asked, but Jason suspected she already knew that wasn't the problem. He wondered how many calls like this she'd had. Neither she nor her boss appeared as shocked as they might have been.

''They didn't say. Go. I can read any proofs that have to be done today. What I don't finish, you can do tomorrow.''

Dana dropped Jason's hand and grabbed her jacket. ''Thank you.''

''You'll let me know what has happened?'' Mr Keane asked.

Jason sensed that behind the abrupt facade, the man was genuinely fond of Dana and concerned about Sammy. Obviously, though, he didn't want her to know how much.

''I'll call you later,'' she promised, as she ran through the shop. Outside she headed straight for the bus stop.

''No. I'll drive you,'' Jason said, surprised that for once she didn't argue. She simply nodded and turned toward the car. Obviously, where Sammy was concerned, she would make a pact with the devil himself if that's what it took to reach her errant brother.

Once she'd given him the directions to the school, though, she clammed up. With her gaze fixed on the passing scenery and her hands clasped tensely in her lap, she looked as if she were struggling against tears.

For what seemed the hundredth time since he and Dana met, Jason wanted to throttle Sammy for putting that worried crease in her forehead. He searched for some way to comfort her, but words seemed totally inadequate. Besides, anything he could think of to say about Sammy right now would not be a comfort. It would only infuriate her and deepen her pain. Since he couldn't think of a consoling alternative, he remained as silent as she was.

As they turned the corner in front of the old building, she said stiffly, "Thanks for the lift. You can let me out here."

He ignored the request, finally pulling into the school's parking lot. "I'm going with you," he said blandly, not entirely certain why he felt this need to stick by her. Maybe it was that flicker of fear in her eyes that told him her strength was about at its limits. He told himself if there'd been anyone else she could have turned to, he would have happily left her, but he wasn't nearly so sure it was as true today as it might have been just yesterday.

Afraid or not, her gaze shot to meet his at last. "No."

"Save your breath. I'm going."

"Jason, why? This doesn't concern you."

"It concerns you, doesn't it? If it concerns you, it concerns me."

"Sammy will just resent your involvement."

His temper flared and he muttered a harsh curse under his breath. "Frankly, at this point, what Sammy feels doesn't matter a damn to me."

Alarm filled her eyes. "I won't have you yelling at him."

"He'll be lucky if I don't break his neck."

"You don't even know what he did."

"I know that when you heard the school had called, you turned absolutely pale. I have to assume you think it's pretty bad."

For an instant she looked as if she was going to argue some more, then her shoulders sagged. "Maybe he just has the flu."

"You don't believe that."

"I want to," she said so wistfully that it wrenched Jason's heart.

His tone softened and he gently brushed away the single tear that had dared to track down her cheek. "I'm sure you do. Let's go see what's going on. There's no point sitting here speculating. Whatever it is, we'll handle it."

"*I'll* handle it."

The words were filled with Dana's usual spunk, but Jason couldn't miss the despair in her eyes, the dejection in the set of her shoulders. For just an instant her lower lip quivered, then as if she'd resolved to tough it out as she always did, she gathered her composure. Clenching her purse so tightly her knuckles turned white, she left the car and stormed off toward the principal's office like some sort of avenging angel, not waiting to see whether Jason followed. He couldn't decide whether he wanted to shake her or kiss her. The woman had so much honor, so damned much loyalty, albeit seriously misguided from what he'd seen of Sammy.

Jason could practically hear his father's voice reminding him that not everyone in the world had it as good as he did and that Hallorans owed it to the less fortunate to give them a helping hand. Up to now his idea of charity had been writing several large checks and putting them in the mail. Maybe it would be good for him to see firsthand what it meant to deal with a troubled kid.

Everyone in the office seemed to recognize Dana the instant she stepped through the door. Gazes met hers and skittered nervously away. Jason did not consider that a good sign. It seemed to confirm his suspicion that these visits happened all too regularly.

"Hi, Ms. Roberts. I'll get Mr. DeRosario," the clerk working at the reception desk said. "He wants to see you before you pick up your brother."

"Is Sammy okay?" Dana asked.

Though the woman looked sympathetic, her only comment was a terse, "Mr. DeRosario will explain."

Jason took an instant liking to the tall, kind-looking man who stepped out of his office and headed toward them. Though the man's expression was serious, his eyes were gentle, suggesting a personality that blended discipline and compassion in equal measures. Jason didn't know much about the education system, but he imagined that the combination was sorely needed in today's overburdened urban schools.

The man greeted Dana with a smile, then glanced curiously at Jason.

"I'm Jason Halloran, a friend of Ms. Roberts," he told the principal. "I came along in case there might be something I can do to help."

"Good."

"Mr. DeRosario, what happened?" Dana asked. "Is my brother all right?"

"Your brother is fine, but I'm afraid I'm going to have to suspend him."

"Suspend him?" Dana echoed. She drew in a deep breath, then asked, "Why?"

''He had a knife, Ms. Roberts. He pulled it during an argument with another student.''

''A knife?'' she repeated dully. Tears pooled in her eyes, but she managed to keep her voice steady. ''Was the other student hurt?''

''No. Thankfully it never went that far. But I cannot tolerate this kind of behavior. We've discussed this before. I've done my best to make allowances for Sammy's circumstances, but I won't allow him to put the other students at risk.''

Dana nodded wearily. ''I understand. How long will he be suspended?''

''Two weeks this time.''

''This time?'' Jason questioned, barely controlling his own dismay. ''He's done this before?''

The principal nodded. ''Sammy seems to feel the solution to his problems is violence. He's instigated several brawls already this school year.'' He turned to Dana. ''I understand that things have been difficult for you, but I strongly urge you to get him some counseling.''

''I tried. He won't go.''

''He'll go,'' Jason muttered, daring Dana to contradict him. ''Thank you, Mr. DeRosario. I think I understand what's been happening here. If Sammy can go now, we'll take him home.''

Mr. DeRosario nodded. ''I sincerely hope you can reach him. He's a bright boy, but he's going to have serious problems if his attitude isn't dealt with soon.''

''I assure you it will be,'' Jason said.

As soon as the principal had gone after Sammy, Dana whirled on him. ''How dare you interfere like that! This has nothing to do with you.''

''It does now.'' He wondered if he was losing his

mind. Why would a sane man willingly get involved in the salvation of a kid who used a knife to solve his problems? Maybe there was more of Kevin Halloran in him than he'd ever realized. He'd always chalked his father's do-gooder tendencies up to leftover sixties social consciousness.

"Jason!" Dana protested.

"We'll discuss it later," Jason said quietly. "Right now, you and I are going to show your brother a united front."

"Just why are we going to do that?" she snapped, obviously fuming at his intrusion into what she considered a family matter.

He cupped her face in his hands, barely resisting the desire to kiss away the last traces of tears. "Because if we don't, Sammy might never have a chance." He said it slowly and with enough conviction that Dana swallowed whatever she'd been about to say next. She looked thoroughly shaken and, for the first time since he'd met her, she looked defeated. That look touched his soul.

But when Sammy walked out of the principal's office, Dana squared her shoulders and leveled a no-nonsense look straight at him. Sammy started to protest his innocence, but she glared at him and he fell silent.

"I'll see you back here in two weeks," the principal said, his hand on Sammy's shoulder.

"Whatever," Sammy said, his tone sullen.

"Think about what we discussed."

"Yeah, sure."

Sammy backed toward the door, then whirled and sprinted outside. They caught up with him at the bottom of the steps. No one spoke until they reached the car, then Sammy balked.

"I'm not riding with him," he said to his sister.

"I've had just about all I can take from you for one day. Get in the car. Now!" she said, all of her fury spilling out in that one order.

Sammy took one quick glance at her stormy expression and began to look uncertain for the first time. He climbed in.

When they finally reached Dana's apartment, the tension in the car swirled like a thick, dispiriting fog. Dana started to open the door, but Jason put his hand over hers.

"In a minute," he said. "I have to go back to the office, but I want to say something first." He turned to face Sammy. "I'm sure you love your sister and I'm sure you don't set out to make her unhappy, but you have. I don't want it to happen again, so you and I are going to make an effort not only to get along, but to fix that lousy attitude of yours. We're starting tonight. I'll pick you up at eight."

"Not a chance," Sammy said. "I didn't commit no crime. I don't need a probation officer."

"Actually you *did* commit a crime. You'll be very lucky if the other student doesn't press charges, so don't smart-mouth me on that score. It's me or a counselor. Take your pick," Jason said, his voice clipped. Where the hell was his father when he needed him? Was he going about this the right way? All he had to guide him were his instincts and that faint glimmer of hope that was finally sparking in Dana's eyes.

Sammy turned pale. He studied Jason closely, as if measuring the chances for a reprieve, then glanced at Dana. Whatever she was thinking about Jason's plans, she didn't contradict him. Apparently Sammy decided that his choices truly were limited to those two. "I'll be ready," he said resentfully.

Jason nodded. "Good. Bring your gym clothes and sneakers."

Sammy looked startled. "Why?"

"Just bring them." He squeezed Dana's hand. "I'll talk to you later, okay?"

She nodded. All the way back to the office, Jason had to fight the image of the fearful expression in her eyes when he'd mentioned the possibility of assault charges. How many times had she walked into that school dreading such an outcome? How much longer could Sammy escape serious jail time? If it took being pals with a juvenile delinquent to wipe away Dana's fears, then that's what he was going to do.

For one fleeting instant Jason wished like crazy that he'd had the good sense to override his grandfather's manipulating moves and refused to work with Dana. What he knew about dealing with a kid as troubled as Sammy would fit on the head of a pin. As for what he knew about a woman like Dana, his expertise failed him there as well, but he was definitely learning fast.

"Cute girl," Brandon Halloran observed when Jason finally got to his office. "Reminds me of someone I used to know."

"I'm surprised you lived to tell about it," Jason muttered.

Brandon chuckled. "I think you'll be surprised at just how easily you adapt."

"I don't want to adapt."

"But you will," Brandon said with confidence. "You will. By the way, I've been thinking it's time to bring your father up to speed on this whole marketing thing we've got working. You know how he gets if he thinks one of us is keeping secrets from him. He's been meaner than a tied-up pit bull these last few weeks. Any idea what's going on with him?''

''I think he and Mom had some sort of disagreement. Neither one of them is saying much, but the last time I dropped by their house the tension was pretty awful.''

''Think we ought to have a man's night out at my club and get to the bottom of things?''

''I think if we try, Dad will just clam up or tell us to mind our own damned business.''

Brandon grinned. ''Never let that stop me before. No need to stop now. You free tonight?''

''Not really,'' he began, then caught sight of the expression on his grandfather's face. He forgot all too often how lonely things must be for his grandfather since his wife of nearly fifty years, Jason's grandmother, had died in the spring. Though Brandon put on a good front most of the time, there were times, like now, when his sorrow was unmistakable.

''Tonight would be great, if we can make it early.''

''Early is best for me, too,'' Brandon said. ''Say six-thirty. You tell your father. Hog-tie him if you have to.''

Jason chuckled at the idea of making Kevin Halloran do anything he'd set his mind against. Of all of them, his father was the most stubborn. ''I'll do my best,'' he said.

It looked to Jason as if his entire evening was likely to be spent with men who, with the exception of his grandfather, weren't particularly interested in sharing his company.

Chapter Eight

Dinner was not a success. Kevin Halloran maintained a stoic silence throughout the meal, responding to questions in terse monosyllables whenever he could get away with it. He barely touched his prime rib, but steadily sipped the cabernet sauvignon. Jason's frustration matched that of his grandfather's tone when Brandon finally snapped, "Son, what the hell is wrong with you?"

Raking his hand through blond hair shot with silver, Kevin glared at his father. "Nothing I care to talk about."

"Well, you've made that clear enough. Since when can't you open up with family?"

His expression utterly exhausted, Kevin rubbed his hand across his eyes. "Dad, please. Drop it. Let's talk about anything else—the weather, sports—I don't give a damn. Just leave my state of mind out of the conversation.''

''Granddad's just worried about you,'' Jason reminded him. ''So am I. You've been like this for weeks now. Are you feeling okay? Have you seen a doctor lately?''

Kevin threw down his napkin and shoved his chair back. ''If I'd wanted to be psychoanalyzed, I could have gone home,'' he snapped. As if horrified by what he'd revealed as well as the uncharacteristic display of raw anger, he mumbled, ''I'm sorry, Dad. Jason. I have things to do. I'll see you both at the office tomorrow.''

He stalked off, leaving Jason and Brandon to stare at each other in open-mouthed astonishment.

''What do you suppose that was all about?'' Brandon said finally. ''Kevin's not a man to lose control.''

''You don't suppose he and Mom are really having problems, do you? That crack about being psychoanalyzed at home sounded pretty bitter.''

Jason had never been more shaken. The thought that his parents' marriage might be in serious trouble threw him for a loop. He'd always viewed them as a perfect example of marital harmony. They'd been married nearly thirty years, had known each other since childhood. When he'd been growing up, his home had been filled with laughter and genuine affection. He'd considered himself one of the luckiest kids around. Had something gone terribly wrong in these last two months, something that in his absorption with his own life he had failed to notice?

''Damned if I know what to think,'' Brandon responded, his expression bewildered. ''I do know that it won't do us a bit of good to try to pry any more information out of him, while he's in this mood. Your father's a proud man. Never was one to share his problems. Never did like anyone to catch him down."

Brandon suddenly looked weary, every one of his sixty-eight years showing. "Guess I made a mistake in pressing for answers."

"You were just trying to help. We both were."

"Maybe so, but I should have known better. It looks like we just made things worse."

"I'll talk to Mom," Jason promised. "Maybe she'll tell me what's going on."

Brandon sighed. "I wish I were closer to your mother. She's a good woman."

Jason stared at him in astonishment. "I've always thought the two of you got along just fine."

"We've done pretty well at maintaining a truce, but there was a time when she didn't owe me the time of day. I suspect you know I tried to keep your father away from her. It's one of my real regrets."

Jason had heard bits of the story before. He knew that Lacey Grainger Halloran had long since forgiven his grandfather for his interference, that family had always been every bit as important to her as it was to his grandfather and she'd worked hard at mending fences. He'd always thought his grandfather recognized that bond.

"Granddad, she doesn't hold that against you. Not after all this time."

"Wouldn't blame her if she did." He met Jason's gaze. "You run along. I know you have plans."

"I don't want to leave you."

"Don't worry about me. I think I'll stay here and have a brandy. I saw some of my friends go into the card room a while back. Maybe I'll join them. Haven't played bridge since your grandmother died.''

Jason felt torn. He didn't want to leave his grandfather alone when he was in this strange melancholy mood, but he didn't dare cancel the plans with Sammy, either. The idea of asking his grandfather along crossed his mind, but he dismissed it at once. If his grandfather had tried to keep his father and a woman as sweet as Lacey Grainger apart, who knew what he would do if he met Sammy while he was at his rebellious worst. It might forever change the way he felt toward Dana and, for some reason he couldn't entirely explain, Jason didn't want that to happen.

He squeezed his grandfather's shoulder. ''Try not to worry. Dad will be okay.''

Brandon placed a hand over his. ''At my age worrying about family just comes naturally.''

As Jason drove across town to Dana's, he knew exactly what his grandfather meant. All through dinner Dana and Sammy had never been far from his mind. Family. His family. The thought brought him up short. Where the hell had that come from?

When he got to the apartment, he bounded up the stairs and rapped lightly on the door, wondering if he shouldn't be taking the first flight out of town instead.

Dana looked surprised to see him. ''I thought you were going to call first.''

''I said I'd be here at eight. Is Sammy ready?''

''He's not here.''

Jason's gaze narrowed. ''What do you mean he's not here?'' he asked slowly, fighting to keep a lid on his temper.

She held up a hand. ''Don't get angry. He's just

downstairs. He'll be back in a minute. I want to talk to you before you leave, anyway."

He shoved his hands in his pockets and waited for the explosion of outrage over his arrogant interference. Dana watched him for a minute, then said, "I'm sorry."

He blinked. "Sorry?"

Her smile was rueful. "Don't sound so shocked. You know perfectly well I owed you an apology. I overreacted at the school this afternoon. You were just trying to help. I don't know why you'd want to get mixed up in this, but I'm grateful."

He brushed an errant hair away from her face. "Why did my wanting to help upset you so much in the first place?"

As if to escape his touch, she began to pace. "I thought you were convinced I couldn't handle it myself. Since I was already feeling like a failure, it was like rubbing salt in a wound. I've done a lot of thinking since then. If you can accomplish something with Sammy that I can't, then that has to be my first priority. I won't interfere."

Jason heard the stoic resolve and sensed the deep hurt behind it. "Dana," he said, stepping in front of her and taking her hands, "you have not failed anyone, least of all your brother."

She regarded him anxiously. "Then why does it feel that way?"

"Because parents—and for all intents and purposes that's what you are—parents always seem to blame themselves when things go wrong for their kids. I just spent a couple of hours with my grandfather, who's feeling guilty for mistakes he made years ago with my father. Sammy isn't a child anymore. He's making choices for himself, choices you can't control."

"But they're such bad choices."

"Yes," he agreed, seeing no reason to sugarcoat the obvious. "And between us, we are going to make him see that."

Uncertain whose need was greater, he pulled her into his arms and simply held her. At first she was stiff, but then she melted against him, her arms tightening around his waist, her cheek resting against his chest. Jason felt the distinct stirring of desire at the press of her breasts, the warm brush of her thighs. As if he was no longer in control, his hands slid down her back to cup her bottom more tightly against him. He felt an immediate rush of heat and drew in a ragged breath. This felt far too right. What would happen when he could no longer get his common sense to outweigh this attraction that was growing day by day? What worried him most was that it was deepening on all levels, not just the physical. As he became more and more entangled in Dana's life, he saw her strengths more clearly. She was beginning to bring out traits in him that he hadn't even known existed. Just being here tonight was a perfect example, but spending an evening with Sammy was the last thing on his mind at the moment.

Jason tilted Dana's chin up and gazed into her eyes. "I want you," he said bluntly, so there could be no mistaking his intentions.

Her eyes widened. "Where did that come from?"

Though his body ached for her, he tried to laugh off the desire. He loosened his hold, but he couldn't quite bring himself to release her. "I'll be damned if I know," he admitted. "Sometimes I'm just as stunned by it as you are. Something tells me that sooner or later we're going to have to deal with these feelings, though. We can't go on denying them."

Dana wasn't sure whether her heart was hammering from Jason's nearness or from his promise. It was something she wasn't likely to discover tonight, either.

Jason stepped away just as the door opened and Sammy burst in. His glance went from Jason to Dana and back again. For an instant he looked as if he wanted to make an issue out of the embrace he'd interrupted, but apparently he read something in Jason's expression that stopped him. Dana was grateful for that. She didn't think she could stand another outburst on a day that had been filled with emotional peaks and valleys.

Though he kept one hand on her waist, Jason focused his attention on Sammy. "You ready, pal?"

"Where are we going?"

"To the gym. If you feel like fighting, I'm going to show you a way to do it that will keep you out of trouble."

Dana saw the reluctant spark of interest in Sammy's eyes and heard the eagerness in his tone when he asked, "You and me are gonna fight?"

"That's right," Jason said.

Somehow the prospect of her brother and Jason going at it tooth and nail did not strike Dana as a wildly terrific idea. Jason would expect to play by the rules. Sammy would not. "I'm coming, too," she announced, grabbing her jacket.

Both men stared at her. "Why?" Sammy asked. "You don't like it when I fight."

"That's right. Besides, I will not have either of you

knowing moves that I can't counter,'' she said, giving Jason a meaningful look.

''Dana,'' he protested.

''Don't even try to stop me. I've made up my mind. I'll get my things.''

As she left the room, Jason and Sammy exchanged a *what-do-you-expect-from-a-woman* sort of look.

''Okay,'' Jason said with obvious reluctance. ''Let's go.''

At the sight of the seedy gym, Dana began to have second thoughts. For some reason she'd been hoping for some fancy health club, maybe a sterile martial arts studio with mirrors and mats. She had not been expecting a place with punching bags that looked as if they'd been through a half century of practice, a decrepit barn of a building where the smell of sweat and the sound of painful grunts were clearly commonplace. What startled her even more than the grime and low-class atmosphere was the fact that Jason seemed perfectly at home.

Half a dozen men in boxing shorts, their bare chests gleaming with perspiration, greeted him and stared at her with open curiosity. She halted just inside the door. ''Maybe this was a bad idea,'' she said, though she had to admit to a certain fascination.

''Oh, no, you don't,'' Jason said with a grin. ''You're not backing out on us now. Just try to keep your eyes off all the other men.'' He turned toward the grizzled old man who was working with a gigantic black man. ''Hey, Johnny, since we're short on ladies' dressing rooms around here, do you mind if my friend uses your office to change?''

''It's okay with me, as long as she doesn't try to tidy up.''

"I wouldn't dream of it," Dana declared, though she had cause to reconsider when she saw the mess the office was in.

Apparently paperwork was not Johnny's forte. Stacks of it, most with yellowed corners and faded type, were piled on what was most likely a dining room table. Nothing that looked remotely like a file cabinet existed, though there were a dozen or so boxes scattered on the floor. It seemed as though someone had once made a haphazard attempt to turn those boxes into a filing system. They were lettered A-F, G-I and so on. Most contained boxing gloves and what looked to be bottles of liniment. Dana itched to make order out of chaos, but settled for changing into shorts and a T-shirt.

It took a certain amount of courage to step back out into a room filled with sweaty, macho men in what suddenly seemed to be fairly revealing attire. She quickly realized, though, that Jason seemed to be the only one paying much attention to her legs. The look in his eyes made her pulse race. At this rate she wouldn't have to bother with aerobics to get her heart rate up—the sight of Jason's bare chest, with its whorl of golden blond hairs, was enough to do that. She'd never expected to discover such well-developed muscles under those sedate clothes he seemed born to wear.

He provided her and Sammy with boxing gloves, then led them to a punching bag. He demonstrated in slow motion, then gestured for them to try it. Dana drew back and slammed her fist into the bag. She felt the shock all the way up her arm. Determinedly she punched again.

"Get a rhythm going," Jason suggested to Sammy,

who seemed intent on knocking the bag from its mooring in the ceiling. "This is all about finesse, not just brute strength."

Sammy's attention kept straying toward the ring in the center of the room. "When do you and me get to fight?" he asked Jason with what Dana thought was an entirely too bloodthirsty tone.

"When you know what you're doing," Jason said. "You haven't even worked up a good sweat yet."

Dana, however, was dripping from the effort. She'd had no idea how out of shape she was. With her schedule there was no time for running, much less the money for an expensive health club and the forms of exercise available there.

Breathless, she grabbed a towel and sank down onto a chair just outside of Johnny's office. Jason followed her.

"You okay?"

"I'm okay now. Something tells me tomorrow will be a different story."

"A nice hot shower will do you good."

Something in his tone brought her head up. "Here?"

"You'll catch cold if you go back outside without changing into dry clothes."

"But you said there wasn't a women's dressing room."

"I could come in and keep the place clear for a few minutes."

"Why don't I think that's an entirely benevolent offer?"

He grinned. "Because you understand me too well. However, I'm unlikely to try to ravish you or even join you in the shower with so many witnesses, including your brother. You'll be safe enough.''

Dana had to admit that a steaming shower sounded like heaven. ''Are you sure the guys won't mind?''

''They'll wait.''

''I'll get my clothes,'' she said.

At the door to the locker room, she experienced another moment of doubt. Going into a male domain struck her as being on the cutting edge of a danger she wasn't sure she wanted to experience. Then again, Jason was going to be there to see that no one bothered her. For all of his teasing and innuendoes, she knew from his support at the school today and from what he was now doing for Sammy, that she could trust him with her life. She'd never before known a man who could inspire that kind of trust.

''Five minutes,'' she promised.

''Take your time.'' He stationed himself protectively in the doorway.

''You did check inside, right? No one's in there?''

''I guarantee it. Believe me, if I'm stuck out here, no one else is going to share that shower with you.''

Dana couldn't resist patting his cheek. ''You are so noble.''

''No,'' he said softly, ''I'm not. Remember that.''

The low warning with its hint of intimacy doubled the temperature in the shower. Dana wasn't sure whether the steam arose from the water or her thoughts. Whichever it was, she decided she didn't dare linger. The sooner she got outside, where the cold air could snap her back to reality, the better off she'd be.

She toweled herself dry, tugged on her clothes and

exited the locker room to discover that Johnny was posted as guard.

"Where's Jason?" she asked the old man, who grinned at her.

"Over there." He pointed toward the ring.

Jason was in the center squared off with a man who had a good twenty pounds and six inches in height on him. Sammy was standing ringside, his gaze fastened on Jason with something akin to awe on his face as Jason's blows landed with speed and obvious cunning. Dana winced as his opponent directed a punch straight at Jason's jaw, then followed with one to his midsection. Jason countered with a hit that rocked the other man back on his heels. He staggered and sank to the mat.

Grinning, Jason held out his hand and gave the other man a boost up.

"That was awesome," Sammy said, when Jason left the ring. "How'd you learn to fight like that?"

"My father and his father before him. We were all on the boxing teams at our colleges."

"How long before I can be that good?"

Jason shrugged. "Depends on how hard you're willing to practice."

"Could I come back here, maybe after school sometimes?"

Though Dana wasn't really certain how she felt about boxing as a sport for Sammy, she was more than ready to give anything a try that would keep him off the streets and away from his old friends. "It's okay with me," she said. "Jason, is it possible?"

Jason nodded. "Let's go talk to Johnny. Maybe he'll work with you when I can't be here."

Dana watched as they crossed the gym. The two

men who meant the most to her, she thought as her breath seemed to catch in her throat. Her brother, who'd been everything to her from the day he was born. And the man who, unwillingly or not, seemed destined to become an integral part of her life.

Sammy was standing just a little taller than usual, and for the first time in weeks the note of hostility in his voice had vanished. He actually seemed excited about something. She owed Jason for that. She wasn't entirely sure why he had done it, but the reason mattered far less than the outcome. The motivation worried her, but she couldn't deny that the gift was precious.

What would he expect in return, though? There was every indication that he was beginning to want her in his bed. A man as virile and attractive as Jason would have a healthy love life. Undoubtedly he wasn't used to a woman saying no. Despite all of her qualms about deepening the bond between them, Dana couldn't deny that they appeared destined to make love sooner or later unless they stopped seeing each other altogether. The attraction grew hotter with each meeting. She was beginning to experience this odd, aching emptiness each time his kisses ended, an emptiness she suspected only Jason could fill. And the look in his eyes told her he wanted her every bit as badly. It was a turn of events she definitely hadn't counted on.

She couldn't allow herself to confuse wanting with love, though. Unexpected attractions sprang up between all sorts of mismatched people. That didn't mean they had to break their hearts by falling in love. If she kept her eyes wide open, if she experienced the wild sensations promised by Jason's touches just once, she could walk away with her heart unscathed.

Rot! She was deluding herself and she knew it. But because of Sammy, she couldn't walk away now, while the damage would be minimal. Jason was proving to be a good influence, and she wouldn't rob her brother of a chance to get his life in order. She would just have to be strong enough to withstand Jason's best efforts to woo her.

That was easier said than done, she decided an hour later as they sat in a tiny Italian restaurant that smelled of garlic and tomato sauce. A huge pizza loaded with everything sat in the center of the table. Sammy was greedily eating his fourth or fifth slice. Her first slice sat half-eaten on the plate in front of her. Jason's eyes were on her, as if he found her far more tempting than anything the restaurant had to offer.

Fortunately Sammy kept up a non-stop stream of questions that diverted Jason's attention for five- and ten-minute spurts, just long enough for her to catch her breath. He answered distractedly, but his gaze never wavered from her. That avid attention was enough to give a woman wild ideas about her attractiveness, yet Dana knew she couldn't look all that great after a workout and a shower that had soaked her hair.

As if he'd read her mind, Jason leaned close and murmured, "You look gorgeous with your cheeks all flushed like that. Throwing a few punches obviously agrees with you."

She thought of the punch she'd thrown the day they'd met and grinned. "I can think of some occasions when that's been true."

Obviously following her thoughts, he grinned back. "Maybe teaching you the rudiments of boxing is not such a hot idea, after all. As I recall, you packed a pretty good punch without it.''

Sammy looked intrigued. ''You hit him?''

''She did,'' Jason answered for her. ''I was just standing there minding my own business and your sister came up and slugged me. Apparently starting brawls is a family trait.''

Sammy's gaze narrowed. ''Why'd she hit you? Were you coming on to her?''

''Actually she was defending your honor. She thought I was the creep who sold you that stolen VCR.''

Her brother squirmed uncomfortably. ''You know about that?''

''Yes. I assume that you've seen the last of that guy.''

''Yeah, I guess.''

''You guess?'' Jason repeated, his voice rising ominously.

''I haven't seen him for a while now,'' Sammy said quickly to Dana's relief.

Jason nodded. ''Look, although I think the guy ought to be turned in, I'm not going to force you to rat on him. However, if I find you that you've been within a mile of him again, you and I will go a few rounds and I guarantee you won't like the way your face looks when I've rearranged it.''

Dana waited for a rebellious outburst and was stunned when Sammy struggled against a giggle and lost.

''You heard that in some old movie, right?'' he demanded. ''James Cagney, Edward G. Robinson, one of those guys.''

Jason shook his head. ''Nope. That was pure Jason

Halloran and I meant every word. If you doubt that, just try me.''

Sammy's grin faded.

''So,'' Dana began hurriedly. ''It's probably time we got home.''

After one last measuring look, Jason and Sammy nodded.

When they reached the apartment, Sammy took off for his room without another word. Jason dropped his coat over the back of a chair and headed straight for the kitchen. ''Do you have any coffee?'' he called over his shoulder.

''Make yourself at home, why don't you?'' Dana muttered as she trailed after him.

In the kitchen she took the can of coffee from his hands and scooped some into the pot. When she'd turned it on to perk, she faced Jason. ''Thank you for everything you're trying to do, but be careful, Jason. Don't push him too hard. He'll just rebel.''

''If I let up on him for even a second, I'll lose the edge. Right now he's giving me a sort of grudging respect because no one has ever been this tough with him before. I want him to understand the ground rules.''

She regarded him oddly. ''Is that how you were raised?''

''Hardly. My parents were just one step away from being the kind who thought a child should be allowed to express himself, even if that included tearing down the house. There were a few times when I really wished someone would set down a few rules, so I'd know what the hell was expected of me. Fortunately my grandfather wasn't shy about doing just that. I used to love to visit him because I always knew exactly what I could and couldn't do. And I always knew he and my grandmother loved me, even when I crossed the line.''

''You think I've been too lenient with Sammy,'' Dana said.

''Maybe. Maybe not. I just see a kid now who's crying out for someone to point him in some direction. If it's not you, then it'll be those thugs he considers his friends.''

Dana poured the coffee, then sank down across from Jason. ''Sometimes I get so damned tired of being responsible,'' she said wearily.

Jason reached for her hand. ''You're not in this alone anymore,'' he said softly. ''From now on we'll share the responsibility.''

Although everything in her screamed that she had to remain strong, had to remain independent, she couldn't bring herself to voice the words that would keep him at bay. She felt his strength pouring into her, felt the warmth and concern that surrounded her like a velvet cloak and wanted with all her might to draw it closer.

When he raised her hand to his lips and pressed a kiss against her knuckles, she felt like the most cherished woman on the face of the earth. The sensation was too intoxicating by far to turn away. She would indulge herself, just for tonight, in the fantasy that Jason would always be around to protect her.

Chapter Nine

Feeling an unfamiliar need for a long, friendly chat that might help her to put things with Jason into perspective, Dana walked over to Mrs. Finch's bookstore on her way home from work at the print shop a week later. Although she didn't really need an excuse for dropping by, she had one all prepared. She'd finished the bookstore's latest flyers. Mr. Keane had run them off on the copying machine just before closing.

Glancing in the shop's window before entering, her mouth dropped open. Wearing slacks and a dress shirt, Jason was scrunched down in one of the faded chintz chairs that were placed here and there for browsing customers. His tie was loose, his collar open. He was holding a china cup of tea that looked completely out of place in his big hands, but his expression was rapt as he listened to Mrs. Finch. Dana couldn't imagine what the two of them had to talk about.

Except her, she thought with horror, rushing inside.

"Agatha Christie is the very best mystery writer ever," Mrs. Finch was declaring to Dana's relief.

"John D. MacDonald," Jason countered. He glanced up and shot Dana a warm look. "And there's Dashiell Hammett. What do you think, Dana?"

She regarded the two of them warily, not entirely convinced of the innocence of the conversation. "I don't have time to read mysteries."

"I've tried," Mrs. Finch said apologetically as if Dana were one of her failures. "I sneaked one of Christie's best into her sack last time. She brought the book back the next day. Said I'd mixed it in with her books by mistake."

"Didn't you even peek?" Jason teased.

"No," Dana said, then amended, "Okay, I peeked. I read the first few lines…and a little bit at the end."

Mrs. Finch looked delighted. "Oh, my, I'll have you hooked yet."

"Don't count on it," Dana warned. "And don't even think about trying to get me addicted to those romances you love so much. They're frivolous."

"Only if you don't happen to care about human relationships," Mrs. Finch informed her.

"Interesting how she keeps bringing those romances up, isn't it?" Jason observed, giving the bookstore owner a deliberate wink. "Do you suppose she's developed an obsession with romance lately?"

Dana looked from one to the other, scowling, then muttered something about looking for a new design book. This visit was doing absolutely nothing to ease her mind. If anything, she felt more ganged up on than ever. Obviously her friend had chosen sides. What puzzled her was that there were even sides to choose.

A week ago Jason Halloran hadn't even wanted to spend a few hours in an office with her. Now he was popping up every time she turned around. Was the man trying to drive her nuts?

"Certainly, dear. Look all you want," Mrs. Finch said, clearly already distracted by her handsome visitor. "You know where they are."

Jason didn't even bother to comment. He jumped right back into the mystery discussion they'd been in the midst of before her arrival.

Suddenly feeling thoroughly out of sorts, Dana went down the narrow aisle to the back of the store. She plucked books off the shelves, scanned them without seeing the words, then put them back. After she'd been through half a dozen books, she realized she was straining to listen to Jason and Mrs. Finch. They seemed to be having a grand time without her.

Dana edged closer, then sat in an old armchair that invited customers to curl up. She'd spent hours in this chair on other occasions, lost in the design books that she suspected Mrs. Finch had started to stock just for her. Though she held one of the newest books now, all of her attention was riveted on the chattering pair at the front of the store. They were just out of view, though occasionally she glimpsed Jason's blond hair when he leaned forward to make a point.

She supposed it was nice that a man as busy as Jason would take the time to visit a sweet little old lady. No, there was no supposing about it. It *was* nice. So why did she seem to resent it? Why was she so suspicious of this sudden change of heart?

Actually she'd been increasingly disgruntled this whole week when Jason had ignored her and spent his spare time with Sammy. Her brother had come home filled with stories about Jason's excellent left hook, his fancy footwork in the ring, his awesome sucker punch. Dana wondered idly where those punches had been when she'd slugged him at Washington's Tavern. She should probably consider herself lucky that she'd escaped that day without a scratch.

At any rate it seemed that Jason was slowly but surely winning Sammy over. She couldn't very well begrudge her brother the male attention he so badly needed, but she was beginning to wonder exactly where she fit in. It bothered the daylights out of her that it seemed to matter.

The truth, she finally admitted with a sigh, was that she was feeling left out. Downright lonely, in fact. In a life that had been crowded with work and school and raising Sammy, it was a totally new and not particularly welcome sensation. Mrs. Finch was the closest thing she'd ever had to a grandmother. Sammy was *her* brother. For reasons that escaped her, Jason seemed intent on adopting both of them.

As for Jason's plans where she was concerned, his precise role in her life seemed to defy description. In another era, he would have been described as a beau, one who'd already made his intentions perfectly clear. In this bolder day and age, he might have been her lover by now, if both of them hadn't had serious reservations about such a drastic move. For the past week he'd been virtually ignoring her. Had he lost interest? Wasn't that what she'd wanted? Since she wasn't able to put him—or her own emotions—into a nice, neat little compartment, he was troublesome.

She glanced wistfully toward the front of the store. She could just walk up and join them. They hadn't deliberately shut her out of the conversation earlier. In fact, the expression in Jason's eyes had been warmly welcoming. In a way, she supposed, she envied them their uncomplicated conversation, their free and easy laughter. Whenever she was with Jason the conversation always took a dangerously intimate turn, and the laughter had a wickedly provocative edge to it that set off fireworks deep inside her, even when they were arguing. Sometimes *especially* when they were arguing.

"Where did you go?" Jason asked softly, coming up and hunkering down in front of her. He braced his hands on her thighs, sending a jolt of awareness through her. Those fireworks exploded in fiery splendor.

Dana's pulse scrambled at the probing look in his eyes.

"I've been right here," she said.

"Maybe physically, but your mind must have been a million miles away. You looked, I don't know, a little sad, I guess."

Dana wasn't about to admit to the oddly jealous turn her thoughts had taken. Instead, she said, "Who won the battle over the mystery writers, you or Mrs. Finch?"

"We agreed to disagree. I promised to read old Agatha with a more open mind and she's going to reconsider MacDonald's Travis McGee series." A spark of pure devilment lit his eyes. "I was hoping she'd offer me one of those romances with the sexy covers."

Dana chuckled at his disappointed expression. "I'll just bet you were. Carrying one of those around would have done astonishing things to your image."

"Think it would counteract the stodgy coat?"

Without thinking about what she was doing, Dana reached over and fingered the hair that had fallen over his eyes. As she smoothed it back into place, she felt his skin heat beneath her touch, detected the sudden leap of his pulse. Knowing that she could stir him so readily gave her an unexpected sensation of power. Why was it Jason who made her feel so much like a woman? What quality did he have that wreaked havoc with her best intentions? Compassion? Gentleness? Strength? He had them all.

And that terrified her.

''There's nothing wrong with the image that coat projects,'' she told him, tracing the line of his jaw with her fingertips.

''Oh?'' he said, his voice suddenly whisper rough. ''I was under the impression you considered me and my coat deadly dull.''

''A week ago I might have,'' she admitted.

''And now?''

''I don't know what to think of you anymore,'' she said, sounding bemused. ''Sometimes...sometimes I can't even think when I'm around you.''

Jason looked every bit as bewildered as she felt. He captured her hand and drew it to his chest. She'd never touched material as soft as the fine cotton of his shirt. Beneath it she could feel the powerful thunder of his heart as his gaze held hers.

''But you feel things when you're with me, don't you?'' he asked quietly. ''Tell the truth, Dana. Aren't you the least bit tempted?''

Something in his tone pleaded for honesty. She owed him that much, even knowing she couldn't commit to more than this one costly admission.

"Tempted to go to bed with you? Yes," she confessed.

He shook his head. "No, to fall in love with me."

"Oh, Jason," she whispered, wishing she could admit this truth as readily: she wasn't just tempted, she was already falling. And it scared her silly.

All of these tantalizing glimpses and teasing remarks were beginning to torment Jason. He'd deliberately kept his distance from Dana for the past week, hoping that this craziness would go away, that he'd awake in the morning and Dana would no longer appeal to him. He had a sinking feeling that changing the color of his eyes or the rhythm of his heart would be easier.

Last night in the bookstore he'd sensed that she was on the edge, struggling with deep emotions that were clearly as foreign to her as they were to him—emotions neither of them were ready to accept.

She'd looked so lost and alone that he'd wanted to take her into his arms and swear to her that she would never be lonely again, that he would always be there to offer comfort and strength and love. He wasn't sure, though, that it was a promise he could keep. He had no track record with commitment and responsibility. As for handling the implications of love—not just sex—between a man and a woman, he was every bit as inexperienced as she.

And then there was Sammy. His respect for the boy's intelligence was growing, even as his frustration mounted. For all the progress the two of them had made in recent days, the kid was hardly ready for sainthood. Jason suspected that their outings to the gym might only be giving Sammy the skills he would need to tough it out on the streets. Jason doubted the teen actually saw boxing as an alternative to the thrill of real violence. Every time Jason tried to speak to Sammy about making a serious change in his attitude and his companions, the youngster's overt hostility returned.

Faced with the least attractive side of Sammy's personality, Jason continually had to remind himself that he was doing this to prove to himself that he was capable of being totally unselfish for once in his life. Maybe it would be a sign that he'd finally grown up.

The bonus, of course, was the approval and relief that shone in Dana's eyes with each tiny bit of progress he made with her brother. It made him feel ten feet tall. He hadn't realized how badly his self-confidence needed such a boost.

He had started doubting his own common sense. Maybe he'd misjudged how wrong Dana was for him. He'd felt revitalized the past couple of weeks. Maybe it wouldn't be so terrible to risk deepening their relationship.

Convinced of that, Jason left work early with his blood pumping just a little harder as he contemplated a very romantic evening ahead. He found a florist who'd managed to rush the season with an abundant assortment of spring flowers. Jason filled his arms with red tulips and golden daffodils, picked up a bottle of wine, then stopped at a meat market that dealt only in the choicest steaks and chops.

It occurred to him to call ahead to be sure Dana would be home. But he felt certain she'd find a dozen excuses for turning him down. He skirted the most obvious one by buying a third steak. He figured there was no escaping Sammy's presence. Jason appreciated the irony in having the kid as a chaperon.

It was dusk when he reached the neighborhood. The nearest parking place was an unsavory two blocks away. Jason gathered his purchases from the back seat, then started toward Dana's. He had just started to cross the entrance to an alley, when he heard a commotion and sensed a violent undertone. One glance into he gloomy alley brought his heart to his throat.

Dana was pressed against a brick wall. A trio of unkempt youths were taunting her. A fourth, his back to Jason, was hanging back, oddly silent. From where Jason stood at the entrance to the alley, there was no question at all about their intentions—they were going to rob her or worse.

Jason was filled with such a murderous rage, his hands shook. Every instinct shouted at him to rush to her rescue. His muscles ached from the tension of listening to his head, which warned him that rushing in against these odds wouldn't help Dana and might even get her hurt.

As he considered what to do, his heart pounded so hard he was sure they would hear it. Anger rushed through him with raw, primitive force. If they laid one finger on her, one finger, he would delight in taking them apart.

"You don't want to do this," Dana said. She was pale, but there wasn't the slightest quaver in her voice. Jason winced at the spunky declaration. Didn't she know she was just daring them to contradict her? Didn't she have enough good sense to recognize the very real danger she was in? Maybe it was just as well. He was terrified enough for the two of them.

He'd never felt more helpless in his life, trying to

cling to reason when all he wanted was to strike out blindly, to pay them back for threatening her. In that instant he realized with a sense of shock that he was falling in love with her.

And, with horrifying clarity, that he could lose her.

"Hey, did you hear that, Rocky? We don't want to do nothin' to the lady." The punk who said it leered at her and inched closer as if to contradict her statement. His fingers swept down her cheek. Jason felt sick to his stomach as he thought of how easily the boy could have wielded a knife instead.

Finally, his hands knotting into fists, the boy hovering in the background spoke. "Leave her alone, Vinnie."

Vinnie didn't look inclined to take his advice. "Kid, stay out of this."

At the hint of a split in their ranks, Jason took heart. Maybe the odds weren't so uneven after all. Suddenly, with a move so swift it took both Vinnie and Jason by surprise, the boy leaped. He began pummeling the ringleader, obviously fearless or determined to pretend to be. Jason recognized the attitude even before he picked up on the slim build and blond hair. Sammy, coming to his sister's defense without regard to the consequences to himself—or to her, for that matter.

With Vinnie occupied, Dana flew at the one called Rocky. Just as the remaining youth prepared to come to the assistance of the gang leaders, Jason tore down the alley and slammed the guy into the wall. The boy managed one glancing blow to Jason's head that drew blood. Then Jason grabbed the boy's arm and twisted it behind his back until he heard a satisfying grunt of pain.

"I think maybe you should plan on sitting this one

out,'' he said as he wound his tie around the youth's wrists, then looped it around a drainpipe. Satisfied that this one was out of commission, Jason went to Dana's assistance. He decked Rocky with a blow that the kid didn't even see coming. The crunching shot gave him a mild sense of satisfaction.

Even before the thug crashed to the ground, and with barely a glance at Jason, Dana moved on to help Sammy. The two of them were all over Vinnie. They didn't look as if they needed any help from him in winding things up. In fact, Dana actually looked as if she was enjoying her moment of revenge on the scum who'd threatened her. Jason had no intention of denying her the pleasure. He figured the punk had it coming.

With blood dripping from the gash above his eye, Jason settled on a garbage can to watch. He pressed a clean handkerchief to the scrape and admired the uppercut that Sammy delivered to Vinnie's jaw, while Dana held his arms pinned behind him. Vinnie sank slowly facedown into a bank of gray slush. Apparently out of some misguided concern for the punk's life, they rolled him over before walking over to Jason, whose temper was kicking in at full steam now that the danger was past.

''My heroes,'' Dana declared, looking downright invigorated by the success of the brawl. She had a scrape down one cheek and scratches on her hands. Other than that she looked none the worse for wear. It took everything in Jason to keep from crushing her in an embrace.

Instead, he glared at her. ''Heroes, hell. Sammy, what were you doing here in the alley with those guys when they went after your sister?'' he demanded.

Dana looked shocked by Jason's implication. "He wasn't with them."

"Oh, wasn't he?" He leveled a look at Sammy, who had the good sense to look uneasy. "You were right in the thick of things until you realized it was Dana they'd dragged back here, weren't you?"

"No. I saw 'em and followed," he swore unconvincingly. His gaze never met Jason's directly. "That's all."

"You don't know these boys?" Jason pressed.

Dana regarded him oddly, her expression puzzled. "Sammy is not on trial here. He threw the first punch to protect me."

"The police might think otherwise. Sammy, you haven't answered my question. Do you know these guys or not?"

"I've seen 'em around."

"Are they part of a gang?"

"I guess."

"What about you?"

Sammy looked from his sister to Jason and back again. "I'm not in any gang."

"But you want to be."

"Dammit, Jason, leave him alone," Dana said protectively. "I'm telling you he came to my rescue. You were here. You must have seen it."

"In the end, yes, he did," Jason admitted, then sighed. "We'll talk about it later."

"There is nothing to discuss," Dana declared. "Sammy, go call 911 and get a policeman over here so I can file assault charges."

Sammy's expression went from hostile to scared in an instant. "Sis, can't you forget about it?" he pleaded, confirming Jason's belief that he'd been up to his skinny little neck in the activities of this gang of hoodlums.

''No, I cannot forget about it. If I don't press charges, they could do this to someone else. Get the police now.''

Sammy ran off. As soon as he'd gone, Jason said mildly, ''I seriously doubt that the police will show up here anytime soon.''

''Of course they will,'' Dana said. ''Why wouldn't they?''

''Because Sammy won't call them, not if he expects to hang out with his friends ever again. These guys don't rat on each other.''

Fury flashed in Dana's eyes. ''And I'm telling you that you're wrong about that. Just because a kid's had it tough in life, doesn't mean he automatically turns into some criminal. I thought you were his friend.''

''I'm trying to be. That doesn't mean I turn a blind eye to his faults.''

''The way I do?'' she asked resentfully.

''I didn't say that, but yes, the way you do.''

Dana's lower lip trembled. ''I see his faults. I've told him…''

''Telling him isn't enough.'' He reached for her hand, but she stiffened. ''Dammit, Dana,'' he said impatiently. ''There have to be consequences. Can't you see that, even after this?''

''What kind of consequences did you have in mind? Jail? Beating him with a belt? What?''

Jason raked his fingers through his hair. ''No,'' he said wearily.

''What then?'' She perched on the lid of the garbage can next to him. ''Take tonight. He came to my rescue. Am I supposed to punish him for that?''

"No, but you'd better make darned sure you know who his friends are from now on."

"And just how am I supposed to do that? I work two jobs at the moment. I can't stick around all afternoon and do background checks on the kids he spends time with after school."

Jason sighed. There was no denying the complexity of the problem. "You're right," he admitted. "I don't know what the answer is. I just know that he's headed for trouble."

"I thought the time he was spending with you was helping."

Jason grinned ruefully. "Sure. Didn't you see those punches he threw? The kid's a natural. On one hand, I'm damned proud of him. On the other, I want to shake him until his teeth rattle." He glanced sideways. "There may be one thing you could do to improve things."

"What's that? I'll try anything."

"Move. This neighborhood's not safe for you, and it sure as hell isn't doing Sammy any good to associate with the kids around here."

For a fleeting instant Dana's expression brightened, then her face fell. "I can't afford to move."

Before Jason could open his mouth to offer to help, she held up her hand. "I won't take a cent from you."

"Do you really have a choice? If you don't do something, Sammy's likely to end up in jail. Let me help. If you won't take money, then move into my place."

Her eyes widened. "You have to be kidding."

Actually Jason thought he might be slightly insane, but the longer he toyed with the idea, the more he saw it as the only solution. Once Sammy was removed from these surroundings, the kid might actually have a chance. As for Dana, at least she would be out of danger. Of all of them, he was the one most likely to be endangered by such a move. The feelings that had slammed into his gut when he'd faced the prospect of losing her would be on the line if she were in close proximity. He had to risk it, though. For her sake. And Sammy's.

"Just temporarily," he said, giving both of them a needed out. "Just until you save enough to get a better place in a better neighborhood. There are plenty of bedrooms. You and Sammy can both have your privacy."

He allowed his gaze to linger until he saw the rise of desire in her eyes. He dropped his voice. "If you want it."

Dana seemed to shake off the spell she'd clearly been succumbing to. "Not a good idea," she said, but there was a breathlessness to her voice that contradicted the declaration. She was tempted. He would just have to make her see the logic of it.

At the first stirring of Vinnie and his cohorts, Jason glanced toward them and asked pointedly, "Do you have a better idea?"

"No, but..."

"Just promise me you'll think about it."

With her gaze locked with his, she finally sighed and nodded. "I'll think about it."

"By the way, are you ready to concede that the police are not headed our way? If so, I suggest we take off before these guys decide they'd like to go another round. If they ask for more, I'm not at all sure I won't be the one in jail with a murder rap hanging over my head. With any luck, we can make that call ourselves and get the cops down here before these jerks vanish.''

Dana's chin inched up. ''I'll wait. You call the police.''

''Oh, no,'' Jason said. ''You're not staying here another minute. And since we've already established that there are very valid reasons for not leaving me within a mile of these guys without witnesses, we're going together.''

''What if they escape?''

''Then we'll just have to convince Sammy to tell us who they are. Now let's go.'' He groaned as he leaned down to pick up the bag with the steaks in it. They were about the only thing he could salvage from his romantic offerings. The bottle of wine had broken when he dropped it to go after Vinnie. The bouquet of flowers had been trampled. Dana stared around at the mess, seeing it for the first time.

''Flowers?''

''For you. Sorry they didn't make it.''

She picked up one spunky daffodil that was less bruised than the rest and held it gently. ''They're beautiful,'' she said. ''Thank you.''

''I'll buy you more.''

''No. I like this one. It's a survivor.''

Jason shook his head wearily and admitted with grudging admiration, ''Like you.''

Sometimes Dana's fight-to-the-end philosophy scared the daylights out of him. Protecting a woman like that took more ingenuity than most mortal men possessed. He was trying, though.

And with a little divine intervention and a whole lot of patience, maybe he'd survive Dana's stubborn determination to fight him every step of the way.

Chapter Ten

After the incident in the alley, Jason could barely bring himself to let Dana out of his sight. He was astounded by the deep feeling of protectiveness she aroused in him. Again and again he tried to tell himself it wasn't because he was falling in love with her. He couldn't be. He was a man who always used his head, and his head had warned him from the outset to steer clear of her. His heart, though, was another matter. He couldn't seem to control it the way he could his thoughts.

The only thing keeping him from forcing the issue of a move was the knowledge that Dana's reaction to pressure was likely to be withdrawal. She didn't seem to trust simple generosity. It had taken him a long time to understand that. It was Halloran tradition to reach out, to give something back to the community, to help those in need. In Dana's world, though, she'd learned to look for the ulterior motive.

Jason had no idea how to break through that kind of instinctive self-protection except to give her time. Since she was about to start working full-time for the Lansing Agency, and thus for him, on Monday, he didn't want to do anything that would scare her off. Once they were locked into a day-in, day-out pattern, he could look after her the way he wanted to without arousing her fiery streak of independence.

That didn't keep him from calling as many times each day as he could justify. It was astonishing the number of excuses he could manufacture. If Dana suspected his motives on this too, she never let on. On most occasions, she actually sounded glad to hear from him, at least until he tried to delve into anything personal. She dodged those questions with the skill of a shady politician. When he brought up Sammy, who'd refused any more boxing lessons, she turned downright testy. Jason wondered if they would ever be able to agree on anything having to do with her brother.

That didn't stop him from trying, though he was rapidly reaching his wit's end. Not even the lure of tickets to a Celtics game had improved Sammy's mood, which seemed surlier than ever. He'd refused the invitation. As a result, Dana had begged off, too. Jason had gone to the game with his father, hoping that the night out would lead to confidences that would help him understand what was going on with his parents.

To his frustration, he'd struck out on that as well. The only thing his father seemed remotely inclined to discuss was the basketball game, and even then he'd kept his comments terse. Jason was more convinced than ever that things weren't right between his parents. On one level he realized he was no more ready to deal with that aloud than his father was.

It was after midnight when Jason finally got home, too late to call Dana. After the tense standoff with his father and the close Celtics' victory, he was too wired to sleep. Disgruntled as well by his lack of progress with Dana, he tried to read over the marketing and advertising plan he'd been finalizing in preparation for Dana's first day on the job.

No matter how hard he tried, though, he couldn't seem to concentrate. For some reason he felt this odd sense that Dana needed him, that she was in trouble. He tried valiantly to ignore it, but time and again he glanced at the phone, debating with himself. He'd finally convinced himself to call and was already reaching for the phone, when it rang.

"Yes, hello," he said, instantly convinced that his instincts had been accurate. No one ever called him this late unless there was a problem.

"Jason," Dana said in a voice that sounded sandpaper husky from crying.

His heart slammed against his ribs. "What's wrong?"

"It's Sammy. I know I shouldn't call you after the way he's acted, after the way I've acted, but I didn't know what else to do. There isn't anyone else who could help."

"What's he done?" To his regret, his antagonistic tone sounded as if he were anticipating the worst.

"He hasn't *done* anything," she said, clearly bristling. "He's just gone. I came home earlier and he was out. I didn't think much about it until a couple of hours ago. He knows he has an eleven-o'clock curfew on weekends unless we discuss a later one. He always calls if he's going to be late,'' she said staunchly, as if to defend him from an attack she knew Jason was likely to make.

''I'll be right there,'' Jason said, already reaching for his clothes.

''Thank you.''

Dana sounded so tired, so vulnerable. Jason felt something tear lose inside his chest as he considered the state of panic she must be in. This time he was going to shake Sammy until his teeth rattled. Dana didn't deserve this kind of treatment from a kid she'd spent years protecting and nurturing, a boy whose needs she'd always put above her own. If Jason had anything to say about it, Dana was through making sacrifices that went unappreciated.

He reached her apartment in record time and raced inside. At the sound of his footsteps pounding up the stairs, she had the door open before he reached the top. Her expression wavered between relief and disappointment when she saw it was him. Jason could understand the ambivalence. Obviously she'd been praying it was Sammy. Jason's help came in at a distant second best.

Jason took one look at the tears tracking down her cheeks and swept her into his arms. For some reason she felt almost fragile, as if fear alone had robbed her of her usual strength. There was no hint of the famed Dana Roberts spunk.

''Any news?'' he asked gently.

He felt the subtle shake of her head, the sigh that shuddered through her.

''Let's go inside and think this through.''

"I want to go look for him," she insisted stubbornly.

"Running around the streets at this hour won't accomplish anything unless we have a plan. Come on. Make some coffee and tell me every single place you think he might be."

In the kitchen she scooped up the coffee, then spilled it from a spoon that shook uncontrollably. Jason retrieved the spoon, urged her into a chair, then wiped up the coffee and started over. When the pot was on the stove, he pulled a chair close to her and enfolded her trembling, icy hands in his.

Looking downright miserable, Dana met his gaze and said, "He's never done anything like this before—never. What if he's hurt?"

"Don't worry. We'll call the hospitals and the police. We'll find him."

She looked thunderstruck. "The police?"

"To see about reported accidents."

She nodded reluctantly. "Okay. Wouldn't they have called me, though? He has ID with my name and number for emergencies."

Jason could think of several reasons, all of them bad, that no one had called Dana. He evaded. "Not necessarily."

She started to get up. "Shouldn't we be doing that now?"

"As soon as you drink a little coffee. Have you eaten anything tonight?"

"A sandwich." At his skeptical glance, she added, "Honest. I really didn't start worrying until eleven when he was due in."

"Okay, then. Drink the coffee and let me make a few calls. Where's the phone book?"

"In the living room by the phone."

"You stay here and try to relax. I'll be right back."

Naturally she didn't stay put. Though Jason worried that listening to question after question would only add to her stress, she weathered the next hour fairly well. In fact, she seemed to grow calmer, more determined. That strength in a crisis was an admirable trait, but Jason almost wished she would cry or scream—anything to wipe away that increasingly bleak, stoic expression.

The police had no record of Sammy either being picked up or in an accident. After the last futile call to a hospital, Jason sighed. "No luck."

Dana's expression did brighten slightly then. "That's good, though, isn't it? It means he's not hurt and we already know he hasn't been arrested."

What it meant to Jason's way of thinking was the kid had absolutely no excuse for not calling. None. If he did turn out to be okay and just exercising his selfish independent streak, Jason very well might put him in the hospital himself.

"You're right. I'm sure there's no reason to worry," he found himself saying, hoping to put a little color back into Dana's pale, drawn face.

She wasn't quite that easily consoled, however. The next thing he knew, she was on her feet and reaching for her jacket. "I'm going to look for him. He has to be someplace."

"Dana, no."

"I can't just sit here."

"You can." When she continued toward the door, her expression defiant, he said, "Stay. I'll go look. He could come back or call and you should be here."

Only when he'd promised to search the neighborhood thoroughly did she remove her coat and sit back down, drawing her knees up to her chin and circling them with her arms. He squeezed her hands and dropped a feather-light kiss on her cheek. "Try not to worry. I'll check in every half hour and let you know what area I've covered. See if you can think of any place he might go, some friend he might visit."

He left her staring at the phone.

As the hours wore on toward morning with no sign of Sammy, Jason grew almost as alarmed as Dana. Sammy might infuriate him, and Dana's blind, unwavering defense of the boy might drive him to distraction, but he wouldn't want anything to happen to him. The kid had so much untapped potential. It was that waste more than anything that caused Jason to lose patience with Sammy so readily. How could he so casually throw away not only his own natural gifts, but the opportunities Dana struggled to offer him? What in God's name would it take to reach him?

Each time Jason called with no news, he could hear the mounting fear in Dana's voice. By the time he got back to the apartment at dawn, she was in a state of near panic. He was nearly as frazzled himself.

"He probably spent the night with one of his friends," he said, though somehow Sammy didn't strike him as the type to go on some innocent sleepover at a friend's house.

Dana didn't seem to buy the explanation any more than he did. She tried her best to look hopeful, but the effort fell discouragingly short. Jason would have dragged home moonbeams, if they would have cheered her up. He doubted it would have mattered.

"Are you hungry?" she asked dutifully. "I have some eggs."

He shook his head. ''No, just give me some more coffee, so I can warm up a little. Then I'll go out again.''

''You don't think we're going to find him, do you?'' Dana said, her voice flat.

Jason considered lying to her, but couldn't do it. Pulling her close, he said as gently as he could, ''Not unless he wants to be found. He's sixteen and pretty ingenious. My guess is he'll come home when he's good and ready.''

''Why would he have left in the first place? We didn't have a fight. Everything was just fine when I went out.''

''Sweetheart, it may have absolutely nothing to do with you. Maybe he had a run-in with that gang of his and figured he needed to hide out. It's hard to tell how a teenager's mind works. Maybe he did something he knew would upset you and was too ashamed to admit it. When he gets hungry enough and lonely enough, he'll figure out that running's not the answer.''

''I wish I could be as sure of that as you are.''

Jason wasn't sure of much of anything, just that he would have given his life to save Dana this kind of heartache.

''You don't suppose he would call *you,*'' she said, a sudden spark of excitement in her eyes. ''I mean if he were in trouble, he might think you could get him out of it.''

''I think I'd be the last person he'd call.''

''But he might,'' Dana insisted. ''Is your answering machine on?''

''Yes.''

''Check it for messages. Please, Jason.''

Jason thought it was a waste of time, but he called,

then punched in his security code. The tape rewound through one lengthy message and began to play.

"Jason, it's Johnny. You know, over at the gym. I know it's early, man, but I found that friend of yours, you know the kid, over here. He was asleep in the locker room. I'm trying to get him to hang loose, but he's jumpy as a cat. Get over here as soon as possible. I figure you're with his sister, but the kid won't tell me how to reach her. Make tracks, buddy. I have a feeling the kid's in some kind of trouble."

Jason closed his eyes in relief.

"What is it?" Dana demanded. "He called, didn't he?"

"No, but Johnny from the gym called. He found Sammy when he went in this morning. He's trying to get him to stick around, but we'd better get over there. If Sammy figures out that Johnny called me, Johnny's afraid he'll split."

Dana already had her coat and was sprinting for the door. As Jason followed, he wondered if he'd been right about Sammy's reaction to Johnny's call. Maybe there was a significance to the fact that he'd chosen the gym to run to, knowing that Johnny *would* call Jason. If so, maybe Sammy was finally beginning to trust him, beginning to reach out to him. He had a feeling this was a turning point. No matter what, he had to control his temper long enough to give Sammy the chance to open up.

At the gym they found Johnny pacing out front, looking grim. His expression brightened the minute he spotted them. "Thank goodness. I was beginning to think I was going to have to tie him up."

"Is he okay?" Dana asked, her brow creased with worry.

"Looks okay to me, but if everything were peachy, he wouldn't have been conked out in the back room, would he?"

"I want to see him. Where is he?"

"In my office. I talked him into eating. I brought him back some eggs and pancakes from the fast-food place down the block."

"Dana, let me talk to him," Jason said.

"No. Sammy's my brother. It's my problem."

"You made it mine the minute you called me. Now let me see if I can find out why he's hiding out. It may be something he doesn't want to involve you in."

Even as the words came out of his mouth, Jason knew that he'd hit on the answer. But what could possibly be so bad that Sammy would fear telling Dana? Like his sister, the boy tended to think he was invincible, that he could handle anything.

Dana looked reluctant, but she finally nodded. "Jason, please don't yell at him."

Yelling at the kid was the least of what he had in mind, but he nodded. "Get Johnny to teach you a few punches. It'll work off the frustration," he suggested, squeezing her hand before he went inside.

The door to Johnny's office was wide open and for an instant Jason panicked. What if he'd been wrong? What if Sammy had spotted them and gone out the back while they were outside? Dana would never forgive him for letting him get away. He crossed the gym in a dozen strides, then quietly stepped into the office.

Sammy was still there, the empty breakfast container shoved aside, his head on Johnny's desk. He'd fallen asleep again. He was snoring softly. In sleep, with that crazy hank of blond hair falling over his eyes, he had the look of an innocent kid. Jason found it almost possible to believe that it really wasn't too late to turn his life around.

He shut the door softly, then pulled up a chair and sat down between Sammy and the only escape route. He reached over and shook his shoulder. "Wake up, son."

Sammy mumbled something, then lifted his head and stared at Jason through groggy, sleep-filled eyes. Instantly alarm filled those blue depths. He slid his chair back, glancing around frantically for a way out.

"You might as well sit back down. You're not going anywhere."

"That no-good, lyin' so..." The words were tough, but the tone was halfhearted.

"Cut the crap," Jason said. "You knew Johnny would call me. That's why you came here, isn't it?"

Sammy's mouth clamped shut and his defiant expression faltered.

"What kind of trouble are you in?"

"I can handle it," he said with one last bit of bravado.

Jason nodded and softened his tone. What was it with these Roberts siblings? Both of them had to do everything on their own. "Maybe so," he said to Sammy. "But why not let me help if I can."

"I don't need help," he insisted, then amended, "Not for me, anyway. It's Dana."

Jason felt his heartbeat slow. "What about Dana?" he questioned very quietly, his hands slowly clenching into fists.

"The guys who attacked her in that alley, they threatened to come after her again. They wanted to know where we lived. I got away, but I think they wanted me to. They thought I'd go home, but I saw them followin' me. That's why I came here. I couldn't go back to the apartment. I was afraid they'd hurt her and I wouldn't be able to stop them."

Suddenly Sammy's expression grew even more worried. "She's okay, isn't she? They didn't find her?"

"She's okay," Jason reassured him, keeping a tight leash on his fury. This was the last straw. "She's right outside with Johnny."

"What are we gonna do?"

Jason had to give him credit. He sounded genuinely distressed. Maybe Sammy had grown up a little tonight, realized that there were consequences to his actions not just for him, but for his sister.

"We're going to convince your sister that it's time to move. With any luck we'll have the two of you out of that apartment by the end of the day and neither of you will have to worry about those thugs again."

Sammy looked skeptical. "I don't think Dana's gonna go for it. Moving costs money."

"Money's the least of our problem."

Sammy managed a little half smile. "Maybe for you. But Dana worries about it a lot."

"She won't have to, not anymore."

"What are you gonna do? Give her a loan? I don't think she'll take it."

Jason nodded. "You're probably right. She's turned me down before. Think we can talk her into moving the two of you into my place?"

Sammy's mouth dropped open. "You want us to move in with you?" His gaze narrowed speculatively. "Both of us?"

Jason chuckled. "You don't think she's likely to come without you, do you?"

"No, but I just can't imagine you and me in the same house. We don't exactly see eye to eye."

"We both care about your sister, don't we? Maybe we should concentrate on that. It would make your sister happy if we got along."

"What's your real scam?" Sammy suddenly looked very grown up. In a sober tone he demanded, "You plannin' to marry her or somethin'?"

"The thought has crossed my mind," Jason admitted, as much to his own astonishment as Sammy's. "Think she'd go for it?"

Sammy seemed to consider the idea, then shook his head. "Not a chance. It doesn't make much sense to me, but she's got this crazy idea that she has to do everything the hard way. I don't think marriage is in her plans."

"Then I guess I'll just have to change her mind," he said, knowing that Sammy was right on target with his analysis. "First things first, though. We've got to convince her that this move is for your good. It's the only way she'll go for it."

"Isn't that like lyin' or something?" Sammy asked, his expression too knowing, in Jason's opinion.

The kid had certainly picked a fine time to develop scruples, Jason thought. "It's not entirely a lie," he informed Sammy. "After all it won't hurt you to find some new friends."

"Right," Sammy said skeptically, then opened the door and went to find his sister.

Jason followed slowly, trying to figure out the right way to phrase the decision he and Sammy had reached.

"Oh, no!"

Dana's voice echoed throughout the gym and Jason

realized the phrasing had been taken out of his hands. Obviously Sammy had already told his sister about their plan. She didn't seem to be taking it well. She was marching across the gym with fire in her eyes.

"What kind of hogwash were you filling his head with in there?" she demanded, backing Jason into a corner.

"Hogwash?"

"You are not going to use my brother to get to me. We are perfectly safe living where we are—a lot safer than I would be living with you."

There was safety and then there was *safety*. Jason refrained from trying to explain the difference to her. "Dana, my house could accommodate a dozen people. You'll have all the privacy you want. You have to admit, it would be better for Sammy to get away from the influence of those creeps."

Admittedly the prospect of having the kid under his roof gave him pause, but it was a sacrifice he was prepared to make to keep them both safe. It was way too soon to think much beyond that.

"It's happening, isn't it?" she demanded. "You've got some crazy idea about rescuing me. Well, I won't have it. I can stand on my own two feet. I always have."

Jason could see her reasoning, at once, and she was right. She had awakened some white-knight fantasy in him. That didn't mean the idea was a bad one. "I'm not trying to rob you of your independence," he said tightly. "Think about your brother, dammit. He's the only person in the whole blessed world who matters to you, and you seem willing to throw away his chances out of some stubborn need to handle everything on your own. Talk about selfish!"

Dana stared at him, obviously stung by his outburst. Slowly the fight seemed to drain out of her. "You're probably right about moving," she conceded grudgingly. "But we'll find an apartment in another neighborhood. I'll pick up today's paper on the way home and check out the ads."

"That takes time. Stay with me until you find another place. I don't like the idea of those guys tracking you down. They won't give up easily." An idea flashed through his mind and he added determinedly, "If you don't come to my place, I'll have to move into yours and then we really will be in close quarters."

There was a flash of defiance in her eyes, but apparently she recognized that he wasn't budging on this one. She finally nodded. "Okay. You're probably right. That would be the sensible thing to do."

Jason's pulse leaped.

"But it will only be temporary, just until I find a new apartment."

"Absolutely," he agreed.

With any luck he could keep her so busy she wouldn't have time to look for weeks.

Dana couldn't imagine what had possessed her to think that living in the same house with Jason would work. Even as a stopgap measure to protect her brother, it struck her as a dramatic, foolhardy move. The whole time she was packing enough things to get them through the first few days, she practiced excuses for backing out. Every time she started to say one out loud, Jason shot her a forbidding look that caused the words to lodge in her throat.

Okay, so she could make the best of anything for a

few days. That's all it would be. She would find a new apartment no later than Friday. She and Sammy could move next weekend, her sanity intact. She would thank Jason profusely for his trouble and run like crazy. No problem.

That was before she saw the house.

Settled on a block of gracious old town houses, there was a wide bay window in front which guaranteed the window seat she'd always wanted inside. There were fireplaces not only in the living room, but in all of the bedrooms. The high ceilings would welcome the tallest Christmas tree. She stood in the living room after touring the house and tried to hide the delight that spilled through her. It wouldn't do for Jason to ever discover that he owned her dream house, the one she'd spent countless hours fantasizing about while sitting on her own graffiti-decorated front steps.

Fortunately he seemed unaware of her speechlessness. Sammy was keeping Jason occupied with a series of awed questions. He'd gaped in astonishment when Mrs. Willis, the smiling housekeeper, had shown them a kitchen that was almost the size of their entire apartment. She'd taken one look at Sammy's skinny physique and immediately gone to work. She'd shooed them all into the living room with a promise of sandwiches and pie.

As she looked at the obviously pricey antiques, Dana worried that her rambunctious brother, who was just growing comfortable with his new height, would clumsily destroy something valuable.

''Well, what do you think?'' Jason asked quietly, his hands resting on her shoulders as she gazed longingly at the window seat that was just as she'd always imagined.

"It's lovely," she said honestly.

"Think you'll be comfortable here?"

She shook her head at the anxious note in his voice. "Jason, you saw the way we've been living. How could we not be comfortable?" Determined to make it clear, though, that this was a temporary measure, she added firmly, "We'll try to stay out of your way. There's no need to change your routine for us."

"Dana," he said, his voice a low warning. "What's wrong with you? Why do you look so edgy? We even have chaperons. There's Sammy, and Mrs. Willis lives in."

"You didn't mention her before."

"I didn't think of her as a selling point. Of course, she and Mrs. Finch do share a fascination with romances."

"Terrific," Dana muttered. She glanced around and realized they were alone. "Where's Sammy?"

"Back in the kitchen. I believe he wanted to be sure the sandwiches weren't anything sissy like watercress."

Despite her nervousness, Dana chuckled. "Sammy's never even heard of watercress sandwiches. Why on earth would he think they might be?"

Jason looked guilty. "I believe I might have planted the possibility in his head."

She scanned his face. "Why?"

"So I could be alone with you. Come on. Let's sit over here."

He drew her to the window seat which was wide enough for both of them to sit with their backs to the sides, their legs brushing as they faced each other. Outside, rain had started to fall with the promise of snow by night. Dana felt a rare warmth and coziness steal through her. Living in a place like this would make her soft. She would grow too complacent.

"Why did you want to sit here?" she asked, wondering at his perfect choice in a room filled with comfortable-looking chairs.

"Because you haven't taken your eyes off it since you came in."

Unwilling to admit to the fascination with the window seat, she asked, "How long have you had this house?"

"Forever, it seems. It's the home my parents had when they first married. When we moved into a bigger place, they kept this one. For years it was rented, but I insisted on having it when I got out of college. I bought it from them. Some of my best memories come from the years we spent here. I used to sit in this window seat and read on rainy days. I'd read adventure stories and imagine that I was the hero. You have no idea the number of dragons I slayed in this very place."

Dana smiled. "And you're still slaying them, aren't you?"

"I'm trying," he admitted.

"Why?"

"I think you know the answer to that. Do you want me to say it out loud?"

"No," she said hurriedly. Somehow she knew what he'd say. And hearing him say aloud that he loved her here in this wonderful house, in this perfect setting would distract her from her goals. It would make her dreams actually seem within her grasp.

And anyone from her neighborhood knew all too well that dreams didn't come true, not unless you made them happen yourself. If Jason gave them to her, she would lose something, though exactly what was beginning to elude her.

Chapter Eleven

Dana had every intention of starting her new job as scheduled on Monday. Jason had other ideas. In fact, he had the perfect ruse. He convinced John Lansing to let her complete a project for him before filling out all the necessary paperwork at the Lansing Agency. That left her free to spend the entire day Monday making arrangements for Sammy to transfer to a new school. Last night she and Jason had devoted long hours to arguing about the transfer. She'd insisted that there was no point in pulling him out of his old school until she knew where they were going to be moving. Jason had countered that leaving her brother where he was would defeat the whole purpose of getting them out of the old neighborhood.

Even though they'd disagreed, Dana had felt an odd sense of relief at being able to share the burden of decision making. It frightened her how easily Jason was weaving himself into the fabric of her life, how readily she was willing to relinquish her responsibilities. It just proved what she'd known all along: she didn't dare let a man like Jason into her life. It would make her weak.

As it turned out, Sammy's suspension complicated matters. The new school didn't want to take him until he'd completed the punishment. Overhearing Dana's dilemma, Mrs. Willis offered to tutor Sammy until he could start classes again. Since she also offered to reward him with chocolate chip cookies, Sammy readily agreed to continue his lessons at home.

Dana watched in astonishment as Sammy and the housekeeper immediately disappeared into the kitchen. Sammy had his arm draped around the older woman's shoulders as he tried to convince her that he needed food first if he was to study properly. Chuckling, Mrs. Willis agreed. She seemed destined to play the same grandmotherly role in his life that Mrs. Finch played in Dana's.

With Sammy settled for the moment, Dana spent the remainder of the afternoon at loose ends, wandering through the house. It was the first time she could recall when she didn't have a dozen things that had to be done. She found a leather-bound copy of *Treasure Island* in one of the living room shelves and settled into the window seat to read. Caught up in the adventure, and imagining Jason reading the story in the very same place as a boy, made her feel closer to him than ever. It was a dangerous allure.

Jason didn't arrive home until after six. From her place on the window seat, Dana watched him, feeling unexpectedly shy as he came into the living room looking for her. As if they were an old married couple, he dropped a kiss on her brow, then handed Sammy a bag filled with the latest computer games.

Sammy emptied them onto the sofa, his eyes widening. "Hey, these are radical! Are they for me?"

Jason grinned. "They're yours. Maybe you can teach me to play them after dinner."

"Sure. Hey, sis, did you see?"

"I saw." She shot him a pointed glance. Sammy responded with a puzzled expression, then jumped up.

"Oh, yeah." He held out his hand to Jason. "Thanks, man."

"You're welcome. I thought maybe they'd keep you busy until it's time to go back to school."

Sammy groaned. "Who's got spare time? Did you know Mrs. W. used to be a teacher? She gave me more assignments than I ever had in school. I'll be up till midnight."

Anxious to get to the computer games, neither man seemed inclined to waste much time lingering over the housekeeper's beef stew. Amused that Jason seemed every bit as excited as Sammy, Dana went back to her place in the window seat to watch the two of them as they hunched over the computer. Sammy couldn't believe that Jason had never played a computer game before. He delighted in patiently explaining the rules, then beating the daylights out of Jason. Listening to their heated exchanges, she decided it was a toss-up which one was influencing the other.

Curious about the games, she got up and took a closer look. The game they were so intent on masked a geography lesson, one of Sammy's poorest subjects.

"Pretty sly," she told Jason, when Sammy finally went to his room, leaving the two of them alone.

Jason came over and nudged her legs aside, so he

could sit across from her. Dana was all too aware of the way their knees intimately bumped, her faded jeans a sharp contrast to his expensive wool slacks.

"I haven't the foggiest idea what you're talking about," Jason said.

"Oh, really? I suppose it was just an accident that the game focused on geography."

"True," he said, his expression all innocence. "It looked like fun. I'd seen a lot about it in magazines and on public television. I'd just never gotten around to trying it."

"You're a crummy liar, but thank you. For the first time, I think Sammy realized learning could be fun. He's never loved books the way I have. He's just wanted to experience things, to see them firsthand."

Jason tucked her sock-clad feet in his lap and began massaging them. The deep strokes were both soothing and oddly exciting. Tingles shot from her toes straight to her midsection.

"There are some who say that his way is right, that people who get all their education from books never really learn about living," he said as if it were no more than an idle thought. His caresses said otherwise.

Dana's breath had gone perfectly still. "Is that what you think? Do you think I've been missing out on life?"

His gaze met hers. "It doesn't really matter what I think. What do you think?"

Dana had to try very hard to stay focused on the train of the conversation. "Maybe I've missed out on some things, but not the important ones."

Jason's hands slid beyond her feet and began a hypnotic caress of the bare skin just above her socks.

She'd had no idea just how shivery sensitive that part of her anatomy was.

"What about love?" he said as matter-of-factly as if he'd asked about the likelihood of snow. "Isn't that one of the most important things?"

"I suppose. What about it?" she asked, her voice suddenly choked. That increasingly familiar ache was back again, that deep-down need that was aroused in her by Jason's most casual touches.

"Don't you think that's one of those things you have to experience to understand? You can read about it, but until you've felt your heart open up to another person, you don't really know what it is. I'm just beginning to realize that myself. How about you?"

"Maybe." Her voice was a near whisper as she succumbed to the delicious warmth spreading through her. With the fire crackling in the fireplace and Jason's intoxicating touches, she felt as if she'd discovered paradise. If ever she was going to allow herself to love a man, it would be this one. He could be exasperating and arrogant and stuffy, but his heart and his touch were gentle.

His fingers came to rest just above her knee. Her stomach quivered in anticipation. Yet nothing more happened.

Why wasn't he finishing what he started? she wondered, filled with a frustration she couldn't quite explain. Why, for the first time in her life, wasn't she afraid of what might happen next? Could it be that she was actually ready to admit she needed another person in her life and that Jason Halloran was that person?

Fending off male advances had become second nature to her by the time she was twelve. The guys in her neighborhood hadn't been respectful of age or innocence. Dana had known intuitively that the first time she gave any one of them the slightest encouragement, she would become fair game for them all. That's when she'd learned exactly where to hit to prove that no meant *no.*

To her confusion, she wasn't the least bit interested in saying no now. On some level she couldn't explain, it was as if she'd waited her whole life for this moment, yet Jason was holding back. His touches teased, inflamed, then left her wanting. Agitated by the sensations and her own unexpected response to them, she dared to meet Jason's gaze. At once she saw the turmoil, saw her own turbulent desire reflected there.

"Jason?"

"What?"

"I think I need you to kiss me."

A half smile came and went, then his mouth slowly covered hers with exquisite tenderness. His tongue coaxed her lips apart, and Dana's senses went spinning. It was a response she'd come to expect and, again, she wasn't afraid.

Nor was she satisfied. There was a sweetness to the kiss, a gentle persuasiveness, but she knew there had to be more, and she wanted it, desired it with a fierce intensity that shook her to her very core. She wasn't ready to label the wanting love, wasn't ready to think at all beyond tonight. Tonight, though, she wanted to be held in Jason's arms.

The daring prospect was fraught with obstacles. Sammy, for one. She couldn't make love to Jason with her brother in the same house. And what would Mrs. Willis think if she discovered that Dana's bed hadn't been slept in?

Those were just excuses, she told herself. Jason's

master suite was at the opposite end of the house from the rooms she and Sammy had taken. As for the housekeeper, Mrs. Willis wouldn't see anything out of the ordinary if Dana's room was tidy when she first entered it tomorrow. Dana was too used to making her own bed to leave it for someone else to do. Even this morning everything had been neatly in place before she'd ever walked out the door. Though Mrs. Willis was clearly inclined to pamper her while she was there, Dana had explained that she was used to doing things for herself.

There was nothing, then, to stand in the way of her spending the night with Jason. Except maybe Jason himself. She gazed at him and saw the banked desire still lingering in his eyes, felt the hesitation in his touch. He was every bit as troubled by the prospect of taking this next step as she was. Maybe it was his willingness to hold back that touched that part of her heart that had always said no in the past. She would never find a man who cared more about her feelings than Jason.

Sliding toward him, she took his face in her hands and slanted her mouth across his. She felt the heat climb in his cheeks, felt the urgency mount in his kiss as he matched her hunger.

Then his hands covered hers and he pulled back, no more than an inch, but the separation was too much. She felt bereft. She tried to close the gap, but he held back. "What do you want, Dana?"

"You know," she said, lost in the first whisper of a smoldering sensuality she was just beginning to discover. "Can't you tell?"

"I want you to say it. I need to know that you mean it."

She swallowed hard. "I want you to make love to me." She began faintly, but by the end she managed to sound bold and convincing.

Against her hands, Jason's fingers trembled. "You're sure?"

"Very sure."

"You aren't doing this out of some misguided sense of obligation because you're staying here?"

"I'm doing it because I think I'll fly apart if I don't experience what it's like to have you love me."

The words had come from her heart—her poor, misguided and probably soon-to-be-broken heart. Apparently they were enough. Jason scooped her into his arms and carried her up the steps. "You can back out anytime," he said, but the look in his eyes pleaded with her not to.

There was no chance she was going to change her mind now, anyway. Dana felt a shimmering feminine awareness that pulled like a magnet. It was all she could do to keep her hands from roaming down Jason's shoulders to explore his chest. Curiosity mixed with desire made her bold. Whatever shyness she might have been expected to feel had long since vanished, swept away by wave after wave of deep longing. All of the warnings she'd given herself just this morning seemed unimportant when compared to the discoveries she was about to make—about herself, about Jason, about making love.

With the door to Jason's room firmly locked behind them, she stood on tiptoe to draw him into a kiss from which there could be no retreat. She was desperate to know where passion led, where this tantalizing spiral of white-hot sensation peaked.

Lifting Dana gently and putting her on the bed, Jason scanned her face, his gaze intent. ''No regrets?''

''Not now. Not later,'' she promised. And if there were, she would keep them to herself, knowing instinctively that there would be worse regrets if they never shared this moment.

His fingers looped under the hem of her sweater, then slowly drew it over her head. The casual brush of his fingers against her bare midriff left a trail of heat. He traced the swell of her breasts, teasing until she was sure she would die if his touch didn't reach the sensitized nipples. With one deft movement, he unhooked her bra and for a moment he simply stared, his expression rapt. If Dana had ever worried about her attractiveness, that look put her worries to rest. Fascinated, he touched one swollen, rosy peak, first with the pad of his thumb, then with his tongue. Dana's back arched as a riot of new sensations shimmered through her.

But for every feathered touch and every deep caress, satisfaction was followed too quickly by a rising sense of need. Like the climber who always discovers new peaks the instant the last has been attained, Dana discovered that each glorious, thrilling sensation only hinted at one even more spectacular.

She lost track of where one stroke ended and the next began, caught up instead in a never-ending wave that crested, then eased gently away before building again, higher than ever. Still there was this emptiness that she didn't understand.

Jason's flesh burned every bit as hot as her own. His desire was written on his face, but he seemed determined to take his time, determined to tease and taunt until neither of them could wait an instant longer for fulfillment. That time was fast approaching.

Up until the last possible second, Dana waited for the fear to ruin what was happening between them. She was so sure that her conscience and common sense would kick in and rob her of Jason's tenderness, of his love. As her body lifted toward his, seeking the elusive fulfillment he withheld, she realized that behind the desire in his eyes there was worry. He, too, was waiting for her to change her mind, giving her time for thought to overrule sensation.

She reached for him then, boldly caressing, telling him without words that there would be no retreat. He couldn't hold back a low moan as her strokes became more insistent. And then he was chuckling.

"I get the message," he murmured as he held himself above her.

"I certainly hope so," she said. "There's a lot to be said for anticipation, but I think it's time you make a commitment."

The word with its multitude of meanings crept out before she realized how Jason would interpret it. Satisfaction flared in his eyes as he eased into her at last. There was one brief, searing instant of unexpected pain, then Dana was filled with that sense of completion that had eluded her for so long. Lost to the sensations, she forgot all about her foolish slip of tongue, forgot everything except the wild racing of her heart, the rush of heat and, finally, the most incredible release—as if she'd just discovered a way to catapult over rainbows.

The night was all about giving—and learning to accept. It was morning before her last teasing remark came back to haunt her. She woke to find Jason propped up on his elbow, staring at her. His sleepy, sensual smile made her stomach flip over.

"So, let's talk about commitment," he said, drawing a fingertip over her breast.

"I can't talk about anything when you're doing that," she said.

To her regret he opted for talking over touching. "How do you feel about commitment?"

Suddenly all too aware of the silver-framed family photographs that lined his dresser, she was shaking her head before the first words were out of his mouth. "Are we talking in general? I think it's a fine idea…for some people."

"But not for you?"

"Not for me."

"Then why are we here?" he demanded mildly. "Why did you make the choice to make love last night, when it's a choice you've obviously never made before?"

"Because I…" She saw the expectant look on his face, but she couldn't bring herself to say the words she knew he wanted to hear. "Because I trust you. Isn't that enough for now?" she said wistfully.

For a minute his gaze clashed with hers, but then he sighed. "For now," he agreed. "But I want more than an occasional night in bed with you, Dana."

"It wasn't all that long ago that you dismissed me as a flake. Why the abrupt change?"

"I wish I could explain it," he said. "All I know is that for the past few weeks I've felt alive for the first time in months. You've brought out a side of me I never even knew existed. I may be a lot of things, Dana, but I'm not stupid. I recognize a good thing when I have it within my grasp. I will give you anything you ask, do anything you want, but I'm not known for my patience."

"Tell me about it," she muttered.

He scowled at her. "All I'm trying to say is that I can wait only so long."

Dana was shaken by the unspoken threat underlying his words, but she put on her bravest front and resorted to teasing. "You'll do anything, huh?"

"Anything," he vowed.

"Well, that presents some intriguing possibilities."

There was just enough time for him to show her one of them before they left for work.

The expression on Dana's face made Jason very nervous.

"Okay, spill it," he said finally, sensing that he was about to pay for his impetuous early-morning promise to give her anything she wanted. "What's up?"

"I was talking to Harriet just now," she began slowly.

"Harriet?" he repeated blankly. "You've been conspiring with my secretary?"

"I wouldn't call it conspiring and don't look so stunned. She's really very nice."

"Harriet?"

"Will you stop it and listen? She told me about this part-time job, in the mailroom."

"You have a job," he said tightly. He was not going to encourage her to take a second job, just so she could afford to move into a fancier place of her own that much sooner. Besides, she barely had enough time to sleep as it was—especially when she was occupying his bed, which was where he intended she stay.

"Not for me," she said patiently.

Suddenly he realized why she looked so nervous. "Oh, no," he said, coming out from behind his desk. "I will not give your brother a job."

She laced her hands behind his neck and gave him an imploring look. "It's just a part-time messenger job. He could come in after school, earn a little of his own money, learn about accepting responsibility—it would be perfect. How much trouble could he possibly get into?"

Jason eased away from her and raked his fingers through his hair. He couldn't think straight when she had her arms around him like that, and this situation definitely called for straight thinking.

"You're asking this about a boy who a few short weeks ago was ready to go into business selling stolen goods. The same boy who was thrown out of school last week for pulling a knife on a classmate. The same kid who's this close—" he held up fingers a scant inch apart "—this close to getting into a gang that mugs people for kicks."

Dana remained undaunted by the facts. It was one of her more endearing and infuriating qualities.

"Just look how he's blossoming now that he's out of that environment. He's already taking his studies more seriously with Mrs. Willis there to tutor him. Haven't you ever made a mistake?" she demanded. "Or is the difference that Hallorans have enough money to cover up any little indiscretions they might make?"

"This isn't about money or family."

"No. It's about second chances."

The whisper-soft tone of her voice was persuasive. The look in her eyes could have converted sinner to saint. Jason sighed.

"He won't do it."

"He will," she said, throwing her arms around him. She gave him a tantalizing peck on the cheek. "I'll call and tell him to come over this afternoon. Thank you, Jason. You won't regret it."

He already did. The mere thought of that little punk on the loose at Halloran Industries made him shudder. It was one thing to have Sammy living in his house, where Mrs. Willis could keep her stern eye on him and only Jason would have to pay for any of his royal screwups. It was another thing entirely to inflict him on the family business. What sort of magic was this woman working, Jason wondered, that would make him even consider such an idea?

On the other hand, he thought slowly, maybe Dana was right. Maybe this was an opportunity, a challenge. The one thing he and Dana argued about more than anything else was her brother. Maybe by taking one giant leap of faith in Sammy, he could eliminate the bone of contention between them and further cement a relationship that was coming to mean everything to him.

One look at Sammy's sullen expression a few hours later and Jason wasn't so sure. Whatever progress they'd made at home seemed to have been lost. He wondered if Sammy viewed this as punishment, rather than a chance.

After a cursory nod, Sammy sprawled in the chair across from Jason and regarded him with open hostility. His attitude improved only slightly when he turned his attention to the computer, the fax machine and the calculator. Jason could practically see the larcenous wheels spinning in his head.

"Don't even think about it," he warned in a low voice.

Sammy looked startled. "Hey, I was just checkin' the place out."

"I'm sure you were. However, if one item in this office moves by so much as an inch, I will know where to look. Do we understand each other?"

Sammy shrugged. "You're the boss."

"That's right."

"What am I gonna do?"

"It's a messenger job. You'll see that the mail is picked up from the offices, sorted and distributed. Once in a while you might be asked to take something into town."

"How? You plannin' to loan me your car?"

"No. I'm planning to give you bus fare."

"What's this job pay?"

Jason named the minimum wage figure.

"You're kiddin' me, right?"

"I'm not kidding you."

"I could make more than that busing tables in some dive."

"Maybe. Is that something you're interested in doing? I have a couple of friends who own restaurants."

Sammy seemed startled by Jason's willingness to give him a choice. "I thought this was a done deal. Now I get it. You're just doing my sister a favor—again. The minute I screw up, I'm out, right? If you can pawn me off on one of your friends, you won't need to mess with me at all and you'll still be square with Dana."

It was a long speech for Sammy. To Jason's surprise, he realized that there was an edge of real hurt in the boy's voice. Jason wondered how many times people had made snap decisions about Sammy, had promised him something only to yank it away again.

"Sammy, let's back up a minute. Do you really want a job?"

Sammy shrugged. "Dana works too hard. I should help out."

"That's an admirable attitude. Now, if you really had a choice, if you could do anything in the world you wanted to, what would it be?"

Sammy rolled his eyes. "I'm just a kid."

"You're sixteen years old. You're almost a man. Surely you've thought about what you'd like to do when you get out of school."

"Not really."

"What is your best subject?"

"Math, I guess. I like English, too. I get good grades on all my essays."

There was no mistaking the faint spark of enthusiasm. Sammy tried hard to maintain his distant, nonchalant attitude, but Jason detected the slight shift in his mood from boredom to interest.

"What if we rethink this job situation a little, then? How about working three hours after school? You spend the first two hours taking care of the mail. Then during the last hour each day we'll let you spend some time in different departments around here. You could start in accounting, maybe spend some time with me in marketing, helping me with some writing I have to do. If you're interested, I'm sure my grandfather would be happy to teach you about the manufacturing process, too."

"We're still talkin' that minimum-wage stuff, though, right?"

Jason grinned. "At first. But if you catch on quickly

in any of the departments and want to move up, we'll talk about a salary increase then."

"I suppose that would be okay."

His tone was lukewarm, but there was a rare spark of excitement in Sammy's eyes.

"You'll start tomorrow?"

"Why not," Sammy said, then added with studied nonchalance, "I got an hour to kill now, if there's somethin' you want me to do."

"I'll have Harriet take you down to personnel and you can fill out some forms. Then, if you still have some time, I'll show you around."

He buzzed for Harriet, then watched Sammy leave with her. To his astonishment, the boy actually seemed to be walking a little taller. Jason heard Dana's greeting in the outer office, then the quick rush of questions about how the interview went.

"No problem," Sammy said, his tone cocky. "I'm a tough negotiator, sis. You're lookin' at one top-notch executive trainee."

Jason was still chuckling when Dana stepped into his office, her eyes sparkling.

"Executive trainee?" she said. "I thought you were having trouble with the concept of messenger."

"Actually Sammy was having more trouble with that than I was. Minimum wage did not appeal to him. We compromised. He still gets minimum wage, but he'll rotate through the departments so he'll get a little experience in various things. Who knows, maybe he'll find his niche." He regarded her hopefully. "Do you suppose there's any chance we could talk him into a more normal haircut before my father sees him?"

Dana chuckled at the wistfulness in his voice. "I

doubt it. You know, Jason Halloran, you're not nearly as tough as you like to pretend to be.''

''Oh, but I am,'' he said. ''I intend to make the person who got me into this pay.''

''Pay how?''

He reached for her hand and tugged her closer. ''Like this,'' he said softly and pulled her into his arms. ''I think for a few more kisses like this, I might be willing to make Sammy head of marketing.''

Chapter Twelve

For a man who'd always been determinedly grounded in reality, Jason had developed a surprisingly fanciful habit of imagining Dana's voice whenever he started feeling lonely. This morning, however, he was certain that for once it was not his imagination playing tricks on him. They didn't have an appointment, but he was willing to swear she was in his outer office. He poked his head out and discovered her in the midst of what looked like a very conspiratorial group—Sammy, an astonishingly lighthearted Harriet and his grandfather. Brandon looked like the sassy cat who'd just swallowed the canary.

"What kind of trouble are you all getting into out here?" Jason demanded. "And why wasn't I included?"

Four moderately guilty faces turned in his direction. Brandon was quickest on his feet. He'd had years of experience twisting tricky situations to his own advantage.

"You can't possibly begrudge an old man a little time with your girl," he said. "However, if you're jealous, you can come along. We're about to go on a tour of the plant."

"Harriet has worked here for the past twenty years. She's seen every nook and cranny of the place," Jason reminded him. "And Dana saw the plant from top to bottom just a couple of weeks ago."

"Not through *my* eyes. You probably did one of those wham-bang tours that barely touched the tip of the iceberg."

"I did leave out all the nostalgia," Jason admitted, grinning at him. His grandfather was clearly in his element, relishing the prospect of an attentive audience. Jason turned to Dana and her brother, who was slouched on a corner of Harriet's desk twisting paper clips out of shape. "I hope you know what you're in for. His version could take hours."

"You could come along," Dana coaxed. "Maybe it would improve your skills as a tour guide—add a little color. Tours could become a great marketing device. Dozens of little fifth-graders parading through here every day. Just imagine."

Jason shuddered at the thought. But he'd discovered lately that when Dana got that impish look on her face, he found it impossible to refuse her anything. His intentions to reform and become a dutiful company official flew out the window. He forgot all about the stack of work on his desk. Maybe, if he got lucky, he could sneak a kiss behind one of the giant looms.

"Yes," he murmured. "Just imagine."

Draping an arm around Dana's shoulder, he gestured to Brandon. "Lead on, Granddad."

Jason listened with tolerant amusement as his grandfather launched into a family history that started back in England before the turn of the century. Dana and even Sammy listened raptly as Brandon talked about his grandfather's textile mill in England and his struggle to build a name for himself.

"His son, my father, had bigger dreams. He'd heard there was newer, faster equipment to be had in America and he had a spirit of adventure. He came to this country with little money in his pocket and a lot of desire. His uncles had been here for years, working for one of the mills that had been around for decades. It was founded by a competitor of Francis Cabot Lowell right around 1816, 1820. In those early years most of the country's wholesale wool trade was handled right out of Boston.

"Anyway, James and the uncles pooled their money and bought the plant. The equipment wasn't as up-to-date as some, but they knew where to go in England and Scotland for the best wool, and pretty soon they developed a reputation for the finest fabric. That was the start of Halloran Industries.

"Nowadays, this place is something of a dinosaur. Most of the big mills from before the turn of the century went south. We decided to stay right here. We were never interested in quantity or in producing cheap material. We've concentrated on making the best."

He plucked up a handful of soft gray hairs and showed them to Sammy. "You know what this is?"

"Looks like a bunch of old hairs to me."

"Expensive old hairs. Here, feel them. Feel how

soft they are. That's cashmere, son. It comes from Himalayan goats in Tibet. We blend this with wool to make some of the winter fabric.''

He led Sammy to another loom. ''Now you watch this. It used to be done completely by hand. Just imagine that. All that spinning and weaving took days just to get enough material to make a coat or a dress.''

Jason watched in astonishment as Sammy's expression turned from boredom to fascination. He seemed to be hanging on Brandon's words. Brandon seemed equally delighted to find someone who'd actually listen to all his old stories with rapt attention. How had they so easily found the rapport he'd had to struggle for? Maybe it was because his grandfather was genuinely accepting of other people, flaws and all.

''I thought most textile manufacturers specialized,'' Dana said. ''Halloran Industries does woolen fabrics, silks and cottons. Isn't that more expensive?''

''Sure,'' Brandon agreed. ''But remember what I said. We wanted to do quality, not quantity. The decision to diversify goes back to my father. The truth of the matter was he was fascinated by the techniques. Every time he'd see a piece of fabric that intrigued him, he'd set out to learn how it was made. He even traveled to the Far East to learn more about silkworms.''

''I've been trying to convince Granddad and Dad for ages that we ought to concentrate on one specialty,'' Jason said. ''Then Granddad goes off on one of his vacation trips and, just like his father, he comes home with some ancient French woodblocks for printing cotton and we add a new line. It's not cost-effective.''

Brandon shrugged. ''If I wanted to manufacture the

material for cheap bed linens, I'd have gone south years ago and set up shop near a cotton field. Top designers and decorators come here when they want something rare and spectacular for their finest customers. We'll work to order, match a dye to suit the customer. Few places can afford to do that."

"*We* can't afford to do that," Jason countered.

Brandon chuckled. "You sound more like your father every day."

Jason couldn't help grinning back at him. "Now that is a depressing thought."

Sammy had wandered over to a bale of Sea Island cotton waiting to be processed. "This stuff actually turns into material?" he asked, his expression incredulous. "Like my shirt or somethin'?"

Brandon studied Sammy's faded plaid shirt and said, "Maybe not that shirt, but you've got the idea. First it's carded, then it goes through three more steps before we spin it." He showed him the stages, leading up to the final woven material. "Feel the difference between ours and yours. It's all in the thread count." He scowled at Jason. "Can't seem to make *some people* understand the importance of that."

He moved across an aisle. "Now look over here. We're handprinting it. I found these woodblocks at a mill that was closing in France last year after four centuries. What do you think of that?"

"Awesome," Sammy said. "Tell me again about the wool. Where's that place the sheep come from?"

The two of them went off together, Brandon responding animatedly to Sammy's rapid-fire questions.

Jason watched them go with something akin to wonder spreading through him. "I think Granddad has finally met a soul mate. Dad and I have always been more fascinated with the business end of things. Granddad just loves the product. He inherited that obsession with the textiles themselves from his father and who knows how many generations before him.''

Suddenly he realized that Dana was barely listening. She was scribbling rapidly on the notepad she'd carried during the tour.

''What are you doing?'' he asked.

''Some of this information might be helpful when we design that new campaign, don't you think?''

''You're probably right, but this minute I'm much more fascinated with these silk threads you've got caught in your hair.'' He reached up to brush away strands of pale pink silk. ''Did you tangle with a silkworm somewhere along the way?''

''Actually I was peeking under something to see how the machinery worked.''

''Can I see your notes?'' he said, holding out his hand. ''They must be fascinating.''

Dana handed him the notebook. A half dozen pages had scrawled notes on them, but what Jason found incredible were the sketches. ''These are amazing.''

''You really think so?''

''I can't believe you did them in just the little bit of time Granddad spent in each area. We could use these in the next brochure instead of photographs. Let's go back to my office and rough out an overall design, while the idea's still fresh.''

As they walked back to his office, Jason was astounded at his mounting excitement. He couldn't help but be struck by the change in his attitude, the sense of fulfillment he suddenly felt. Whether it was having Dana at the office or simply having her in his life, those days of boredom and dissatisfaction seemed like a distant nightmare. Maybe it was simply a matter of seeing his world through fresh, unjaded eyes. Or perhaps it was simply finding a focus. At any rate, for the first time in his life he truly felt a part of something bigger than his own selfish interests.

They were bent over Dana's sketchbook an hour later, when the door to his office burst open. Jason glanced up and caught his father's agitated expression, the quick head-to-toe examination to which he subjected Dana before mentally dismissing her.

''Hey, Dad, come on in. I want you to meet the new artist who's working with us. Dana Roberts, this is my father, Kevin Halloran.''

Kevin's fierce expression softened slightly as he shook Dana's hand. ''Son, if you've got a minute, I think you and I need to talk.''

There was an edge to his father's tone that worried Jason. Kevin rudely turned his back on Dana and went to stare out the window as he waited for Jason to create the sort of privacy he'd requested.

Jason bit back a furious retort and said quietly, ''Sure. Dana, we can finish this later. I think you've got the right idea now, anyway.''

When she was gone, Kevin turned back. Before Jason could say a word about his father's rudeness, Kevin snapped, ''What's this I hear about some woman moving in with you?''

Jason froze. ''Where did you hear that?''

''Actually I believe your mother heard it from one of her friends, Marcy Wellington's mother.''

Jason recalled the visit he'd had the previous evening from Marcy. Always more aggressively interested in him than he'd been in her, she'd stopped by hoping to spend the evening, perhaps even the night, with him. She'd even expressed a willingness to forgive him for what she described as that humiliating evening at the symphony gala. Discovering Dana on the premises had brought out her cattiest nature. He wasn't surprised that the news had traveled this fast.

"How could you take a step like this without informing us?" Kevin demanded. "Your mother's distraught."

"I doubt that," Jason countered. It was his father, not his mother, who tended to worry about appearances. "Don't you think I'm a little old to be called on the carpet about my living arrangements?"

"Not when they reflect on this family. Not when you're living in our house."

"It's not your house. I bought it, remember? And having Dana and her brother living under my roof is hardly likely to damage the Halloran reputation."

Kevin stared at him in astonishment. "That's the one? That girl who just left here is living with you?"

Jason bristled at the demeaning tone, but managed to keep his own tone even. "She needed to get out of her old apartment. She's staying with me until she can find her own place in a better neighborhood. If I have my way, she'll stay on indefinitely. I'm planning to ask her to marry me, Dad."

Kevin regarded him as if he'd lost his mind. "You're *what?*"

Jason wasn't sure exactly when he'd made up his mind. Maybe it was simply hearing his father's demeaning tone that had formalized the decision. "I'm asking her to marry me. She'll probably turn me down, but I intend to keep on trying until she says yes."

"Well, thank goodness one of you is displaying some sense. Are you determined to ruin your life?"

Jason's voice dropped to a low, ominous tone. "If I recall, there was a time when Granddad said the same thing about Mother. You of all people should understand what kind of havoc an outdated attitude like that can wreak. Are you planning to follow in his footsteps, anyway?"

The charge had the desired effect. Kevin's face fell. He rubbed a hand across his eyes and sank into a chair across from Jason's desk. When he finally met Jason's gaze again, he looked genuinely contrite. "I'm sorry. I don't know what's gotten into me lately."

Worried at the gray cast to his father's complexion, Jason pulled a chair up opposite his father and sat down. "Dad, can't you talk to me about what's going on?"

His father shook his head. "No. I'm not sure I even understand it myself."

"Why don't you and Mom come to dinner tomorrow night? You can spend some time with Dana and her brother. I want you to see how truly special she is. I'll ask Granddad, too. He's out in the plant with her brother now. He and Sammy have really hit it off."

His father didn't look thrilled with the prospect of a family dinner, but he said, "I'll talk to your mother and let you know, okay?"

"Please try, Dad. It's important to me."

Kevin stood up and squeezed his shoulder. "I'll do what I can."

As he left Jason's office, though, Jason couldn't help wondering if his father had any intention at all of passing along the invitation. To make sure that the dinner came off, if for no other reason than to provide an opportunity to see his parents together and get a sense of what was troubling them, Jason dialed his parents' number.

"Mom, I was just talking to Dad about a family dinner at my place tomorrow night. There's someone I want you to meet."

"The woman who's living there?" she said, though her tone was far less judgmental than his father's had been.

"Yes. You'll really like her. Her brother's a little—" he searched for a word "—unexpected. So is Dana, for that matter. You'll come, won't you?"

"If it's important to you, we'll be there," she promised, though he could tell her heart wasn't in it.

Still, that was two down and three more to go. His grandfather would probably be delighted to have the opportunity to spend more time with Dana and Sammy. And Sammy could be persuaded to do anything that involved Mrs. Willis's cooking. Dana, however, was another story. He had a hunch she was going to take one look at the Halloran clan gathering and head for the hills. For a woman who craved family the way she obviously did, she seemed deadly earnest about avoiding any personal connection with his.

He debated telling her at all, then decided she'd never forgive him if she turned up for dinner in jeans and discovered his whole family at the table.

He broached the subject at the dinner table that night, after Sammy had left to spend an hour playing computer games before doing the assignments Mrs. Willis continued to heap on him.

Dana listened to the plans, then repeated, "They're all coming here? Tomorrow?"

"Yes. You already know Dad and my grandfather, right? And you'll love my mother."

"I don't think so. Sammy and I will go out for the evening."

"The whole point of this dinner is to have everyone get to know you."

Her gaze narrowed. "Why?"

Sensing that he'd made a tactical blunder, Jason tried to backtrack. "I want you to meet my family. It'll help you understand what Hallorans are all about."

"Professionally?" she inquired hopefully.

"Exactly."

"I suppose that does make sense, but..."

For the first time since he'd known her, she suddenly looked totally at a loss. "But what?" he prodded.

"Nothing," she said finally.

Jason suspected he knew what *nothing* meant. He'd seen her one dressy outfit and suspected she was already finding fault with it, trying to imagine how she could possibly fit in with his family, wearing discounted clothes. He vowed then and there to find her something special first thing in the morning. What good was manufacturing the finest fabric, if you couldn't call in a favor from a designer every now and then?

Dana imagined she knew what it felt like to be walking toward a guillotine. Despite Jason's reassurances that this family dinner was nothing more than an opportunity for her to understand the Hallorans, she knew she was the one being trotted out for inspection. Not even Sammy was under the kind of unspoken pressure she was facing. He'd greeted news of the dinner with blasé indifference, then had gone back to one of the books Brandon had loaned him about the history of the textile industry.

Determined to strive for the same kind of nonchalance that Sammy was affecting, Dana didn't even bother to go home from work early. What was the point? She had one decent skirt, one reasonably fashionable sweater, one pair of high-heeled shoes. With no feminine dawdling over choices to factor in, it would take her about twenty minutes to shower and dress.

That was her thinking right up until the minute she walked into her room and discovered the boxes stacked in the middle of her bed—a bed she'd slept in only once since moving in with Jason. She stared at the assortment of packages in wonder.

Never, not once in her life had she received this many presents at one time. What was she supposed to do about them? She couldn't take gifts from Jason. She might not have been to finishing school, but she knew what was proper. Even in her neighborhood, a woman took presents like this only when she was willing to have her reputation compromised. Hers might be shaky at the moment, but so far she hadn't done anything she might regret later. These packages represented regrets.

She scooped them up in her arms and marched down the hall to Jason's suite. Since her hands were full, she kicked the door until Jason came to open it.

"What's all this?" he questioned, feigning innocence.

"I might ask you the same thing."

"Haven't you opened them?"

"No. I can't accept them."

"You don't even know what's inside."

"I can guess," she said stubbornly. She dumped the boxes onto the bed, then turned to glare at him. "If I'm not good enough for your family the way I am, then I don't need to be at this dinner tonight. And if you're ashamed of me, then you'd better say so now, because I will not allow you to try to pretty me up just so I'll fit in."

Her point made—rather emphatically she thought—she stalked toward the door.

"Whoa!" Jason said, putting his hands on her shoulders and spinning her around. "Let's get one thing straight right now. I am not ashamed of you. I want you to like my family and vice versa, but if that doesn't happen, so be it. I bought these things for you because I want you to feel comfortable, because you deserve to have beautiful things. If you'd rather wear something else—if you want to wear your jeans and one of your sweaters—it's okay with me. I love those jeans. They do great things for your legs."

The sincerity in his voice reached her. Her temper slowed to a simmer, then finally cooled altogether. "Maybe I could at least look in the boxes," she said cautiously.

Sammy at his most indifferent couldn't have been any more casual than Jason when he shrugged. "It's up to you."

"I'll look."

She opened what appeared to be a shoebox first. Folded inside layers of tissue paper were the slinkiest, highest silver sandals she'd ever seen. She recognized the label from one of the city's swankest shoe stores.

"Ohmigosh," she murmured, trying to imagine wearing the shoes without feeling a little like Cinderella in her glass slippers. If the shoes were this incredible, what on earth did the rest of the boxes contain?

"More?" Jason inquired lazily. He'd sprawled in a chair to watch. His posture was relaxed, but there was a tension beneath the surface that suggested he couldn't wait for her reaction to the rest.

Suddenly Dana grinned and gave in to temptation. How often did fairy-tale extravagances happen to a woman like her? "Oh, what the hell? Let's go for it."

She tugged open the biggest box and discovered a slinky black dress that shimmered with silver beads on the shoulders. She held it up and moved in front of the full-length mirror. She swallowed hard when she saw her reflection. She looked glamorous. She turned slowly back to Jason. "If this is what you had in mind for a simple family dinner, I would never have forgiven you if you'd let me go downstairs in jeans."

"I had my own jeans out, just in case."

The remaining boxes contained the sheerest, laciest lingerie Dana had ever seen. She tried to picture Jason shopping for it, but her imagination failed her. "You bought these?" she asked holding up one of several pairs of virtually nonexistent panties. The pair dangling from her finger was black. There were others in the sexiest red, the richest cream, the most virginal white.

He grinned. "Had the time of my life doing it, too. You just have to promise you'll wear them under your jeans. The image will drive me wild. In fact, if you don't get them out of here this very instant, you and I are going to be very late for dinner and that will really take some explaining."

Dana gathered the clothes up from the bed and started out the door. At the next instant she looked back and caught the pleased expression on Jason's face. "Thank you," she said softly. "I feel like Cinderella."

"There's a difference, sweetheart. You're already home."

Dana couldn't get Jason's words out of her head all through dinner. She barely noticed that Sammy was wearing new slacks, a dress shirt and a tie that he kept trying to tug loose. There was a new confidence about him that even in her distracted state was impossible to miss. He watched Brandon Halloran and mimicked every move the older man made. Brandon was careful to include Sammy in the conversation, for which Dana was grateful.

Everything about the evening was perfect. Everyone admired her dress. Mrs. Willis's menu was superb, even if Dana didn't know what half the things were. Lacey Halloran went out of her way to be gracious to both Dana and Sammy. After his initial reserve, even Kevin Halloran opened up. It had taken several glasses of wine to accomplish that, but whatever the cause, Dana was grateful. After his behavior in Jason's office, she'd been prepared for open disapproval.

Jason sat back and watched the byplay with the satisfaction of a man who'd put all of his chess pieces into motion and was waiting for certain victory. When they moved into the living room after dinner, he poured brandy for everyone—even Sammy, who choked on the first sip and asked for a soda.

Lacey Halloran set her own snifter of brandy on an end table and leaned toward Dana. "Jason tells me you had to leave your old apartment."

"That's 'cause these guys I knew said they were gonna come after her," Sammy piped up. "Jason and

I figured it wasn't so safe for her to be there anymore.''

Jason's mother looked nonplussed for an instant. ''That must have been very frightening,'' she said finally.

''You get used to the violence in a neighborhood like that,'' Dana responded.

''I'm sure living here is a vast improvement,'' Kevin said. It sounded to Dana as if he were accusing her of something, though his expression was perfectly bland.

''Actually I don't expect to be here all that long. Sammy and I will find a place of our own.''

Lacey Halloran looked confused. ''But I thought...''

''There's no rush,'' Jason said, interrupting his mother.

Dana had a terrible hunch she knew exactly what the woman had been about to say. Apparently Brandon Halloran was not the only one with a mistaken understanding of where her relationship with Jason was headed. They'd probably taken one look at this fancy dress she was wearing tonight and leaped to all sorts of wrong conclusions. They probably thought she intended to take Jason for everything she could get. Unfortunately there was no way she could correct their impressions without embarrassing Jason and making matters worse.

It was one of those rare times when retreat seemed the most prudent course.

She stood up. ''If you'll excuse me, I really should be going up. I have work to do and I'm sure you all would like to spend some time together without an outsider around. Sammy, I know you have homework."

Jason was on his feet at once. "Dana..."

"No, really. I have to get those sketches finished tonight. It was very nice meeting all of you."

She was halfway up the stairs before Sammy caught up with her, his expression puzzled. "Are you mad about somethin', sis?"

Dana sighed. "No. I'm not mad."

"Then why'd you run out like that?"

"We're not Hallorans, Sammy. We can't let ourselves forget that."

"But..."

She hugged him tight. "I don't think I mentioned it earlier, but you look very handsome."

His eyes lit up. "You really think so?"

"I really think so. Good night, Sammy. I'll see you in the morning. Don't stay up too late."

Unfortunately she wasn't able to take her own advice. She changed into an oversized T-shirt, climbed into bed, than stared at the ceiling for what seemed like hours. When sleep continued to elude her, she got up and, dragging a blanket with her, curled up in a chair by the window.

She was still sitting there, staring out at the inky darkness when she heard the faint tap on her door, then saw it inch open. Jason didn't wait for a response before sliding inside. Dana's breath lodged in her throat.

It was an instant before his eyes adjusted to the darkness, before he spotted her in the chair. When he did, he crossed the room in three angry strides, then hauled her up against him and slanted a bruising kiss across her mouth. Dana was so stunned by the onslaught of sensations, by the rough demand, that it was an instant before she fought to free herself.

Breathing hard, she stepped away from him and demanded, ''What the hell was that all about?''

''Just a reminder,'' he said in a low, warning tone.

''Of what?''

''A reminder that you're not some stray border in this house. You're here because I love you and want to marry you. That gives you every right to be here.''

Her heart hammering, she held up a hand. ''Jason, please. You have to slow down. Where did all this talk of marriage come from?''

He looked every bit as startled as she felt. ''Okay, it didn't come out quite the way it should have, but I meant every word. I want to marry you. I won't have you acting like some second-class citizen around here.''

Since the thought of marriage was too troubling to deal with, she murmured, ''I'm sorry if I was rude.''

He plunged his fingers through his hair. ''Dammit, Dana, this is not about being rude. It's about understanding that you belong. No matter what anyone thinks, what anyone says, you belong.''

She sighed and rested a hand against his cheek. ''I wish that were true, Jason. I really wish it were true.'' And for the first time since she'd met him, she admitted to herself that she'd done the unforgivable: she had fallen head over heels in love.

Chapter Thirteen

Dana had taken a real liking to Brandon Halloran. She would have been grateful to him for no other reason than the way he treated Sammy, but there was more to it. He was a lot like Jason. Impetuous on the surface, but rock solid underneath. There was something comforting in thinking that Jason would be just like him in another forty or so years.

She thought of his lively humor, his loving meddling, his sage advice, and she wished she had a grandfather like that. Since she didn't, she wished she could adopt the man sitting across from her, who was regarding her so pensively.

She'd been surprised when he'd invited her to lunch. No, invited was the wrong word. He'd insisted on it, latching on to her coat and her elbow with a determination that had left her with little choice. She couldn't say she was sorry to be with him, though, even if he had brought her back to Washington's Tavern where her relationship with the Hallorans had begun so inauspiciously.

"Okay," Brandon said finally, pinning her with one of his no-nonsense gazes. "Let's talk turkey, young lady. What was that little speech all about last night?"

Dana's spoon fell from her fingers, splattering clam chowder in every direction. Cleaning up the mess gave her time to think. Even with the extra time, the best she could manage was, "What speech?"

"Don't play dumb with me. Your exit lines. All that garbage about leaving us Hallorans alone."

"It was obvious to me that there were things you wanted to talk about, personal things. There was no room for strangers." The same argument hadn't worked on Jason, but perhaps Brandon would be more gullible.

He gave a rough hoot. "Young lady, who are you trying to kid? You're hardly a stranger. Looks to me as if my grandson is intent on marrying you. And if I know Jason, he'll have his way."

"That's wishful thinking on your part," she countered.

He regarded her intently. "You trying to tell me you're not interested?"

Dana tried. She gathered up all the appropriate denials and tried to force them past her lips, but the lies wouldn't come. "I wish I weren't," she said finally.

"Why?"

Dana ignored the question in favor of asking, "Did he put you up to this?"

"Up to what?" he inquired innocently. "So far all I've asked is a simple question. Are you in love with the man or not? I'll admit I'm biased, but he seems like a fine catch to me. No real faults, unless you count that stubbornness he gets from me. Actually, I see that as a beneficial quality.''

''He is a fine catch, as you put it. My reasons are between Jason and me.''

''Not entirely,'' he said. ''In this family we all care what happens to one another. Haven't you noticed how much meddling has gone on trying to figure out this mess between Lacey and Kevin? We still don't have a clue. It's a damned shame, too. There was a time they were so much in love, they lit up a room just by coming into it. I was blind to it then, but I'm not blind to what's going on between you and Jason. You have the same effect on each other.''

Dana settled for agreeing with his observation about Kevin and Lacey Halloran. Even if Jason hadn't told her how worried he was about his parents, she would have sensed the undercurrents last night. Even so, it was none of her business. Or theirs. She reminded Brandon of that.

''I've also noticed that they're telling everyone to butt out,'' she said.

''True, but that doesn't mean we won't go on trying. Now let's get back to you and Jason, a subject you seem determined to avoid, I might add. Only explanation I can think of is that I'm hitting too close to the truth. You are in love with the boy, but something's holding you back from saying it.''

Dana really wished he'd drop the subject, but she couldn't see any way of avoiding the discussion short of getting up and walking out of the restaurant. So, even though the conversation was likely to make her miserable, she would sit here and listen while he extolled his grandson's virtues. She doubted he even knew half of them. She knew them all. One of the most important was his family loyalty. She also understood Brandon's need to protect his own. They were two of a kind on that count.

"Well, girl, what do you have to say for yourself?" he was demanding again. "What's wrong with marrying into this family?"

"It seems to me you're the one with all the answers," she retorted. "You tell me."

"My guess is you're scared."

She nodded reluctantly. "On the mark so far."

"Of what, for goodness' sake?"

"You've seen how Jason is. He gets all caught up in being protective."

"What's so terrible about having a man cherish you like that?"

"What if I forget how to take care of myself?"

There was a twinkle in his eyes. "You aiming to give up your career and stay home and eat bonbons?"

"Of course not."

"You planning to cut out that razor-sharp tongue of yours? I've heard you've given my grandson what for more than once."

"I usually say what's on my mind. I guess that wouldn't change," she conceded grudgingly.

"Then it must be that you think you're not good enough to be part of this highfalutin Boston clan. Let me straighten you out on that right now. We've always been a family of scramblers. Ain't nothing ever been handed to us. I think you'd fit right in."

He regarded her slyly. "Besides, if you love my grandson, that's all it takes. I learned my lesson long ago, when it comes to making hasty judgments and interfering in other people's lives. I walked away from love once in my own life. I know how that can change a person forever. I don't want to see you and my grandson waking up one day with regrets the way I do.''

Dana's eyebrows rose a fraction.

''Don't you smart mouth me,'' he said.

''I never said a word.''

He nodded, his expression turning complacent. ''Okay, then. Here's the deal. You think you need to make a contribution, something beyond the fact that you're making Jason happy, something more important than giving our old company a spruced-up image. Am I right?''

Though she wanted to argue just on principle, Dana had no ready comeback for the truth. She folded her hands and waited. Whatever this sneaky old man had in mind was bound to be a doozy.

He grinned at her stubborn silence. ''I'll take that for a yes. So, that being the case, I'm going to let you buy into Halloran Industries. You'll be a partner right along with the rest of us.''

Dana couldn't help it. She laughed. ''With what, pray tell?''

''With the money you're going to make designing a whole new line of sweaters.''

She stared at him incredulously. ''Sweaters?''

''That's right. You've got an eye for what young people like and a flair for the dramatic. Take the one you have on now. Cheers the whole place up. I've snapped a few photos over the past few weeks. Showed them to a friend of mine. He'll make you an offer to carry the line, if you're interested. You can do whatever you want with the money, but if it'll make you feel more like a part of the family to invest in Halloran Industries, we'll work it out.''

His gaze pinned her. ''Or you can make Jason the happiest man in the world and accomplish exactly the same thing by marrying him.''

''You can't bribe me into becoming a Halloran.''

Brandon regarded her indignantly. ''Who's bribing you? It's a fair deal. If you think about it, you'll realize that. This is one time you shouldn't let bullheadedness get in the way of what's best for your future. Those sweaters would give you and that brother of yours a mighty fine stake.''

It was only later, when she'd mentally stripped the scene of her emotional reaction, that she realized how much faith Brandon Halloran had in her—and in Jason's love for her. Granted, Brandon was somewhat biased, but it was probably the most objective opinion she was likely to get from someone who knew all the parties involved.

Yet it still wasn't enough.

''So how was lunch with my grandfather?'' Jason wanted to know the minute Dana got back to his office. ''Why did he want to see you?''

She regarded him closely. ''You don't know?''

''Know what?''

''He made me an offer. He wants Halloran Industries to produce a line of sweaters that I will design. He figures if he gives me a stake in the company, I'll feel like I belong. I think he was proposing on your behalf.''

After an initial spark of excitement, Jason's expression faltered. ''You turned him down, didn't you?''

''No,'' she said, still feeling pressured. ''I told him

I'd think about it. I'm not blind to the opportunity he's offering me. I'm just worried about the strings."

"There are none, Dana. My grandfather doesn't operate that way and neither do I. He obviously sees this line as an excellent way of expanding our presence in the marketplace. He's been itching to tackle something new for a long time now. I've had a hunch from the day he saw that first sweater of yours that he was plotting something like this."

Dana began to pace. "It's ridiculous. I don't know a thing about designing sweaters."

"Oh, really?"

She noticed him glance over at the one she was wearing, the one his grandfather told her cheered up a room. It was bright red with yellow accents and one bold streak of blue. She had to admit her spirits had risen when she'd been making it. She'd used the yellow yarn simply because it had been left over from another project. The instant she'd begun knitting it in, though, she'd known it was right.

"Who came up with that one?" Jason asked.

"I did."

"And the other half dozen or so I've seen you wear?"

"I did."

"Ever get any compliments on them?"

"Yes," she said slowly. "Quite a few people have asked where I bought them."

Jason nodded. "What did my grandfather suggest? A limited line, sold in exclusive boutiques?"

"Actually I didn't let him get that far. He did say he knew someone who was interested in the line."

Jason picked up his phone and rang his grandfather's office. Dana was so busy trying to imagine seeing her sweater designs in some fancy boutique, she barely heard his end of the conversation. What would it be like to have unlimited resources at her command? To be able to select a color and create a dye that matched exactly what she saw in her mind's eye? To choose yarns that felt soft, rather than those on sale? She was surprised to discover that the idea tempted.

Jason whistled softly at something his grandfather said. "I see," he said. "Yeah, I will definitely tell her that."

She glanced at him as he hung up.

"Granddad told me who he showed your sweaters to."

"And?"

Jason named a designer whose clothes were sold in the most exclusive shops in the world. Dana's mouth dropped open. "You're kidding, right?"

"I'm not kidding. He'll take any one-of-a-kind design you make by hand as exclusives for his private customers. He thinks the ski crowd will flip over them. Then he'd like at least four other designs in limited production for his ready-to-wear line that's going into department stores for the first time next year."

Dana couldn't even grasp the fact that this man wanted to sell a few of her sweaters, much less the fact that Brandon Halloran was willing to commit his company to producing four designs in quantity. She shot Jason a puzzled look.

"Won't it be incredibly expensive just to set up the equipment to make these sweaters? It's not the same as making a bolt of cloth, is it?"

Jason grinned. "As Granddad sees it, that's just part of the fun. We'll be doing something new and exciting."

"You'd probably prefer that he stick to weaving woolens."

Jason sighed. "A month ago, maybe even a few days ago, I would have said yes. I'm starting to look at things differently now. Sure, Halloran Industries is a business and we want it to be profitable, but if you're going to spend your life doing something, you'd really better like it as well. It won't kill us if we make a little less. And at the kind of prices Granddad intends to charge, we definitely won't go broke."

"What kind of money are we talking about?"

"I'd say your share ought to enable you to do just about anything you'd like to do," he said, naming a figure that would have seemed beyond the realm of possibility just a few short months ago.

Dazed, Dana nodded. "I've got to go," she said. "I'll see you at home later."

Jason's expression grew puzzled. "Are you okay?"

"For a woman who feels as if she's been hit over the head with a baseball bat, I'm doing just fine."

She walked for hours, oblivious to the cold, oblivious to the snow that swirled in the air. What Brandon Halloran was offering to her was total financial independence for the first time in her life. She would truly be free to make choices, to give Sammy the kind of life she'd wanted for herself growing up, including a college education. They'd be able to live almost anyplace they wanted. Maybe not in a house as fine as Jason's, but certainly in one that was comfortable, that had its own fireplace and maybe even a bay window.

So, why wasn't she shouting for joy? Why wasn't she racing to look through the classified ads for apartments? Why wasn't she picking up a sketch pad to draw sweater designs, rather than brochure layouts?

Was it because the thought of walking away from Jason left this lonely emptiness deep inside her?

When she finally went home, still with no answers, she slowly climbed the steps to her room. Inside, she pulled out all of the sweaters she'd made over the years and spread them on the bed. She studied each one, recalling the exact moment when she'd come up with the idea, the hunt for the right yarn in some discount store, the frustration when she couldn't find the exact shade she'd had in mind. She rubbed her fingers over uneven stitches and careless seams in her first faltering attempts.

Somewhere along the way these bold sweaters had become a part of her, an expression of all of her bright dreams for the future. How could she bear to give away—even for a bundle of money—something that was her? Wouldn't she lose herself in the process?

There was no question, though, that an opportunity like this knocked once in a lifetime. Only a fool would turn it down. It would give her options she'd never even imagined. She could leave the Lansing Agency. Or stay. She could leave this house.

Or, she realized with a start, she could stay. If she stayed, she could pay her own way and Sammy's. She would have the financial independence she'd always craved, even here in Jason's home. As for emotional independence, that didn't look nearly as attractive to her as it once had.

The freedom to choose. Wasn't that all she had ever really wanted? And given the choice, wasn't Jason the only man she could imagine loving? It kept coming back to Jason and the depth of the feelings that had flourished despite her best attempts to fight them.

For a woman who had left the house this morning

convinced that there was no way for her to have a future with a man like Jason, a few hours had made an undeniable difference. She had hope now. She could finally see that letting Jason into her heart was not the same as losing a part of herself. For the first time in her life, she could see that love gave people strength. It didn't rob them of it.

Chapter Fourteen

When his mother called and asked him to lunch, Jason didn't know what to think. She wasn't in the habit of meeting him in the city. On top of that, it had been less than forty-eight hours since he'd last seen her. Although he was having a horrible day, with no promise of improvement even if he were to put in sixteen hours straight, something in her tone told him to make the time for her.

"Could we do it here? I'll have something sent in," he suggested, reluctant to alter his new routine now that he was finally energized about work.

"I'd rather not," she said. "This won't take long, but it is important, and I'd prefer a little privacy. What about that little French restaurant up the street. We won't be interrupted there, will we?"

Jason sensed she was asking about more than the size of the restaurant's crowd at noon. Was she truly trying to avoid his father? "No one from here goes there, if that's what you're asking."

"I'll see you there, then."

Now that Jason was sitting across from her, he felt an ominous sense of foreboding. Lacey Halloran looked uncomfortable. No, Jason thought, studying her more closely. She looked miserable. Though she was dressed cheerfully enough in a becoming rose-colored wool dress with her mane of caramel-colored hair falling in loose waves to her shoulders, there was an air of despair that was unmistakable. There was no hint of the usual sparkle in her blue eyes. He had a hunch that skillful makeup hid dark shadows under those eyes as well.

"Mom," he began quietly, "what's bothering you? You aren't worried about Dana and me, are you?"

She glanced up from the consommé she'd been idly stirring for the past five minutes. For the first time since he'd arrived there was a spark of animation in her eyes. "No, absolutely not. I like her. She has a lot of spirit. I used to be like that once."

She sounded so melancholy and sad, as if she'd lost something precious and didn't know how to get it back. Jason felt his stomach knot. He laid a hand on hers. Hers was like ice. "Are you okay?"

She closed her eyes for an instant, and Jason's worry mounted. When she opened her eyes, that unmistakable sadness was there again.

"I really don't know how to get into this with you," she said finally. "I told your father I wanted to be the one to tell you, but now that the time has come, I can't seem to find the words."

Jason's heart thudded. "What is it? Are you ill?"

She shook her head, reaching over to squeeze his hand. "No, it's nothing like that."

"Is it Dad, then? He's okay, isn't he?"

She drew in a deep breath. "I've moved out," she blurted finally. "Yesterday."

Jason felt as if she'd slammed a fist into his midsection. If she'd declared that she'd burned the place down, he would have been no more shocked. Even after that awful dinner with his father a few weeks earlier and the tension in his own dining room just two days earlier, he wasn't prepared for this announcement.

"What?" he said blankly, praying he'd misunderstood. "I don't understand."

"I've moved out of the house. I just wanted you to know so you wouldn't go over there looking for me. Not that you drop in unannounced," she murmured. "Oh, who am I kidding? I was terrified you'd see it in some gossip column. I'm sure there are a few people who won't be able to wait to share the news of a split in the Halloran clan."

The prospect of publicity was the least of Jason's concerns. "Why did you move?" he asked weakly, thinking of all the signs he'd seen that things weren't right between his parents. He'd blinded himself to them because he didn't want to believe there was anything seriously wrong. "What did Dad do?"

He tried to imagine his father having an affair and couldn't. Kevin Halloran was not a philanderer. Jason would have staked his last dime on that. Kevin did spend too many hours at the office. Maybe that was it. His father had turned into a workaholic and his mother was lonely.

Funny how he'd always thought his parents' marriage so solid, so free from the kinds of problems and pressures that split other families apart. He could see now that they were only human and it shook him more than he could say.

"Your father didn't do anything, not really. It's complicated," she said.

"That's not good enough, Mom," he snapped in frustration. At her startled, hurt look, he said, "I'm sorry, but there has to be a reason."

"I would explain it to you if I could, but I can't. Not entirely." She gazed at him apologetically. "I'm sorry to spring this on you now, when you've just met someone you really care about. This should be the happiest time in your life. I'm sorry for spoiling it. I would have waited until, I don't know, after you were engaged, maybe even married, but there's no telling just when that would happen. I decided postponing the move wouldn't change anything. The longer it went on, the more I felt as if I were suffocating."

"I'll talk to Dad," he said, ignoring the denial she'd made too easily. "Whatever he's done, he can fix it."

Lacey smiled sadly. "No. I've told you this is not his fault. Not entirely, anyway. At any rate, it's between your father and me. Promise me you'll let it be. This is the right thing for both of us."

"How can moving out be the right thing?" Jason exploded in frustration. "Isn't that just running away? Or are you filing for divorce? Have things gone that far?"

"Not yet."

It suddenly occurred to him that perhaps he'd been trying to cast blame in the wrong direction. What if his mother…? Dear Lord, it wasn't possible that she had found someone to fill the lonely hours when her husband was at work. ''Mom, is it...you haven't... there's not...''

No matter how he tried to phrase it, he couldn't get the words out. It was clear, though, that his mother understood. Suddenly she was reaching into her purse. ''I really have to go.''

Jason spotted the tears welling up in her eyes and felt more helpless than he'd ever felt in his entire life. ''Mom?''

She brushed a kiss against his cheek, then hurried from the restaurant. She hadn't even told him how he could get in touch with her.

He spent the afternoon closeted in his office with the door shut, trying to make sense of what had happened. It took everything in him to keep from going down the hall and slugging his father. Unfortunately he couldn't seem to make up his mind whether or not he deserved it. His mother had never once said that his father was to blame for anything. But no matter how hard he tried, he couldn't imagine his mother walking away from the family that had always meant everything to her, unless his father had committed some terrible sin.

He barely looked up at the tap on the door. He didn't bother responding. Harriet would send whoever it was away. He'd told her he didn't want to be disturbed.

The door opened a crack. ''Jason?'' Dana said softly, then added more anxiously, ''What are you doing sitting in here in the dark?''

He glanced around and realized the room was filled with shadows. He hadn't even noticed. ''What time is it?'' he asked wearily.

''Past six. Are you okay?''

"No," he said. "I am definitely not okay."

"What's wrong?"

"I had lunch with my mother today. She's moved out of the house." He looked at Dana and astonishment filled his voice. "She's actually left my father."

The startled expression on Dana's face reflected his own feelings exactly.

"I don't understand," she said.

"Neither do I. She didn't see fit to explain it." He shook his head. "No. That's not fair. I think she was too upset to talk about it."

"What does your father say?"

"I haven't talked to him. I was afraid I'd hit first and talk later."

"Maybe it's not his fault."

"It has to be somebody's fault," he said, itching to cast blame and unwilling still to pin it on his gentle, sensitive mother. The fact that she hadn't denied the suggestion that she was having an affair nagged at him like a hangnail. He toyed with the idea until the pain was nearly unbearable.

"Maybe it really is no one's fault," Dana said, coming up behind his chair and beginning to massage away the tension in his shoulders.

The brush of her fingers against his neck had his pulse bucking. Though he was certain she meant to relax him with the kneading strokes, the effect was anything but soothing. Every nerve in his body craved the magic of her touch.

When he could stand the tantalizing, innocent caresses no longer, he swiveled his chair around and pulled her down onto his lap. Before it even registered what he intended, his mouth was covering hers with a desperation that might have frightened him if he'd recognized it. Instead he was just acting on his feelings, hungry for the taste of her.

The kiss was bruising, needy and it wasn't nearly enough. He shoved her sweater up until he unhooked her bra. Her breasts spilled into his hands. He took the rosy tip of one into his mouth, urging it into a hard bud, then did the same with the other. The silk of her skin burned hot beneath his touch.

As if she sensed his need, Dana unbuttoned his shirt with matching urgency, her hands stroking and teasing with renewed purpose, this time to inflame. Her mouth found his masculine nipples and teased with the same desperate intensity. Jason had never before been aroused so fast. He felt as if he were going to explode if he couldn't bury himself inside her.

He gathered her into his arms and carried her to the sofa. With hands that shook with emotion, he stripped away her jeans, then his own slacks, until he was able to enter her with a quick, powerful thrust.

With each desperate stroke some of his anger and confusion began to fade. With each caress he thought less and less about his parents' failure and more about his own future, here in Dana's arms. How could emotions this powerful ever die? Surely this kind of intensity couldn't be lost.

With one last shred of sanity, he slowed, only to have Dana quicken the pace again, luring him over the edge with an instinctive understanding of his need.

When they were both spent, tangled in rumpled clothes and slick with perspiration, he cradled her in his arms. The peace he'd craved hadn't come. If anything, he felt worse than before because he'd used a woman he loved without regard for her feelings.

"I'm sorry," he whispered, distraught by the uncaring way he'd treated her. He tried to find the words to explain, settling finally for the simple, raw truth. "I needed you so much."

"I know," she said gently.

"That's no excuse for being so thoughtless, so rough."

"You weren't rough. Just demanding." She gave a little half smile, the kind which Mona Lisa had been enchanting people with for years. "You always are, you know. I think that's what I love about you. You don't hold anything back. I always know how much you want me."

"I gotta tell you, Dana, right now that scares the hell out of me."

"Because of what's going on with your parents."

"Exactly. If they can't make it after all these years, after so damned much history, nobody can. Nobody."

There was a bleak finality in his tone, a weariness. If his well-suited parents couldn't hold on to their marriage, how could he possibly expect to have a future with someone so much his opposite? Perhaps in the end his first instincts had been right. The only future he and Dana were likely to have would be whatever days they could grab before their differences inevitably caught up with them.

After that evening in his office, Jason never even hinted about wanting to marry Dana. She had no doubts about his love for her, no doubts that he still wanted her. Each night in his bed proved the depth of his hunger for what they had found together. But it was as if a switch had been turned and he no longer saw marriage as an option.

She had absolutely no idea what to do about it. Her

sense of helplessness was all the worse because she had finally admitted to herself that she loved him, that she wanted a life with him. At least she was ready to take the risk, because for the first time she had realized that Jason needed her every bit as much as she needed him.

That's what love was all about, she had realized with astonishing clarity that evening in his office when he'd come to her with all of his insecurities and desperate yearnings on the line. That moment had solidified all the emotions she had recognized over the past days. There would always be times when one person needed and the other person gave, and times when they would reverse roles. Right now it was critical for her to find some way to make Jason see that what was happening to his parents was not an indictment of marriage, but proof that love wasn't something ever to be taken for granted.

Troubled, she found herself turning to Brandon Halloran for advice. "I think he's going to walk away from what we have," she told him, her expression bleak.

"Because of this nonsense between Kevin and Lacey?"

"It's shaken his faith in love."

"But not in you," Brandon reminded her. "You're still sharing that house with him. You ready to make it permanent?"

Dana smiled ruefully. "Yes. My timing's lousy, isn't it?"

"I don't think it could get much better actually. He needs you now. The fact that you haven't abandoned him ought to tell him what he needs to hear."

"He's not listening. I don't think he's comfortable

with needing anything from me. He's used to being the one needed."

"Seems to me the real test of love is surviving the crises."

"And this is one of those crises, right?"

"Looks like it to me."

Dana gave him a swift hug on her way out. "I'll let you know how it turns out."

"Just tell me when to show up at the church. What this family needs all the way around is a good wedding."

"You're an old romantic."

"Damn right, I am. I want some great-grandchildren before I'm too old to enjoy 'em, too."

Dana groaned. "Let's take this one step at a time, okay?"

She could think of only one sure way to snap Jason out of his mood, a way that would only work if he loved her as much as she thought he did. That night she sent Sammy to a movie with Mrs. Willis, set the table with the finest china and candles, and wore the slinky black dress Jason had given her.

He glanced around, took in the seductive setting and regarded her warily. "What's this all about?"

"I need to talk to you about something."

"If you're serving prime rib, I'm really going to start worrying."

Dana carried two plates of medium-rare prime rib in from the kitchen.

"Okay. Spill it," he said. "What's going on?"

"Actually, I've been thinking about getting my own place."

Jason's fork clattered to the table. "You've what?" His voice rose ominously.

"It's clear I'm just in the way here. You can't be expected to put up with Sammy and me indefinitely. I've picked out a couple of apartments. I was hoping you'd agree to go with me tomorrow to take a look at them. I could use your advice."

"No. Absolutely not."

"Why not? Don't you have the time?"

"This has nothing to do with time." His gaze narrowed. "I thought you were happy here. I thought we had something."

Dana shrugged. "I thought so, too, but lately..." She allowed her voice to trail off.

"Lately I haven't been paying enough attention to you."

"That's not it."

"What then?"

She studied him regretfully. "If you can't figure it out, then I'm not going to explain it. Look, if you don't want to go with me to look at apartments, it's okay. Sammy and I will go in the morning. We should be able to move in a week or two."

Jason threw his napkin on the table and stormed from the room. A minute later the front door slammed. Fortunately he left before he caught the smile of satisfaction on Dana's lips.

She cleaned up the dishes, then went into the living room. She sat in the window seat, her legs tucked under her and watched for Jason to come home. It was nearly an hour later before she saw him coming up the front walk. When he caught sight of her in the window, he paused and squared his shoulders. His step became even more determined.

The front door shook on its hinges, when he closed it behind him. He strode into the living room and straight over to her. Hands on hips, he faced her with a familiar stubborn spark in his eyes.

"You are not moving out of here tomorrow or any other time and that's final."

"Excuse me?"

"You may think you'll be better off someplace else, but I'm not letting you out of my sight. I love you. If you're not ready to marry me, that's fine. I'll wait. But I will not let you run off."

He was still ranting when Dana rose from the window seat and shut him up by covering his mouth with her own. After one startled instant, his arms circled her waist. He leaned back with an unexpected glint of amused understanding in his eyes.

"Who won that battle?" he inquired.

"We did," she said. "I finally got you to admit that you still loved me."

"There's never been any doubt in my mind about that."

Dana shook her head. "Oh, I think you've been questioning a lot lately. I just wanted you to see that the most important thing in loving someone is not ever taking them for granted."

Jason chuckled. "How could I ever take a woman like you for granted? There's not a day that goes by when I don't realize how lucky I am to have found you."

"It's possible then that given time your parents will remember they once felt that way, too. We'll just have to help them."

"So, now that you've brought me into line, you're ready to take on my parents. I suspect Granddad will want to have a hand in that, too."

''Last time I saw him he was more worried about having great-grandchildren.''

A slow smile spread across Jason's face. ''I think we can accommodate him on that score, don't you?''

Dana took his hand and led him toward the stairs. ''Frankly, I thought you'd never ask.''

* * * * *

HONOR

Prologue

Even at forty-eight Lacey Grainger Halloran was still one hell of a woman, her husband thought with pride and a sense of wonder as he watched her begin the long walk down the carpeted aisle of Whitehall Episcopal Church. She had never looked more stunning or more confident.

More than twenty-five years of marriage, Kevin Halloran thought. So many troubled times, shared and apart. Yet it felt as if they were starting out fresh, as if this were the very first ceremony in which they would make a commitment for life.

Last time, like so many of their friends in the mid-sixties, Kevin and Lacey had skipped the traditional prayer book, church wedding in favor of a hastily arranged outdoor ceremony atop a country hill alight with the colors of spring. Kevin's family, firmly entrenched in tradition, had been appalled. Throughout the brief service, with its unorthodox but heartfelt vows, their faces had radiated disapproval. But at least they had come.

Though Lacey had sworn it didn't matter, Kevin had known that deep down she had feared his family would stay away, publicly writing off the match as a bad one. It had nearly broken his heart to see the relief and hope in her eyes when she'd seen his parents join the small gathering on that sunny hillside.

Today's ceremony, a renewal of their vows, was every bit as significant as that first wedding day. His father and his son stood next to him, each nervously awaiting their own brides.

Kevin had been astonished to discover that long ago his father had been deeply in love with a woman whose name Kevin had never even heard mentioned. Now, just a few years after his own mother's death, that woman—Elizabeth Forsythe Newton—had reappeared in his father's life. Today they would be wed as his father had longed for them to be all those years ago.

With a sense of amazement, Kevin watched the transformation of his father's stern face as his bride began the walk down the aisle. After two long years of sorrow and loneliness, Brandon Halloran looked downright invigorated by life. His damn-the-world, full-steam-ahead energy was back, and everyone was having difficulty keeping up with him.

Something warm stole through Kevin as he realized that it was possible for love to endure through so many years of separation.

Filled anew with a surprising sense of hope, Kevin glanced at his son and caught the expression of open adoration in Jason's eyes as he waited for his wife to join him to renew their own vows. Within weeks Jason and Dana would be blessed with a child of their own—a boy if Kevin knew anything at all about the Halloran genes. The cycle would begin again.

All in all, it was quite a day for the Hallorans, Kevin thought as he took his wife's slender hand in his. Lacey was trembling, he realized with a faint sense of amazement. He gazed into her eyes, blue and bright with unshed tears, and realized anew how very deeply he cared for her and how devastated and lost he would have been had they not found their way back to each other.

Squeezing Lacey's hand for reassurance, Kevin began to speak. With his voice choked with emotion, he tried to find the words to tell her exactly what she meant to him, to express the strength he found in their marriage, had always found in her love. They were words he hadn't said nearly enough through the years, words he had almost lost the chance to say at all.

"Lacey, from the day I first saw you back in the fifth grade, there has been no one like you in my life. You have been my friend, my confidante, my lover and my wife. I am a better man for knowing you and loving you. I beg your forgiveness for the times I have forgotten that, for the times when I have lost sight of all that truly matters."

The memory of how hard his gentle Lacey had fought to save their relationship brought a smile to his lips. "I can't begin to find the words to tell you how much I admire the courage it took to shake up our marriage in the hope that we would find something even better. From now on I promise you days that will only get better with each passing year."

As a tear spilled down her cheek, he gently brushed

it away, his own fingers trembling. Then he said in a voice that finally held steady, ''I, Kevin, take thee, Lacey, a woman who has stood by me through hard times and good, who has provided love and understanding, I take thee again to be my wedded wife. For the blessing of your undying love, I thank God. For the joy of our family, I thank you. And I promise to honor you and all that you have meant to me all the rest of my days.''

As the solemn vows echoed in the old Boston church, his thoughts drifted back over those dark and lonely days when his own stupidity had almost cost him the most important thing in his life.

Chapter One

"Dad, you're killing yourself."

Kevin Halloran tore his gaze away from the bleak Halloran Industries financial report he'd been working on for the past twelve hours and met his son's troubled eyes. "Jason, I am not having this discussion. Go home. It's after eight. Dana will be wondering where you are."

To Kevin's deep regret, his son defiantly removed his jacket and loosened his tie with the obvious intention of settling in for a lengthy chat. Kevin had a hunch they were headed over the same familiar turf. The sorry state of his marriage had been the primary topic of conversation for two weeks now. His son and his father couldn't seem to stop their meddling no matter how rudely he tried to cut them off.

Kevin reached for a cigarette, then caught Jason's disapproving frown as his son eyed the mound of butts already overflowing the ashtray. Kevin drew his hand back and settled for another sip of cold, bitter coffee. The acid pitched in his stomach.

"Dana knows exactly where I am," Jason said, complacently ignoring his father's dismissal. "She sent me. We're both worried about you, Dad. You look like hell. You're smoking too much. You're living on caffeine. I doubt you're getting enough sleep. Face it, you haven't been yourself since Mother moved out of the house."

The cold knot that formed in Kevin's stomach every time he thought about home and Lacey came back with a savagery that stunned him.

"I don't want to talk about your mother," he countered bluntly and reached for the cigarette, after all. When it was lit and he'd drawn the smoke deep into his lungs, he deliberately forced his attention back to the stack of work on his desk.

If he buried himself in reports and figures, maybe, just maybe, Jason would give up and go away. More importantly, maybe he could forget the emptiness Lacey's leaving had created inside him, the echoing silence that greeted him each night when he returned home.

In theory it should have worked, but Kevin had discovered that theories and paperwork didn't mean a damn thing in the middle of another god-awful, lonely, silent night. That didn't mean he was willing to talk, not to Jason. Lacey had been the only person in his life to whom he could open up. She had had the most amazing knack for listening without making judgments.

Jason obviously thought that his cool, analytical approach would help, but in Kevin's experience, talking about emotions never accomplished a thing. To his way of thinking, airing problems only exposed a man's weaknesses right at a time when he needed every shred of pride he had left.

Besides that, dissecting things a man couldn't change only made the hurt worse, Kevin thought, still careful to avoid Jason's increasingly impatient gaze. There were even times, in the dark, lonely hours of the night, when the pain became a blind rage, when he wanted to strike out, to break things. The only thing stopping him was the certain knowledge that he had only himself to blame for the way things were between him and Lacey. She'd made that clear enough before she'd gone.

"*I* want to talk," Jason said, still on the same relentless track despite his father's obvious unwillingness to open up.

His tone was deceptively mild. Kevin recognized the stubborn streak his son had inherited from a long line of mule-headed Halloran men. Even as Kevin glanced up, Jason was settling more comfortably into the chair opposite him, his jaw squared, his expression determined. He took Kevin's just-lit cigarette and deliberately ground it out, his hard look daring his father to challenge the action.

"Not once in all these months have you explained why Mother moved out," his son said.

"That's between your mother and me," Kevin responded stiffly, unwilling—unable—to say more. Then, because he needed desperately to know despite everything, he asked, "What has she told you?"

"About as much as you have," Jason admitted with obvious disgust at the continued parental secrecy.

"Did you two make some sort of pact of silence, the way you always did when I was a kid?"

"We never did any such thing."

"Perhaps it wasn't a formal contract, drawn up by the Halloran legal staff, but it was a pact nonetheless. You never wanted me to guess that the two of you were quarreling. Instead, the house got quiet as a tomb for weeks on end." He shook his head. "It was awful."

Unable to bear his son's distraught expression, Kevin stood up, walked to the window and stared out at the Boston skyline in the distance. Lights were just now blinking on. Was one of them Lacey's? he wondered. What was she doing in that ridiculously cramped apartment of hers? How could she hope to find happiness there, when he'd given her everything a woman could possibly want and it hadn't been enough?

He sighed and turned back, just in time to hear Jason say, "When Dana's mad at me, she puts all her cards on the table, usually at the top of her lungs. There's not a chance in hell I won't know exactly what's on her mind. With the two of you, though, I don't know." He shrugged helplessly. "I think I'd have liked it better if you'd broken the china."

"And risked your grandfather's wrath?" Kevin retorted with a faint smile. "That china came over from England more than a century ago."

Jason didn't smile back at the weak attempt at humor. "I'm not interested in the china. I'm interested in what the hell happened to my parents' marriage."

Kevin sighed, a bone-deep weariness stealing through him. "Son, if I knew that, maybe I could make it right."

When Jason started to probe more deeply, Kevin shook his head. "I will not talk about this," he warned with quiet finality. "Go home to your wife. She's expecting your baby. She needs you there."

"The baby's not due for another three months. I hardly think Dana's desperate for me to get home and watch her as if she might break. Besides, every time she gets the least little bit queasy, so do I. We're running out of crackers."

"Then buy some and go home," Kevin said flatly.

This time it was Jason who sighed. "Okay, but if you need to talk, Dad..."

Kevin might not be able to explain what had happened, or his own feelings, but he couldn't ignore the pain and confusion in Jason's tone. He relented as much as he could. "I'll come looking for you, son. I promise."

Finally, after several endless minutes, Jason nodded, his expression resigned. He stood in the doorway and said, "If you want her back, Dad, you're going to have to fight for her."

"I know that." What he didn't say was that he wasn't at all sure he had the energy left for the battle.

Jason left finally, shutting the office door very quietly behind him.

That careful exit, more than anything, told Kevin just how upset his son was. Jason slammed doors. From the time he'd been able to walk, he'd raced through life, hitting doors at full tilt, letting them crash behind him. The quiet closing of Kevin's door with its implied hint of defeat was just one more sign that both of their worlds had suddenly gone topsy-turvy.

When Jason had gone, Kevin leaned back in his chair and wondered why it had taken a crisis of this magnitude to begin to open the lines of communication with his son. If nothing else came from this damnable separation, at least perhaps he would have the new bond that had formed over the last few months between him and Jason.

After years of distance and a sense that they never connected, Kevin had been stunned to realize that his son truly did love him. It had been equally surprising to realize that Jason had matured so much. Kevin gave Dana a lot of credit for that. She had given Jason a sense of direction. Besides that, his daughter-in-law was every bit as determined as Lacey had once been to see that the Halloran family ties remained close-knit.

Jason, Dana, even Kevin's father used every opportunity to try to push him into reconciling with his wife. Right now, though, Kevin wasn't up to explaining that the choice wasn't his. He couldn't cope with explanations, period. The fact of the matter was that he couldn't cope with anything these days. There was an aching, leaden sensation in the middle of his chest that never seemed to go away.

If Jason didn't understand his separation from Lacey, it was a thousand times worse for him. How could a love that had begun in the fifth grade, a marriage that had lasted over twenty-five years, fall apart in a split second?

The day a year earlier when Lacey had moved out of their huge house and into a tiny apartment of her own, Kevin had been stunned. Sure, they'd had a few fights. She couldn't seem to understand the demands of running a business like Halloran Industries. In her own quiet way she had badgered him to let up, to spend more time with her, to think of his health.

The next thing he knew, Lacey was forcing his hand, trying to recapture a time long ago, a time when, as he saw it now, he'd avoided responsibility, rather than accepting it. Her harsh all-or-nothing ultimatum—Halloran Industries or a marriage—had taken him by surprise. His inability to make the decision she'd demanded had been answer enough, it seemed. In her view, with his silence, he had chosen the generations-old family textile business over her.

Lacey had made good on her threat, too. Kevin didn't have to understand her decision to know that it was final. Lacey appeared easygoing and flexible, but beneath that gentle facade was a stubborn streak a mile wide. He'd recognized it the first time he'd seen the defiant lift of her chin, despite the sheen of tears in her eleven-year-old eyes. That fierce determination, that willingness to spit in the eye of her own fears had made her a perfect match for a Halloran.

It was up to Lacey to explain her moving out to Jason, though. Kevin wasn't about to try. He would never be able to hide his anger or this raw, gut-wrenching feeling of utter helplessness that was totally alien to him. He might understand the most intricate details of business administration, but over the past year he'd come to realize he didn't know a damn thing about women, not even the one woman who'd captured his heart so very long ago.

And, to his profound regret given the circumstances, the woman who held it still.

"Mom, I just don't get it. What happened? Why did you move out? I thought you'd go back long ago. Haven't you made your point yet?"

How many times was Jason going to ask her that?

Lacey Halloran wondered. How many times would she have to give the same stupid, evasive answer because she couldn't bear to get into the truth?

"Jason, that is between your father and me," she said, her tone gentle as she busied herself repotting a bright red geranium to keep her son from seeing how her hands shook. It wouldn't do at all for him to see how much she feared the empty days ahead, an emptiness she had brought on herself.

Lacey couldn't blame Jason for being confused. She'd felt that way herself for months now, maybe even years. She'd felt her relationship with Kevin sliding not just into a rut, but into some deep, dark ravine. Finally she couldn't take it any longer, couldn't bury the memories of the dear, rebellious young man who'd set himself up as her protector when they'd been barely eleven.

In those days Kevin had been noble and brave and adventurous. They'd roared through the sixties with spirit and love and idealism. Even now she wasn't sure exactly when he'd started to change or when she'd first noticed the shift in priorities, the abandonment of values they'd once shared.

Maybe it was when he'd caved in to pressure from his father to join Halloran Industries. Brandon had used every trick in the book to lure his son into taking his rightful place in the family business. He'd finally played on Kevin's guilt, convincing him that he was doing a disservice to his wife and son by not giving them everything they deserved. None of Lacey's protests had been able to allay Kevin's fear that his father was right.

Maybe it was after that, when he'd ignored her open distaste and bought that huge, monstrous house that was more like a mausoleum than a home. Kevin had wanted a place suitable for entertaining business associates, a palace for her, he'd said. Brandon's realtor had taken them to showcases. Ironically, Kevin had chosen the one most similar to the lonely status symbol of a house in which he'd been raised himself.

There were other symptoms of the chasm widening between them. Determined to prove himself, to exceed Brandon's high expectations, he'd begun spending longer and longer hours at the office. Lacey had even suspected, but never proven, that he was having an affair.

There were desperate times when she even pinpointed something as silly and unimportant as the moment when he'd traded folk songs and rock for classical music as an indication of all that was going wrong with their marriage.

Somewhere along the way, though, the life she'd anticipated with Kevin had changed. She had never expected to be caught up in a whirlwind of social, business and charitable demands. She had never expected to see Kevin's decency and strength lost to ambition.

As CEO of Halloran Industries, Kevin had become a respected member of Boston's elite establishment. But ideals they had once cherished, dreams they had worked for together, had been lost. Worst of all, Kevin seemed blind to the significance of the changes and the destruction of all they once held dear.

In the heat of that last, bitter argument, he had accused her of not keeping pace, of being unwilling to change, unable to accept the reality of getting ahead in a world that respected nothing so much as success.

If that was a flaw, so be it, Lacey thought, angrily

snapping off a dead geranium leaf. What was so terrible about wanting to help others? Wanting to make a home for her family?

Wanting a husband to stop killing himself?

She sighed. Was there anything more important than love and family and commitment? It might be old-fashioned, but dammit she would fight to her dying breath to preserve those simple ideals, to get her husband to wake up before it was too late. She wanted that special, wonderful man she'd loved for so terribly long back again.

Even so, even though it had broken her heart to watch his rare, generous spirit wither and die, she might have forced herself to accept the changes if only Kevin had seemed happy. In lives otherwise rich with love, she might have accepted that no one ever stayed the same, if only his complexion hadn't taken on that deathly pallor.

Instead of being happy and energetic, he'd merely seemed driven. The effect on his health was devastating. He'd already suffered one heart attack, a mild one that the doctor described as a warning.

Rather than modifying his life-style, though, Kevin had become even more obsessed. They had argued again and again. Lacey had pleaded with him to stop killing himself, for him to at least try to make her see why he felt so driven. His response had been to avoid the arguments by spending even longer hours at the office. There had been one last explosive argument and then she had gone, unable to bear even one more day of watching him die before her eyes, one more lonely evening waiting for a call from some hospital emergency room.

Lacey couldn't say all that to Jason, though. He

hadn't even been married an entire year yet himself. How could a mother explain the tarnish that eventually robbed love of its shine to a man for whom it still held a shimmering beauty? Instead she deliberately asked about Dana and watched his expression soften, heard the warmth steal back into his voice, replacing the despair that had been evident only moments before.

"Dana's glowing," he said. "She considers this pregnancy the grandest adventure in her life. Quite a statement given her decision to raise her brother on her own."

Lacey chuckled. "It certainly is an adventure. You're both happy about it, then? I wondered. It seemed a little soon. You have so many adjustments to make, especially with her brother living with you."

"To my astonishment, Sammy is no trouble at all. He spends every spare second with Granddad. The other night I found them crawling around under one of the looms at the plant. Granddad was trying to explain how to get a white-on-white pattern on damask."

"Does Sammy even know what damask is?" Lacey asked, trying to imagine the sixteen-year-old hell-raiser with the outrageous haircut being familiar with fine fabrics.

"Actually that's how the subject came up in the first place, as I understand it. Sammy wanted to use Granddad's tablecloth for a ghost costume for some play."

The image brought a smile to her lips. "I can just imagine Brandon's reaction to that."

Jason shook his head. "No, you can't. He actually got the scissors for him. But before he'd let Sammy ruin the tablecloth, he insisted on showing him how it was made. Off they went to the plant, leaving dinner still sitting on the table. Needless to say, Sammy changed his mind once he saw that the cloth wasn't some old rag Granddad had gotten from a discount store."

Lacey tapped the soil gently around the geranium's roots, then put the pot aside and reached for another. The rich scent of earth and the pungent aroma of the flowers had begun to work their soothing magic. She could almost forget her life was no longer complete.

"I saw Dad last night," Jason said, all the laughter gone from his voice, replaced by a cautious note.

Lacey drew in a deep breath. Her hands stilled. The announcement brought a shuddering end to her tranquility. "How is he?" she asked finally.

"Terrible, though he won't admit it. Mom, you still love him. I can see that. And he's still crazy about you. How long are the two of you going to let this go on?"

"As long as it takes."

"As long as it takes to do what?" Jason demanded, his tone filled with frustration. "Do either of you have the faintest idea why you're apart?"

"We're apart because that's the way it has to be."

Before she could stop him, Jason crushed the bright red petals of a geranium between his fingers. She wasn't even sure he was aware of what he'd done until he glanced down. Then he impatiently tossed the mangled bloom aside.

"That doesn't make a damned bit of sense," he said, raking his fingers through blond hair the same shade his father's had been at that age.

"Stop." Lacey put her hand over his.

"Are you trying to find yourself? Is that what this is? Some crazy mid-life crisis?"

Lacey drew in a deep breath. "I couldn't watch it

anymore,'' she admitted quietly, giving in to Jason's desperate need to understand something that was almost beyond explaining. ''I couldn't sit by and watch your father destroy his health. I was dying bit by bit, right along with him. I tried everything I knew, but nothing worked.''

Her son stared at her, his eyes filled with astonishment. ''Are you saying that you wanted to shock him into letting up?''

Tears misted in her eyes. She blinked them away. ''I hoped that our marriage would matter enough, that *I* would matter enough, to make him stop killing himself.''

''But you *are* the only thing that matters to him.''

She shook her head. ''Not anymore. Not enough. Have you seen any signs that he's changing? Admit it, since I left, he's only working harder.''

''Because he has no reason to go home. Don't you see? You've created a catch-22.''

''So what should I do? Go home and watch him die? Give him permission to do it? I won't do that, Jason. I can't.''

''Can't you talk about it? Compromise?''

''Not about this.''

Jason ran his fingers through his hair again in the gesture he'd picked up from his wife. ''Damn! What an awful mess.''

''I'm sorry. I'm sorry you're caught in the middle. I would give anything for that not to be.''

''I love you both. I want to see you happy again, the way you used to be.''

Lacey's lips curved into a rueful smile. ''No one wants that any more than I do. I promise you that.''

They were still talking when the phone rang. Lacey

picked it up and heard a cool, impersonal voice inform her that Kevin Halloran had just been brought into the hospital. ''He's in the cardiac intensive care unit. He wanted you to know.''

''Oh, God,'' she whispered softly, sinking into a chair, her own heart pounding.

''Mom, what is it? Is it Granddad? Dad?''

''Your father,'' she said, taking his hand, needing his strength to ask into the phone, ''How is he? Will he make it?''

''His condition is critical.''

Leaving had accomplished nothing, Lacey thought bitterly. Nothing.

Then, with a rush of panic, she tried to bring herself to face the very real possibility of losing forever the man she had loved nearly her whole life.

Chapter Two

The ten-mile ride across town to the hospital was the longest Lacey had ever taken, even though Jason drove like a maniac. His expression was grim, and she was certain she'd detected accusation in his eyes from the moment she'd told him about his father's heart attack. Whatever he thought, it was no worse than what she was mentally telling herself. She felt as if the guilt were smothering her.

The deep sadness, the sense of magic lost that had pervaded her entire being for so long had vanished in the brief seconds of that phone call, replaced by a gut-wrenching fear. Kevin couldn't die, not like this, not with so very much between them unresolved.

"It's my fault," she said when she could stand the silence no longer. "I moved out. Maybe if I'd stayed..." But she knew deep down it wouldn't have mattered. Kevin had made up his mind to tempt fate.

And he'd lost. Dear God, she prayed, don't let him pay with his life. Make this just one more warning. Give him one more chance.

Jason glanced her way. "He's going to be okay, Mother. Stop beating yourself up over this. Casting blame isn't going to do Dad any good. Did the hospital call Granddad?"

She realized she hadn't asked, that she had no idea where Kevin had been when he'd had the heart attack or even how he'd gotten to the hospital. "I don't know. I don't know any more than what I've told you."

"Maybe Granddad was with him. Knowing the two of them, they were probably still at the office."

Jason seemed to take comfort from the possibility that Brandon had been with Kevin, that he might even now be with him. Lacey was less certain how she felt about seeing her father-in-law. She dreaded another confrontation. They'd already had one monumental set-to over her decision to move out.

Brandon had ranted and raved, even questioned her sanity. She knew it killed him that he couldn't manipulate them all like puppets on a string. She wasn't sure she could stand another meeting like that, especially tonight.

The bottom line, though, was that in his own way Brandon loved Kevin every bit as much as she did and wanted what was best for him. Unfortunately, they tended to differ on what that was.

Despite their differences, he had every right to be at Kevin's side. Knowing Brandon, though, he would figure he had more of a right to be there than she did. Maybe that was true. She didn't know anymore.

"It's my fault," she said again as Jason sped into

the parking lot by the emergency entrance and screeched to a halt in the first space he could find.

"Stop it," Jason said impatiently, slamming the car door and coming around to join her. "You did what you thought you had to do. I may not agree with your methods, but I know you did it out of love."

"Maybe I did it out of selfishness," she countered and bit back a sob as guilt clogged her throat. "Maybe I was only thinking of my needs, not his."

"You don't have a selfish bone in your body," Jason said, taking her by the shoulders and giving her a gentle shake. He scanned her face. "Are you going to be okay?"

Lacey drew in a deep breath. She slowly, consciously pulled herself together and gave him a tremulous smile. "I'm not the one in intensive care. I'll be fine." She took his hand. "Let's go see your father."

Upstairs they found Brandon Halloran pacing the long, empty corridor outside of cardiac intensive care. Not even he could bluster his way past the restricted visiting hours posted on the door. Pale and shaken, his expression was bleak as he waited for word on his son's condition.

Jason put an arm around his grandfather's shoulders and steered him toward the waiting room, but Lacey held back, uncertain of Brandon's mood.

Years ago, before she and Kevin had even married, they had been the closest thing to enemies. Brandon had blamed her for so much that was wrong with his relationship with his son. Since then they'd forged a cautious friendship, which appeared to have splintered into a million pieces because she'd abandoned his beloved and only son.

Hesitant, Lacey stood in the doorway of the waiting

room until Brandon held out his hand. Then she moved quickly, anxious for news, anxious for a little of Brandon's towering, unshakable strength. Clasping his firm but icy hand between her own, she asked, "How is he? What have they told you?"

"Not a damned thing," he grumbled. "As much money as I give to this place, you'd think I could get a straight answer out of someone."

"What happened?"

A shadow seemed to pass over his eyes as he remembered. "Found him at his desk, all slumped over. Thought for a minute he might be dead. The guard got the paramedics there and we brought him here."

"Was he conscious?" Lacey asked.

"Part of the time. Said he wanted to see you. I don't pretend to understand what's been wrong between the two of you, but I want you to put it aside for now," he said, giving her a warning look that Lacey recognized from a dozen different occasions.

Brandon Halloran had strong opinions on family loyalty and just about everything else. He wasn't afraid to voice them. He had the confidence of a man who'd done well with his life and knew it. In fact, he thought the world would be a whole lot better if everyone would just accept the wisdom of his plans for them. It had galled the daylights out of him that Lacey and Kevin had dared to go their own way, at least in the beginning.

As much as she might have resented it once, Lacey found there was something almost comforting about the familiarity of his response to this crisis. That strength of purpose, that single-minded clarity of vision was welcome tonight in a way it never had been before. If there was any way in hell Brandon Halloran could buy salvation for his son, he would do it.

"I do love him," she said gently. "That's never been the problem."

Brandon scowled at her. "Well, I'll be damned if I know what is. I listened to all that double-talk you gave me months ago, chewed it over in my head every second since then and, by God, I still can't make a bit of sense of it. You got some sort of complaint about the life-style he gave you?"

"No," she whispered, stung by the harsh accusation. "Not the way you mean."

"I didn't notice you turning down the house, that fancy sports car."

Little did he know how she had fought both, Lacey thought but refused to say. Kevin had insisted. Brandon would never believe that, though. Even at the best of times in Brandon and Lacey's tenuous relationship, she'd been very much aware that he expected the worst of her, that he didn't entirely understand that someone could be motivated by something other than money and status, especially someone who'd brought nothing more than the strength of her love to a marriage.

"What then?" he demanded roughly. "Make me see why a woman would walk out on a man who's provided her with everything money could buy."

"I only wanted my husband back," she told him, but she could see that Brandon couldn't fathom what she meant. He started to speak, but Jason cut him off.

"Granddad," he said, "this isn't the time."

The fight seemed to drain out of Brandon as quickly as it had stirred. "No. No, it's not." It was the closest he was likely to come to an apology. He asked Jason, "You called Dana yet?"

Jason shook his head. "I don't want to upset her."

"She'd want to be here," Lacey told him. "Go call. We'll be okay."

With Jason gone, the look she and Brandon exchanged was measuring. She suspected he was trying every bit as hard as she was to avoid starting another pointless argument. But the only way around it was small talk or silence. She didn't have the stomach for small talk. Neither, she suspected, did he.

"Damn, I hate this waiting," he said finally. "You want some coffee or something?"

Lacey shook her head. "Nothing."

"How do you suppose he ended up in a fix like this? He's a young man yet."

"It's not the first time," she reminded him. "If anything, he took worse care of himself after the first attack."

"And I suppose you're blaming that on me."

"Casting blame won't help," she said, repeating what Jason had said to try to comfort her. It didn't work on Brandon, either. He took up his impatient pacing again.

If someone didn't come out and talk to them soon, Brandon was likely to call up the hospital board's president and demand a change in administration, she thought. He'd wave another endowment under the president's nose for effect. Waiting was always hardest on a man who was used to making things happen.

Lacey hated it, too, because it gave her time to think, time to remember the way it had once been between her and Kevin, back at the very beginning.

It had been her first day at a new school. Worse, it

was the middle of the year. Friendships had been made and she was an outsider. She was eleven years old, tall, skinny, shy and awkward.

She had been so sure that the other kids would make fun of her, that they would see that the clothes she wore were hand-me-downs, that her hair had been clipped impatiently by her mother, rather than in some fancy salon. She was terrified that they would discover that her last classmates had labeled her a brain and left her out of anything fun.

It had taken every ounce of bravery she'd possessed to slip into the classroom and scurry to a seat in the back, hoping no one would notice her. Then the teacher had singled her out, introduced her as a newcomer and made her move right smack to the middle of a room in which students had been seated in alphabetical order. She'd felt all those inquisitive, judgmental eyes on her and she'd wanted to cry.

She'd rushed too fast, trying to slide into her assigned seat without anyone taking further notice of her. Instead, she'd spilled her books in the process and had to listen to the taunting laughter that had made her feel more an outsider than ever. She'd kept her chin up, but hadn't been able to stop the tears from filling her eyes. She'd desperately tried to blink them away before anyone saw.

But a boy with tousled golden hair and a smile that revealed a chipped front tooth had seen. He had knelt down, picked up the books and placed them on her desk.

''Thank you, Kevin,'' Mrs. Niles had said, while the other boys in the room had made wisecracks about his gallantry.

Lacey had felt awful, knowing that he'd been embarrassed in front of his friends just for coming to her rescue. She had given him a hesitant smile and felt her eleven-year-old heart tumble at the impish, unworried grin he shot her in return.

From that moment on Kevin Halloran had been her protector, her knight in shining armor. He'd withstood a lot of teasing for befriending her. He'd fought a lot of playground battles on her behalf, had chosen her for teams when others wouldn't, had badgered her to try out for cheerleading when she'd known she wasn't pretty enough or popular enough to make it. To her amazement, he'd been right. She had cheered loudest and longest when he'd raced for the goal line.

Later, he'd ignored a lot of wealthy, admiring teenaged girls to date her, apparently preferring their quiet, serious talks to the adolescent wiles of her peers.

Then he'd dared to fall in love with her.

Brandon Halloran had thrown one of his inimitable fits about the engagement. He'd declared that no son of his was going to marry some little nobody who was only after his money. He'd vowed to do everything in his power to see that they split up. In the lowest moment of her life, he had offered her a bribe. When that hadn't worked, he'd sent Kevin off to college at Stanford, hoping that distance would accomplish what his ranting and threats had not.

None of it had dimmed Kevin and Lacey's determination or their love. Sometimes it astonished Lacey that at that age they had stood firm against the power of Brandon's opposition. In anyone else it might have been sheer stubbornness, but with Kevin it had been a deeply ingrained conviction that Lacey brought something into his life that he could never hope to find with another woman. At least that's what he'd told her when he'd insisted that they would get married with or without his parents' approval. He'd defiantly exchanged his class ring for a tiny chip of a diamond, rather than use parental funds for something splashier.

Where had that steadfast sense of commitment gone? The love hadn't died. As she sat in a corner of the cold, dimly lit hospital waiting room, terrified of losing him forever this time, Lacey could admit that much. She also knew that they couldn't go on as they had been, drifting farther and farther apart with each day that passed, fighting bitterly at every turn.

Jason returned just as Dr. Lincoln Westlake came out of the cardiac unit. Lacey froze at the sight of his grim expression. Even Brandon looked uncertain. It was Jason who finally dared to ask how Kevin was doing.

"I won't lie to you. He's in pretty bad shape. If I had to guess, I'd say he didn't take that last attack seriously and did everything in his power to ensure he'd have another one."

Brandon gazed at him in astonishment. "Are you saying he tried to bring this on?"

"In a way."

"That's absurd. Why that would be the next best thing to suicide."

"Mr. Halloran, your son is a bright man. He knew the risks and he did nothing to minimize them." He glanced at Lacey, and his tone gentled. "Did he?"

She sighed. The truth was that he'd even canceled half a dozen follow-up appointments with the doctor. She'd finally given up trying to make them.

"No. Nothing," she admitted. Damn him, she said

to herself. Damn Kevin Halloran for trying to play God with his own life!

"Can I see him?" she asked, when she could keep her voice steady.

"For five minutes. He's resting now and I don't want you to wake him. If he's to have any chance at all, he needs to stay as quiet as possible."

Lacey nodded. "Thanks, Linc. If anyone can pull him through this, I know you can."

"I'm going to do my damnedest. If he'll give me a little help, we might have a chance. You come on in, when you're ready."

As he walked away, Lacey started toward the cardiac unit after him. Brandon stepped into her path. "Remember what the doctor said, girl. Don't you go upsetting him!"

"Granddad!" Jason warned.

Lacey put her hand on her son's arm. "It's okay." She met Brandon's gaze evenly and saw the worry and exhaustion in his eyes. "I'll tell him that you're here and that you're praying for him."

Brandon nodded, then sighed heavily and sank into one of the cushioned chairs. He motioned for Jason to sit next to him, then looked up at her. "You tell him we're all praying for him," he said.

Lacey nodded. She pressed the button that allowed the automatic doors to the unit to swish silently open, then stepped into a high-tech wonderland that was both magnificent and frightening.

Like the spokes of a wheel, small, softly lit rooms surrounded a central desk banked with monitors. Hushed voices competed with beeping equipment and the steady gurgle of oxygen.

She spotted Linc through one of the doorways, a

chart in his hand, his troubled gaze riveted on the bed. Drawing in a deep breath, she walked to the doorway. Linc gave her a reassuring smile and motioned her in. Her steps were halting, but she finally approached the bed.

It took every last ounce of her courage to glance past the tangle of wires, IV tubes and oxygen to her husband.

Against the startling white of the pillow, Kevin's handsome, angular face had a grayish cast. His golden hair, shot now with silver, was mussed, its impeccable cut wasted. Without the armor of his custom-tailored suit, his designer shirt and silk tie, he looked vulnerable, every inch a mortal, rather than the invincible hero she'd always thought him to be.

He was so terribly still, she thought, fighting panic. The man who had always seemed so alive, so filled with energy looked like a shadow, quiet and lifeless. Her gaze shifted desperately to a monitor and fixed on the steady rhythm. She had no idea what the up-and-down movement of the lines meant except that they were proof her husband was still clinging to life.

Lacey stepped closer and took Kevin's one free hand, curving her fingers around his, trying to share her warmth with him. Her own heart lurched anew at his vulnerability, then filled to overflowing, first with love, then with rage—at him and at her own impotence.

Damn you, Kevin, she thought. *You were always my strength. I'm not sure I know how to be yours.*

She whispered, "Fight, Kevin. Dammit, you have to live. You have a grandchild on the way. You have to be here to teach him how to ride a bicycle, how to throw a ball. You know I'm not good at things like that.''

She closed her eyes and thought of all the plans they'd made. She kept her voice low as she reminded him, willed him to live to see them come true.

''Don't you remember how we always looked forward to spoiling our grandchildren? There were so many things we were going to do. We were going to spend long, lazy days walking on the beach. We were going to read Shakespeare's sonnets and visit Walden Pond. Don't you dare make me do those things alone.''

She felt Linc's hand on her shoulder. ''That's enough for now,'' he said gently. ''Let him rest.''

''Not yet,'' she pleaded, terrified Kevin would slip away if she weren't there to hold on to him. ''Another minute, please. I won't say another word. Just let me stay.''

Linc studied her silently, then nodded. He reached for a tissue and handed it to her. ''Another minute,'' he agreed. ''No more.''

Lacey brushed away the tears she hadn't even realized were there until she had the tissue in her hand. Very much aware of her vow to remain silent, she tried bargaining in her mind with Kevin and then with God.

With her gaze riveted on her husband's face, she was aware of the first subtle blink of his lashes. Hope burst inside her. That's it, she cried in her heart. You can do it, Kevin. I know you can.

She knew her minute's reprieve was long over, but she didn't budge, waiting. It was a minute more and then another before Kevin's eyes finally blinked open and his gaze searched the room before finally focusing on her.

He managed a feeble smile that was only a faint shadow of the smile that had captivated her heart all those years ago. Even so, Lacey's heart filled to bursting and she felt tears of relief spill down her cheeks. In that instant she knew beyond a doubt that whatever it took, her husband was going to make it. He would fight to live.

But the struggle to save their marriage was yet to come.

Chapter Three

Lacey spent a long, uneasy night in the hospital waiting room, refusing to go home, desperately needing the few precious minutes every couple of hours that Linc allowed her to visit Kevin. She couldn't rid herself of that first sense of shock at his pallor, that initial horror that he might give up and slip away. Fear welled up inside her and abated only when she was by his side, willing her strength into him.

It had been nearly midnight when she had insisted that Jason take Dana home. She tried futilely to get Brandon to go with them. She was worried about the exhaustion that had shadowed his eyes. It reminded her all too vividly of those first grief-stricken weeks after he had lost his wife. For all that Brandon thought otherwise, he was not invincible.

Now, even though he was resting, he looked miserably uncomfortable on the waiting room's too-short sofa. Lacey couldn't help thinking he would have been far better off in his own bed, in his own home with Mrs. Farnsworth, his housekeeper of thirty years, fussing over him. Still, she could understand his need to stay close to Kevin. Despite all she and Kevin had been through lately—all the bitterness and recriminations—she'd felt the same way.

Though Kevin hadn't awakened again through the long night, Lacey had been comforted simply by seeing him, by listening to the steady sound of the monitor tracking his heartbeat. Now, her throat dry, her stomach growling, she went off in search of tea and toast for herself and her father-in-law. If Brandon was going to insist on staying until the crisis passed, he would need all his strength.

Brandon was awake when Lacey returned, his cheek bearing the pattern of the sofa's piping, his clothes rumpled to a state that would have given his personal tailor palpitations. His eyes were brighter, though.

"Wondered where you'd gone," he said, accepting the cup of tea and ignoring the toast.

Even in this crisis he obviously had no intention of veering from his Spartan routine, Lacey thought with a mix of admiration and frustration. No wonder Kevin found his father such a tough act to follow.

"The doctor was by a minute ago," he said, interrupting her thoughts. "Can't believe that boy who used to climb trees in my backyard is a cardiologist these days. You suppose we ought to call in someone else?"

"Linc is one of the best and you know it."

"I suppose." He still looked doubtful.

"What did he say?"

"He thinks the worst is past. If Kevin stays stable

another forty-eight hours, he'll consider moving him to a private room.''

''And then what?'' she asked, more to herself than Brandon.

His sharp gaze pinned her, the blue eyes glinting with a challenge. ''Then we'll all do whatever it takes to help Kevin get his health back. All of us, you hear me?''

Lacey shook her head ruefully. An order like that was all too typical of her father-in-law. ''Brandon, you can't bully us into a happy marriage.''

He scowled and waved a finger under her nose. ''Maybe not, but I can damn well see that you stick it out until this crisis is past.''

Determined not to let him see how his threat disturbed her, Lacey returned his fierce expression.

''I will not argue with you about this,'' she said, carefully setting her tea on the table, then turning and walking away. Maybe it was the cowardly thing to do, but she couldn't see any other choice. The stress of the present on both of them was bad enough without battling over the future.

Outside the hospital, where winter hadn't quite given way to spring, a bed of purple crocuses were forcing their way through the still-icy earth. Lacey circled the grounds, holding her thin jacket closed against the damp breeze. The nip in the air cleared her head. She reminded herself that for all his blustering, Brandon couldn't control whatever decision she and Kevin reached about their marriage.

That decision, however, was far in the future. Brandon was right about one thing: the most important task now was to see that Kevin pulled through, that he took this latest warning more seriously than he had the last.

She, more than anyone, wanted to see his masculine vitality restored, to see his pallor replaced by the healthy glow he'd once had.

She recalled the way he'd looked on their wedding day, his hair too long by his father's standards and tousled by a spring breeze. Used to seeing him in jeans and denim jackets, she'd thought he looked outrageously sexy and impressive in custom-tailored gray slacks and a blue dress shirt. She'd never guessed he owned clothes like that, though it stood to reason he would, given the family's business in textiles and their social standing. Usually, though, Kevin had rebelled at anything that hinted at his privileged background.

Most of all, Lacey recalled the expression of adoration on his face when she'd joined him on that blustery hillside. She had been so proud to become his wife, so touched by the tender vows he'd written himself. The emotions she had felt that day had only deepened with time. In the end she had loved him enough to leave, loved him enough to risk everything she cared about on the one slim chance that the desperate measure would force him to face the dangers of his present life-style.

Steeped in bittersweet memories, Lacey walked until it was time to go back in to see Kevin. She avoided the waiting room and Brandon, going instead straight to the cardiac unit.

She found Kevin with his eyes closed, his expression more peaceful. His jaw was shadowed by the first faint stubble of a beard that under other circumstances she might have found sexy because of its ruggedly sensual look. It would have reminded her of the rebellious, bearded young man who'd marched for peace at a time when his father was backing the Vietnam

War. Today it only reminded her of how sick he was, because that shadow emphasized his pallor.

Seated by his bed, his hand in hers, Lacey's thoughts began drifting back again. She was startled when she heard him whisper her name.

"Lacey, is that you?"

"It's me, Kevin."

"You stayed," he said, gently squeezing her hand. He sounded surprised.

"I stayed," she murmured, then added wearily, "but dammit, Kevin Halloran, did you have to go to this extreme just to get my attention?"

"You're here, aren't you?" he responded with that familiar teasing note in his weakened voice. His tone sobered. "What's Linc saying?"

"He says you're going to be all right, if you take care of yourself and slow down."

A faint twinkle sparked in his eyes as his gaze met hers. "Sounds like a fate worse than death."

"Don't you dare joke about it," she said furiously, jerking her hand from his and poking it into her pocket. "You scared the daylights out of all of us."

"Does Jason know? He came to see me at the office. Was it last night? Or before? I've lost track of the time."

"It was two nights ago. He came to see me last night. He was with me when the hospital called."

"I'm afraid we had words."

"So he mentioned. He's frustrated and confused. He wants to help, but he doesn't know how."

Kevin sighed heavily. "That makes two of us."

Lacey bit back a retort that would match the faint edge of bitterness in his. If she started saying all that was on her mind—the whole jumble of fury and regrets—Linc would throw her out of intensive care.

"Lace?"

She met Kevin's troubled gaze. "Yes."

"You haven't forgiven me, have you?"

Faced with that unblinking, uncompromising stare, she could only shake her head. Instead of saying more, she deliberately changed the subject.

"Your father is outside. He's been here all night. In fact, he was driving the staff crazy because he had to wait to find out what was going on. I think he thought he ought to be in here telling them how to get the oxygen started."

Lacey waited for Kevin's familiar grinning response to tales of his father's efforts to manage life on his terms. Instead he winced. Lacey caught his effort to hide it and asked, "Are you in pain? Should I call the nurse?"

He grimaced. "I feel as if I've been run over by a truck."

"You look like it, too."

He reached for her hand again and when she finally placed it in his, he held on tight. "You were right, weren't you, Lace?"

"About what?"

"The work. I got my priorities all screwed up."

Lacey hadn't wanted to wring an admission from Kevin like this. Besides, the truth of the matter was that work was only part of the problem. Worse was the fact that the man who'd been her lover and best friend had too often seemed little more than a stranger.

"Now's not the time to talk about that," she told him.

"Can we talk about it, though?" he said, a sense of urgency in his voice.

"I always thought we could talk about anything," she replied softly, unable to hide the regret.

Blue eyes pinned her. "Until I shut you out," he said.

"I never said that."

"But it's the truth. I did. I'm sorry."

"Kevin—"

"I want us to start over. When I get out of here, I want to go away, take a long vacation and make things right between us again. I've missed you these past months, more than I can say." His voice faltered. "I just…I wanted you to know."

When she didn't say a word, couldn't squeeze a sound around the tears that clogged her throat, he prodded, "Lace, what do you think? Can we give it a try?"

A part of her thought it was too late. A part of her wanted to scream that this sudden change of attitude was too easy, a quick reaction to a health crisis that would pass as soon as he felt more like himself again.

And yet a part of her yearned for the way it used to be between them, wanted to believe it was possible to recapture the richness of their love.

"We'll talk about it when you're out of here," she said evasively.

Every bit as stubborn as his father, Kevin wouldn't let it go that easily. "You won't back out?"

Lacey drew in a deep breath and met his gaze evenly. "Of talking?" she asked. "No. I won't back out."

Kevin sighed then, obviously content with that much of a commitment. His eyes slowly drifted closed. He was still clinging to her hand, the touch apparently as much comfort for him as it was for her.

Kevin knew he was going to have a fight on his hands. He'd seen that much in Lacey's brilliant blue eyes, even when she'd reluctantly agreed to talk about the future. For some reason a fight didn't scare him anymore, not half as much as the thought of losing her forever.

Besides, nothing about his relationship with Lacey had ever been easy, not from the day he'd told his parents about her, anyway. Before that, they had spent long, quiet hours talking, sharing innermost thoughts that no boy dared to share with his buddies. Lacey's gentle smiles had brought sunshine into his life from the day they'd met.

More than simply his friend, she was his social conscience. She was the first person to make him realize that not everyone was as fortunate as he was, that he had an obligation to look beyond his own narrow world. From the first moment she had looked at him like a hero, he'd wanted to prove himself worthy of her.

Then Brandon had started throwing his weight around, threatening Lacey, scowling at Kevin, swearing that the Halloran name would be sullied forever if he dared to marry a woman lacking the requisite Boston pedigree.

The truth of the matter was that Brandon had been afraid. He'd spent his whole life making plans for the day when Kevin would take his rightful place at Halloran Industries. But Kevin hadn't been interested. Brandon had blamed Lacey for that. He'd accused her of ruining his son's life, of forcing him to choose between her and his heritage.

Infuriated by the unjust accusation, Lacey had faced Brandon down, her shoulders squared, her chin jutting out, her eyes filled with fire. Only her hands, clenched at her sides, gave away her nervousness.

Her voice steady, she had said, "You're the one making him choose. I want Kevin to be happy. If Halloran Industries makes him happy, it's fine with me. But he says he wants to do something else with his life."

Kevin had never been more proud of her. Brandon had appeared stunned by her spunk and by her blunt words. He'd turned to Kevin. "Is what she's saying right? You don't want to work with me?"

"It's not that, Dad. You think of Halloran Industries as some sort of family dynasty. I need to prove myself. I don't want something that's handed to me."

"You're just one of those damned hippies. Just look at you. Your hair's too long. You dress like a bum."

"I dress like everyone else."

"Not like everyone else in *this* family," Brandon said in disgust. "You think we should be ashamed of having money. Well, dammit, I worked for every penny we have. So did your granddad, and you will, too."

"You're acting as if clothes are the only things that matter. What about having a social conscience? Doesn't that matter at all to you?"

Brandon slammed his fist down on his desk. "You act as if you invented it. You'll have to work for what you get at Halloran, same as I did. And you'll be expected to share with the community, the same way I have, the way your granddad did."

"It won't be the same and you know it. You think writing a check covers you for all eternity. What about fighting for what's right, fighting to make a difference? That's what I care about. That's what I want to do with my life. I just can't see myself making fancy fabrics for the wealthy when people are going hungry."

"And what about the people who have food on their tables every night because we provide them with jobs? You think that doesn't count for anything?"

Kevin had been at a loss to argue that point. Somehow he'd been so certain back then that he could find ways to make his life count, to better things for thousands, rather than the mere hundred or so employed by Halloran Industries.

Lacey had stood by him when he'd walked away from the Halloran money, turned his back on his family. As he remembered, he thought perhaps those were the best years of their lives. They had struggled. At times they hadn't had two nickels to rub together, but it had been okay because they'd had dreams and they'd had each other.

They'd worked side by side to help people who didn't have nearly as much, people who didn't believe in themselves.

Educated in business and drawn by an idealistic notion of making the world a better place, Kevin had applied his skills in a series of low-paying and off-times unrewarding public service jobs. For several years he found the sacrifices he made worthwhile. He was filled with satisfaction and hope. He'd never once been tempted to touch his trust fund for himself.

Then he'd realized that for every instance in which he made a difference, there were a dozen more about which he could do nothing. Increasingly frustrated after nearly fifteen years of struggling, he was finally ready to listen when his father pressed him yet again about joining Halloran Industries.

It hadn't been difficult for Kevin to justify his eventual acceptance of the offer. Perhaps from a position of power, he would be able to make the changes in society that up to now had eluded him. And, as Brandon pointed out with distressing accuracy, his beautiful Lacey and his wonderful son did not deserve to live like paupers just so Kevin could make some obviously misguided political statement.

Like so many other idealistic children of the sixties, he figured he had finally grown up.

Kevin also recognized that Brandon's request was his awkward way of apologizing for misjudging Lacey, his way of making amends for years lost. Whether Brandon had made the gesture for himself or for Kevin's mother, Kevin felt he owed it to his father and to his own family to try to make it work. Lacey had been elated by the reconciliation, if not by the decision to join Halloran Industries.

Kevin had joined the company more than a decade ago and there had been no regrets on his part, not at first, anyway. He threw himself into the job the only way he knew how—heart and soul. Only now, with his marriage and his very life at stake, was he beginning to understand what Lacey had been saying all along, that the cost might have been too high.

When he'd awakened earlier to find Lacey standing beside his hospital bed, he'd been reminded of those early days. He'd seen the familiar tenderness and compassion in her eyes. He'd detected the faint trace of fear that had reminded him of the scared girl who'd stolen his heart when he'd been a mere boy.

He had wanted more than anything to tell her everything would be all right as he had so often in years past. But for the first time in his life, he wasn't so sure he could rectify things. He just knew he had to try, that the vows he'd taken nearly thirty years ago still meant something to him.

Kevin could only pray that they still meant something to Lacey, as well.

Chapter Four

Lacey heard the phone ringing through a bone-deep haze of exhaustion. The shrill sound brought her instantly awake.

Kevin! Something had happened to Kevin, she thought as she fumbled frantically for the phone, her heart hammering.

"Yes, hello," she said, her voice still scratchy with sleep.

"Lacey, it's Dana. I'm sorry if I woke you."

Lacey tried to shake off her grogginess. "It's okay, dear. I was just taking a nap. I didn't get much sleep at the hospital last night. Is there news? Is Kevin okay?"

"He's doing well," her daughter-in-law reassured her. "Jason called about an hour ago. He'd been in to see him earlier. He said Kevin looked a hundred percent better than he did when we left last night. What about you, though? Are you okay? Yesterday must have been—'' she hesitated, then said ''—well, it must have been difficult with things the way they've been between you and Kevin.''

The last part was said in an uncertain rush, as if Dana wasn't sure she should even broach the subject of Lacey's relationship with her husband.

Hoping to avoid any further probing, Lacey deliberately injected a cheerful note in her voice. ''Other than being tired, I'm just fine.''

The reply was greeted with a skeptical silence. ''Could we have lunch?'' Dana asked finally. ''I'll pick something up and bring it over, if you don't feel like going out.''

''Maybe another time,'' Lacey said evasively. Dana had an uncanny knack for getting to the heart of things. Her directness was one of her charms, but Lacey wasn't sure she was ready to talk about what she was feeling—not until she understood it more clearly herself.

Before last night, it had been months since Lacey had seen Kevin. Then to see him in a hospital bed. It had been her worst nightmare come true. Anxiety, anger and love had each taken turns, leaving her thoroughly drained and confused. How could she feel so much for a man she didn't even think she knew anymore?

''Are you anxious to get back to the hospital?'' Dana questioned.

Lacey might have grabbed at the excuse, if she hadn't known the implications. ''No. Actually I hadn't planned to stop by until this evening.''

''Then there's no reason for me not to come over,'' her daughter-in-law declared decisively. ''I won't let you put me off. You need someone to talk to and it might as well be me. Who knows these Halloran men better than you and I do? I'll be there in an hour.''

She hung up before Lacey could think of a single thing to say to keep her away. Besides, maybe Dana was right. She did need to sort things out, and Dana knew as much as anyone what these Halloran men were like once they started with their bulldozer tactics.

Brandon's warning, combined with Kevin's plea for another chance had taken their toll. Lacey was already dreading going back to the hospital, fearing that she would succumb to the combined pressure without giving the decision nearly enough thought. Maybe Dana could help her to stiffen her resolve.

A shower did its part to revive her. By the time the doorbell rang, she'd swept her hair back in a French braid and pulled on gray wool slacks and the cheerfully bright, blue sweater Dana had given her last Christmas.

At the door Dana shrugged out of her coat, then looked Lacey over from head to toe and nodded in satisfaction. ''Everyone should have a mother-in-law who looks like you. You're a walking advertisement for my designs.''

Lacey grinned. ''You look pretty snappy yourself. How much longer do you figure you'll be able to wear that outfit?''

''About another hour, if I skip lunch,'' Dana complained as she headed for the kitchen with her armload of carryout food. ''I couldn't get the waistband snapped as it is. Fortunately the sweater covers the gap. If I'm this bad with three months to go, what will I look like by the time I deliver? Jason will have to roll me to the hospital on one of those carts they use for moving heavy crates."

"Believe me, he'll be too excited to worry about how you look." She studied Dana's sweater, a bold swirl of hot pink on a neon green background. "A new design? Just looking at you cheers me up."

"That's the idea. It's for the mass market line. What do you think?"

"I think you're going to make a fortune for that designer who's added them to his collection and for Halloran Industries. Brandon must be ecstatic."

Dana rolled her eyes as she spread a selection of deli salads on the kitchen table. "Actually Brandon is more interested in the timetable for producing his great grandchild. I swear he would take Lemaze classes with me if Jason would let him. Jason has already had to stop him from checking the references of the instructors."

"That man needs to find a woman of his own. Maybe then he'd stop meddling in all our lives," Lacey said as she put plastic plates, mismatched stainless flatware and paper napkins on the table.

Dana's eyebrows rose a fraction. "Still roughing it?"

"It is a far cry from the Halloran china and silver, isn't it? You should have seen Kevin's expression when he saw it."

"He's been here, then?"

"Yes, when I first moved in. He left convinced that I'd lost my mind. Brandon agreed. Jason, also, probably, though he's too polite to say it to my face."

"Well, we know why Kevin would hate it. As for Brandon, he can't imagine anyone not being madly in love with his son or grandson. He also thinks the Halloran life-style is the primary selling point. I agree with you that he needs to find some woman and fall in love again. Better yet, he should have to fight to win her over. I told him exactly that just the other day.''

''What did he say?''

''That a girl my age shouldn't be meddling in the love life of her elders. I don't think he saw the irony.''

''He wouldn't,'' Lacey agreed. ''Brandon thinks his interference is a God-given right as patriarch of the Halloran clan.''

Dana's expression turned quizzical. ''Do I detect a note of bitterness?''

''Bitterness, resignation, maybe a little frustration.''

''He's been cross-examining you about the separation again, hasn't he?''

''Brandon, Jason, even Kevin from his hospital bed. None of them seem to get it, even after all this time.''

''I do,'' Dana said with such quiet compassion that it brought tears to Lacey's eyes.

She blamed the rare display of emotion on stress and gave her daughter-in-law a watery, grateful smile. ''I think maybe you do. I didn't leave out of spite. I don't hate Kevin.''

''Quite the contrary would be my guess,'' Dana said. ''It hurts, doesn't it? It hurts to see someone you love changing before your eyes and feeling totally helpless to stop it.''

Not for the first time, Lacey was astounded by Dana's insightfulness. ''For a young woman, you sound very wise.''

Dana shrugged off the compliment. ''I watched my mother fade and then die after my father walked out on us. Then I saw Sammy turn from a wonderful kid into a teenager destined for real trouble. No matter what I said or did, it never made a difference. In the end all I could do was love them, anyway. Thank God Jason came along when he did. He's the one who finally got through to Sammy."

Lacey patted her hand. "I'm sorry I never knew your mother. She must have been something for you to turn out to be so special."

Lacey caught the unexpected tears shimmering in Dana's eyes before she turned away. The rare show of emotion surprised Lacey. Her daughter-in-law always seemed so composed.

"Thanks for saying that," Dana murmured. "Sometimes I forget what she was like before she changed. It's good to be reminded that she wasn't always so defeated, that there was a time when she was terrific and fun to be around."

Finally she faced Lacey again, the tearful, faraway look in her eyes gone. "You never met my mother and yet you have an instinctive understanding of her. At the same time, I wonder if you see the side of Kevin that I see at work."

"Meaning?" Lacey questioned cautiously.

"Did you know that he personally went to the hospital to visit the child of one of the Halloran workers, when the boy was diagnosed with leukemia?"

Startled, Lacey shook her head. It was something the old Kevin would have done in the blink of an eye, but now? She wouldn't have believed it, if she hadn't known that Dana would never make up such a story.

"It's true," Dana said. "Jason told me he also gave the woman time off with pay to be with her son. And he sent the whole family off to Disneyworld for

Christmas because the boy had always wanted to meet Mickey Mouse."

"Kevin did that?" Lacey asked softly.

"He did. From what I've seen since I started working there, Kevin likes to make everyone believe that he's all business, that the only thing he cares about is the bottom line. I don't think there's a worker at Halloran Industries, though, who hasn't been touched by his kindness at one time or another." She smiled at Lacey. "I thought you should know. Maybe it will help to put things in perspective."

Lacey nodded. "Thank you for telling me. Kevin never did."

"He wouldn't. He takes it for granted that it's part of his job. That's what I admire so much about him. He doesn't think that being considerate, that caring deeply about his employees' welfare is unusual. It's just the way he is."

"Yes," Lacey said, more shaken than she could say by the reminder of a generosity of spirit she had thought was lost, "it is the way he is."

Was it possible that things weren't quite as hopeless as she had imagined?

Kevin thought he detected something new and oddly hesitant in Lacey's blue eyes when she came to visit him that evening. She regarded him as if she weren't quite sure what to make of him. Her assessing glance puzzled him.

"I like your hair like that," he began tentatively, wondering if it was past time to be wooing her with compliments, no matter how sincerely spoken. He yearned for the right to brush back the silken strands that had escaped the pulled-back style. "You look like a girl again. That sweater becomes you, too. It matches your eyes. One of Dana's designs, I'll bet."

A blush of pink rose in her cheeks as she nodded, making him regret how long it had been since he'd told her how beautiful she was. "It's true," he continued. "Sometimes I look at you and it's as if time had stood still."

She grinned at that. "What's gotten into you today? Is there a little Irish blarney in that IV?"

"They don't tell me what sort of concoctions they put in there. Maybe it's truth serum. I do know I've felt a powerful need to see you. I worried you might not come back."

"I told you I would."

"Are you here because I'm at death's door or because you want to be here?"

She regarded him impatiently. "You are *not* at death's door, so don't try playing on my sympathy. You're going to be just fine."

"If I rest," he reminded her.

"Exactly."

"Who's going to make me?"

"You're a grown man. No one should have to make you listen to reason."

"Maybe I've forgotten what it's like to rest. Maybe I need someone around to show me." He met her gaze and held it. "I need you, Lacey."

Her lips parted, but before she could speak, Brandon slipped into the room. Kevin managed a rueful grin. "Your timing's lousy, Dad."

Brandon looked from Kevin to Lacey and back again, then nodded in obvious satisfaction. "Interrupting your courting, am I? I'm sure you'll remember right where you left off. Just wanted to say goodbye before I go get some sleep. These old bones of mine can't take another night on that poor excuse of a sofa in the waiting room.'' He glanced at Lacey. ''Remind me to order up some new furniture for this place.''

''I'm sure they'll appreciate it,'' Lacey said, already edging toward the door. ''Why don't I leave you two alone. I don't think Linc wants two of us in here at a time.''

''Lacey,'' Kevin said, stopping her before she could flee, ''I won't forget.''

''Forget what?''

''I won't forget what we were talking about,'' he answered meaningfully.

She scurried out the door, reminding him of the only other time he could recall seeing her flustered—the day he'd asked her to marry him. She had wanted so desperately to say yes. He'd been able to read that much in her eyes. She'd tried to weigh that desire against the implications, from Brandon's wrath to the certain end of his future in the family business.

''Yes,'' she had said hesitantly, then before he could whoop for joy, ''No. Oh, Kevin, I couldn't bear it if our being together ruined your relationship with your father.''

''Dad will survive this little setback to his plans. He always does.''

''But there's nothing more important than family.''

''We'll have our own family. You and I. Our children. It'll be enough for me. Will it be enough for you?''

''All I've ever wanted in my life was to love you.''

''Then that's our answer, isn't it?'' Kevin had said with the naive faith only a twenty-year-old can have. ''All I've ever wanted is to make you happy.''

For so many years love had been enough. Only lately had he realized that sometimes marriage took more than love. It took patience and understanding and a willingness to struggle through the bad times. It took listening and sharing and compromise.

Kevin knew, then, what he had to do, what it would take to win Lacey back, to convince her that what they had now was just as strong as what they'd had back then.

When Jason came in later, Kevin asked him to make arrangements to open their house on Cape Cod. "Call the caretaker and have him stock the refrigerator and put in a supply of firewood. I'm going there when I get out."

Jason's expression was concerned. "Shouldn't you stay in town, closer to your doctor?"

"I need to get away. I can't bear the thought of going back to that huge house again. Your mother hates it. Did you know that?"

Jason looked startled. "She does?"

"Always has. I insisted on buying it after I went to work with your grandfather. I thought we needed to make a statement, live up to the corporate image, some such nonsense. She put up with it when you were growing up, but once you'd moved out, she started talking again about moving, getting something smaller."

Kevin took a deep breath as he made another decision. "I want you to put it on the market. Maybe then she'll see that I'm serious about wanting a reconciliation."

"Dad, are you sure? I thought you loved that house."

"I loved what I thought it represented. Turns out it's just a house, and a lonely one at that."

"Are you planning to stay on the Cape?"

"If I can convince your mother to stay there with me, I just may."

Jason grinned. "You always could twist her around your little finger."

Kevin shook his head ruefully. "No, son. You've got that backward. All it took was a smile and she could make me jump through hoops. Guess I'd forgotten that because in recent years I haven't given her much to smile about."

"Want to tell me what that means?"

He grinned at his son. "No."

Lacey would know and that was all that mattered.

The next morning Kevin waited impatiently for Lacey's visit. She didn't come. She wasn't there when he moved into a private room. Nor had she arrived by the time he got his pitiful excuse for a dinner.

When Jason arrived at seven-thirty, Kevin swallowed his pride and asked, "Have you seen your mother today?"

"No. Why? Hasn't she been here?"

Kevin shook his head. "You don't suppose she's sick?"

"I'll check on her on my way home."

"Go now."

"But I just got here."

"I'll feel better knowing that your mother is okay. Maybe the stress of the past few weeks caught up with her. That terrible flu is going around."

Jason threw up his hands. "Okay, I'll go, but I think you're worrying about nothing. Dana usually talks to her during the day. I'm sure if anything were wrong she would have let me know."

Kevin watched as Jason pulled his overcoat back on. "You'll call me?"

"I'll call you. Now stop worrying and eat your dinner."

Kevin glanced at the bland scoop of mashed potatoes and the colorless chunk of chicken. "This is not dinner. It's a form of torture dreamed up by Linc Westlake. I don't suppose you could sneak me some of Mrs. Willis's chicken and dumplings?" he inquired hopefully, thinking of Jason's housekeeper's delicious cooking.

Jason grinned at him. "I'll check with the doctor. If he says it's okay, I'm sure Mrs. Willis will be thrilled to make it for you. Get some rest, Dad. Don't tire yourself out with worrying. It won't help."

Jason had been gone less than twenty minutes when the door opened and Lacey walked through, her expression harried.

"Hi," she said cheerfully. "You're looking better."

"Where have you been?" Kevin asked, unable to control the edge in his voice.

Lacey regarded him sharply. "You sound angry."

"Worried," he corrected. "And if I sound worried, it's because I was. I expected you hours ago."

"Expected?" she echoed softly.

Kevin heard the warning note in her voice, but couldn't keep himself from adding, "If you couldn't get by, you should have let me know. I just sent Jason to check on you."

"Why on earth would you do that?"

"I told you. I was worried."

Kevin could see that Lacey was fighting her temper.

She'd always been independent. No doubt she'd grown more so during their separation, when she'd been accountable to no one for her actions. She drew in a deep breath and pulled a chair close to the bed. He noticed she didn't take off her coat, as if to indicate to him that she wasn't here to stay.

"Kevin," she began in that patient tone he'd heard her use on Jason when he was five and misbehaving, "I'm sure you are bored to tears in here," she continued, "but I can't be here every minute. I have other obligations."

"One of those committees, I'm sure."

The sarcastic barb brought sparks into her eyes. "May I remind you that I am on those committees because you thought it would be the thing for the wife of a Halloran to do."

He winced. "Sorry. You're right. Is that where you were?"

"No. As it happens, I've gotten involved with something else."

Something or some*one,* he couldn't help wondering. Kevin felt an ache deep inside as he realized that this was probably just one of many things he didn't know about how Lacey spent her time.

"Tell me," he said. He saw her slowly relax at the genuine note of interest in his voice.

"Another time," she said. "For now, tell me how you're feeling. You must have had a good day, since Linc moved you out of intensive care and into a private room so quickly."

"The day's better now that you're here."

Kevin reached for her hand. After a hesitation so light that only a man deeply in love with his wife would notice, she slipped her hand into his. Contentment swelled inside him and he realized with Lacey here he could sleep at last.

Later he would never be sure if Lacey's gentle kiss was real or something he had dreamed.

Chapter Five

Over the next several days Lacey realized her feelings about Kevin's continued rapid recovery were oddly mixed. Day by day his strength returned. It was almost as if he applied the same obsessive attention to healing that he did to everything else. It was both astonishing and reassuring to see.

Though Lacey hated herself for even thinking it, she couldn't help wondering what would happen when he was well, when she no longer would have these hospital visits as an excuse for seeing him. The prospect of letting go for the second time daunted her. And yet there was no going back, not on the basis of a few quick promises, which were all too likely to be broken. She'd made up her mind about that.

Unfortunately, there was a troubling and unmistakable glint of determination in Kevin's eyes every time he looked at her. She'd often seen that expression right before he or Brandon scored some business coup. Kevin was scheming and it made her very nervous. Worse, she had the sense that Jason was conspiring with him. Together, the two men she loved most in the world were formidable opponents.

"Okay, enough is enough. What are the two of you up to?" she demanded when she found them with their heads together at the end of Kevin's first week in the hospital.

Jason looked from her to his father and back again. Guilt was written all over his face. "I'm out of here," he said hurriedly, backing toward the door.

Hands on hips, Lacey stepped into his path. "Not so fast."

He gave her a quick peck on the cheek. "Gotta go, Mom. Dana's waiting for me in the car."

"She can wait another ten seconds."

"Couldn't you just ask Dad, if you want to know something?" he suggested hopefully. "He's the one with all the answers."

She glanced at Kevin and saw the old familiar twinkle in his eyes. It made her heart tumble, just as it always had. That twinkle was downright dangerous.

Lacey recalled the first time she'd seen that glint of mischief in his eyes. He'd used some super glue to seal their fifth-grade teacher's desk drawer shut. That drawer had held their report cards. Kevin hadn't been anxious to take his home.

Now he was scowling with mock ferocity at Jason. "Traitor," he murmured, but there was a note of laughter in his voice.

"Bye, Mom. See you, Dad. Good luck."

Lacey approached the bed cautiously. "Now just why would you be in need of luck?"

"I'm a sick man," he said in a pathetically weak tone that was so obviously feigned, Lacey almost burst out laughing.

"I need luck, prayers, whatever it takes," he added for good measure.

"Nice try," she said.

Kevin managed to look genuinely dismayed. "You don't believe me?"

"I don't believe you," she concurred. "Try again."

"Have you seen Linc today?"

Her gaze narrowed as the first faint suspicion flickered in her mind. "What does Linc have to do with this?"

"He's agreed to let me out of here on Sunday."

"Kevin, that's wonderful!" she blurted out instinctively before she caught the glimmer of satisfaction in his eyes.

"What's the rest?" she asked slowly.

He folded his hands across his chest and inquired complacently, "What makes you think there's anything more?"

"Oh, please. I know you. If it were a simple matter of getting out of here on Sunday, you wouldn't look so smug."

"Smug? I was aiming for helpless."

"You couldn't look helpless if you tried. Come on, spill it. What's the rest?"

"There's a condition to my release."

Lacey got an uneasy feeling in the pit of her stomach, as suspicion replaced amusement. "What condition?"

"That I have someone around to look after me."

She ignored the return of the obvious gleam in his

eyes and asked briskly, "Isn't our housekeeper there?"

At the quick shake of his head, she very nearly moaned. He'd never liked the stiff, unyielding woman, but he'd never been willing to fire her, either. "Kevin, you haven't fought with her, have you?"

"Actually, I had Jason send her off to visit her sister in Florida."

"Tell her to come back. I'm sure she'd cooperate under the circumstances."

"Afraid not."

"Why?"

"Well, the truth of the matter is that I fired her."

"You what?"

"I was never there, anyway," he said defensively. "So you see, I can't go home."

"Then you'll go to your father's. Mrs. Farnsworth would love the chance to fuss over you."

"I suppose that would work," he said. "But you know Dad. It wouldn't be long before he'd want to have business discussions over breakfast, lunch and dinner."

There was more than a little truth in that, Lacey conceded reluctantly. She knew now exactly where Kevin was headed, had known all along that some version of this game would come up sooner or later. Even so, she didn't have a ready, convincing alternative.

"Jason has room," she said desperately.

"What about Sammy?" he countered neatly.

Obviously he'd planned this as skillfully as a master chess player, Lacey thought, trying to muster up her fading resolve as he went on.

"I'll need peace and quiet," Kevin added for good

measure. ''You can't expect a kid that age to be on good behavior for days on end. Besides, Dana shouldn't have to take care of a sick father-in-law when she's trying to prepare for a baby.''

''I think she'll have plenty of time to prepare after you're fully recuperated,'' Lacey retorted dryly.

She didn't have a strong argument where Sammy was concerned, however. Kevin was right to be worried about Dana's younger brother. He would probably try to engage Kevin in heated video games. With her husband's spirit of competitiveness, he'd land right back in the hospital.

''You could be right about Sammy, though,'' she admitted reluctantly. ''Maybe Jason could loan you Mrs. Willis and you could just stay at home.''

''I have a better idea,'' Kevin said cheerfully.

''Why doesn't that surprise me,'' she muttered darkly, envisioning the two of them in her cramped little apartment or, worse yet, back in their own home.

''I thought you and I could go to the Cape. It would be peaceful there this time of year.''

Peaceful? she thought, stunned by the suggestion. The two of them alone on Cape Cod? No, that wouldn't be peaceful. It would be lunacy.

Cape Cod was where they'd made love for the very first time. Cape Cod was where he'd proposed to her. Cape Cod was where Jason had been conceived. Cape Cod was chock-full of memories. She had no intention of subjecting herself to that kind of torture.

''No,'' she said adamantly, ''absolutely not.''

''It would be good for us, Lacey. You have to admit that.''

Lacey felt as if the walls of the room were closing in on her. It wasn't just the early memories. Later, nostalgic for all they had shared on Cape Cod, they had bought a house there. It was the one outrageously expensive indulgence that she had approved of totally.

They had made a pact that no business problems could ever follow them there. That house had become their refuge, a place for quiet talks, long walks and slow, sensuous sex. Kevin had kept his part of the bargain—until the day he'd stopped going because he no longer had time for the simple pleasure of a relaxing, intimate vacation.

Of all the suggestions he might have made, this was the most wickedly clever. The memories they shared there were among their most powerfully seductive.

She met his gaze and saw that he knew exactly what he was asking of her.

"Please, Lacey," he coaxed. "You did promise we would talk."

She was shaking her head before the words were out of his mouth. "I didn't promise to move back in with you. It won't work, Kevin."

"It will if we want it to. I'm ready to try. What about you?" He studied her closely, then added, "Or have you given up on our marriage?"

There was no mistaking the dare. Lacey cursed the tidy way Kevin had backed her into a corner. He knew how desperately she wanted to salvage what they'd once had. If she turned him down, she was as much as admitting that she'd given up hope.

Or that she was afraid.

She couldn't deny the fear that curled within her at the thought of what might happen if she gave in to his plan. If she accepted, if she went to the Cape and nothing had changed, she wasn't sure she could bear the pain of another separation and inevitably a divorce.

Now at least the worst days were behind her. She'd begun picking up the pieces of her life, creating a world in which Kevin was no longer the center. She liked the strength she'd discovered within herself.

But if that strength were real, if she'd truly gained her independence, wouldn't she be able to cope no matter what happened? She could practically hear him taunting her with that, though in reality he said nothing. Maybe it was simply her brain arguing with her heart.

All of the questions and none of the answers flashed through her mind in no more than an instant. Lacey studied Kevin's face and saw the uncertainty, the wistfulness in his eyes. It mirrored what she felt in her heart, the hope that had never died.

"I'll go," she said finally. She'd thought the risk of leaving Kevin had been dangerous enough. The risk of going back was a thousand times greater. She had to try, though. She would never forgive herself if she didn't.

"Thank you," he said simply. And she knew from the way time seemed to stand still as she met his gaze that her decision had been the right one, the only one.

No matter how much it might hurt later.

Kevin had the entire, endless night to think about Lacey's answer. He knew what it had taken for her to overcome her reluctance. The look in her eyes had spoken volumes about the struggle that raged inside her. He swore that he would do whatever it took to overcome her doubts. He viewed the coming days as a honeymoon of sorts, a chance to put their marriage on a new, more solid footing.

And he began making careful plans.

"I'll take care of everything," Brandon announced the following morning when he learned of their arrangement, which he clearly viewed as permanent. "Over the years I've learned a thing or two about patching things up after a spat."

"I'm sure you have," Kevin agreed, recalling the flurry of expensive gifts that would pour in whenever his father and mother argued.

His mother would point to a piece of jewelry and say, "This was for the time he stayed the whole night through at the factory and forgot to call. And these earrings were for that time he didn't tell me he'd invited guests for dinner and showed up with two of his most important customers."

Kevin grinned at the memories, but held up his hand. "Slow down, Dad. I think I'll handle this one my way. Besides, Jason's already called the caretaker. The house will be ready for us."

"What about flowers? Never was a woman who could resist a few bouquets of flowers."

"Like the five dozen roses you sent Mom, when you forgot your anniversary? Or the orchids that came when you missed her birthday?"

Brandon scowled at him. "Okay, so I had a lousy head for dates. Your mother loved those flowers just the same."

"Yes, she did," Kevin said softly, "because they came from you. Let me deal with Lacey my own way, Dad."

Brandon went on as if he hadn't heard a word Kevin was saying. "Maybe I ought to take a drive out there and check on things. You can't trust strangers to remember everything."

Kevin groaned as he envisioned his father standing

in the doorway to welcome them. Lacey would no doubt turn tail and run. Although, on second thought, she might welcome a buffer between them. Either way, Kevin had no intention of letting Brandon meddle in this particular scenario.

"Forget it, Dad. For a man who spent years trying to keep us apart, you're suddenly awfully anxious for us to get back together."

Brandon didn't rise to the bait. "I'm not one bit afraid to admit I've made mistakes in my life. A few of them have been doozies. I know what I did back then to try to ruin what you two had was wrong. Lacey's a fine woman. You couldn't have done better."

"I know that. I'm glad you can see it now, too."

"You think this plan of yours is going to work?" he inquired, his brow furrowed. "Seems mighty chancy."

Kevin sighed. "It is a risk. If it doesn't work, I'll just have to come up with another idea. I'm not going to let her go without a fight, Dad. Not a second time. Come on. Let's go for a walk around the corridor. I'm going to need all my strength back if I'm going into battle tomorrow."

As they walked the length of the hospital hallway, Kevin saw the elevator doors slide open. He paused and watched, unwilling to admit how much he was hoping Lacey would be among those getting off. When she emerged behind a group of nurses, he spotted her at once, astonished at how youthful she looked with her honey-blond hair skimming her shoulders, her cheeks tinted pink from the March winds.

She started toward his room, then noticed him out of the corner of her eye. She turned his way, a smile spreading slowly across her face.

"I like the fancy new pajamas," she said, grinning at the outrageously expensive pair Brandon had brought him from a British collection made with Halloran fabrics.

Kevin would never have worn them if the only alternative hadn't been one of those indecent hospital gowns. In fact, as he thought back, the last pair of pajamas he'd owned had had bunny rabbits on them and he'd been going to sleep with a pacifier.

"What's wrong with them?" Brandon demanded. "This is one of the finest cottons we make. Do you have any idea what they charge for these things?"

"Settle down, Dad. I'm sure Lacey is truly awed by the quality."

"Awed isn't quite the word I had in mind," she teased. "I think I saw a pair just like these in some forties movie with Claudette Colbert. Or was it Katharine Hepburn?"

"Okay, enough, you two," Brandon grumbled. He shot a pointed glance at Kevin. "You could be walking up and down these hallways with your bottom bare."

Kevin sneaked a look at Lacey, whose lips were twitching as she fought the urge to laugh. She refused to meet his gaze. Brandon sniffed.

"Think I'll go off and leave you two alone. It's obvious you don't need me around anymore."

"Goodbye, Dad."

Lacey gave him a peck on the cheek and murmured something Kevin couldn't quite hear. From the amusement that immediately sparked in his father's eyes, Kevin had a hunch it had something to do with the damned pajamas.

When she finally turned back to Kevin, her expression was as innocent as a new baby's.

"What'd you say to him?" Kevin demanded.

"That's our secret."

"I thought secrets were taboo in a healthy marriage."

"Some secrets are taboo. Others add spice."

"You and my father have a secret that's going to add spice to our marriage?"

She grinned at him impishly. "You never know."

He regarded her indignantly. "You know, Lacey Halloran, it has occurred to me that locking myself away in a house on the Cape with you could drive me nuts."

"Not my fault," she claimed innocently. "It was your idea."

"And you intend to make me pay for that, don't you?"

"The regimen I have planned for you will make basic training seem like child's play."

He watched the play of light on her streaked blond hair and the sparks of mischief in her eyes. "What does Linc have to say about this plan you have?"

"Who do you think gave it to me?"

She waved several booklets without allowing him to catch a glimpse of the titles. He had to take her word for it when she flipped through them.

"'Cholesterol Management.' 'Triglycerides and You.' 'Exercise for the Healthy Heart.' 'The Low-Fat Diet.' And my favorite, 'Heart-Friendly Fruits and Vegetables.' I can hardly wait."

"I could still go to Jason's, you know. Sammy's beginning to look like a saint compared to my wife."

"I hear he has the newest video game. You very well might want to reconsider," she said agreeably.

He stopped where he was and framed her face with his hands. He could feel the heat climb in her cheeks. "Not a chance, Mrs. Halloran. Not a chance."

Chapter Six

The promise of long, quiet, intimate days on Cape Cod with Kevin terrified Lacey. It was possible—likely, even—that their expectations were entirely different. Anticipation and worry made the drive from the hospital to the Cape seem longer than ever.

What if Kevin only intended to lure her back, but hadn't thought beyond the challenge of the chase? she worried, when the first deadly silence fell.

She had little doubt that he could seduce her, that he could scramble her emotions and turn her best intentions to mush. Even in the worst of times, she had responded all too easily to his touch. The loving had been wonderful, but toward the end it hadn't been nearly enough. Now it would be a short-term solution at best.

A trip like this was what Lacey had been longing for, but now that Kevin had made the commitment to spend time with her, she wondered what would happen if they couldn't recapture what they had lost. In a last-ditch desperation, were they pinning too much on this time alone? Was she expecting something from Kevin that he couldn't possibly give?

As she clutched the steering wheel with white-knuckled intensity, her thoughts tumbled like bits of colored glass in a kaleidoscope, leaving her hopelessly confused.

Beside her, Kevin had settled back in the seat and closed his eyes, no more anxious to continue the struggle for nervous, meaningless small talk than she was.

With a bone-deep sorrow, Lacey couldn't help noticing the contrast to other trips they had made, times when the car had been filled with laughter and quiet conversation as they made the transition from their harried life-style in Boston to the relaxation of Cape Cod. Then even the silences had been lazy and comfortable. The anticipation had been sweet, not mixed with a vague sense of dread as it was now.

She breathed a sigh of relief when she finally pulled into the driveway of the rambling old house with its weathered gray shingles and white trim. A few hardy geraniums bloomed in the window boxes, the splashes of red against gray reminding her of an Andrew Wyeth painting she particularly loved.

She vividly recalled the precise moment when she and Kevin had first come upon this place, choosing it over all the others they had seen because of its haphazard wandering over a spectacular oceanfront piece of property. Later in the spring there would be daffodils and tulips everywhere and the scent of lilacs from a bush near the kitchen window.

Lacey glanced over and saw that Kevin was awake,

his intense gaze closely examining the house that had once been so special to them.

"It looks neglected," he observed ruefully. "When was the last time we were out here?"

"Together?" she questioned pointedly. "Three years ago. We drove out for the day."

He regarded her with astonishment. "Surely that can't be."

"You've been too busy," she reminded him, trying—and failing—to keep the note of censure out of her voice.

He sighed. "That excuse must have worn thin. I remember how much you always loved coming here, especially this time of year before the summer crowds came back."

Kevin leaned closer, his breath fanning her face. He trailed his knuckles along her cheek, stirring her senses. She turned into the caress, and his fingers stroked her skin. The pad of his thumb skimmed provocatively over her lips.

"I'm sorry, Lace. I truly am."

She could tell from the look in his eyes that he really meant it, and something deep inside her shifted, making room for emotions she wasn't yet prepared to handle. Trying to ignore the trembly feeling he could still evoke in her, Lacey swallowed hard. She pulled away and summoned a smile.

"No more apologies, remember? We're here now." Her tone turned brisk. "We'd better get you inside. Linc wasn't all that thrilled that you wanted to come here, rather than stay in Boston."

"He just hates the fact that he won't be able to run up my bill with all those house calls," Kevin said as he opened the door and got out, following her to the trunk.

Instinctively he reached for a bag as they began the familiar ritual of unloading the car. Worried about the strain on his still-healing heart, Lacey quickly waved him off. "I'll get these."

A rare flash of anger rose in his eyes, then died just as quickly. "You're right," he said stiffly. "I'll go unlock the door. I should be able to manage that much at least."

Lacey cursed the fact that she'd reminded him that for now he wasn't as vital and healthy as he'd always been. Kevin had never been able to cope with so much as a cold, hating the slightest sign of weakness in a body he'd always tested to the limits. He looked so strong, with his powerful shoulders and well-sculpted legs, that she herself could almost forget that inside he was not yet healed.

Tennis, sailing and, years earlier, football—he had played them all with demanding intensity. How difficult it must be for him now to defer the simplest tasks to her. Still, Linc's instructions had been specific, and she intended to follow them to the letter.

There was no sign of Kevin as she made the half dozen trips to carry their luggage inside. He had vanished as soon as he'd opened the front door for her.

After an instant's hesitation, Lacey placed his bags in the master bedroom and her own in the guest room across the hall. The width of that hall was no more than three feet, but she saw it as symbolic of the ever-widening chasm between them in their marriage.

Worried that Kevin was still not inside—on such a chilly, blustery day—his first out of the hospital—she went in search of him.

She found him at last in back of the house, standing atop of a distant sand dune. Wearing only a thin jacket, a knit shirt and jeans, he had his hands in his pockets, his shoulders hunched against the wind. He was staring out to a white-capped sea that roared its strength as it crashed against the shore.

Guessing a little of what he must be feeling, Lacey walked to his side, hesitated, then tucked her arm through his.

"It certainly is setting up a fuss today, isn't it?" she observed.

At first she didn't think he would answer her, either out of some lingering resentment or because he was lost in his own thoughts. Finally he glanced at her, then back to the ocean and said, "I'd forgotten what that sound is like, how it fills up your head, driving out all petty annoyances."

"Like a symphony. Isn't that what you told me once?"

Kevin shook his head, clearly bemused by the words. "Was I ever that poetic?"

"I thought you were."

He turned and met her gaze then. Lacey thought for a moment she could see straight into his soul. Such sadness. It made her ache to think of him hurting so deeply. Yet her own sorrow was just as deep, just as heart-wrenching.

"Past tense," he noted wearily.

This time she lifted her fingers to caress his cheek. "Don't," she said softly. "Please don't. We have to make a pact to stop looking back. We have to look ahead."

"I'm not sure I dare."

Surprised by the genuine note of dismay in his voice, she asked, "Why?"

"What if there's only emptiness? Without you, that's all it would be, you know."

Hearing him say the words, hearing him admit how much she meant to him should have made her feel deliriously happy. But she was no longer that shy, innocent girl who'd given her heart so freely. Instead, knowing all she did, she felt this terrible pressure—pressure to forget the differences that had brought them to this moment, this place.

A part of Lacey wanted to give in now and promise him that everything would be as it always had been. She desperately needed to believe that coming here had been enough to reassure her. But the part of her that listened to her brain, rather than her heart, knew it was far too soon for either of them to make a commitment like that. Despite the pretty words, Kevin was no more ready for promises than she was.

She touched his cheek again, her splayed fingers warm against his chilled flesh, the gesture meant to comfort, not to promise. Their gazes met, caught, lingered. The silent communication was filled with hope and wistful yearning.

"I'm going to start dinner," she told him after several seconds passed. "Don't stay out here too long. It will be dark soon and the air is already cold and damp."

His gaze once again on the sea, he nodded and let her go.

Inside, Lacey found the refrigerator already well stocked with groceries, including a container of clam chowder left by the caretaker with a note saying it was from his grandmother. She poured it into a cast iron kettle on the stove, turned the flame on low and went to check more thoroughly on the rest of the house.

Everything had been readied for them. A fire had been laid and extra wood was stacked beside the hearth. Without the salty haze that would be back again within hours, the just-washed windows glistened with the last soft rays of sunlight. The wide plank floors had been rubbed to a soft glow, the furniture polished with something that smelled of lemons.

Best of all, a huge basket of her favorite spring flowers—daffodils, tulips and lily of the valley—added a cheerful finishing touch. Brandon's romantic idea, no doubt.

If Lacey hadn't known how long the house had stood empty, she might have believed she and Kevin had been here only yesterday. As it was, she hadn't been able to bear more than a quick day trip now and again. Alone, she had been all too vividly reminded of what she and Kevin had lost. The ache in her heart had been too much so she had never lingered.

Now she touched the automatic lighter to the kindling in the fireplace. Within minutes, the flames had caught and a cozy warmth stole through the chilly room.

Back in the kitchen she grabbed a handful of silver and a pair of placemats and set places on the coffee table in front of the fire. When they were here alone, they rarely ate in the formal dining room or even in the huge old kitchen, preferring the intimacy of meals in front of the fire's warmth. Only on the hottest days of summer did the routine vary and then they moved to the beach, where they could listen to the waves and watch the stars as they ate by candlelight.

Kevin came in just as she was pulling a loaf of

crusty, homemade bread from the oven. His eyes lit up as he shrugged out of his jacket and tossed it over the back of a chair.

"Is that what I think it is?" he asked, coming closer to sniff the wonderful aroma.

"Mrs. Renfield's homemade bread," she confirmed. "And her New England clam chowder. Your favorites."

"What can I do to help?"

"If you'll take the bread in, I'll bring the soup. That should do it."

"I don't suppose she left one of her peach pies in the refrigerator."

"Sorry," Lacey said, amused at his immediately disappointed expression. "Looks like a cherry cobbler to me. And don't tell me you didn't know perfectly well that she was going to leave all this for you. You probably called her up and pleaded with her."

"I did no such thing."

"Then you had Jason do it."

He grinned at her. "Okay, maybe I did suggest he drop a few hints."

"Are you sure he didn't do more than that?"

"Such as?"

"Sending her a few bolts of that outrageously expensive fabric she loves so much."

Kevin grinned guiltily. "A few yards, not a few bolts."

"Do you realize that that seventy-five-year-old grandmother uses that cloth to whip up fancy pot holders for the church bazaar?"

"She does not," he said, his expression clearly scandalized at the waste.

Lacey picked up one of the pot holders she'd used

to carry in the steaming bowls of chowder. "Recognize this?"

Kevin groaned. "Oh, dear Lord. Don't ever let Dad see that."

"Too late. He bought up every one she had at the bazaar last year. He was terrified one of Halloran's customers would see them and realize they were designing ball gowns made out of the same material."

Lacey felt her lips curving into a smile as Kevin's laughter bubbled forth. It had been so long since she'd heard him sound genuinely happy.

"Can you imagine Miriam Grayson discovering that her latest couture creation matched Mrs. Renfield's pot holders?" Kevin said, still chuckling. "Her designer would wind up skewered with one of her lethal, pearl-tipped hat pins."

"I believe Brandon mentioned the same scenario. For about thirty seconds he actually seemed tempted to risk it."

"I'm not surprised. Old Miriam is a pompous pain in the you-know-what. However, her designer is one of Halloran's best customers. Dad obviously had second thoughts the minute he envisioned the impact on the company's bottom line."

As silly and inconsequential as the conversation was, Lacey couldn't help thinking it was the first time in months that she and Kevin had actually shared so much carefree laughter. She would have to remember to thank Mrs. Renfield by slipping her a few yards of that emerald-green silk that would go so well with her bright eyes—after warning her to use it on a dress, not pot holders.

The tone of the evening seemed set after that. Kevin and Lacey reminisced about other trips and other neighbors. They recalled clam bakes and bake sales, art festivals and favorite restaurants. Here, unlike Boston, they had always felt part of the quiet, casual rhythm of the community, had had time for neighborly visits and lingering over tea.

Lacey felt Kevin's gaze on her and regarded him quizzically. ''What?''

''This is the way I always think of you,'' he said, brushing a strand of her hair back and letting it spill through his fingers.

''How?'' she said. Her breath caught in her throat as her pulse scrambled wildly.

''The firelight in your hair, your eyes sparkling, a smile on your lips. Are you happy to be here, Lacey?''

Unable to speak, she simply nodded.

''With me?''

That question was more difficult to answer honestly. Being here with Kevin was bittersweet at best. She could almost believe things were perfect. Almost.

And then she would remember.

He sighed. ''Obviously, I shouldn't have pressed,'' he said, his voice tight.

Stricken by the hurt in his eyes, she said, ''Kevin, this isn't a quick fix. It's a beginning.''

He nodded, then stood up. ''I'm more tired than I thought.''

Lacey started to force him to stay, force him to confront the very real ordeal ahead of them. Then she bowed to the exhaustion on his face. ''Your things are in the master bedroom.''

''And yours?'' he asked very slowly.

''Across the hall. I thought it was best.''

''As always, I'm sure you're right,'' he retorted not attempting to conceal the sarcasm. He pivoted then and walked away, leaving Lacey alone to face the fire and the long, empty hours ahead before sleep would claim her.

Kevin stood at the window of the master bedroom, his eyes gazing blankly into the darkness of a moonless night. The sound of the waves did nothing to soothe him.

Maybe this had been a terrible idea, after all. Maybe instead of bringing him and Lacey closer, staying here would only remind her of what had gone wrong.

What did she want? he wondered angrily. Lacey had always expected him to live up to some impossible ideal, and he'd tried. Lord, how he had tried. But in the end, he'd proven himself to be a mere mortal. Maybe that would never be enough for her.

He listened as the door across the hall closed softly, and he found his hands balling into fists.

Rest, Linc had told him. How could he rest, when the woman he loved was holding him at a distance, when his body ached to feel her next to him again?

He hadn't grown used to the emptiness of their huge bed in Boston. Though this one was smaller, it would be just as cold and unwelcoming without her there beside him. He stared at it bleakly, and for one brief second he considered grabbing his blankets and sleeping in one of the other guest rooms.

Kevin saw the folly of that at once. He could sleep in any bed in the house and Lacey's nearness would taunt him. He would sense her presence in his very gut. The unmistakable, seductive scent of her favorite floral perfume was everywhere in this house. He would lie there surrounded by her, yet unable to touch her.

Exhaustion finally propelled him across the room. He stretched out on the bed, the sheet skimming his naked flesh and reminding him all too clearly of his wife's first, delicate caresses. The aching arousal was almost painful, but in its own way reassuring. If the attraction burned this brightly for him, surely it could not have died for Lacey. It would take time, that was all. Time to discover each other anew. Time to heal.

Time to fall in love all over again.

Chapter Seven

If they had ended the previous evening walking on eggshells, the morning was starting out to be a hundred times worse. Lacey was so painfully careful and polite Kevin was sure he was going to scream.

Not that he could blame her after the way he'd treated her when he'd found out about the sleeping arrangements. Morning had given him a different perspective on how he'd handled things. Had he honestly expected her to tumble into his arms just because she'd agreed to come to the Cape with him? Hoped, maybe. Expected, no.

As he'd anticipated, their bed had seemed incredibly empty without her. He'd lain awake for hours wishing she were close enough to touch, wishing he could feel the soft feathering of her breath against his skin. He'd ached for just a hint of their old physical intimacy. Toward dawn he had reconciled himself to the unlikelihood of that happening for weeks, maybe longer. Not until she trusted him again.

Even though Kevin accepted much of the blame for the way things were between them, the saccharine politeness to which Lacey was now subjecting him grated.

"More decaf?" she inquired, every bit as solicitous as a well-trained waitress, and just as impersonal.

"No," he responded curtly. He blamed the surliness in his tone on the hours he'd spent counting sheep and trying not to think of Lacey in that bed across the hall.

"Another piece of toast?"

"I've had plenty."

"Did you want the A section of the paper?"

"No."

"Sports?"

"No."

Lacey nodded and retreated behind the local section. In self-defense Kevin grabbed the section atop the stack in front of her. Business, he noted with a modicum of enthusiasm. Maybe that would keep his mind occupied. He could concentrate on mergers and takeovers, instead of the way Lacey's ice-blue sweater clung to her curves and brought out the color of her eyes.

One of the hazards of being in the textile business, he'd discovered long ago, was the need to scrutinize fabrics. When they were worn by his wife, it was doubly difficult to focus his attention elsewhere.

Damn, he hated the last instruction Linc had given him. No sex, the doctor had warned. At Kevin's horrified expression, he'd added, "Soon, but absolutely not right away. A little patience won't hurt you."

That was easy for Linc to say. He wasn't seated

across the table from a woman he hadn't held in his arms for months, a woman who had never seemed so desirable or so aloof. Kevin knew that if he could just hold Lacey, caress her, then the distance and uneasiness between them would melt away.

Instead, he was going to have to rely on his wits. The prospect daunted him. Maybe if he thought of this as a deal he needed to close, a strategy would come to him. The thought of Lacey's reaction to being compared with a business deal brought a smile to his lips.

She folded the last section of the paper and apparently caught him still grinning.

"What's so funny?"

"Nothing," he said hurriedly. "What would you like to do today?"

"Do?" she repeated blankly. "You're here to recuperate, not to fill up every spare minute. It's called relaxation. You do remember how that works, don't you?"

"Barely," he admitted.

She nodded and he could see from the amusement in her eyes that the dark mood had lifted. He wasn't deceiving himself, though. It could return as quickly as it had gone.

"Then lesson one is that we make no plans," Lacey said. "We do whatever we feel like doing. For starters, there's a stack of new books in the living room. And since it looks as if it's going to pour any minute, that makes this the perfect day to curl up in front of the fire with a good book."

"Sounds good to me. Did you bring that new management book? I haven't had time to get to it yet."

Lacey shot him a disapproving frown. "No management books. Try mysteries, political thrillers, maybe a biography, as long as it's not about some titan of industry. Remember when we used to spend all day sitting out back, doing nothing more than reading and sipping iced tea?''

''Vaguely. Are you sure I wasn't reading management books?''

She grinned. ''Positive.''

''Political tracts?''

''Afraid not.''

''I was reading fiction?'' He was incredulous.

She nodded. ''At the beach you read fiction. Actually I take that back. If I recall correctly, you fell asleep with the books in your hands. I can't swear that you read any of them.''

''No wonder not one single plot comes back to me.''

She smiled, then, and leaned closer. To his surprise she laced her fingers through his.

''It's going to be okay,'' she promised. ''This awkwardness will pass.''

''Will it?'' he questioned doubtfully. ''Sometimes I feel as if I'm an amnesiac trying to recall a part of my life that's completely blanked out. You seem to have such a vivid recollection of the way things used to be.''

Lacey sighed and withdrew her hand. ''Maybe I do live too much in the past. Maybe it's wrong to want to go back. But I think about how perfectly attuned we were, how much we treasured quiet moments, and I can't help having regrets. Now we can't even get through a single evening without arguing.''

Kevin couldn't deny the truth in that. ''We aren't the same people we were when we met. Lacey, we were eleven years old. We were kids.''

''We were the same way when we were twenty-one, even thirty-one,'' she reminded him, suddenly angry. ''We were on the same wavelength. We shared everything. We could practically finish each other's sentences, though thank God we didn't. It all started to change—''

''When I went to work at Halloran,'' he finished for her, his own temper flaring. How long did she intend to throw that decision back in his face? ''Why is going to work for my father so terrible? Jason's there, too. I don't hear you criticizing him for making that choice.''

''It was his *choice,* Kevin. It was what he always wanted. You were railroaded into it by Brandon.''

The last of Kevin's patience snapped. ''Was our life so rosy before that? Don't you remember the way we had to squeeze every last penny out of every dollar we made? Don't you remember the nights I came home so frustrated and angry that my jaws ached from clenching my teeth? Don't you remember how we both woke up one day to the fact that no matter what we did, no matter how hard we worked to fight the system, the system wasn't going to change unless we worked within it?'' He slammed his fist down on the table. ''For God's sake, Lacey, we aren't idealistic children anymore.''

Her eyes widened during his tirade, then slowly filled with hurt. ''Is that what you think, that I haven't grown up? Is that it, Kevin? If so, then maybe we're wasting our time here, after all.''

Her jaw set, she picked up the breakfast dishes and carried them to the counter. Her back to him, he could see the deep sigh shudder through her in the instant before she slammed the dishes down so hard it was a wonder they didn't shatter. She grabbed her jacket from a peg by the back door and stormed out, leaving him filled with rage and the uneasy sense that this brief but cutting argument might well have been their last.

He hadn't meant to accuse her of immaturity. It wasn't that at all. But it was true that she tended to cling to ideals, rather than deal with the practicalities. Looking at Halloran's bottom line had put things into the right perspective for him. He'd been able to provide for his family, give them the way of life they deserved. He had helped Brandon to make the company even stronger, kept him from at least some of his own wild schemes that would have cut deeply into their profits. Jason would have a legacy now, as would his child. What more did Lacey want from him?

Kevin waited anxiously after that, starting each time he thought he heard a sound. He wanted to finish the argument, make her see his point of view for once.

His frayed nerves grew worse with each passing hour. By mid-morning, with rain pelting the windows with the force of sleet, he was worried sick. Where was she?

He consoled himself with the thought that no one would stay outdoors in weather like this. Surely she had taken refuge with one of the neighbors. He glanced repeatedly out the front window to reassure himself that the car was still in the driveway, that she'd hadn't taken it and fled.

When Lacey wasn't back by noon, worry turned to anger. She had to know what she was doing to him, he thought. She could have called, let him know that she was safe and dry.

As quickly as the fury rose, though, it abated. What if she weren't safe? What if she had fallen and hurt herself? What if she were cold and wet, stranded on the beach somewhere, caught by a rising tide? *What ifs* chased through his mind and turned the canned soup he'd forced himself to eat into acid in his stomach.

It was nearly one o'clock when Kevin heard Lacey's footsteps on the back porch. He threw open the door and found her standing there looking soaked and bedraggled. Even as he met her gaze, he saw her shiver, her whole body trembling violently. The patches of color in her cheeks were too vivid. Her lips had an unhealthy bluish tint. She looked as if she might keel over into his arms.

"My God," he murmured, pulling her inside. "Did you decide to go for a swim?"

Her teeth chattered as she tried to answer.

Fury evaporated as he focused on her needs. There would be time enough for recriminations later. "Never mind," he said. "Let's get you out of these clothes and into a warm tub."

He reached for her jacket, but she pushed his hands away. "To-o-o c-c-old," she murmured.

"Well, this soggy mess won't do much to change that. Come on, Lacey, take it off. I'll go get you a blanket and you can sit in front of the fire while I run the bath water."

Teeth still chattering, she nodded finally and began working at the buttons. Satisfied that she was going to follow instructions, Kevin went into the bedroom and pulled the quilt off his bed. When he got back to the kitchen with it, he halted in the doorway, his expression stunned.

Lacey had stripped down to her underwear—scraps of lace that hid nothing, including the fact that her nipples had peaked into hard buds from the chill air. He drew in a ragged breath and forced himself to sacrifice his need to study every inch of her lovely, fragile body that had changed so little through the years. He wrapped her in the quilt and held her close until the violent shivering stopped.

With his chin resting on the quilt draped over her shoulders, he asked, "Better?"

"Much," she said, her voice finally steady.

"Then go sit in front of the fire, okay?"

Lacey nodded, then turned to meet his gaze. "Thanks."

"For what?"

"For not telling me what a fool I am."

He grinned. "I'm saving that for later."

After an instant's pause she managed a wobbly grin of her own. "I should have known."

When the bath water had been drawn and the tub was filled with her favorite fragrant bubbles, he called her into the bathroom. She drew in a deep breath of the steamy air.

"Heaven," she declared.

"I'll warm up some soup for you. Don't stay too long," he said, wishing he dared to linger, wishing she would invite him to join her in that oversized tub as she had so often in the past. Imagining her skin slick and sensitized beneath his touch made his body grow taut.

Her gaze rose to meet his, and he could tell from the smoldering look in her eyes that she remembered, too, and that she could see exactly what the memories were doing to him. "I won't be long," she promised.

Reluctantly Kevin closed the door, then leaned against it, suddenly weak with longing. Oh, how he ached for her. How badly he wanted to hold her, to caress her, to claim her once more as his own. The longing spread through him, a slow flame that warmed and lured. If he knew anything at all about his wife, she too was burning. She too was filled with a sweet, aching need that nothing short of tender caresses and uninhibited passion would satisfy.

He forced himself to go back into the kitchen, to throw Lacey's soggy clothes into the washer, to pour a healthy serving of soup into the saucepan on the stove. The routine got him through the worst of the wanting. He was even able to have a perfectly rational discussion with himself about the dangers of rushing things.

Not that it meant a hill of beans when Lacey walked back into the kitchen with her blond hair curling damply around her face, her skin glowing from the fragrant steam. His body told him exactly what he could do with all of his rationalizations.

The only thing that saved him from making an absolute fool of himself was the way his wife pounced on the soup as if she hadn't eaten in days. Only when she'd finished the entire bowl, sighed and leaned back to sip a cup of tea did he dare to speak.

"Where did you go this morning?" He was proud of the casual tone.

"For a walk on the beach."

"In the pouring rain? Were you that furious with me?"

She shrugged. "I was furious, but the truth of the matter is that it wasn't raining when I left. I was a couple of miles up the beach before it got really bad. I started to head back, but by then the tide had come in and I couldn't get around the point. When I realized it wasn't going to let up anytime soon, I climbed the cliff."

Kevin's eyes widened. "You're terrified of heights."

"I'm not so thrilled with the idea of catching pneumonia, either. I figured climbing was the lesser of two evils. I only panicked once when I made the mistake of looking down. It wasn't all that far, but it looked damned treacherous and slippery."

"It *is* treacherous and slippery. You could have broken your neck."

"But I didn't," she said, looking pleased with herself.

He hesitated, then finally said, "Should we talk about what happened this morning?"

Her smile faded. "Not now. I'm exhausted."

Though he was reluctant to put the discussion off any longer, he nodded. "Go on and take a nap then. I'll clean up here."

She shook her head. "I think I'll go sit in front of the fire instead."

She stood up and started for the door, then turned back. "Kevin?"

He stopped halfway between the table and the sink. "Yes?"

"Will you come join me when you're finished?"

Irritated that even this small overture aroused him to a state of aching desire, he nearly refused. Then he caught the wistfulness in her eyes and realized that to deny them both a moment's pleasure was absurd.

"I'll be there in a minute," he promised.

Lacey wasn't entirely sure what impulse had made her ask Kevin to join her in the living room. Goodness knew the man had infuriated her earlier with the suggestion that she was behaving immaturely just because she wanted her husband healthy and happy again. Of course, she'd only added proof to his claim by running out. She should have stayed and talked, held her temper and listened to his explanation. That was the only way this was going to work.

They needed so desperately to talk. She needed to comprehend why he'd been so quick to condemn her attitude. He needed to understand exactly what she was trying to recapture. They both needed to discover if there was any common ground left at all. They couldn't do that without putting all their cards on the table, even the ones most likely to hurt.

She was too tired now to get into it again, but asking Kevin to join her in the living room had been an overture, at least. It had been impossible to miss the longing in his eyes when he'd come upon her in the middle of the kitchen with nothing but bra and panties keeping her decent. That longing had turned to desire as he'd stood beside the tub watching her lower herself into the foam of lilac-scented bubbles. Lacey knew exactly what Kevin was feeling, because it had taken every ounce of willpower she possessed to refrain from inviting him to share the bath with her.

All the talking and listening would have to wait, though. Now she wanted nothing more than to curl up on the sofa and stare at the mesmerizing flames. She wanted only to let the fire's heat soak into her bones.

As it did, she could feel herself relaxing, feel her eyes drifting shut. She blinked and forced herself awake. She wanted to stay awake until Kevin was by her side, but tension, exercise and fear had exhausted her. Her eyes closed again.

She had only the vaguest sense when Kevin joined her on the sofa. When he whispered her name, she thought she responded, but couldn't be sure. Then she felt herself being resettled in his arms, and it was as if she'd come home at last. A sigh trembled on her lips, and then she slept as she hadn't slept in all the lonely months they'd been apart.

Chapter Eight

Kevin stood in the doorway of the kitchen watching the play of sunlight on Lacey's hair. She'd left it loose, not bothering to tame the haphazard curls that framed her face. It shimmered with silver and gold highlights, reminding him of the way it had looked on their wedding day.

There was something radiant and serene about her today, just as there had been then. However she felt about yesterday's disagreements, she had obviously pushed them out of her mind. She looked beautiful, despite the fact that she was elbow-deep in dirt that was still damp from the previous day's rain.

"What on earth are you doing?" he inquired as she scowled fiercely at something she saw.

In response, a clump of weeds flew over her shoulder and landed at his feet.

"I'm trying to make some order out of this mess.

The weeds have taken over,'' she muttered without turning to look at him.

''Why don't you call Rick Renfield and have him do it? Isn't that what we pay him for?''

''We pay him to keep an eye on the house, to make sure the pipes don't freeze, to see that the grass is cut. I doubt he knows the first thing about gardening.''

''And you do?''

Lacey turned, then, and swiped a strand of hair out of her face with the back of her wrist. The impatient gesture left a beguiling streak of dirt across her cheek. The curly wisp promptly blew forward again.

Unable to resist, Kevin walked closer and knelt down. His fingers brushed the silken strand back, then lingered against her sun-kissed skin. With the pad of his thumb, he wiped away the smudge of dirt. He could almost swear he felt her tremble at the innocent caress.

She gazed up at him and his heart stilled.

''You've forgotten that I was the one who put in all the flower beds at our first house,'' she said. ''I landscaped that entire yard.''

He regarded her with a faint sense of puzzlement. ''I thought you just did that because we didn't have the money back then to hire somebody.''

''I did it because I enjoyed it,'' she said almost angrily, backing away from his touch. ''When we moved, you hired a gardener and I never had the chance again. Tomas wouldn't even let me near the rose bushes to clip them for the house, much less indulge me by letting me plant something.''

''Why didn't you say something?''

''To him?''

''No. To me.''

"I did," she said. "You never listened."

He heard the weary resignation in her tone and winced. "I'm sorry. I guess I thought you'd prefer to spend your time on all those committees you were forever joining."

"And you were wrong," she said curtly. "I joined those committees because you wanted me to and because there was nothing left for me to do at home. We had a gardener and a housekeeper. If Jason had been younger, you probably would have insisted on a nanny."

Kevin stood up and shoved his hands into his pockets. "Most women would kill to have full-time household help, especially with a house as large as ours and with all the entertaining we needed to do."

"I am *not* most women."

For emphasis she jammed a trowel into the rain-softened earth and muttered something more, something he couldn't quite make out. He decided it was just as well. He doubted it was complimentary.

Again Kevin wished that their first tentative steps toward a reconciliation weren't so incredibly awkward. So many things seemed to be blurted out in anger, complaints long buried. Once minor, now they seemed almost insurmountable.

He wondered if Lacey was right. Had she told him all this before? Had he failed to listen, sure that he was giving her what she wanted, rather than what he thought she deserved?

There were times he felt as if he were learning about this woman all over again, rather than simply picking up the threads of a relationship that had weathered more than a quarter of a century. He tried to accept that it was going to take time, that two people who had apparently lost the ability to communicate what was in their hearts weren't going to relearn the skill overnight.

"I was thinking of going for a walk on the beach," Kevin said finally, unwilling to pursue the dangerous direction of their conversation on such a beautiful afternoon. They needed time just to be together, not a nonstop confrontation.

"It's a beautiful day for it," Lacey said, then added sternly, "Remember not to overdo it. Even though you've made remarkable progress, Linc wants you to take it easy."

That said, she seemed to be waiting, but for what, he wondered. An invitation? Surely she knew she was welcome. Then again, nothing could be taken for granted as it once had been. "Want to come along?" he asked.

For an instant he thought she was going to refuse, using the gardening as an excuse. He could see the refusal forming on her lips when she turned her face up to meet his gaze, then something shifted. Her mouth curved into a faint smile.

"Sure," she said, taking off her gardening gloves and tossing them aside. "Let me get a sweater. The wind is probably colder down by the water."

Kevin nodded and watched her go inside. When she emerged, a bulky red sweater topped her snug-fitting jeans. He had a hunch it was one of his daughter-in-law's designs. It was certainly far bolder than what Lacey usually wore in town. There she tended to stick to cashmere and pearls, as understated and elegant as any society matron in the city.

In fact, with his hours at work and his business commitments, he had seen her more often in sleek designer evening wear than anything casual. With her quiet grace, her stunning figure and youthful complexion, she had done the name of Halloran proud, after all. Even Brandon had admitted that.

Kevin thought it was odd that he was only now realizing that he liked her better this way. It reminded him of the girl he'd fallen in love with, the girl in hand-me-downs who'd felt the needs of others so deeply, the girl who'd learned to overcome her shyness in order to fight for the things in which she believed with all her heart.

Including their marriage.

As much as it troubled and angered him, Kevin knew that's what Lacey had been doing when she'd walked out the door of their Boston home months ago. She hadn't left in defeat or even fury. She had left with the hope that her daring ultimatum would get his attention as nothing else had.

If it hadn't been for this most recent heart attack, he wondered if they would be here today or whether his stubborn refusal to acknowledge the validity of her claims would still be keeping them apart.

Knowing that somehow he had to fight for each precious moment until he could regain her trust, he held out his hand. After an instant's hesitation, she took it. They climbed over the dunes to reach the hard-packed sand by the water's edge.

The ocean was quieter today, its pace late-afternoon lazy as it shimmered silver gray in the sun. He felt good holding his wife's hand again as the sun's warmth kissed their shoulders and a cool breeze fanned their faces.

"Remember," he began at the same time she did.

He glanced into her eyes and saw the laughter lurking in the blue depths. "You first."

"I was just remembering the first time we came here."

"To this house or to the Cape?"

"To this house. Your hand shook the whole time you were writing out the check for the deposit. I think in the back of your mind you viewed it as selling out to the establishment. You spent the whole weekend looking as if you expected the activist brigade to catch you and make you turn in your young idealist credentials. I was terrified you were going to back out."

"I still get a pang every now and then," he admitted candidly. "Especially when I think of how many people are homeless."

"Which explains why, the very next week, you donated money to create a homeless shelter. For a few anxious days I was afraid you were going to try to donate this place."

"Back then if it hadn't been for the zoning problems, I probably would have."

"And now?"

"I'm grateful you talked me into it. It's the one place where I feel as if we connect."

Lacey nodded. "I feel that, too. It's because it's the one place where we have only happy memories. We never allowed our differences to follow us here."

Kevin returned her gaze evenly, pained by the depth of hurt that shadowed her blue eyes.

"And when the differences got to be too much to put aside, I just stopped coming," he admitted, certain that she would be angered or at the very least hurt by the brutal honesty. To his surprise she was nodding as if it were something she'd realized long ago.

"I know," she confirmed softly. "That made me saddest of all. We've lost three years here, years we can never get back. We missed the flowers blooming in the spring, the lazy summer days, the change of the leaves in the fall. Even before we were married, Cape Cod was where we always came to witness the changing of the seasons. Now the seasons just rush by."

"Don't," he whispered, pausing by the edge of the water and cupping her chin. "Don't count them as lost. We can learn from them. We can build on a foundation that's all the stronger for having weathered this crisis."

As tears welled in Lacey's eyes, Kevin drew her slowly into his arms, holding her loosely. At first she was stiff, but in no more than a heartbeat she began to relax, her arms circling his waist, her head resting against his chest, where he was sure she could hear his heart thunder.

The scents of salt water and flowery perfume swirled around him as he gave himself over to the sensations that just holding her stirred. His blood roared in his veins, then slowed as contentment stole over him. When had he last felt this peaceful? Months ago? Years?

"When you say it like that," she murmured, the words muffled against his chest, "I can almost believe we will work things out."

"Believe it, Lacey. I want it with all my heart."

"So do I."

But they both knew that wanting alone was not nearly enough.

Lacey was standing in front of the kitchen counter up to her elbows in bread dough and flour. She studied the mess and wondered what had possessed her to try to bake bread, when the best bakery in the universe was less than a mile away, to say nothing of Mrs. Renfield, who would gladly trade one of her home-baked loaves for more of that fancy material.

Maybe it had something to do with the confession she'd made the day before. It was true that she had resented giving up the claim to her own kitchen, her own gardens. She had spoken out, but obviously not forcefully enough if Kevin had no memory of it. Maybe she had just given up, once it was clear that he'd made up his mind. Maybe it was her own fault, as much as his. For all of his talents, he wasn't a mind reader. If she had capitulated, he must have thought it was simply because he'd convinced her.

Maybe she was baking bread because she was still shaken by the way she had felt with Kevin's arms around her. Each time he touched her, each time he gazed into her eyes, each time she felt his kindness surrounding her like the warmth of a quilt, he stripped away some of her defenses. After that, Lacey had desperately needed a project that would give her time to re-group. What better way to do that than tackling something she'd never tried before?

Just as she was resolving never to give in so easily again to his persuasive arguments or his touches, she heard Kevin's muffled chuckle behind her and whirled on him. She shook a warning finger at him, sending out a fine mist of flour.

"Don't say it. Don't even think it."

His eyes sparkled with amusement. "I was just admiring your domesticity. I suppose this is one of those other things I robbed you of by hiring a housekeeper."

She heard the note of good-natured teasing in his

tone, but she was in no mood for it, not with this mess spread out around her. "Do you recall my ever baking bread?"

"Nope."

"That's right. I never once attempted it, even before you hired the housekeeper. Thank goodness you never wanted to live in one of those communes where everyone baked their own bread and lived off the vegetables they grew themselves."

"Without toxic pesticides, of course."

She grinned. "Of course."

"So why are you baking bread now?"

"Because I should have learned," she said, aware as she said it how ridiculous she sounded.

"Excuse me?" Kevin queried, justifiably confused by her convoluted logic.

"I know how you like home-baked bread. It was something I always meant to learn, but first one thing and then another came along and I never did."

"So you're learning now?"

She swiped her hand across her face. "More or less. I stopped by Mrs. Renfield's while you were resting this afternoon and asked her for the recipe."

"Maybe you should have asked her for another loaf of bread."

Lacey scowled at Kevin for echoing her own thoughts. "Go away."

He nodded agreeably. "No problem. When should I come back?"

"Try breakfast. I figure I ought to have some semblance of bread figured out by then."

"We haven't had dinner yet."

"Don't you think I know that? I forgot about all that rising and kneading and stuff. It takes time."

"I'd really like some dinner." At her fierce expression, he quickly amended, "Not right away, but soon. Say, by eight?"

"So order a pizza," she growled.

His eyes lit up. "A pizza! Great idea." He reached for the phone.

"Wait!"

He turned back. "I knew it was too good to be true. No pizza, huh?"

"Chinese. Call for Chinese. Nothing fried, nothing with eggs. That should be healthy enough. I think there's a menu from a carryout place by the phone in the living room."

He then left her alone to pummel the damn dough and rue the precise moment when she'd had this brainstorm. She slammed her fist into the doughy mound sending a spray of flour into the air. There was a certain amount of satisfaction in the action. Maybe she ought to recommend it to Kevin as a way to work off tension at the end of a long day at Halloran Industries.

Lacey thought she had the bread under control by the time Kevin came back. She'd actually put the dough into bread pans to rise for the last time. She stood back and admired them, breathing in the yeasty scent. Suddenly she realized she was starved.

"What did you order?" she asked him as he came over to examine the end result of her labors thus far.

"Chow mein, lemon chicken and for you fried rice with shrimp."

"Sounds heavenly."

"I placed another order while I was in there, too," he said, tossing a catalog onto the table. "Check out page five and see what you think."

Lacey's gaze narrowed as she picked up the brochure from a store famous for its kitchenware. She flipped the first couple of pages until she found the item he'd circled: an outrageously expensive automatic bread maker.

"You didn't," she said, laughter bubbling up as she looked at his smug expression.

"I did. If baking bread is going to make you happy, you might as well have the right equipment."

"There are some who'd say this is cheating."

"I prefer to think of it as modernization."

She grinned at him. "I'm not sure your motive is all that altruistic. I suspect you're just hoping I'll convert so you'll have some chance of getting your meals on time."

"Not me," he said piously. "I could live on love."

"I suppose that's why we're having Chinese carryout tonight."

"Exactly. I *love* Chinese carryout."

Lacey caught the devilish twinkle in his eyes and suddenly felt warm all over. In moments like this she felt the deep, abiding pull of her love for Kevin all over again. She knew a lot of women who would regard a kitchen appliance as a sorry excuse for a romantic gift. She also knew that she would always see it as the first concrete evidence that the sensitive, considerate man she'd fallen in love with still existed.

Chapter Nine

Lacey drove into town for a much-needed break from Kevin's gentle attentiveness. After nearly two weeks, she was finding it more and more difficult to ignore her mounting desires and keep her resolve.

Simply wandering the aisles of the grocery store kept her mind on more mundane matters. It was virtually impossible to feel particularly romantic in the frozen food section of the supermarket. It was also good to see other people, many of whom she recognized from past trips.

She had just turned the corner of the canned goods aisle, when she ran into Mrs. Renfield. Dressed in a blue-flowered cotton blouse, a matching sweater the shade of Texas bluebonnets, gray slacks and sensible black shoes, the seventy-five-year-old widow didn't look a day over sixty. There was scarcely a wrinkle on her face, a testament to the floppy-brimmed hat she always wore to work in her garden and to walk on the beach. Though her gray hair looked as if it might have been chopped off with hedge clippers, the short style was actually very becoming.

"Lacey, dear, how wonderful to see you. How did your bread turn out?"

"It was edible," Lacey said ruefully. "But it wasn't nearly as good as yours."

The older woman waved off the compliment. "You'll get the hang of it soon enough. Wouldn't you and Kevin like to drop by for tea this afternoon? I've just made another cherry cobbler. I know how much you both love it. There's even enough for Jason and that new wife of his. Are you expecting them anytime soon?"

"Maybe this weekend, in fact. Kevin mentioned after he talked to Jason this morning that they hoped to drive out on Saturday morning."

"Then you must come by and collect the cobbler. Besides, I haven't seen Kevin once since the two of you came out here."

"I know," Lacey said. "He's been sticking pretty close to home. He's still trying to get his strength back."

"Well, there's nothing better for that than fresh salt air and a brisk walk on the beach. You bring him by for tea and I'll tell him so myself."

Lacey grinned at her. "If I were you, I'd keep my advice to myself. Kevin is getting tired of being told what to do."

"Fiddle-faddle. He can grumble all he wants at me. I can take it. I raised six boys and you'd better believe they all still listen when I have something to say."

"I'm sure they do. I'll see how Kevin's feeling

when I get home. I'll call if we can make it over. If not today, soon. I promise.''

Mrs. Renfield regarded Lacey intently and patted her hand. ''My dear, you mustn't take it to heart when he loses his temper. Men never can deal with being sick. They take it out on whoever's closest to them.''

With that reassurance given, the elderly woman was on her way, pushing her grocery cart briskly down the aisle without a backward glance. She was stopped twice more by friends before she reached the end of the row.

How had she known? Lacey wondered. How had a woman she knew only slightly guessed that Kevin was scowling impatiently every time Lacey dared to mention that he was pushing himself too hard?

She shrugged finally. Maybe it wasn't some odd psychic power. Maybe it was simply a matter of understanding the nature of the beast. After all, from the time Jason was old enough to talk, he'd always been a bear, too. He moaned and groaned so pathetically, it might have broken her heart if she hadn't known that he was dealing with a cold or measles and not something fatal. She thought it was poetic justice that he was suffering from morning sickness right along with Dana.

As for Kevin, the worst of it was probably over. Day by day his strength was clearly coming back. After the first week, she had been able to see it in the energy he found to walk on the beach every morning and afternoon. He'd begun to tackle small chores around the house with some semblance of his old enthusiasm.

Lacey might have worried more about the demands he was placing on his still-healing heart, if he hadn't balanced it all with quiet hours of reading. Just last night a techno-thriller had kept him up until the wee hours of the morning. She had seen the light under his door each time she'd awakened. Today at breakfast he'd been anxious to discuss every detail of the fast-paced plot with her.

With Kevin's energy increasing, she wondered how much longer she would be able to keep him idle on the Cape, how much longer before they would have to face making a final decision about their marriage. She knew he'd started making daily phone calls to Brandon and to Jason, though he tried to mask them as nothing more than casual chats. The fact that he felt the need to hide his business calls worried her almost as much as the increasing activity. If he couldn't confide even that, how could they expect to communicate about the really important issues facing them?

When Lacey came home from the store an hour later to find Kevin atop a ladder, clinging to the roof, she felt her heart climb in her throat. As she watched, he saw her and waved, his expression cheerful, his balance at the top of that ladder more precarious than ever.

''I'll be down in a minute,'' he called as she left the car door open and rushed across the yard to steady the ladder for his descent.

When he finally reached the ground and her own pulse rate slowed to something close to normal, she whirled on him. ''Kevin Halloran, are you out of your mind?'' Hands on hips, she stood toe-to-toe with him. ''What did you think you were doing?''

''Checking the drainpipe for leaves,'' he replied nonchalantly. He dropped a casual kiss on her forehead. ''No big deal.''

The Best of the Best™—Here's How it Works

Accepting your 2 free books and gift places you under no obligation to buy anything. You may keep the books and gift and return the shipping statement marked "cancel." If you do not cancel, about a month later we will send you 4 additional novels and bill you just $4.24 each in the U.S., or $4.74 each in Canada, plus 25¢ delivery per book and applicable sales tax, if any.* That's the complete price, and — compared to cover prices of $5.50 or more each in the U.S. and $6.50 or more each in Canada — it's quite a bargain! You may cancel at any time, but if you choose to continue, every month we'll send you 4 more books, which you may either purchase at the discount price…or return to us and cancel your subscription.

*Terms and prices subject to change without notice. Sales tax applicable in N.Y. Canadian residents will be charged applicable provincial taxes and GST.

If offer card is missing write to: The Best of the Best, 3010 Walden Ave., P.O. Box 1867, Buffalo, NY 14240-1867

NO POSTAGE
NECESSARY
IF MAILED
IN THE
UNITED STATES

BUSINESS REPLY MAIL

FIRST-CLASS MAIL PERMIT NO. 717 BUFFALO NY

POSTAGE WILL BE PAID BY ADDRESSEE

THE BEST OF THE BEST
3010 WALDEN AVE
PO BOX 1867
BUFFALO NY 14240-9952

Lacey felt her temper climb. "No big deal. *No big deal!* You could have fallen and no one would have been here to help. You're not supposed to go up and down steps, much less ladders. What if you'd gotten dizzy?" she demanded, listening to the hysterical rise of her voice, but unable to control it.

"I would have held on until the dizziness passed," he said so calmly that she nearly missed the glint of anger in his eye. "You have to stop hovering over me, Lacey. I can't take much more of it. I won't let you make me out to be an invalid."

She felt as if he'd slapped her. Unshed tears stung her eyes.

"Hovering?" she repeated furiously, Mrs. Renfield's wise advice a distant memory. "Is that what I've been doing? Well, I'm sorry. I thought I was just thinking about your welfare. I thought I was just trying to make sure that you recuperated the way Linc wanted you to. I'm sorry all to hell for worrying about you!"

If she'd had the groceries in her arms, she would have thrown them at him. Instead, she turned and stomped off, only to have him catch her by the arm and twirl her around to meet his equally furious gaze.

Before Lacey could catch her breath, Kevin's lips were on hers, hard and urgent. There was a raw, primitive anger behind the kiss, a battle for possession and control.

She had known the kiss was coming for days now, known that their mutual desire could be banked only so long. She wanted desperately to fight his claim, but her body's needs wouldn't let her. She had hungered for far too long to feel Kevin's mouth on hers, to feel his heat rising, drawing her closer with the certain lure of an old lover. Day by day that hunger had grown, controlled only by stern lectures and rigid willpower.

Now, with the decision taken out of her control, her hands fisted, clinging to the rough denim of his shirt. He dragged her closer until their bodies fit together as naturally as two pieces of a puzzle. Her mouth opened too eagerly for the sweet invasion of his tongue. Within seconds the punishing kiss became a bold, urgent caress that set off a fire low inside her. Her blood rushed to a wilder rhythm.

It had been so long, so terribly long, since she had felt this alluring heat, since his clean, masculine scent had teased her senses. Her responses were instinctive, as doubts and warnings fled. This was the way she and Kevin had once been together—sensual creatures who stirred to passion with the most innocent touch, the most casual glance. This had been the crowning glory of their love, a lure so powerful that nothing, *nothing* could have stood in their way.

Thinking, as she had, that it had been lost, she exhilarated in the sensations pulsing through her body, the quick rise of heat, the questing hunger, the aching need. And all because of a kiss—a single, long, deep, slow kiss.

She moaned as he drew away, moaned and clung to his shoulders, her knees weak, her breathing uneven, her emotions in turmoil.

Reluctant to end the moment, Lacey was slow to open her eyes, slow to search Kevin's expression for some sign of what he was feeling. Even so, it was impossible to miss the naked longing in his eyes, the ragged rise and fall of his chest, the still-angry set to his lips.

"I want you," he said, his voice gruff. "I want you

more than I've ever imagined wanting a woman." He took her hand and pressed it against him. "This is what you do to me still, after all this time."

Lacey swallowed hard against the emotions that were crowding in her chest. Her fingers lingered against the roughness of denim, lingered against the evidence of her own powerful sensuality. If she could still affect him like this, if she could still make him yearn to touch and caress and love, weren't all things possible?

Maybe. Maybe not, she thought with a sigh as she slowly withdrew. At her age she knew better than to equate passion with the forever kind of love. Knew better, but wished just the same. Oh, how she wished that these few moments of uncensored desire were proof that she and Kevin were almost there, almost back to the way they had been.

As if the rare display of vulnerability had cost him dearly, Kevin refused to go to Mrs. Renfield's for tea, but insisted Lacey accept the invitation. Lacey went through the motions, listening to the latest gossip, pretending that everything in her own life was fine, accepting the cobbler because it would have hurt the older woman's feelings to turn it down.

When she returned, Kevin was careful to avoid her, as if he feared, as she did, that the raw emotions that had rushed to the surface earlier would disrupt their tenuous hold on an atmosphere of calm.

If they dared to allow passion to run its natural course, would they ever take the time to search their hearts for the answers they needed to make their marriage work? Lacey knew that soul-searching talks were something they had to do. The time was fast approaching when their discussions would have to reach deep, in order to bring all the old hurts into the open. Without such brutally painful honesty, they would never clear the air once and for all.

Lacey spent the last hours of daylight trying to stay out of Kevin's path, not yet ready for a confrontation that would rip open wounds just now healing. Nor was she ready for more of the bittersweet temptation she felt each time he was near—a temptation that taunted all the more now that she knew it was based on reality, not memories.

Kevin retreated emotionally as well as physically. Perhaps, she thought, because his own pride was at stake. He had shown himself to be vulnerable, and she doubted he would allow her to see his need again. Like boxers they had gone to their respective corners to soothe their wounds and prepare for the next round.

That night their unspoken truce was still uneasy. The conversation at dinner was stilted and confined to the barest attempt at politeness. More than once Kevin looked as if he wanted to say something more important than "Pass the pepper," but each time he snapped his mouth closed, leaving the words unsaid. He left the table before dessert, declaring that the cobbler should be saved for Jason and Dana.

Lacey and Kevin sat on opposite sides of the living room, unopened books in their hands, both of them staring at the fire. It was Lacey, nerves unbearably taut, who finally broke the silence.

"I picked up a movie at the video store earlier. Would you like to watch it?"

Kevin shrugged. "We might as well. You put it on. I'll be back in a minute."

When he hadn't returned after a few minutes, she

went looking for him. She found him in the kitchen with the refrigerator door open wide. He was scanning the newly filled shelves.

"What are you looking for?" she asked.

"Something to eat while we watch the movie."

She knew what he meant by that. To his way of thinking, carrot sticks, apples and celery were not snacks. A bowl of chocolate chip ice cream, a bigger bowl of buttered popcorn or a handful of crackers with cheddar cheese went with old movies. So did Mrs. Renfield's latest cherry cobbler, which just an hour earlier Kevin had vowed to save. Yet in the midst of a snack attack, she doubted he would remember the promise.

Lacey also knew that she dare not offer advice on the subject of his diet. He'd already indicated what he thought of her interference. She consoled herself with a reminder that Kevin was a grown man. If he was going to improve his health, it would have to be a conscious choice on his part. It was time to let go of her own need to protect him, a need based on her desperate fear of losing him. It was no easier than Jason's first day at school or his departure for college. In so many ways it was more important than either.

Kevin glanced back at her, his expression defensive. "No comment?" he inquired.

"None."

He muttered something under his breath, reached into the refrigerator and withdrew the carrot sticks. Lacey let out the breath she'd been holding. Kevin put a handful of the carrots on a plate, regarded them with disgust and slammed the refrigerator door.

"This better be one helluva a movie," he grumbled as he stalked past her.

''Bogart and Bacall,'' she reminded him. ''How could it be anything else?''

In no time at all Kevin was so absorbed in the film that he didn't even reach for the remaining carrots. Just as Lacey had finally begun to relax, the phone rang. She grabbed it as Kevin cut off the VCR and headed for the kitchen.

''Lacey, it's Paula. Is this a bad time?''

''No, it's fine.'' Unless Kevin was using it as an excuse to sneak the last of that cobbler, she thought. ''What's up?''

''We could really use your help tomorrow. Is there any chance at all you can get to Boston?''

Lacey had a hunch it would be good to allow Kevin some space, more than she'd given him even today. Not only that, she knew she could do with a real break. The nonstop tension of fighting Kevin and her own emotions was beginning to get to her.

''I may be late, but I'll be there,'' she promised.

''Are you okay? You sound funny,'' Paula said, quick to pick up on Lacey's mood.

''I'm just tired. I'll get a good night's sleep and be fine by the time I see you.''

''If you say so,'' her friend said skeptically. ''Is Kevin okay?''

''Getting better all the time,'' she responded honestly.

''And you don't intend to say any more than that with him there,'' Paula replied. ''Okay, I'll let you go for now, but be prepared to discuss this in depth tomorrow.''

Lacey's laugh was strained. ''Don't threaten me, pal. I could stay here tomorrow. They're predicting seventy degrees and sunny, a perfect day for the beach.''

''But I know you won't let me down. See you.''

Lacey was slow to hang up. She should tell Kevin about the remarkable housing project in which Paula had involved her. Paula and her husband Dave had never lost the idealistic fervor that had once gripped Kevin and Lacey. Tonight would be the perfect opportunity to fill Kevin in on what their old friends had been doing. Maybe he would even want to ride into town with her, take a look at a project that really worked.

When he hadn't rejoined her ten minutes later, she got up and went to look for him. He wasn't in the kitchen so she walked down the hall and saw that the door to his room was closed.

She opened it a crack. ''Kevin,'' she said softly, as worry sneaked up on her.

After a moment's silence, during which all she heard was the quickened beating of her own heart, he said, ''Yes?''

''Are you okay?''

''Just tired,'' he answered tersely.

His tone concerned her almost as much as the admission. ''You're sure that's all it is?''

''Yes. Good night, Lacey.''

There was no doubt that he had dismissed her.

''Good night, Kevin,'' she said, an unmistakable strain in her voice. She sighed and reluctantly closed the door.

She tried watching the rest of the old movie, but couldn't keep her attention focused on the flickering black and white images. Finally she gave up.

In her own room, with the book she'd been reading

discarded, she stared at the ceiling and wondered how they could possibly hope to salvage their marriage when more often than not they treated each other like strangers, no doubt because neither of them dared to force the issues they really needed to resolve. Instead they skirted their problems, like drivers avoiding dangerous potholes.

No more, she vowed with determination—most likely because she knew already that tomorrow offered yet another reprieve. She would use the time in Boston to think through the best way to broach things with Kevin. She would organize her thoughts, if not her emotions.

Her plan decided, Lacey tried to sleep. Unfortunately the emotions she'd vowed to dismiss wouldn't release their hold so easily. Every sigh of the wind, each creak of the bedsprings, every crash of waves was enough to bring her wide awake again.

And awake, Kevin's face was always there, and the memories of his caresses were as tantalizing as the reality.

When dawn broke at last, she couldn't wait to run.

Chapter Ten

After the unending tension of the previous evening and the sleepless night, swinging a hammer actually felt good to Lacey. Admittedly she was doing it with more energy than accuracy, but she relished the pull on her muscles, the warmth of the sun on her shoulders.

All around her were the sounds of electric saws, hammers and the blare of sixties rock 'n' roll. The hammering seemed to take on the rhythm of the music.

Simply being among a group that was mostly strangers made it easier not to think about Kevin. During their time on Cape Cod, there had been too many bold glances that unnerved her, too many innocent caresses that tempted, too many whispered words designed to lure.

Especially yesterday. That kiss had very nearly been her undoing. Lacey felt as if she'd been walking a tightrope, trying to maintain her equilibrium above a sea of temptations.

Now with sweat beading on her brow and tracking between her breasts, she put all of those confusing sensations out of her mind to concentrate on the task at hand. It was either that or risk slamming the hammer on her thumb instead of hitting the nails she was supposed to drive into place in the drywall. She'd already done that twice. The result was a throbbing, black and blue thumb, but she was determined not to quit until her assigned section of the house was complete. She knew how anxiously some family was waiting for the day they could move in.

When Paula Gethers had called months ago and pleaded with her to pitch in on a unique housing project that would ultimately provide renovated, low-income homes, the concept had intrigued Lacey. And the timing couldn't have been better. She had just left Kevin, and her days were filled with endless hours of loneliness and regrets.

When Paula had said she didn't want Lacey to do fund-raising, didn't want her to write a check, Lacey had regarded her skeptically.

"What then?"

"I need you to hit nails, paint, maybe lay some tiles. Who knows, maybe I'll have you learn to install plumbing."

Lacey had burst out laughing at that. "You've got to be kidding."

Paula had shaken her head. "Nope. Come take a look."

Lacey had gone that day and been relegated to wielding a paintbrush. She'd ended up with more paint in her hair and on her clothes than on the walls, but she'd been hooked.

The calls had come steadily after that until Lacey was involved almost as closely with the project as her old friend. Last night's call had been more welcome than all the others because it provided her with an excuse to put that much-needed space between herself and Kevin.

At one time she had been on a dozen different committees, all of them demanding, all of them worthwhile. With none of them, though, had she felt such an immediate sense of satisfaction. Never before had she been able to stand back at the end of the day and look at the results of her labors and see so clearly that her contribution of time and energy truly made a difference for some family. Lacey felt good knowing that each house might become a first home for a family previously relegated to a ramshackle public-housing project.

Admittedly there had also been a sense of poignancy. Maybe if such a program had existed years ago, there would have been help for her own family. They had lived in a cramped, run-down, rented apartment, unable to afford anything better, yet too well-off to qualify for assistance.

Lacey would never forget the first time she had gone home with Kevin. She had circled the huge Halloran home as if it were a museum, studying the paintings in Brandon's collection with a sense of awe. The furnishings were perfect, down to the last crystal vase and the matching gold lighter and cigarette case. It was the first time she had truly realized how very different their lives were, and it had terrified her.

For weeks after the visit, she had tried to break

things off, tried to put some distance between them. Kevin would have none of it. Intuitively he had known how she felt and even at eighteen he had been determined.

To her horror, he had spoken to her mother and wrangled an invitation to her home for dinner. There, amidst the garage-sale collection of furnishings and the strong aroma of garlic, he had looked as out of place as a Renoir amidst paintings on velvet.

If he had been appalled, though, he hid it well. He had been lavish with his praise of her mother's cooking. With the composure of someone who'd been brought up with all the social graces, he had talked about unemployment with her father, an assembly line worker who feared each and every day would be his last on the job.

Slowly Lacey had relaxed as his charm had touched them all. The evening had been a resounding success. Only later had she realized that that night had been the start of Kevin's transition from being solely her protector to his commitment to broader change for society itself. His fervor had ignited her own and they both had developed a sense of purpose that was all the stronger because it was something they shared.

How long ago that all seemed now. Lacey tugged at the red bandana she'd tied around her neck and pulled it free, then used it to mop her brow. If Kevin could only see her now, she thought. He wouldn't believe the streaks of dirt, the paint and sawdust that clung to her hair, the aching muscles that were proof that on this project at least she was pulling her own weight.

She wasn't sure why she hadn't forced the issue last night and told him where she intended to spend the day. Because he'd slipped away during her conversation with Paula, then taken refuge in his room, she had felt more defeated than she had in a long time. When he'd dismissed her at the doorway, she'd consoled herself that there would be time to explain in the morning.

But when morning came, she had been almost relieved to discover that he was still asleep. Rather than waking him, she'd left an innocuous note on the kitchen table beside a bowl of high-fiber cereal.

"Had to go into town. Back by dinner. L."

A zillion years ago, he would have known where she was going, would have cared about a project like this, would have been among the first to volunteer. Her subconscious decision to keep it to herself now spoke volumes about how she felt his priorities had changed.

Or, more likely, how she feared his reaction would disappoint her. If he showed no interest or, worse yet, if he belittled the effort, it would be irrefutable proof of how much he had changed.

Maybe she was selling him short, though. Maybe if she gave him a chance, he would share in her excitement. There was only one way to find out. She vowed then and there to tell him every detail over dinner. And if his response was only to pull out his pen and write a check, at least the cause would benefit.

"When was the last time you actually hit a nail?" Paula inquired, her low, throaty voice filled with amusement. She sounded as if she ought to do sultry voice-overs for commercials, rather than spend her days on a construction site. "If everyone worked at this rate, the house wouldn't be ready until next year," she said.

Lacey glanced at her old friend and laughed. "What

can I say? Volunteer help starts slacking off when the sun goes down."

"We're a good hour from sunset, lady." Paula handed her a soft drink and settled on the bottom rung of a ladder. "You okay? You looked lost in thought, a little sad."

"I was just wondering what Kevin would think if he could see me now."

"Probably that you'd lost your marbles. That's what Dave thinks about me, and he's been right here every day. He still can't believe that a woman who used to get her nails done twice a week when she was in high school now has none and isn't hysterical over it." She held up her hands, displaying the blunt-cut nails that were free of polish. Tiny cuts and specks of paint had turned them into a worker's hands. "They may not be as pretty, but I figure I've earned every battle scar."

She regarded Lacey closely. "Why haven't you told Kevin about this?"

"I'm not sure," Lacey admitted. "I was just thinking that I'd tell him tonight."

"You might have a glass of brandy nearby in case he swoons from shock the way Dave did. Or you could just bring him by sometime," she suggested slyly. "That's how I sold Dave and you and just about everyone else who's gotten involved."

Lacey grinned. "A pretty sneaky trick, if you ask me."

"I'll use whatever it takes if it means getting these houses fixed up faster. I've fine-tuned my approach to the contractors so they start saying yes when they see me coming. You should have heard the number I pulled on the mayor. I've never been more eloquent, if I do say so myself."

"Has he committed any city funds yet?"

Paula shook her head. "I'm not counting on the city for anything. This is all about private citizens helping each other. I wanted him to cough up his own bucks and a few weekends of his time. I figured he'd be the ideal role model for all the other politicians and give this program some much-needed visibility."

"Did he agree?"

"It's an election year. Just imagine the photo opportunities," she said dryly. She glanced at her watch. "If you're going back out to the Cape tonight, you'd better get started. It will be dark soon and we'll have to shut down for the night, anyway."

Lacey nodded. "I'll try to get back later in the week, by next weekend for sure."

"Who knows? Maybe you'll have Kevin along."

"Yes. Who knows," she said, but she couldn't mask her very real doubts.

If the furious expression on Kevin's face when she drove up was any indication, Lacey figured she'd better not count on him for much of anything. As she crossed the lawn, he opened the screen door and stepped outside.

When she was close enough, he waved her note under her nose. "What is this?"

She immediately bristled at his curt tone. "The note I left for you."

"Is this supposed to give me the first clue about where to find you? What if there'd been an emergency? What if I'd wanted to get in touch with you? Was I supposed to call all over Boston and hope I lucked out?"

She stopped in mid-step and studied him, worry

washing through her. "Was there an emergency? Are you okay?"

"Dammit, this is not about my health. It's about your lack of consideration. It's about your running off without so much as a word to let me know where you were going and when you'd be back."

Lacey swallowed the angry retort that rose automatically to her lips. Maybe now he would know how she felt more often than not, shut out and filled with loneliness and longing.

"Well," he demanded, "what do you have to say for yourself?"

"Nothing," she said softly. "You're obviously too upset to listen to reason."

"Don't you dare patronize me."

"We'll discuss it over dinner," she said with deliberate calm as she left him standing in the front hall.

"Oh, no," he said, catching up with her in the doorway to the kitchen and moving quickly into her path. "We'll discuss it *now.*"

Lacey drew in a deep breath and lifted her gaze to clash with his. "Kevin, for the past decade you have not once beat me home in the evenings. I have always left a note just in case. Today I did the same thing. I told you I had gone out, and I told you when I'd be home. I figured you wouldn't be any more interested in the details than you usually are."

Despite her best efforts, she hadn't been able to keep the bitterness out at the end. He looked stunned.

"Not interested?" he repeated softly. "I'm always interested in everything you do."

"No," she said evenly. "That was true once, but not recently. As long as I was there to greet you every evening, as long as I never disrupted your plans, you never once asked a question about how I spent my days."

"I assumed you went to those meetings," he muttered defensively.

"*Those meetings,* as you refer to them, were a sorry substitute for having any real purpose in my life. I know that I am as much to blame for allowing that to happen as you are, but the fact of the matter is that for too long now I have been frustrated, lonely and bored to tears. While you've been climbing the corporate ladder of success, I've been searching for some niche I could fill. Thanks to Paula, I've found it."

For an instant he looked puzzled. Puzzlement slowly turned to incredulity. "Paula Gethers? The one who used to organize peace marches? I didn't know the two of you even saw each other anymore."

"Actually we see each other quite a lot. I'm helping her to renovate houses."

Kevin's mouth dropped open. "You're what?" he asked, not even trying to hide his astonishment and disbelief.

"Renovating houses," she repeated a bit more emphatically.

"You mean hiring contractors, decorators, that sort of thing?"

"No. I mean picking up hammers and paintbrushes and screwdrivers." She held out her hands for his inspection.

He took her hands and examined them, slowly taking in the specks of paint that had escaped her cleaning, the blister on one finger, the black and blue under the nail of her thumb.

"My God," he breathed softly, as he gently

smoothed his fingers over the rough spots. ''You're serious, aren't you?''

Lacey withdrew her hand before his touch made her forget how irritated she was. ''Never more so,'' she said with a hint of defiance.

''But why? You could hire anyone you wanted to do that sort of work.''

''Not for this. There's no money involved. The work is done by volunteers. The materials are donated. Then the houses are turned over to needy families. Paula's more familiar with the financial arrangements made with the families, but I do know they have to help with the construction.''

The last traces of anger vanished from Kevin's eyes. Lacey could tell the exact instant when his imagination caught fire. Her breath caught in her throat. A radiant burst of hope spilled through her.

''Sit down and tell me,'' he said, urging her to the table. He poured them each a cup of coffee and sat down opposite her. ''How does it work? Who's involved?''

Kevin's sudden burst of enthusiasm was catching, reminding her of long-ago nights when they had sat just like this for hours on end. Her words tumbled over each other as she shared her excitement about the program with him. All the things she had longed to describe to him for so long came pouring out.

''I was there the day they turned over the first house I'd worked on,'' she said. ''A single mother was moving in with her three kids. There were tears in her eyes as she walked from room to room just touching things. She said she'd never before seen anyplace so clean.''

Tears welled up in Lacey's eyes as she remembered that day. ''Oh, Kevin, if only you could have been there. Knowing that that house was hers filled her with so much pride and so much determination. You could see it in her face. This is the kind of social program that really works, that doesn't spend a fortune on overhead. It gets down to one of the very first basics of life, shelter.''

''I want to see for myself,'' Kevin said when she was finally done. He got up and began to pace, just as he always had when he was trying to work out a complex problem. ''Maybe there's some way Halloran can get involved,'' he said finally. ''We could donate fabric for draperies, underwrite some of the costs to buy up land or old houses. What do you think? Would that help?''

Lacey felt a wellspring of emotion rise up inside her. *This* was the Kevin she'd fallen in love with. *This* was the man who was touched by the plight of others and wanted desperately to help.

''Thank you,'' she said, feeling as if a boulder had lodged in her throat.

He seemed puzzled by her emotion. ''Lacey, it's only some fabric and a few dollars. Halloran makes donations like that all the time.''

She shook her head. ''You're wrong. It's much more.''

''I don't understand.''

''Kevin, it's more proof that the man I fell in love with still exists. Don't you see? If we could work together on this, it would be a start, a new beginning for us.''

As understanding dawned, he clasped her hands in his and lifted them to his mouth. He kissed each speck of paint, each blemish until Lacey was sure the earth was falling away beneath her. She wanted to fling her arms around him, wanted to welcome him back from the cold, uncaring, distant place it seemed he'd gone without her. She held back only by reminding herself that this was only a beginning.

They were up until midnight making plans. Dinner was no more than sandwiches hastily slapped together and eaten distractedly. When neither of them could hold their eyes open a minute longer, they were still reluctant to go to bed. In the hallway between their rooms, their gazes caught and held.

Lacey raised her fingers to caress his cheek. "I love you," she dared to say for the first time in months.

"And I love you," he echoed. He glanced toward the door of the master bedroom, then back to her. "Lace?"

Her heart hammered in her chest at the invitation. To spend the night in his bed again, in his arms, would be just this side of heaven. But something inside her whispered that it was still too soon, that to give in to the provocative promise in his eyes would risk everything.

"I can't," she said finally.

She saw the quick hurt in his eyes and wished she could take the words back, but it was too late. Already he was retreating.

How many more times could she bring herself to say no? she wondered. How many more times could Kevin hear it without distancing himself from her for good? Would she even know when it was time to put her heart and soul on the line, no matter what?

The elusive answer to those questions kept her awake most of the night. When the early morning hours came, the questions were still there. And the answers were no clearer.

Chapter Eleven

So many times during the night Kevin was tempted to get up and go across the hall. It was three o'clock when he knew he could no longer deny himself. Lacey was still his wife. He still loved her with all his heart. And he knew in his gut that the longer they allowed this foolishness of separate bedrooms to go on, the more difficult it would be to end.

The longing in Lacey's eyes tonight had been unmistakable. Whatever was holding her back mystified him. She wasn't the type to play games. She never had been. Even when they had made love for the very first time, there had been no coy pretenses between them.

His thoughts drifted back to that long-ago night. It had been here on Cape Cod, the summer after their freshman year in college. Vacation was almost over and they faced another long year of being apart, thanks to his father's determined interference.

They had come to the beach for the weekend with friends, but had quickly abandoned them in favor of privacy. They had gone for a walk on the beach, their way lit by the full moon. When they found a secluded cove, he had spread a blanket on the still-warm sand. Other nights, other summers, they had done no more than sit and talk, often until dawn, but somehow both of them knew that this night would be different. The love that had blossomed between them with a slow, sweet dawning needed expression in a new and exciting way.

Lacey had made the first bold move. With his eyes riveted on her, she had slowly removed her clothes. She had been a virgin, yet there had been no shyness in her that night. She had stood before him, naked in the moonlight, proud, her eyes filled with love.

"Make love to me," she had whispered.

Uncertain, he was the one to hesitate. He had always been so sure that he was the stronger one, but that night Lacey had proved him wrong. She had been bold and daring, while he thought his heart would split in two with the sheer joy of making her his.

Slowly, tenderly he had claimed her, enchanted by the velvet softness of her flesh, intoxicated by the taste of her. He had wanted her for so long, needed her forever it seemed. His hands trembled as they cupped her breasts. His pulse raced as he touched her moist warmth. She had been so hot, so ready for him, so eager to guide him into her.

As he sank into her that very first time, she had cried out his name, not in pain as he had feared, but in unmistakable exhilaration. Surrounded by her heat, thrilled by her pleasure, he had felt his own pleasure build and build until he too came apart in a shattering climax that was beyond anything he had ever imagined.

Just thinking about it now aroused him to a state of breathless, aching anticipation. It was past time for patience, past time for half measures. He stood up and crossed the room in three strides. At the door he hesitated, then shook off his doubts. No, he was right about this. He had to be.

He paused again at the guest room door, then opened it slowly. Inside, a beam of moonlight streamed through the window casting a silvery glow over Lacey's complexion. She was wearing a gown of French lace and Halloran's finest pale pink satin. It was one he had given to her for their last anniversary. Though she preferred a classic, elegant look in public, she had always loved impractical, frothy concoctions for sleeping. In this one, she looked more feminine, more tantalizing than ever.

Tenderness welled up inside him, as he guessed how restless she had been. The sheets were in a tangle. The gown had ridden up to bare one glorious, tempting thigh. Kevin sucked in a ragged breath as desire pulsed through him. She was so incredibly beautiful, so inviting.

And so exhausted, he realized as he inched closer and glimpsed the shadows under her eyes. It was little wonder after the day she had spent working with Paula…and after the torment he had put her through for far longer than that.

Honor warred with need. This time, to his regret, honor won.

Reluctantly Kevin settled for a whisper-light caress

of her shoulder, as he shifted one fallen strap of her gown back into place. Fingertips skimmed over cool, silken flesh, lingered as his pulse skipped, then raced.

Lacey's breath hitched at the touch. He held his own breath in an agony of anticipation, waiting to see if she would wake, hoping against hope that she would. He told himself he would be blameless then.

When she didn't awaken, when the pattern of her breathing became slow and steady again, he sighed.

Tomorrow, he promised himself. Tomorrow they would find their way back into each other's arms.

Lacey spent the morning trying to figure out why Kevin suddenly seemed so nostalgic. It was as if he'd spent the whole night lost in memories, caught up in the same sweetly tormenting dreams that she had had when she'd finally fallen into a restless slumber.

Today it seemed as if he were using those memories to rekindle the desire that had always surged between them like a palpable force.

"What's gotten into you?" she murmured, when his hand curved around the nape of her neck for just an instant as he returned to the breakfast table. The casual touch sent her pulse scrambling. She tried to cover it by spreading jam on her toast.

"I don't know what you mean," he said, pouring himself a second cup of coffee, his expression all smug male innocence.

She regarded him with disbelief, then finally shrugged. "Perhaps it's just my imagination playing tricks with me."

He nodded, rather quickly she thought.

"I'm sure that's it," he agreed, but the gleam in his eyes contradicted the too-casual response.

Her gaze narrowed. "Are you sure you have no idea what I'm talking about?"

His eyes widened. "None. Did you sleep well?"

"I tossed and turned a bit. You?"

"I was a bit restless myself. I looked in on you," he said in a voice that sounded a bit husky.

Surprised, she didn't know what to say, finally settling for a simple, "Oh?"

She reached hurriedly for a section of the Boston paper so she could hide the flush of embarrassment that she could feel creeping into her cheeks. Kevin nudged the paper aside.

"Lacey." His voice was soft and slow as honey, but it held a definite note of command.

She swallowed hard, then forced herself to meet his gaze. "Yes?"

"You looked very beautiful."

This time there was no hiding the heat that climbed into her cheeks. "Kevin Halloran, if I didn't know better, I'd think you were trying to rattle me."

He grinned at that. "Then you obviously don't know me at all. Actually my intentions aren't nearly that honorable. I want to seduce you."

Lacey felt every muscle in her body clench, not just at his words, though those were disturbing enough, but at the spark of satisfaction in his eyes.

"Am I having any luck?" he asked, his tone light.

"The offer is tempting," she admitted.

"That's good."

"It is the middle of the morning, though."

"And what is wrong with making love to my wife in the middle of the morning?"

"Not a thing," she murmured breathlessly, captivated by the possibilities.

She saw his whole body tense at that. He held out his hand. She was about to reach for it when reason intruded. There were a hundred reasons for going to bed with Kevin and a thousand more for saying no. She had remembered them all last night. Today it seemed she had to search her memory for just one.

"We can't, Kevin," she said desperately, thinking of Linc's insistent warning. "It's too soon."

Sudden anger turned his eyes a stormy shade of gray blue. "Too soon?" he repeated in a voice that throbbed with sarcasm. "Too soon for whom? We haven't made love in a year. Maybe more."

Though he had missed her meaning entirely, Lacey was too stunned by his harsh, bitterly accusing tone to explain. Instead, she snapped back, "And whose fault is that? Not mine, dammit. I wasn't the one who spent sixteen hours a day in an office and came home exhausted. I'm not the one who was so caught up in work that nothing else mattered."

"No," he said, his tone and his gaze as cold as a winter morning. "You were the one who walked out."

At that she shoved her chair back from the table and forced herself to be silent. Arguing was no solution. If anything it would only make matters worse. But all of this tiptoeing around their problems for fear of upsetting Kevin was beginning to get to her. How many times could she clamp her mouth shut, holding in her hurt, her anger?

At the sink, Lacey gripped the edge of the counter so tightly her knuckles turned white. She drew in a deep, calming breath before she turned back to face him.

"We have to talk about all of this, but only when we can do it calmly."

"I'm not feeling one damn bit calm," he said furiously. "I am sick and tired of being made out to be the bad guy here. I'm a human being, Lacey. Not some storybook hero. I'm sure I've made more than my share of mistakes, but so have you." He glared at her. "So, my dear, have you."

Before Lacey could gather her wits for a comeback, Kevin was gone, leaving her alone with her anger and with the sad awareness that after all these days together, they were not one bit better off than they had been months ago. They didn't understand each other at all anymore.

Lacey was still in the kitchen, lingering over a last cup of coffee, when she heard a car pull up outside. She heard Kevin open the door and she wandered into the hallway to see who'd come to visit.

Jason and Dana. Dear Lord, she had forgotten they were coming. She viewed their arrival as a mixed blessing. They would serve as a buffer after this morning's angry exchange. At the same time, their presence would create even more tension as she and Kevin both struggled to keep their son and daughter-in-law from seeing how little progress had actually been made toward a reconciliation.

As they hurried inside with their bags, Lacey was all too aware of the anxious glances they exchanged.

"Hi, Mom," Jason said, his voice too cheerful. His gaze searched her face. "You've gotten a little sun."

"I've been gardening," she said, putting her cup down to hug Jason and then Dana. She smiled at her daughter-in-law. "How are you feeling?"

"Much better. Jason's finally stopped getting morning sickness."

"Thank goodness," he murmured fervently.

"All men should have a taste of what it's like to carry a baby," Dana retorted. "It might make them more sympathetic."

"I'm sympathetic, all right. But we're only having the one. I can't go through this again."

"You!" Dana retorted indignantly. "At least you'll miss out on the labor pains."

Lacey decided she'd better step in before the familiar battle worsened. "Enough, you two. Where's Sammy?"

"We left him with Brandon," Dana said. "Sammy said something about teaching him to shoot down some kind of creatures."

"A video game created by a sadistic computer hack," Jason explained. "I was awake until three in the morning trying to save some princess from those same evil guys. They multiply like rabbits if you don't stay on your toes."

"Sounds intriguing," Lacey said. "You'll have to teach your father sometime."

"Not while he's recuperating," Dana warned. "It turns them into glassy-eyed monsters. I'm sure it can't be good for their blood pressure. I dared to interrupt Sammy and Jason for dinner the other night and they both jumped down my throat."

"I was winning for the first time in history," Jason explained. "I wasn't about to lose my competitive edge."

Dana rolled her eyes. "See what I mean?"

Jason put an arm around her waist and hugged her. "I love you, anyway," he said. "Where should I put our bags? The guest room across from yours and Dad's?"

Kevin deliberately turned away, leaving Lacey to respond. "No," she said, all too aware of the puzzled expression on Dana's face and on Jason's. There was no hiding the truth from them, though.

"Actually, my things are in there," she said briskly. "Use the yellow room at the end of the hall. It has the second best view in the house."

Jason shot her a sharp look, but fortunately he didn't make an issue of it. He picked up the bags. "I'll be right back. Dana, please go sit down."

"I've been sitting down," she reminded him very patiently. She regarded Lacey hopefully. "He will get over this, won't he?"

"Kevin never did. He watched me like a hawk all during the entire pregnancy. So did Brandon. It almost drove me wild."

"Fortunately Sammy and I made a pact. He'll keep Brandon busy and I will buy him the latest video games. Hopefully they won't release too many new ones between now and when this little one is born."

She patted her rounded belly. "Do you think there's any chance at all I'll have a girl?" she asked wistfully. "I would sure like to buy dolls, instead of footballs."

"The Halloran genes are against it," Kevin said. "I have to admit, though, that I wouldn't mind having a little girl to spoil rotten."

"There will be no spoiling of this child, girl or boy," Dana said firmly.

Lacey shook her head. "Then you married into the wrong family. The Halloran men take spoiling for granted, especially when it comes to grandchildren. I remember the first Christmas after I met Kevin. His grandfather was still alive then. He gave him the first ten-thousand-dollar installment on his trust fund."

"As I recall, I wasn't that impressed," Kevin countered. "I wanted a new ten-speed bike."

"That's okay. I was awed enough for both of us. I got a sweater and a doll that year. They were both second-hand."

Kevin smiled at her, his eyes gentle and filled with remembering. "You still have that doll, though, don't you? While I gave that money away long ago."

"To buy toys for the Salvation Army's Christmas drive," Lacey recalled. "You'd just turned twenty-one, which meant you could start drawing on the trust. I thought using the money to buy those toys was the sweetest thing you'd ever done."

"Dad thought I'd taken leave of my senses. You were six months pregnant and I was giving away our savings to charity." He shook his head. "Talk about irresponsible."

"I didn't think it was irresponsible," Lacey argued. "We had enough. Those people didn't have anything."

"I agree with Lacey," Dana said, leaning down to give Kevin a kiss on his forehead. "It was a noble gesture."

Kevin reached up and patted her cheek. "That's all it was, a gesture. It didn't really solve anything."

Lacey lost patience. "It gave those families and kids a decent holiday, one they'll always remember. If more people made gestures like those, the world would be a better place. What's happened to you, Kevin? When did you become so cynical?"

"Cynical? No, Lacey. I grew up."

She was about to argue, when she saw the alarm in Dana's eyes. She bit back a sharp retort and shrugged. "I guess we still see some things differently," she said and stood up. "I think I'll get busy on lunch. Dana would you like to help me?"

Her daughter-in-law cast one last confused look at Kevin, then followed Lacey into the kitchen.

"Things aren't any better, are they?" Dana said as they prepared lunch.

"Better?" Lacey echoed with a catch in her voice. "If anything, they're worse than ever."

"But why? I don't understand. Anyone who looks at the two of you can see how much you still love each other."

Lacey shrugged. "When you get right down to it, love may not conquer all."

"Now who's sounding cynical?" Dana asked too gently.

Lacey had to fight off the tears that suddenly threatened. She tried to smile. "Come now, you didn't drive all the way out here just to be depressed. Let's have some lunch and then you and Jason can go for a walk on the beach. It's a beautiful day."

Dana looked as if she wanted to say more, but finally she took her cue from Lacey and busied herself with the lunch preparations.

They all ate much too quickly, anxious to put an end to the charade of cheer they tried to maintain. Jason had barely put his last bite of food in his mouth, when Dana stood up and grabbed his hand. "Let's take a walk."

Startled, he simply stared at her. "Before dessert?"

"Yes," she said firmly. With a shrug, he left the table and followed her from the room.

Kevin glanced across the table, his expression rueful. "I'll bet they can't wait to get back to Boston."

Lacey nodded. "I can't say that I blame them."

He hesitated, then finally looked straight into her eyes. "Do you want to leave, too? Was all of this a mistake?"

A sigh of regret shuddered through her as she thought about the question. "No," she said at last. "But I think we were expecting too much. We need to talk—" When he started to speak, she held up her hand. "No. I mean really talk. And we can't do that if I'm terrified of upsetting you."

"Is that really the problem?"

"It is a lot of it," she admitted. "Every time I think that I'm ready to bring everything out into the open, I remember the way you looked in that intensive care unit. I caution myself to wait, just a little longer, just until Linc pronounces you fit again."

"Is that what you meant this morning when you said it was too soon for us to make love?" Kevin asked, his expression oddly hopeful.

"Yes. Then you took it wrong and the next thing I knew we were shouting. If only we could do this calmly and rationally, but unfortunately there's too much hurt and anger."

She couldn't miss his sigh of regret at her words. "What's going to happen to us, Lacey?" he said.

"We're going to survive all this," she said with sudden certainty. "If we can face it, if we can finally begin to be open and honest about our feelings, then we'll survive. We just have to be patient."

"Not one of my virtues, I'm afraid."

"No," she agreed with the beginnings of a smile. "But maybe it's time you learned a little about patience, for more reasons than one."

He reached for her hand and this time she took it and held on tight.

"You're the best reason I can think of, Lacey," he said quietly. "The very best."

Lacey felt her heart climb into her throat. "Maybe we should make a pact."

"We seem to be doing a lot of that."

"But this one could be the most important of all."

"What, then?"

"Could we pretend, just for a few days, that everything is okay between us? Maybe that would take the pressure off. As it is, we're too demanding of ourselves. Every conversation turns into some sort of cross-examination or psychoanalysis. Maybe we should just forget about all the problems and just be ourselves, have a little fun. We can save the serious talk for later."

Kevin looked skeptical. "Isn't that a little like hiding from reality?"

Lacey laughed. "It's a *lot* like hiding from reality, but so what? Nobody's on a timetable here, right? There's no law that says we must resolve every last problem by a certain date, is there?"

"I guess not," he said slowly. "I don't suppose this plan of yours includes moving back into the master bedroom?"

She stood up and pressed a kiss to his forehead. "Don't push your luck, pal."

"Medically speaking, you mean?"

His arm curved around her waist and tumbled her into his lap. Lacey gazed up into eyes that were suddenly filled with laughter. Serenity stole through her then, for the fist time in days.

"Medically speaking," she confirmed softly just before Kevin's mouth settled over hers in a kiss that was filled with tenderness and promise.

That was the way Jason and Dana found them, still at the kitchen table, still wrapped in each other's arms.

"This is an improvement," Jason commented approvingly from the doorway.

"Jason," Dana muttered urgently, tugging on his arm. "Leave them alone."

Lacey laughed. "Too late," she said as she stood up. "How about a game? Scrabble? Cards?"

"Cutthroat Scrabble," Kevin said with a hint of his old enthusiasm. They had spent many an evening engaged in just such battles before the age of video games.

Jason looked from his father to Lacey and back again, then nodded in satisfaction. "I'll get the board."

"And I'll get the snacks," Dana said.

Jason groaned. "Don't let her, Mom. The only things she likes these days are pickles and brownies."

Lacey patted her son's cheek. "Don't worry. We're fresh out of both."

"Don't be so sure," Jason retorted. "I'm relatively certain that's what she brought out here in that extra suitcase."

Kevin stood up. "Maybe I ought to get the snacks."

This time it was Lacey who groaned.

Kevin grinned at her. "Calm down, my love. There's enough celery and carrot sticks in the refrigerator to feed an army, to say nothing of one pregnant lady, one recuperating man and two nervous nellies."

The first word Lacey played on the Scrabble board was *joy*. It might not have earned as many points as some others she could have made, but it was definitely the one that best summed up the way she was feeling as she was surrounded by her family once again.

From the warm, tender expression in Kevin's eyes when he caught her gaze, it was a feeling he understood—and shared.

Chapter Twelve

Having Jason and Dana around did indeed take off the pressure, Kevin realized on Sunday. Witnessing his son and daughter-in-law's happiness spun a web of serenity around all of them.

Slowly he and Lacey had relaxed. Like old friends rediscovering shared interests, their laughter came more easily. And the looks they exchanged were filled with open awareness, rather than carefully banked accusation.

When they stood in the driveway to say goodbye, his arm curved naturally around Lacey's waist. And when Jason's car was out of sight, it seemed just as natural that their hands met and laced together.

"Feel like a walk on the beach?" he asked, reluctant to go back inside and risk spoiling the lazy, spellbinding mood. "We should have another hour or so of daylight."

"A walk sounds good," she said.

At the edge of the yard they slipped off their shoes, then crossed the dunes to reach the water's edge. The last of the day's sunlight slanted across the beach. Much of the wide stretch of sand had been cast in shadow, making the sand cool against their bare feet. For as far as Kevin could see, he and Lacey were alone in the early-evening shadows.

"Isn't this perfect, when it's like this?" Lacey asked with a sigh. "No one around. It's almost possible to believe that we're the only ones who know about this stretch of beach."

"Remind me to bring you back in mid-July," Kevin said, thinking of the crowds that descended with the first full days of summer and remained until Labor Day at least.

"And spoil the illusion? No way."

They walked as far as they could before the tide caught up with them and forced them to turn back. For the first time in months the silence that fell between them was comfortable, rather than strained. Neither of them seemed to feel the need to cover the quiet time with awkward conversation.

Kevin glanced over and caught the slow curving of Lacey's lips. "A penny for your thoughts," he said.

"At today's rate of inflation? You've got to be kidding," she said, repeating a joke that they'd shared over the years whenever one of them tried to pry into the other's secret thoughts.

"How much are your thoughts going for these days?"

She seemed to consider the question carefully. "A hundred dollars easy."

He reached in his back pocket and pulled out his

wallet. He found the hundred-dollar bill he'd tucked there and offered it to her. "These thoughts of yours better be good."

"In whose opinion?" she countered, nabbing the money and tucking it into her pocket.

"Mine. Pay up."

She grinned at him with a wicked gleam in her eyes. "Chicken," she said succinctly.

"I beg your pardon?"

"I was thinking about chicken. Do you realize that there are at least a hundred different ways to fix chicken? And that's before you get into the ethnic variations."

Kevin regarded her intently. "I just paid one hundred dollars for a dissertation on chicken recipes?" He held out his hand. "I don't think so. I expected something terribly revealing about your romantic soul. Give the money back. You took it under false pretenses."

"Try to get it," she challenged and took off running.

Her pace was lightning quick at first as he stood flat-footed and stared after her in delighted astonishment. Then he took off after her. He was aware of the precise moment when she slowed down just enough to be caught. He fell on top of her as they tumbled onto the sand.

"You let me catch you," he accused, all too aware of the press of her breasts against his chest and the familiar fit of their lower bodies. He captured her hands and pinned them over her head. Her eyes were filled with laughter and her breath was coming in soft, ragged puffs that fanned his face.

"Maybe I did and maybe I didn't," she taunted.

"Lacey Grainger Halloran, you are a tease."

She wriggled beneath him, just enough to confirm the accusation. There was an unmistakable flare of excitement in her eyes, though she did her damnedest to look innocent.

"Me?" she murmured.

"Yes, you," he said softly, and then he lowered his mouth to cover hers. Her lips were soft and moist enough to have him forgetting to be sensible and slow and careful. Her mouth tempted, like the lure of a flame, and the heat it sent spiraling through him was devastating.

Their bodies strained together, hers arching into his in a way that had him aching with an arousal so hard, so demanding that he thought it very likely he might embarrass himself as he hadn't since the first time he'd experimented with sex.

Kevin fought for calm by rolling over on his back, taking Lacey with him so that he could see her face and the gathering stars in the evening sky at the same time.

"Good Lord, woman, what you do to me," he murmured, his hands lightly brushing the sand from her face, then lingering to caress.

"I know," she said, her expression dreamy and open for once. "It's the same for me with you. Sometimes you touch me and I think I'll fly apart. It's always been that way."

"Always?" he teased. "In the fifth grade you had the hots for me?"

She laughed at that. "Of course, only then I thought it was an allergy. I had a hunch a doctor could cure it, but I never quite got around to checking."

"Thank God," he said fervently.

"What about you?" she questioned, smoothing her

fingers along the curve of his jaw. ''Did I make you come unglued in the fifth grade?''

''Only when you hit that home run during the spring baseball tournament. I was ready to marry you after that.''

''Fortunately there are laws about that sort of thing.''

''I'm glad we waited as long as we did,'' he said, his hands stroking over the backs of her thighs and up over her still-perfect bottom. Even through a layer of denim, she tempted. ''I wouldn't have missed the sweet anticipation of those years for anything.''

''Me, neither,'' she whispered, twining her arms around his neck and fitting her head into the curve of his shoulder. ''Me, neither.''

They stayed right where they were, snuggled comfortably together, for what seemed an eternity. Neither of them was willing to move and risk losing the rare and special mood. Despite thick sweaters and jeans, they were both cold and damp through to their bones by the time they finally made the effort to stand up and go inside.

''How about soup?'' Lacey suggested as they stood in front of the fire to warm up.

''Chicken noodle, no doubt,'' he said.

She scowled at him, but her eyes were bright with laughter. ''I was thinking of that white bean soup you like so much. It's thick and hearty, the perfect thing for a night like this. Of course, I could manage chicken noodle from a can, if that's your preference.''

''Is there any of that bread you made left?''

''Yes.''

''Then the white bean soup and bread sounds great.''

"Here, in front of the fire?"

"Yes."

He followed her into the kitchen and helped with chopping onions and gathering silverware. There was something reassuring and cozy about working side by side to prepare a meal. How long had it been since they had done that? Before he'd hired the housekeeper certainly. And long before that? Maybe so.

Possibly from the first moment he'd gone to work at Halloran, when he'd realized that Lacey didn't really want to hear how his days at his father's company had gone.

Before that, early in their marriage they had both rushed in after six and divided up the chores so they could get dinner on the table at a decent hour. Lacey had cooked. He had set the table. And they had used the time to compare notes on everything they'd done while apart.

Occasionally he had fixed dinner and let her catch up on laundry. Without any particular planning, they had had the ultimate liberated household, Kevin realized now with amusement. Still, the rhythm of their evenings had been satisfying in some elusive way he couldn't begin to explain. There had been a closeness, a unity. How had he forgotten that?

The phone rang just as Lacey was ready to ladle up the soup. "I'll get it," he offered and picked up the receiver.

"Kevin?"

"Hey, Dad, how are you?"

He glanced at Lacey and saw her shoulders stiffen almost imperceptibly.

"Fine, now that that rapscallion of Dana's has gone home. That boy wears me out."

"Are you sure it isn't the other way around? What did you two do all weekend?"

"Played some fool video game. A lot of nonsense, if you ask me."

"You must have lost," Kevin guessed.

"The boy whipped the daylights out of me," his father admitted with an indignant huff. "No respect for his elders."

"You wanted Sammy to let you win?"

"Of course not, but he didn't have to humiliate me."

Brandon cleared his throat, always a prelude to saying something he figured the other person didn't want to hear. Kevin waited, his nerves tensed.

"I didn't call up there to discuss video games," his father announced. "Just wanted to see how things are going."

"*Things,*" he mocked, realizing where the conversation was headed, "are going fine."

"You ready to get back to work?"

"Dad, don't start."

"I'm not pushing, son. Just asking."

"With you, it's hard to tell the difference."

Brandon uttered a long-suffering sigh. "It sure is hard to get an ounce of respect in this family."

Kevin ignored the play for sympathy. Finally his father said, "You and Lacey doing okay?"

Now they were really getting down to the reason for the call. Kevin studied his wife out of the corner of his eye. There was no mistaking the tense set of her shoulders now. It was as if she could hear her father-in-law's end of the conversation, rather than just Kevin's innocuous replies.

"Okay," he said, wondering if he was stretching the truth.

"Hear she was staying across the hall."

"Dad! That is none of your business." Only Lacey's presence kept him from saying more. He would speak to Jason first thing tomorrow about spreading tales, especially to Brandon. Jason had had his own bitter experience with his grandfather's meddling. He should have known better.

"Of course it's my business. Your happiness will always be my concern."

"Drop it," Kevin warned.

"Okay, okay. The papers on that deal for the new looms are due in tomorrow. Shall I send 'em on out there?"

Kevin hesitated. Those papers were likely to be like waving a red flag under Lacey's nose. On the other hand, what harm could there possibly be in looking through a contract? Somebody besides Brandon needed to look at the fine print. His father wanted those new looms too badly to worry about whether they were being taken to the cleaners on the deal.

"Send them out," he said finally. "Dad, I've got to go now. Lacey has dinner ready."

"You give her my love, then," his father said. "And tell her to get the hell back in her own bed where she belongs. Better yet, put her on and I'll tell her myself."

Kevin groaned. "You will do nothing of the kind. Good night, Dad."

When he'd hung up, Lacey put their bowls of soup on trays, along with the warm bread. They carried the meal into the living room and settled down on the sofa in front of the fire.

For the first time in the last twenty-four hours the silence that fell between them was uneasy. Kevin was more disappointed than surprised.

"Okay," he said finally, putting his spoon down carefully. "What's on your mind?"

"Who says anything is on my mind?" Lacey asked stiffly.

"Lacey, being evasive won't help anything."

"Okay, what did Brandon want this time?"

"He just called to say hello."

She regarded him doubtfully. "It certainly took him long enough to spit one word out."

"You know what I meant," Kevin said, his irritation beginning to mount. "What is it with you and my father? I thought all that animosity was a thing of the past. I thought you'd forgiven him years ago."

"I did."

"Then why do you react like this every time he calls up?"

"He's trying to get you to start working again, isn't he? Doesn't he realize that the whole purpose of your coming out here was to recuperate?"

With her gaze pinned on him, he couldn't manage a convenient lie. "It's just some papers. It'll take me an hour or two."

"Just some papers. An hour or two," Lacey repeated. "Can't you see that's just the tip of the iceberg with Brandon? Next he'll be pulling up here with an attaché case filled with more papers and a fax machine."

"So what if he does?" Kevin snapped. "I have to get back to work sooner or later. I'll be a helluva lot more relaxed here than I would be back in Boston."

Lacey didn't respond to that.

Kevin threw down his napkin. "On second thought, maybe Boston would be simpler. I wouldn't have to worry about you looking over my shoulder making judgments, would I?"

He stood up and started for the door. "I'm going for a walk."

"Kevin," Lacey called after him.

The last thing he heard before he slammed the front door was her muttered curse.

"Damn," Lacey muttered for the tenth time as she paced and waited for Kevin to come back. How had a simple phone call reopened every wound and shattered the cautious tranquility they had finally managed to achieve?

Because it had been from Brandon, of course. She had heard more than enough to realize he had work for Kevin to do. If she hadn't guessed, Kevin's guilty expression would have told her. She suspected there was more—probably unwanted advice about their marriage, if she knew Brandon.

Even so, it had been stupid to force the issue with Kevin. She couldn't keep jumping down his throat over every little thing.

What on earth was wrong with her? Was she so terrified of losing him that she wanted to wrap him in a cloak of that protective bubble wrap and watch over him for the rest of their lives? What kind of life would that be for either of them? Longer, maybe, but rife with tension.

She was going to have to get a grip on herself. She was going to have to ignore her obviously futile plan to hold reality at bay and start talking. No matter how much the words hurt. No matter how angry they got.

They could not allow their pain to fester any longer. Tonight had been proof of that. After a wonderful day of pretending that everything was normal again in their marriage, they had slammed into reality with one phone call.

Lacey was waiting in the living room when Kevin finally came in. She heard him start down the hall and called out to him. For an instant she was afraid he would ignore her, but finally she heard a cautious movement, then a quiet, "Yes?"

"Will you join me?"

"I don't think so," he said. "I'm tired. I'm going to bed."

"Please, Kevin."

"Why, Lacey? What's the point?"

"Our marriage is the point."

"Right now I don't give our marriage a snowball's chance in hell," he said with bleak finality. "Maybe I'll have a different view in the morning, but I wouldn't hold my breath, if I were you."

He was gone before she could force a single word past the tears that clogged her throat.

Chapter Thirteen

All the pretense, all the games had to end, Lacey reminded herself as she sat at the kitchen table in the morning. She had made a pot of tea and laced it liberally with milk. She didn't need the jagged edginess of too much caffeine on top of everything else today. Her nerves were already shot and it was barely six a.m.

She could hear the first faint sounds of the birds as dawn finally broke beyond the horizon. Black became gray, then purple, then softest pink as the sun edged its way up through the clouds. This was her favorite time of day, a time when anything seemed possible. She needed that sense of hope more than ever as she waited for Kevin to join her.

Lacey thought of all the emotions she'd kept hidden, all the desperate thoughts she had never dared to voice, and tried to pick one above all the others as a place to start.

It would be so much easier if healing could take place without all this airing of past betrayals, she thought wistfully. But it would be false healing, one that could never last.

Above all else, she wanted whatever happened today to be the beginning of forever. Her marriage would be salvaged today.

Or it wouldn't.

Either way, she would go on. Both of them would. They were too strong not to fight for happiness—together or apart.

Kevin was wide awake when he heard Lacey leave her room and go into the kitchen. It was still dark outside, too early to be up on a vacation day, far too early to begin dealing with anything that required soul-searching.

But this was no normal vacation, he reminded himself wearily. He couldn't begin to recall the last time he had taken one of those. As for soul-searching, what difference did it make if he went over and over things here in his head or voiced them aloud to Lacey?

Even so, as he lay on the bed, his hands behind his head, he was struck by an odd reluctance to get up and see what form their confrontation was likely to take. After last night, he doubted they would have anything pleasant to say to each other. There was the heavy sense of impending doom weighing him down. He no longer had any idea whether the fault for that was Lacey's or his own. He just knew, as he expected she did, that they couldn't go on this way.

He'd expected something simple to come of this

trip, something magical. Instead he'd been faced with a hard dose of reality. For a man who prided himself on having outgrown so many naive attitudes, he'd clung to this one about his marriage for far too long.

He heard the whistle of the teakettle, a sure sign that Lacey's distress was as deep and dark as his own. She drank tea only when she needed comfort. He could visualize her sitting at the kitchen table, an old china cup cradled in her hands, her gaze fixed on the splashy display of daybreak, her thoughts…

Well, who knew where her thoughts were? He definitely didn't anymore, not with any certainty.

How he regretted that, he thought with a sigh. He regretted too damned much these days, it seemed.

Then fix it, a voice inside his head muttered. *Fix it now or forget it.*

With understandable reluctance, Kevin finally dragged himself out of bed and pulled on a comfortable pair of soft, well-worn jeans and a fisherman's knit sweater that he and Lacey had bought years ago on a trip to Ireland. He dragged on socks and sneakers, because of the chill in the air, though he would have preferred to be barefoot.

He took as long as he could brushing his teeth and shaving. He even ran a comb through his hair. It was a delaying tactic more than anything. His hair had always fallen where it damn well pleased, unless he tamed it often with a short cut. It had grown past taming over the last few weeks and there was too much silver amidst the blond. Funny how there were days when he truly forgot how old he was. Not that forty-eight was exactly ancient, but at times he felt no more than half that.

Kevin glanced at the bed, considered spending more

time making it up, then admitted the one or two minutes it cost him wouldn't be enough to make much difference. He might as well get into the kitchen and face the music.

It was going to be even worse than he'd thought, he decided as he saw Lacey's exhausted expression. She was clinging to that cup of tea as if it were her only lifeline. Her streaked blond hair tumbled loose across her shoulders, inviting his touch, but the look in her eyes when she saw him was forbidding.

"Good morning," he said cautiously, noting that she'd chosen a bright yellow blouse as if to defy her mood.

"Good morning. Would you like breakfast? I could fix you something."

"Tea and toast will do. I'll fix it."

As he popped the bread into the toaster, poured the tea, then brought everything to the table, he stole surreptitious glances at her. She was as still as could be, but there was nothing calm about her. He sensed that turbulent emotions were seething just below the surface. Her gaze was mostly directed down at the tea, but he could see the sorrow and wariness whenever she dared to glance his way.

"Kevin."

"Lacey."

The blurted words were practically simultaneous. With his glance he indicated deference.

Given her chance she looked uncertain. "We can't go on like this. I thought we could, but I was wrong."

"I know," he agreed.

She looked at him then, straight into his eyes, and to his amazement she looked a little helpless and more than a little vulnerable.

"I don't know where to begin," she said finally.

"At the beginning," he suggested, too glibly, judging from the look she shot him.

"That was too long ago to count," she said, but her tone was just a bit lighter. "Can you remember what it was like when we first got married?"

"Yes. At least I think I can. Why don't you tell me what you remember."

"I remember getting up in the morning filled with excitement and anticipation. I remember rushing through the day, reminding myself of every detail so I could share it with you that night. I remember how we talked about everything, every nuance of our lives, every decision, every hope, every dream." She sighed wistfully. "I thought that was the way it would always be."

"I suppose I did, too," he admitted. "It wasn't very realistic of either of us."

"Maybe not."

"Is that all you want back, Lacey? Just the sharing?"

"No, of course not." Her gaze met his, then slipped away. "We had the same vision, then. Somewhere along the way that's what we lost."

"Did we?" he argued. "Don't we both still want the world to be a better place? Don't we both care about family more than anything?"

"I thought we did."

"But?"

"We have such different ways of acting on it. You see a charity, and you need to write a check. You want a home, so you hire people to run it. You believe in family, but not in spending the time it takes to nurture one."

"So I'm still the one at fault," he said, unable to keep the impatience out of his voice. "Only me."

"Of course not," she said at once. "The difference between us is that I've tried every way I could think of to tell you what I need, but you've never once given me a clue about what you want from me anymore. Whatever the housekeeper fixes for dinner is fine. Whatever I wear is fine. However I spend my days is fine." Her tone mimicked him. Her chin rose another notch. "Even the sex began to seem more like habit than the spontaneous passion we used to have."

Kevin stared at her in astonishment. "That's ridiculous," he said defensively.

"Is it? Is it really?" She drew in a deep breath, then braced her hands against the table, almost as if she needed support for whatever she had to say. "Were you having an affair, Kevin?" she asked point blank. "That would explain so much."

Kevin felt as if she'd punched him in his midsection. Shocked, he simply stared at her. He couldn't imagine an accusation that would have thrown him more.

"Well?" she demanded defiantly.

"An affair? Where on earth would you get a ridiculous idea like that?"

"Come on, Kevin. Don't act too stunned. You wouldn't be the first man to have an affair. I can't even count the number of husbands we know who openly play around on their wives."

"Not me, dammit. Not me."

When she continued to look skeptical, he said, "Lacey, I can honestly say that I never even contemplated breaking our marriage vows, much less acted on the thought."

"Is that the truth, Kevin?" she asked softly, her gaze searching his.

He realized then that perhaps more than all the other complaints, all the other differences, this was the one at the root of all their troubles. She couldn't even bring herself to trust him anymore, not even on something as sacred as their marriage vows.

He could read the vulnerability in her eyes, the fear that he'd turned elsewhere for satisfaction, and the expression in her eyes made him ache.

"Darling, I love you. Only you. No matter what else has happened, that has never, ever changed. I've never wanted anyone the way I wanted you."

"Past tense," she observed ruefully.

"No," he swore, leaving his chair to gather her into his arms. She held herself so stiffly, refusing to yield to a comfort too easily offered.

"Present tense," he told her. "I want you now every bit as much as I did when we were a couple of kids discovering our hormones for the first time. Couldn't you tell that last night on the beach, or the night before that and the night before that?"

Apparently he had found the right words—or the right combination of words and touch, after all. He could see the relief slowly washing through her. The words, though, would never be enough. He had to show her how much he needed her, how beautiful he still found her.

"Come with me," he coaxed, brushing her hair back from her face. All thoughts of other issues, other problems faded in his need to convince her of this much at least. "Let me put this crazy notion of yours to rest forever."

Lacey was slow to accept, and he thought for a moment that she might not, using who-knew-what this time as an excuse. In that brief instant of hesitation, he weighed the future without her against the past and realized that nothing would ever be the same if he lost her.

Kevin slid his fingers through her hair until the silky curls tumbled free. The pad of his thumb traced her mouth, the full bottom lip that trembled beneath his touch.

"Please," he whispered, unable to hide the faint note of desperation. "I need you, Lacey. I need you now."

Her fingers came up and linked with his, and the shadows slid away from her eyes, revealing the sheen of tears. "I need you, too," she said.

He would have swept her into his arms in a romantic gesture if he hadn't caught the forbidding look on her face when she realized his intentions. He grinned ruefully. "It's only a few feet," he reminded her.

"Then surely my knees aren't so weak with longing that I can't walk there on my own," she said, surprising him with the dry humor.

His low chuckle slipped out and then they were both laughing. He slanted a kiss across her mouth, capturing the much too infrequent musical sound of her laughter and the taste of milky tea.

"You could always make me laugh," he said.

"I know," she said with a devilish twinkle in her eyes.

But then her hands were at work on the snap of his jeans and he no longer felt the least bit like laughing. He sucked in his breath when her fingers skimmed across denim seeking the already hard shaft beneath.

"Wait," Kevin said urgently, pulling her down to

the bed with him and pinning her hands away from him. He touched his mouth to hers, savoring again the taste, the texture, the heat. Her lips, her tongue had always fascinated him. He could have spent hours absorbed in no more than the nuances of her kisses. But all the while, he worked to rid her of her blouse, her bra, her jeans and panties, just so he could skim fingertips over velvet flesh and tight golden curls.

Soft whispers turned to anxious moans as he came closer and closer to the moist warmth at the apex of her thighs. She struggled to free her hands and when he released her at long last, she used her hands to torment him, to stroke and caress, to soothe and inflame. She slid her hands under his sweater, tangling her fingers in the hairs on his chest, seeking masculine nipples, her gaze locked with his.

She shifted then, and he couldn't take his eyes off the pale softness of her hands as they curved around him, stroking until he thought he would explode from the intensity.

Each of them battled to give, to shower the other with all the love, all the satisfaction that had been withheld for so long. And when the giving pulled them higher and higher, they had to release that last thread of control and learn to accept the unselfish offering.

Lacey came apart first, her body arching, her skin slick with sweat, her eyes filled with so much joy that Kevin was drawn along with her.

When both of them had caught their breath, when the caresses had slowed, he looked into her eyes and promised more. This time, joined together, they traveled even farther, soared even higher.

He couldn't recall a time when they had asked more of each other or given so much. It was proof, beyond all doubt, that what they had was strong enough to last a lifetime.

They slept then, close together, their breath mingling as morning turned to afternoon.

It was only later, in the aftermath of that extraordinary lovemaking, that Kevin said, "This was never, ever the problem between us, Lace."

He swept his hand over the curve of her hip, lingered on the fullness of her breast to prove his point. He knew at once when her body tensed, knew instinctively that his meaning had registered in a way that went beyond the reassuring simplicity of the words. He had unwittingly opened a new door, rather than closing an old one.

"Then what was it?" she demanded softly. "You can't deny that for a time we never touched, not in any way that mattered. Were you just too busy? Too tired? What?"

Kevin tried to find the answers she needed to hear. He searched his heart for things he had never before been willing to put into words. Maybe even thoughts he'd never dared to acknowledge, even to himself.

"Too distracted is probably closer to the truth. I lost sight of what was important," he admitted slowly, as he carefully sorted through explanations.

"After all those years of rebelling, of making my own way, I got caught up in my father's dreams after all. Halloran Industries became important to me. I wanted to make it work. I wanted to have a legacy for our son."

Lacey sat up then, dragging the sheet around her and knotting it above her breasts. Sitting cross-legged before him, she watched him closely in the way that she had of trying to read his innermost, unspoken thoughts. Apparently she came up wanting, because she shook her head.

"But that doesn't explain it. Why should that have driven a wedge between us? I always wanted whatever it took to make you happy."

"You did," he agreed, "or at least you gave it lip service whenever I tried to discuss my decision about Halloran Industries with you."

"Lip service?" she repeated, obviously stung by the charge.

"Yes. As long as what I wanted didn't change too substantially, you went along with it. But along the way I did change substantially. Not necessarily for the best. My needs changed and, no matter what you said aloud, I could see the way you really felt about those changes. It was as if I'd betrayed you, as if I'd betrayed what we'd once fought so hard against. You kept your ideals. I caved in. The accusation was there every time I looked into your eyes."

As the full meaning of Kevin's words sank in, Lacey was shocked by his interpretation of what had gone on between them. "Did I ever say that?"

"You didn't have to. Like I said, it was in your eyes every time you looked at me. When I went to work for Dad, when I bought the house, I always sensed you were making a judgment and that I was coming up short."

"That was your own guilt talking, not me."

"Then why did you begin to withdraw?"

Withdraw? Her? How could that have been, she wondered. "I never meant to do that," she said with total honesty. "Kevin, I didn't hate your job or that house because they represented some evil standard of living. I worried because it seemed to me that you took the job for all the wrong reasons, that you took it because you thought it was your obligation to your father and to Jason and me.''

''And the house? What about that?''

''I hated the house because it no longer seemed like our home, not the way our first house did. I couldn't keep the new one up, so we hired a maid and a housekeeper and a gardener. All the things I loved to do, all the things that I needed to do to take care of my family, to feel I was making a contribution were in the hands of strangers. I felt as if I'd been cast adrift.''

Her claim hovered in the air until at last he said softly, wearily, ''I never knew that.''

''Because we never talked about it. That was my fault, I suppose. I should have explained how I felt.''

Kevin caressed her cheek, the touch light and fleeting. ''I just wanted you to have everything,'' he explained. ''It never occurred to me that in giving you all that, I was taking away something that you felt was more precious.''

''My identity,'' she said quietly. ''How could you not have known, Kevin, that all I ever wanted was you?''

Something in Kevin's face shut down at her words. Lacey had meant them to be reassuring, but it was clear he hadn't taken them that way.

''What's wrong?'' she asked, as an odd chill seemed to invade her.

For the longest time he didn't answer, and during that time she was sure she could hear every tick of the clock on the bedstand, feel every anxious beat of her heart.

Finally, his eyes troubled, he met her gaze. There

was so much raw anguish in his face that she was trembling even before he spoke.

"I can't be your whole world, Lace. I just can't."

"But that's not what I meant," she protested.

He shook his head. "Isn't it? The pressure of that, it's more than I can handle."

Stunned by the bleak finality of his tone, she could only watch as he left the bed, grabbed his clothes and went into the bathroom. She was still helplessly staring after him when he left the house just moments later.

Chapter Fourteen

No one was more stunned than Kevin at the words that had popped out of his mouth just before he'd left the house. Where had those thoughts come from? How had he gone for so many years without the vaguest sense that there was so much resentment buried deep inside him? A shrink would surely have a field day with that one.

As he walked on the beach, oblivious to the sun's heat and the pounding of the waves, Kevin tried hard not to remember the quick flash of hurt and confusion in Lacey's eyes. His implied accusation that her dependence on him had somehow weighed him down had been cruel, especially since he couldn't even explain what was behind it.

Hell, he was the one who'd carved out his role as her protector early on. He'd liked feeling ten feet tall when she looked to him for answers to everything from math lessons to politics. If some of that uneven balance had carried over into their marriage, wasn't that as much his fault as hers?

What worried him more than casting blame for that was the discovery that he had hidden such feelings from himself. Were they really buried in his subconscious or had they merely been a quick, defensive reaction to the guilt he'd accepted too readily for far too long?

Lacey was perfect. Their marriage was perfect. Wasn't that why he'd wanted so desperately to win her back? Surely he wasn't one of those men who clung to the past, simply because they couldn't bear the thought of change.

But if that were so, if he were convinced that everything was so perfect, why did he have this nagging sense that he'd been fooling himself? Had he simply grown comfortable in the role of martyr, accepting the blame heaped on him and feeling noble for ignoring his own doubts?

No, dammit! He did love Lacey. He tried that claim out in his head. It rang just as true as it ever had. Okay, then, he wasn't stark raving mad. He was just mixed up, confused, maybe a little exhausted from all the tension. He wasn't thinking clearly.

Hard as he tried, though, he couldn't easily dismiss what had happened. Those words had come from somewhere and he'd darned well better figure out where before he went back to face Lacey again. If their marriage hadn't always been so perfect, after all, he'd better be able to explain what had been lacking from his point of view. She knew what she thought of as his failings as clearly as if she'd carried an itemized list of his sins around in her head.

But no matter how desperately Kevin tried to find a precise, clear-cut answer, he couldn't. So, he thought with a sigh filled with regrets, it wasn't going to be so easy for them, after all. They were going to have to struggle for answers.

He supposed they were among the lucky ones. They still had the will to fight for their marriage. They had their love. They had this new-found honesty, as painful as it was. He hadn't a doubt in his head that they would make it, as long as they didn't shy away from the truth.

He walked until the sky dimmed and the wind picked up. The biting chill cut through his jacket, but worse was the chill he felt deep inside.

For years now he had not taken the time to be terribly introspective, but suddenly he had the sense that something very precious was on the line. He had to figure out exactly why there had been that vague anger behind his words, that hint of something too long repressed. Theories weren't the answer. He needed facts. He needed to pinpoint the cause, narrow it down to a specific moment or an evolution. He had to understand what was in his heart as clearly as what was in his head.

Kevin thought back to the early days of his marriage, days crammed with too much to do and so much tenderness and love. He and Lacey had both worked like demons at demanding, and often thankless, jobs. Then they had spent long hours side by side volunteering for causes they both believed in. Each night they had tumbled into bed, exhausted, but filled with exhilaration.

That period of their lives had been incredibly special. There was absolutely no doubt in his mind about that. Thinking about those days brought smiles, even laughter. Never pain.

But that time had been far too short, now that he thought about it. When Jason was born barely a year after the wedding, things began to change. Lacey took her maternity leave and seemed to blossom before his eyes as she took care of their son. She turned their cramped apartment into a real home, and there were tempting, creative dinners on the table.

Soon any thoughts of her returning to work, any time for volunteering vanished in a sea of household demands. They moved into the house Jason now owned. Nothing ever quite went back to the way it had been.

And he'd resented it, he realized with a sense of shock that actually brought him to a standstill. All these years he had resented the way things had changed, and yet he'd never said a word, hadn't even identified the cause of his mild dissatisfaction.

If he had changed as she had accused him of so often, then so had she. They had never once dealt with that.

He thought he understood why. Unlike Lacey, he had kept the resentment so deeply buried that only now could he recognize the subtle way it had affected everything between them.

If Lacey was going to conform to a more traditional pattern, if she was going to content herself with a home and motherhood, then why shouldn't he do the male equivalent of caving in? At least that must have been the subliminal message at work on him when he'd finally made the decision to go to work at Halloran Industries. How many decisions after that had been affected in the same way?

To top it off, he'd then had to deal with Lacey's unspoken disapproval, along with his own burden of guilt about becoming more and more like his father with each day that passed. He'd called it growing up, but obviously deep inside he'd never truly believed it.

Explaining all of this to her after all this time wasn't going to be easy. He needed some time to sort through it all himself, time to be sure that the answers he'd come up with were valid. Time, in fact, to discover if his marriage was something he really wanted to succeed.

The last seemed like blasphemy. Of course he wanted it to succeed. That was the one given in all this, the one thing he'd never questioned.

Until now, he reminded himself. Lord knows, he had questions now. Unfortunately he didn't have the luxury of time to find the answers, time to examine and come to terms with these raw new discoveries about himself. Lacey was waiting for him.

Kevin's pace picked up, almost in spite of all the doubts tumbling through his poor, pitiful, aching head. That alone should have told him something. He needed to get back to her, to share his thoughts and hear her reaction to them. Lacey had always had a knack for cutting through his self-delusion.

Until now, he reminded himself ruefully. Now when it probably meant more than anything.

When he got back to the house, he found her sitting in the living room, almost lost in the shadowy darkness. He flipped on a light and felt his heart wrench at the tears tracking down her cheeks. He wanted to go to her. He wanted to hold her, comfort her.

Instinctively he started toward her, then stopped

himself. They needed to air these raw emotions, not soothe them away with meaningless promises.

"Are you okay?" he asked.

"Sure. Terrific," she said with a defiant lift of her chin. She couldn't hide the way it trembled, though. It reminded him of their first meeting so long ago, and his heart ached for her.

And for himself.

"I think maybe this had been the most difficult couple of hours in my entire life," he said finally, sinking into a chair across from her and dragging a hand through his hair.

Eyes shimmering with tears clashed with his. "It hasn't been much of a picnic for me, either."

"No, I'm sure it hasn't been. I'm sorry."

She shrugged. "For what? For being honest? I asked for it, didn't I?"

"But I think we both thought it was going to be a simple matter of airing a few gripes, vowing to try harder and then forgetting all about it."

"Yeah," she said, "silly us."

"There is a bright side," he told her, trying to earn a smile.

"Oh?"

"We haven't had to pay a fortune for shrinks to get to this point."

"Now that is something to stand up and cheer about," she said, her voice steadier at last.

Tears still clung to the ends of her lashes, but she looked stronger somehow, as if she could withstand anything. Perhaps he'd underestimated her ability to stand on her own and overestimated the depth of her need for him.

Whichever it was, Kevin knew in that instant that

he had never loved Lacey more. Whatever faint, lingering doubts he had had about that had fled. His heart still turned over at the sight of her. His head still demanded that he protect her from the sort of hurt he himself had inflicted on her. Old habits obviously died hard.

"Feel like talking?" he asked. "Or should we take some time out? Go to a movie or something?"

She met his gaze evenly. "Hey, it couldn't get much worse than this. Let's get it all out now. I don't think I could concentrate on a movie, anyway."

Her glib words were sheer bravado, but Kevin knew there would never be a better time, that what he had to say would hurt whenever he said it. It was better to get everything out in the open now, so they could begin to pick up the pieces.

If there were any left to pick up. Dear God, why did that thought creep in so often? It terrified him. Like an earthquake, it seemed to shake the very foundation of his life.

He stared at the fire before he spoke, gathering courage, censoring harsh accusations. "It's funny," he began slowly. "I never knew that I felt quite so angry until the words came out of my mouth earlier."

Lacey regarded him intently, as if she were weighing his words. "I still don't understand," she said finally. "You talk about feeling pressured. Why? What did I ever do to make you feel that way? I built my life around making you happy."

"Exactly. Instead of caring about the world as you always had, you limited your concerns to just me and our family. I guess I felt that you had betrayed me long before it was the other way around."

"Betrayed you how?" she asked, looking wounded. "By loving you? By needing you?"

"By changing," he said simply.

"But I'm not the one who changed," she protested.

"Yes. Maybe you can't see it, but I can. You were always strong and independent. You always had this clear vision of what you wanted out of life, what we should be doing to make the world a better place to live. There we were, these two intrepid souls going off to tilt at windmills. We were so self-righteous, I suppose, thinking that we knew more than our parents, that we could fix all their mistakes."

"We did fix some things," she reminded him, a little sadly it seemed.

"Maybe some," he agreed. "Then we had Jason and everything changed. The entire focus of your world centered on our son and on me."

"We had a new baby, Kevin. What did you expect?"

"I'm not talking about the first month or even the first year. I could have understood that. But that absorption with our own narrow world didn't end. I began to feel pressured for the first time since I had known you. No man should ever have to carry the burden of being totally responsible for another person's happiness."

With a growing sense of shock and dismay, Lacey listened to Kevin's version of what had happened to their marriage and tried to reconcile it with her own. It wasn't that she could not accept part of the blame. It was simply that the way he described the changes in their relationship weren't the way she remembered things at all.

There had been so much magic once. There had

been so many times over the past couple of weeks that she had thought for sure they were recapturing it. Now she knew that had been only a naive dream.

This time, magic wasn't quite enough. Lacey struggled with the fact that the life she'd chosen for herself—the role of homemaker in which she'd been so happy, could never be quite the same again. Jason was married now and her husband didn't need her to see to his every need, in fact resented her devotion.

Could it possibly be true that the very things she accused him of were true of her, as well? Was she no longer the generous person who thought only of helping others? Had she lost the vision they'd once shared, just as she believed he had? It had been only recently that she'd rediscovered a sense of activism in the form of the housing project in which Paula had involved her.

''Maybe I should leave, go back to Boston,'' she said finally, expressing a thought that had already come to her while Kevin had been gone. In fact, her mind was already made up despite the tentative way she'd phrased it.

Kevin regarded her angrily, as if the suggestion were yet another betrayal. ''Leave? Now? Lacey, we're just starting to get somewhere. You can't run away now.''

''It's not running. I just need to find some answers to questions I didn't even realize existed. What you've said makes a lot of sense. I was so busy bemoaning the fact that you were no longer the man I married that I never saw that I was no longer the woman you'd married. I need to go find Lacey Grainger again.''

''Lacey Halloran,'' he corrected sharply. ''I never meant for you to leave.''

Lacey moved to his side, hunkered down and placed her hand over his. She caressed his knuckles, wishing she weren't responsible for the fact that he'd clenched his hands into tight, angry fists.

"I know leaving wasn't your idea. But I have a lot of thinking to do."

"And you can't do it here?"

"No," she said sadly. "When I'm with you, it's all I want and that's wrong. You've said so yourself."

Kevin sighed deeply, then looked resigned. "When will you go?"

"If it's okay with you, I'll wait until morning."

"Sure."

"Will you go back into town with me or do you want to stay out here?"

"I think I'll wait here. If I go back, I won't do the thinking I need to do, either. I'll end up going back to the office."

She nodded and stood up. "I'll go pack."

She was almost out the door when he said, "Lacey?"

"Yes?" she said without turning around.

"The one thing I know without question is that I do love you. I'll be here waiting for you when you're ready to talk again."

She felt the salty sting of tears. Her lower lip trembled. "I love you, too," she said in a voice that quavered slightly.

She couldn't quite bring herself to promise that she would be back. She had no idea where the coming days of self-discovery were likely to lead her.

Chapter Fifteen

Naturally the most depressing day of Kevin's life had dawned sunny and mild. The beauty of the sunrise, the gentleness of the morning breeze seemed to mock him. A day like this should have been gray and gloomy, with the threat of a blizzard maybe. Barring that, a good, steady rain would have done.

Instead, he had to contend with clear skies and a temperature that beckoned. He'd tried his best to make it work to his advantage, but the time was fast approaching when Lacey would be pulling out of the driveway and heading back to Boston.

Saying goodbye to his wife—and quite possibly to his marriage—was one of the most difficult things Kevin ever had to do. It would be a thousand times harder this time than it had been months ago when Lacey had first made the decision to move to a place of her own. Or maybe he'd just forgotten the pain of that goodbye.

Already he had delayed her departure by several hours. He had talked her into one last walk on the beach in the glorious morning sunlight. Then he had convinced her that she had to eat before facing such a long drive. He'd insisted on a picnic on the beach. Then he'd asked her to pick up a few last-minute things in town so he wouldn't have to call on the neighbors. She had seized each excuse far more readily than a woman who was anxious to go.

Finally, though, he had run out of excuses. The only one left to him was a plea for her to reconsider leaving at all, and that one he had promised himself not to use. Though yesterday he had fought her going, he knew that she was right. They needed time apart to sort through everything, to figure out exactly who they were.

"You'll call when you get to town?" he asked as he carefully closed the car door.

"I'll call."

She glanced up at him, her blue eyes shimmering with unshed tears. She blinked hurriedly, then looked away. He could barely hear her when she asked, "You'll be careful? You'll take care of yourself?"

"Of course," he promised. "You don't think I'm going to undo all the good you've done with those nourishing soups, do you?"

"Are you sure you don't want me to take you to rent a car?"

"No. You'll be back before I need one," he said, though there was a forced sound to his optimism. He touched a finger to her chin and tilted her head up until he could gaze directly into her eyes. "I'll miss you."

"Me, too." She hesitated, then reached for the key and started the engine. "I should get started."

"Right. Drive carefully." He stepped back from the car.

"I always do."

He couldn't think of one more thing to say to make her linger. He reminded himself again that her decision to leave was the right one, the only one.

So why did he feel a lump the size of Texas lodged in his throat as he watched her go? Why did he feel this aching sense of abandonment, of loneliness and loss, when the car wasn't even out of sight?

Lacey prayed that she would be able to go back to Boston without anyone knowing. She didn't want Jason and Dana hovering. She certainly didn't want Brandon charging in to save the day. Why hadn't she extracted a promise from Kevin not to tell them? Hopefully he would have his own reasons for keeping quiet.

She turned the car radio on full blast, to an oldies station, hoping to drown out her thoughts. Instead, every song dragged her back down memory lane. She cried all the way home—big, sloppy tears that left her blouse soaking wet and her eyes red.

It was dark when she finally got back into town. She had never felt lonelier than she did when she turned the key in the lock of the apartment she had rented months earlier. She went through the living room, bedroom and kitchen switching on lights. She flipped on the stereo because the silence seemed oppressive. This time, at least, she was wise enough to avoid old favorites.

The apartment wasn't so bad, though after the home she and Kevin had shared, it seemed little bigger than one of their walk-in closets. The furniture was slightly shabby, but comfortable. She reminded herself that in many ways she had been happy during her months here. There had been a contentment, though she'd always felt that something was missing. Not something material, just Kevin.

Just Kevin, she thought mockingly, as if he were no more important than a comfortable bed or a faded print of some masterpiece. The truth of the matter, though, was that she could have been happy here for the rest of her days, if Kevin had been here to share it. She supposed that was just one example of that dependence he'd complained about.

Enough, she decided. Tomorrow would be soon enough to tackle the future. She concentrated instead on settling in. It took her no time at all to put her clothes away, to shove her suitcases into the back of the cramped closet. Making herself a pot of tea wasted ten minutes at best.

And then she had to face the fact that she was really and truly alone. Always before she had known in the back of her mind that leaving here and going home was her decision, that Kevin would welcome her back. It was entirely possible after the talk they had had last night that he would have second thoughts about resuming their marriage.

She was startled when the phone rang. She considered not answering it, then worried that it might be Kevin. He'd looked fine when she'd driven off, but something could have happened since then. And he was the only one who knew she'd left the Cape, the only one who would expect to find her here.

"Hello," she said hesitantly.

"Lacey, it's me."

"Kevin. Are you okay?"

"Fine. More to the point, how are you? You promised to call."

"I'm fine," she said, clutching the phone tightly. So, she thought, they were reduced to polite chit-chat. "I'm sorry. I just got in a half hour ago. I was getting settled."

"Everything's okay, then? You've locked the door? Checked the windows?"

A smile crept up on her. "Yes. Kevin, this apartment is perfectly safe."

"Lacey, the security system consists of an old man who'd sell out his own mother for a bottle of booze."

"That's not true. Charley is very careful about who he lets in. Besides, he's not on at night."

As soon as the words were out of her mouth, she realized they'd been a mistake.

"What do you mean he's not on at night?" Kevin demanded. "Who is?"

"Actually, there's a buzzer system."

"My God."

"Kevin, it's fine."

"Sure, okay. I guess you know what you're doing," he said wearily.

"Thanks for checking on me, though," she said, reluctant now to cut the connection. Kevin's concern, even under these tense circumstances, made her feel warm and cherished.

But of course that was what this was all about—proving whether she could stand on her own two feet without him there to protect her. She wasn't sure which of them needed to know the answer to that the most.

Lacey spent the next day restocking her refrigerator, going through the mail and cleaning the apartment. It gave her one whole day of reprieve from thinking about the agonizing decision she had to make.

By afternoon, a late spring cold front was pushing through, bringing rain and icy winds. The skies turned dark and miserable by five o'clock, mirroring her mood.

By eight she was ready to scream. Fearful of what too much introspection might reveal, she picked up the phone and called Paula Gethers. She sensed that staying busy, that finding a new purpose to her life was going to be the most critical thing to come of the next days or weeks.

"How's the house coming?" Lacey asked without preamble, hoping to get her friend off on her favorite topic before she could pick up on any unwitting signals Lacey might be sending out.

"Okay," Paula said, then promptly added, "Lacey, what's wrong?"

So much for fooling an old friend. "Who says anything is wrong?" she said anyway.

"I do, and I'm never wrong about these things."

"Look, I was just wondering if you could use my help tomorrow. That's all."

"I can always use your help, but something tells me you want to hit nails so you won't break up the furniture."

"If you're suggesting I sound depressed, you're right."

"Actually, I would have said angry."

"Maybe that, too. But I don't want to talk about it," she said firmly. "Not now and definitely not tomorrow."

"Then I will see you first thing in the morning and I will keep my opinion of your sorry state of mind to myself."

Lacey sighed. "Thanks on all counts."

"Hon, you don't have to thank me for letting you work your buns off. As for the rest, you may not want to thank me after you've had time to think about it. You sound like you could use someone to talk to. Just remember, I'm here if you change your mind."

Paula said goodbye and hung up before Lacey could reply that the last thing she needed right now was more talk. She and Kevin had done enough of that to last a lifetime. Maybe if they hadn't spent so darn much time digging below the surface of their problems, she wouldn't be questioning the very foundation of her life right now.

She had built her life on loving and being loved by Kevin. Without him, what was left? Her relationship with her son and daughter-in-law to be sure, but they certainly didn't need her hanging around twenty-four hours a day.

Her thoughts were starting to be so depressing that she made the mistake of grabbing the phone without thought when it rang again. Any interruption would be better than more of these dark reminders of the state of her marriage.

The sound of Brandon's voice snapped her back to the present. Any interruption except this one, she corrected, wondering if she dared to hang up in his ear.

''Good. You're there. I'm coming over,'' he announced.

''Brandon, don't,'' she pleaded, then realized that she was talking to herself. Her father-in-law had already hung up.

If she hadn't been so furious, she might have laughed. Brandon was reacting totally in character. He was as predictable when it came to loving his family as, well, as she was. The comparison was the most amusing thing of all.

Lacey briefly considered fleeing, but figured a stint in the French Foreign Legion wouldn't take her far enough. She satisfied her need for some illusion of control by letting him lean on the buzzer downstairs for five full minutes before letting him in.

Brandon glared at her when she finally opened the door, then breezed straight past her, carelessly tossing his Halloran cashmere coat over the back of a chair. He left his umbrella dripping all over the kitchen floor, then stalked into the living room. It looked smaller than ever with him prowling from one end to the other, a disapproving scowl on his face. He rubbed his fingers over the cheap upholstery on the sofa and shook his head, his dismay unmistakable.

''I'm delighted to see you, too,'' she said dryly, when it looked as if it might be a long time before he got down to saying exactly what was on his mind.

''What's the point of making small talk? We both know why I'm here.''

''I doubt that,'' Lacey retorted.

He shot her a puzzled glance as her implication sank in. ''What the devil's that supposed to mean?''

''It means that you couldn't begin to know what's gone on between Kevin and me the last couple of days, not unless your son has broken a lifelong cardinal rule and confided in you.''

''I know you're here and he's still on Cape Cod.''

''And how did you discover that?''

''I drove out there today.''

Lacey's eyebrows rose at that.

''I had some papers to drop off,'' he retorted without a trace of defensiveness. ''Kevin tried to cover for your absence, but he's a lousy liar. That's enough to tell me you two fools still haven't settled your differences.''

''Brandon, you can't charm me into doing what you want,'' Lacey said dryly.

He gave her a sharp glance. ''I wasn't trying to charm you. Dammit all, can't you stop jumping down my throat for five minutes and listen to what I have to say?''

Lacey drew in a deep breath and apologized. ''You're right,'' she said, sitting down opposite him. ''Would you like something? A cup of tea, maybe?''

''I came here for a real heart-to-heart, not to see if you're up on your social graces.''

''Fine. Say whatever you want to say.''

He nodded in satisfaction. ''Years ago I did you a grave disservice. Nobody's sorrier for that than I am. You and Kevin came pretty close to lighting up a room with the kind of love you had. When the two of you stood up to me, I thought there'd never come a day when something more powerful than me would come along and change that.''

She found herself grinning at the high esteem in which he held his own power.

''What's so danged funny?'' he grumbled.

''Nothing,'' she said. ''Go on.''

"I'm not here to ask you again what your differences are. Kevin's old enough to plead his own case."

To her astonishment, he actually looked uneasy. Before she could figure out what to make of that, he said, "I just want you to know if this has anything at all to do with those old days, I'm sorry for what happened and nothing would make me happier than to see the two of you back together."

Touched by the apology, even though it had come nearly three decades too late, Lacey found herself reaching for his hand and clasping it. "Brandon, this isn't about you. I swear it."

"Halloran Industries then? You never did want Kevin to work there."

"That's not true. I just wanted him to make his own choice, not to be bulldozed by you."

"Well, if it's not me and it's not my company, what is it?" he demanded as if the thought of anything else were totally preposterous.

Lacey burst out laughing at that. "And Kevin complained because *I* had a narrow world."

Brandon glowered at her. "What's that supposed to mean?"

"It means, you crotchety old man, that I adore the single-minded purpose with which you protect what's yours. Kevin obviously inherited that from you."

Brandon was shaking his head. "You think he's anything like me?"

"A lot more than either of you suspect, I think. Thank you for coming by. It means a lot."

"You going back there in the morning?"

"No," she said firmly.

Brandon looked disappointed. "My powers of persuasion must be off a little."

''Don't worry. I'm just a tougher sell than your run-of-the-mill client.''

''What are you going to do?''

''Tomorrow I'm going to build a house.''

He regarded her as if she'd suddenly started speaking in Swahili. ''Am I supposed to understand what that means?''

''No,'' she said, laughing.

''Good. I'd hate to think I'd started losing my wits, when I have some plans for the future I've been thinking about. If I could just get the two of you settled and get that great grandbaby born, I might start thinking about my own life.''

This time it was Lacey's turn to be confused. ''Am I supposed to know what you're talking about?''

He gave her a wink. ''Nope. This business of keeping secrets goes both ways.''

Lacey felt her spirits begin to climb just a little as she arrived at the housing site in the morning. The thought of what the half-finished house before her would mean to some family was gratifying. Maybe she couldn't do much to fix her own life, but she could do her part to help someone else get a new start.

She wandered around the house in search of Paula or Dave, so she could get an assignment. She found Paula atop a ladder. Her husband, his hair tied back in a ponytail, was holding the ladder steady with one hand. The other was sliding slowly up the back of Paula's denim-clad leg in an intimate caress.

Lacey felt the sting of tears as she listened to their familiar bickering. There wasn't a hostile note in the exchange, just the fond give and take of two people who'd found their own shorthand way of communicating.

When Dave's hand reached Paula's bottom, she turned and glared down at him. "You're not helping, David Gethers," she grumbled, but Lacey could clearly hear the amusement in her friend's voice.

"How can you say that?" he inquired innocently.

"Because I need to concentrate on what I'm doing here, instead of wondering where that roving hand of yours is heading."

"Don't you worry about that. You go right on doing whatever you need to do."

"If I have to come down off of this ladder," Paula warned with mock ferocity, "you are going to be one sorry man. Go check on the plumbers or something."

"It's the *or something* I'm interested in."

"Dave!"

"Okay, okay," he finally said with weary resignation. He turned and caught sight of Lacey.

"The woman is a trial," he grumbled. "Maybe you can explain to her that there are more important things than checking shingles or whatever she's doing up there."

Lacey laughed. "I doubt I'm the right person to be giving anyone advice on priorities."

Paula peered down at her and immediately descended. "Good. You're here."

"Ready, willing and able," Lacey confirmed. "What's my assignment?"

"First things first. Come with me," Paula steered her around the corner to an RV that served as a mobile office for the project. Inside, she held up a pot of coffee. "Want some?"

Lacey hesitated, sensing that Paula had more on her

mind than deciding whether to hand her a paintbrush or a screwdriver.

''Sure, why not?'' she said finally. She sat down on a corner of the office's one cluttered desk.

''So what did Kevin think when you told him about our project?'' Paula asked.

''He was very excited,'' Lacey said honestly. ''He wants to find a way to get Halloran Industries involved.''

''So why aren't you whooping for joy? Did you expect him to turn up here first thing this morning with a tool kit?''

Lacey sighed and set the cup of coffee aside. ''No, that's not it.''

''What then? Are you two reconciling or not?''

''I don't know.''

Paula shook her head. ''I don't get it. You love him. He loves you. What could be simpler than that?''

''He wants me to have my own interests.''

''Like this project?''

Lacey shrugged. ''I suppose.''

''Come on, girl. Pick up the pace here. I'm getting lost. What do you want?''

''Let me see if I can figure out how to say this. The best thing about our relationship from the very beginning was that we always shared everything. Now he goes off to Halloran and I come here. I guess if anything, I'm envious of what you and Dave have. You share the same concerns. You work side by side.''

''Can I assume that Kevin does not want to come over here and hammer things?''

''He wants to write checks.''

''Hey, we need people like that, too. Don't even think about complaining about that.''

Even as she and Paula talked, Lacey was struck by the first spark of an idea. Suddenly she felt her energy returning and her spirits mending. She grabbed Paula by the shoulders and hugged her.

"You are a genius," she declared. "I've got to run."

"Hey, I have you down for painting the entire living room today."

Lacey opened her purse and took out the hundred-dollar bill Kevin had given her as a joke a few nights earlier. "Pay someone," she said, handing it over. "I have a long drive ahead of me."

Chapter Sixteen

Lacey didn't waste a second before taking off for Cape Cod. Even though she was wearing paint-spattered jeans and an old blouse, she refused to go back to the apartment to change into something more presentable. What she had to say to Kevin was far more important than the way she looked. Half the time he didn't notice what she was wearing, anyway. She did pull off the bandana she'd tied around her head and ran her fingers through her hair to get rid of the tangles. At least there was no paint in it.

As she drove she considered all the implications of her idea. She couldn't figure out why she hadn't had this brainstorm before. During all those lonely months when she'd had nothing to do but think, no solution to the real problems in her marriage had come to her—probably because she hadn't even know exactly what those problems were. She'd focused too much on

Kevin's health and not on the reasons he might have had for driving himself so hard.

Now, after less than forty-eight miserable hours apart, she had recognized the perfect answer, one that had been staring her in the face all along.

Perhaps the reason it seemed so easy now was because of the time she and Kevin had spent together on Cape Cod. In all of that painful self-analysis, they had brought themselves right to the brink of discovery. They might not have reconciled, but they had certainly laid all of the groundwork.

She had to be right about this, she thought as she reversed the drive she'd made only two days before. This time she felt so much more hopeful, not just about fulfilling her own needs, but about finding common ground that she and Kevin could share again, about recapturing that sense of purpose that had made their relationship so special.

Excitement and anticipation spilled through her. She deliberately turned on the oldies station and sang along with all the nostalgic hits, laughing at the happy memories that came back to crowd out the sad.

Her mood lasted until she turned into the driveway and saw Brandon's huge tank of a luxury car parked beside the house. Why was he back out here today? she wondered with a sinking feeling in the pit of her stomach. Why was he here when she so desperately needed to be alone with Kevin to see if they could finally fix their lives?

She drew in a deep breath and reminded herself that she was the one who'd said quite plainly that she wouldn't be coming back this morning. She had no one to blame but herself if her father-in-law had taken that to mean that it was up to him to keep Kevin company.

Of course, it was unlikely that Brandon was inside making soup or playing cards with Kevin. It was far more likely that he'd brought along a stack of work on the pretense of keeping his son occupied.

Feeling oddly uncertain, Lacey looked down at her old clothes and wondered if she ought to drive to the nearest boutique and buy something new. She could already envision Brandon's disapproval. Only her desire to share her idea before she had second thoughts prevented her from leaving. That and an awareness that it was long past time when she had to impress her father-in-law. His visit last night had finally put them on a friendlier footing that she was sure would last and grow.

She walked slowly up the walk, then found herself ringing the doorbell, rather than using her key. It was Kevin who opened the door.

His face looked haggard, as if he hadn't been getting nearly enough sleep since she'd left. There was a faint stubble on his cheeks that she yearned to reach out and caress. As tired as he looked, he'd never seemed more desirable. She wanted to throw herself into his arms and hold on until the dark days had gone for good.

And there was no mistaking the sudden spark of hope in his eyes when he saw her.

"You're back," he began inanely.

She understood the awkwardness, because she was feeling it as well, that and so much more. Trepidation, hope, love.

"Did you forget your key?"

She shook her head. "No. It's in my purse. I wasn't sure if I should use it."

"Lacey, this is your house as much as mine. More, probably."

She shrugged. "I realized that Brandon was here. I thought maybe, I don't know. I thought maybe I should wait and come back later when we could talk."

"Don't be ridiculous."

Just then Brandon appeared in the doorway to the living room. He searched her face, and then, as if he'd seen something he approved of—maybe her new-found confidence—he nodded. He turned at once and went back. It was more discretion than he'd ever displayed before.

"Come on in," Kevin said. "Dad and I were just finishing up."

"That's right," Brandon said, when they'd joined him. "I'll be on my way in just a minute."

It was clear though, that he had been ensconced in the living room for some time. Files were spread on the coffee table. As Lacey walked in, he punched a long series of numbers into a calculator. He nodded in satisfaction, jotted them down and then stood up.

"I'll leave you two. I'm sure you have a lot to discuss," he said, sounding as if he couldn't wait to get away. "Kevin, your instincts were exactly right. Those figures look good. I'll tell Jason to get on with things."

"That sounds good," Kevin said distractedly, his gaze still fixed on Lacey.

"You don't have to rush off," Lacey felt compelled to say to Brandon, though she wanted nothing more than to see him leave.

He grinned at her then. "You're a lousy liar, girl.

Same as Kevin.'' He grabbed his coat and headed for the front door. ''He's been trying to kick me out since I got here, but was too polite to come right out and say anything to my face.''

''Drive carefully,'' she told him.

''Always do.''

He left the room then, and Lacey stared out the front window while she waited for Kevin to come back. The last thing she overheard Brandon ask was when Kevin intended to get back to work.

''I'll have to let you know about that, Dad.''

Lacey noticed Brandon had left the files and the calculator behind. She was tempted to toss the papers into the fireplace, but she left them on the coffee table, waiting to see what Kevin would do about them.

When he came back into the living room, his expression was cautious. ''I'm surprised to see you back so soon,'' he began, his tone wary. He'd shoved his hands into the pockets of his jeans as if he couldn't quite figure out what else to do with them. He kept his distance, standing over by the fireplace, rather than joining her.

''No more surprised than I am to be back.'' She hesitated, then couldn't keep herself from asking, ''You're not going to let Brandon push you into going back to work too soon, are you?''

He held up his hands. ''Lacey, please don't start on that.''

''I can't help it,'' she said, gesturing toward the mess on the coffee table. ''Just look at what he's brought. There's enough there to keep you busy for a month.''

''It's just Dad's way of making sure I'm not too lonely out here. He needed an excuse to come back.''

Lacey wrestled with the idea of Brandon making up excuses for any of his actions. She couldn't imagine it. Then again, in his relationship with his son, anything was possible. She suddenly realized that ever since Kevin had turned down that job at Halloran Industries years ago, Brandon quite probably had feared another rejection. He had never taken Kevin's presence at the company for granted.

At the same time, she and Kevin had taken each other for granted. They had operated for years now under the misguided notion that their relationship would always remain exactly the same. No wonder the past year had been so rocky.

"Are you ready to go back to work?" she asked finally.

"That depends."

"On?"

"What happens with us."

She shook her head. "No, you can't pin that decision on us, on me. What do you want to do with the rest of your life?"

She thought she knew the answer to that, but she had to hear him say it, had to know if the plan she'd devised made any sense at all.

"Actually, I do want to go back to Halloran," Kevin finally admitted with an obvious sigh of relief. "Tradition seems more important to me now. Working with my father and my son creates a bond that most men never have. I want that in my life. I didn't realize until recently how much I counted on that sense of continuity. I think I understand finally what it must have done to Dad when I walked away from it."

"Then you should go back."

He shook his head. "Not at the cost of destroying our marriage."

"Working at Halloran Industries could only destroy our marriage if we allow it to, if we attach some symbolic significance to it the way we did before," she said with a trace of impatience. "I think we're both past that. The important thing is to keep a balance in our lives, to keep the priorities straight. I don't want you obsessed with our marriage, any more than I want you obsessed with work. Isn't that what you were saying to me earlier?"

"Yes, but—"

"No," she said softly. "No *buts,* Kevin. This is about what you think is right for you."

"But I can't decide that in a vacuum. What do you need? What will make you happy?"

She turned to stare out the window as she searched for a way to explain what she was feeling, all the discoveries she'd made.

"I think maybe I actually have an answer to that," she said, finally turning back from the window and meeting his gaze. "I came back here so I could run it by you."

"So, tell me," he said.

Lacey drew in a deep breath. "I've been thinking, maybe we could form a Halloran Foundation, something we could work on together."

"Give away Halloran money?" Kevin teased, pretending to be scandalized by the very notion.

"Stop," she said. "I'm serious. You and your father have always been very generous, but this could be something we do in a more organized fashion."

Kevin's gaze was suddenly more intense. How many times had he looked just that way when they'd bounced ideas back and forth long ago? Her confidence had grown simply by seeing the way he respected what she thought.

"Go on," he said, the first hint of excitement in his voice. "I think I see where you're going with this."

Now, with that slim bit of encouragement, Lacey couldn't keep the enthusiasm out of her voice. "Okay. The way I see it, we'd set up a trust, an endowment, whatever. That would become the basis of the Foundation. That's where you and Brandon come in. You have to make the commitment to set aside the money to do this."

"And where do you fit in?"

"I thought I could evaluate applications, seek out the organizations and individuals that really need help, help establish programs. All those committees I've served on have taught me a lot about fund-raising and grant proposals and effectively run charities. I think I could weed out those that are poorly operated. I'd handle all the day-to-day things, the paperwork. The Halloran board would okay the grants."

Even as she talked, the tiny seed of an idea took root and flourished. She could see from the excitement in Kevin's eyes that he shared her enthusiasm.

"Yes," he said and added his ideas to hers until the Foundation seemed more a reality than a sudden inspiration that had come to her only hours ago.

"Don't you see, Kevin? The best part would be that we'd be doing it together, we'd share the same focus again, even if it's only one small aspect of what you do at Halloran."

He got up and moved to the window to stand behind her. His arms circled her waist. "I think it's the most wonderful, generous idea I've ever heard."

She turned in his arms until she could study him. She searched his face. ''Really?''

''Really,'' he said, pressing a tender kiss to her forehead. Lacey felt her heart tumble.

''Do you think Brandon will go for it?'' she asked, unable to keep the anxiety out of her voice.

''I think he'll love it.''

''Kevin, I know this doesn't take care of everything. I know it's not some magical solution for us, but it's a start.''

His lips touched hers then, capturing all the excitement and adding to it. Anticipation and joy touched off a spark that sent fire dancing through her veins.

''God, I love you,'' Kevin murmured, when he finally pulled away. ''There are so many things I want to say to you, so many things we can do together, now that we know our marriage is here to stay. That is what you want, isn't it?''

''More than anything.''

''What about the house?'' he asked.

''Which house?'' she asked, thoroughly puzzled by the change in direction.

''The one in Boston. Jason told me there's an interested buyer.''

Lacey just stared at him. ''You put it on the market?''

He nodded. ''Before I left the hospital.''

''Why?''

''It was awfully cold and lonely without you. Frankly, I kind of like it here. You and me, walking on the beach, warming up in front of a fire.''

His hands swept over her, slowly stroking until she could imagine those nights of loving in front of the fire as vividly as he could. Then it didn't matter at all that she'd worn paint-spattered clothes, because he was sliding them off her, kissing every inch of her bare flesh until the fire in the hearth was nothing compared to the one deep inside her.

"Oh, my beautiful Lacey," he whispered, his gaze locked on hers. "I was so afraid you wouldn't come back, so afraid that my stupid pride would keep me from coming after you."

"Would you have come after me?" she asked, her voice breathless as he skimmed his fingers over her breasts.

"Yes. I realized finally that I have no pride at all where you're concerned. You hadn't been gone fifteen minutes when I knew that I was wrong to let you go. The only way to work things out was to do it together."

"Of course, I did do some pretty incredible thinking while I was away from you," she taunted.

"But look how much more clearly you're thinking now that we're back together."

She moaned as his fingers slid lower, over her belly and beyond to the precise spot where she yearned to be touched. She arched into the teasing touch. "This doesn't have anything to do with thinking," she told him when she could manage enough breath to say anything.

"That's not what I heard," he told her. "Making love starts in the head."

She slid her hand up his thigh until she reached the hard evidence of his arousal. "But that's not where it finishes, is it?" she taunted.

"Lacey, dearest, darling..."

"Yes?"

"If you keep that up—"

"That is my intention," she said.

"Lacey!"

"You had something else in mind?" she inquired pleasantly.

Kevin groaned. "No. No, I think you've got it."

"Then come here, please."

She arched her back as he drove into her. He pulled back, then entered her more slowly, establishing a tantalizing pace that was just one shade shy of unbearable.

"You're getting even, aren't you?" she asked him as he withdrew again.

"Would I do that?" he inquired, a glint of amusement in his eyes.

"You would." She concentrated very hard on not letting him drive her over the brink until she could take him with her.

Unfortunately she found it very difficult to concentrate on anything but the sensations that were throbbing through her with increasing intensity. The excitement she'd felt about the Halloran Foundation was nothing compared to the excitement generated by this one Halloran man.

"Kevin," she murmured finally.

"Yes."

"I think it's time to stop playing games."

The spark of amusement in his eyes gave way to a dark, burning desire as he lifted her hips and drove into her one last, exquisitely slow time. She felt herself tightening around him, holding him deep inside her until there was nothing left to say, nothing left to do except give herself over to the thrill of coming apart in his embrace.

For the longest time after their passion was spent,

they stayed right where they were, curled up in front of the fire, the reflection of the flames dancing over their perspiration-slicked skin.

"So what do you think?" Kevin asked eventually.

"About what?"

"The house."

After the past half hour, there was only one possible answer as far as Lacey could tell. "Maybe we could make do with an apartment in the city and live on the Cape. I don't think I want to give up what we found out here."

"I certainly don't want to give up times like this," Kevin agreed.

"Are we really okay, though? I'm not dreaming the way I feel right now, am I?"

"Lacey, if it's a dream, then I'm caught up in the same one."

"But will it last?"

"Who can say? I can only promise you that from now on we'll never take each other for granted again. Maybe what happened to us was all for the best. We both learned to appreciate what we have, and next time we'll both fight harder before we risk losing it."

"Will there be a next time, then?" she asked.

"I'm afraid so. There will always be crises in a marriage. Most people these days opt out at the first sign of trouble. I don't want us ever to do that again."

"Is that your sense of Halloran honor talking?"

"No, Lacey, it's my love."

* * * * *

CHERISH

Prologue

Brandon Halloran had never felt so rich, and for once in his sixty-eight years it had nothing to do with the money or the possessions he'd amassed. Squaring his shoulders, his eyes misted over as he caught sight of his beloved Elizabeth at the back of the old Boston church he'd been attending for his entire lifetime. There was no denying the passage of time, but by God, she was a beauty still.

Petite, vivacious and with an undimmed sense of mischief in those twinkling blue eyes of hers, Elizabeth Forsythe Newton radiated joy as her gaze met his. Her pace picked up just a fraction—one beat ahead of the wedding march—as if she couldn't quite wait, after all this time, to be his.

Oh my, yes, Brandon thought, his own heart filling with anticipation. The wait had definitely been too long. Nearly fifty years had passed, during which he'd married another woman and raised a family. He'd seen his own grandson wed to a spunky girl who'd reminded him so much of his precious Elizabeth that his heart had ached.

Life had a way of making amends, though. Finding Lizzy again after all this time had made Brandon feel twice blessed. When he'd finally convinced her that they weren't a couple of old fools for wanting to get married at this stage of their lives, she'd tackled the plans with the enthusiasm of a young girl. She'd even drawn his beloved daughter-in-law and granddaughter-in-law into the celebration and convinced them to share the day by renewing their own vows.

His heart full, Brandon watched his son pledge to honor his wife. Kevin had almost lost that woman—twice, in fact. There'd been a time when Brandon himself had put obstacles in their path—one of his few regrets. He'd been convinced that Lacey Grainger wasn't the right woman for his son, that she'd been responsible for his rebellion against everything the Hallorans stood for. Only later had Brandon come to realize that Lacey was the mellowing influence, the gentle force that brought out Kevin's best instincts. To Brandon's everlasting relief they had mended their marriage, and after today's ceremony of renewal, he expected it would be stronger than ever.

Now, impetuous, full-of-life Dana Roberts was another story. She'd led his grandson on a merry chase, starting things off by slugging Jason in a quiet, respectable tavern. Word of the ruckus had spread far and wide, to Jason's chagrin and Brandon's own delight. My, but Dana had been a breath of fresh air with her feistiness. She'd been a little rough around the edges, but Brandon had spotted the life in her right off, and he'd watched with glee as Jason struggled against the pull of her offbeat ways. Now they were expecting his first great-grandbaby—any minute by the looks of Dana.

Yes, indeed, he'd had a full and blessed life, Brandon thought. Maybe he'd been missing Elizabeth all this time, but the years hadn't been wasted if they'd all led up to this moment. Maybe Brandon and Elizabeth had come to appreciate what they had just a little bit more. Their path to the altar hadn't been easy. They'd had to learn all over again about trust and forgiveness, but he didn't have a doubt in his mind that it would be worth it.

When the minister turned to him, Brandon clasped Elizabeth's fragile hand and held on tight to quiet an unexpected attack of nerves.

"You are the light of my life," he told her. "We have missed so many years and yet it is as if they never were. What I feel for you today is as strong and as deep as it was on the day I first told you I loved you so long ago. Perhaps those words have even more meaning now that we have known the sorrows of loss, the strife of living, the meaning of forgiveness and the joy of rediscovery."

He raised her hand to his lips and kissed it. "I, Brandon, take thee, Elizabeth, a woman I loved and lost and have been blessed to find again to be my wedded wife. I promise to cherish thee all the rest of my days."

To his surprise there were tears in just about everyone's eyes when he'd finished. He wanted to whoop with joy himself, but knew he didn't dare. He'd caused the rest of them enough alarm over the past few months with his impetuous courtship of the woman who was now, at long last, his wife.

Brandon couldn't hold back a chuckle, though, as he thought of the way he and Elizabeth had shaken things up. By God, they had had a fine time. God willing, there was more to come—for all of them.

Chapter One

It had been an absolute bear of a day, with one last wintry rain to cast a pall over the promise of spring. Exhausted, Brandon Halloran poured himself a stiff drink and sank into his favorite leather easy chair in front of the library fireplace. As he stared into the dancing flames, he tried to empty his mind of all the problems that weren't up to him to solve. Unfortunately he didn't seem to be having any more luck with that now than he had over the past weeks.

He'd spent the whole day worrying anew about whether his son and daughter-in-law were going to patch up their marriage. A few weeks ago a divorce had seemed all but certain, but after Kevin's most recent heart attack, Brandon had seen for himself how much Lacey still loved his son. He couldn't imagine why the two of them were so darned blind to something that was clear as glass to him.

Brandon's hopes had risen when his son left the hospital. Kevin and Lacey had traipsed off to Cape Cod together. Brandon had been reassured that things were finally on the right track for the two of them. Then, just today, he'd found out that Lacey was back in Boston—alone.

He'd confronted her earlier tonight, only to have her remind him that he was butting in where he shouldn't. But if he didn't make them see sense, who would? He was family, dammit, to say nothing of being older and wiser.

It was nights like this that Brandon missed his wife the most. Grace had been good to him, loving and gentle. Given his mulishness, she'd also had the patience of a saint. And she'd known when to exert that iron will of hers to keep him from making mistakes he'd regret.

If he and Grace had lacked a certain passion, well, that wasn't the worst thing in the world. Before she'd died so suddenly two years ago, they'd raised a wonderful son and seen their grandson grow into a fine young man. Maybe it was good she hadn't seen Kevin's marriage hit this rough patch. Her heart would have ached just as badly as Brandon's did.

He and Grace had always been able to talk things through. That was the quality he missed the most. She would have understood this empty feeling in the pit of his stomach better than anyone. She'd always known what trouble he had letting go of anything, whether it was putting an end to the meddling in his son's life or walking away from the textile company he'd inherited from his father. How did these young people today say it? Get a life! That's what he needed to do, let go and get a life.

There was certainly no denying it was time to let go of the business he'd spent a lifetime building. He was sixty-eight years old. Thank goodness he still had his health. He could carry on at the helm of Halloran Industries another decade—at least that's the way he felt in the mornings with the whole day stretched out ahead of him.

The truth of the matter was, though, it was past time to give his son and grandson their chance. He'd first taught Kevin and then Jason the best he could, and now it was time to turn over the reins.

Maybe if he had a different personality, he could keep a hand in, stay in the background. He knew himself well enough, though, to realize that as long as he entered that building, he'd never be able to keep still about the decisions being made inside it. The only way for Kevin and Jason to put their own stamp on Halloran Industries would be for Brandon to walk away and not look back.

Damned if he knew how, though. What the devil would he do with all those long, lonely hours? Travel? What was the fun in seeing the world if there was no one to share the experiences with? He could read, play a little golf, but that would never fill up enough hours. His mind would atrophy in a month without the daily challenge of running his company, without the fun of finding some new fabric to design and work into Halloran Industries' line of quality textiles.

Brandon's "whims," Kevin and Jason called them. Yet those whims had kept their company thriving. They'd given him a reason to go on during the bleak days after Grace's death. He'd had some dandy adventures searching for ways to upgrade fabrics so that designers the world over would seek his company out for their richest, most sophisticated customers. The thought of giving all that up left Brandon feeling lost.

Well, he'd just have to make it work. It wasn't fair to hang on forever, not when his son and grandson had both long since proven their worth.

Brandon studied the scrap of paper he held in his hand and wondered if it had the answer.

Just before he'd left the office, he'd finally gotten a call from the detective he'd hired a few months back. Hiring the man had been an impulsive action, one of those spur-of-the-moment, middle-of-the-lonely-night decisions that didn't make a bit of sense in the cold light of day. Still, he'd gone ahead with it, caught up in a need to finally know, after all these years, what had happened to the one woman he'd never been able to forget. He was sure his beloved Grace would forgive him this bit of foolishness.

"Lizzy," he'd scrawled and then a phone number somewhere in Southern California. Elizabeth Forsythe Newton. It had been Elizabeth Forsythe when they'd met nearly a half century ago. Now, according to the detective, she'd been widowed five years, had two daughters and three grandchildren. She still taught school, substituting now, not full-time. She attended church on Sunday, went to an occasional movie. If there was a man in her life, the detective had made no mention of it. He'd promised to mail his complete report in the morning.

Brandon couldn't ask the detective the one question that was uppermost in his mind: did she remember those long-ago days they had shared, at all? Time blurred most things, but for him the memory of those days with Lizzy were every bit as vivid now as they had been hours or even weeks after they'd occurred.

Not even a long and happy marriage had entirely erased thoughts of what might have been.

His housekeeper rapped on the door, then opened it. "Sir, your dinner is ready."

Another depressingly lonely meal, he thought and then made up his mind. "I know it's late, but can you hold it a bit, Mrs. Farnsworth? There's a phone call I need to make."

"Certainly, sir. A half hour?"

"That will be fine."

Even before she'd quietly closed the door, he reached for the phone and punched in the numbers before he could change his mind.

As the phone rang more than three thousand miles away, Brandon thought back to the summer day he'd first seen Lizzy, racing hell-bent for leather along a cliff overlooking the Atlantic. Her auburn hair caught the sun and gleamed like fire. Her white cotton dress had been hiked up daringly above her knees as she ran barefoot through the damp morning grass. He had been stunned by her beauty, but it had been the sheer joy in her expression that had captivated him.

The image lingered as the phone was picked up.

"Yes, hello?" a tentative female voice said.

Brandon's breath seemed to go still, as a powerful sense of déjà vu swept through him. The sweet, musical tone still held some little hint of bubbling laughter beneath the hesitancy. His heart, which had no business doing such things at his age, lurched and took up a quickened rhythm.

"Elizabeth Forsythe? Lizzy, is that you?"

He heard the faint gasp, then the whispered shock of recognition. "Brandon?"

"Yes, Lizzy, it's me. Brandon Halloran. Do you remember? It's been so long."

"I remember," she said, her voice sounding oddly choked. "You were the only one who ever called me that. Where on earth are you?"

"In Boston."

"How did you find me?"

He thought back to how hard he'd tried all those years ago, only to have her prove elusive. This time he'd taken no chances, spared no expense. "I hired a very smart detective."

"A detective? Oh, my. Why on earth would you do that after all this time?"

Elizabeth sounded nervous, maybe even troubled. It puzzled him, but he dismissed it as nothing more than the surprise of hearing from him out of the blue like this.

"Maybe I just wanted to hear the sound of your voice. You sound exactly the same, as if someone's just told you something that made you want to laugh. I've missed you, Lizzy. How are you? Are you well?"

He knew the answer to that much at least, but he was afraid it was far too soon to ask her the questions he really wanted to ask. Most important, he needed to know why she hadn't waited for him.

As they talked, hesitantly at first and then with their old enthusiasm, the years slid away. They were simply two old friends catching up. Haunting memories came back to Brandon as he listened, then were replaced by sorrow as she described so many experiences they hadn't shared.

"You've been out there how long now?" he asked.

"Since 1942."

"The year we met."

"Yes," she said softly. "The year we met."

Was there a note of wistfulness in her response? "Tell me about your life. You have children?" he asked, needing to hear her confirm every word in the detective's report.

"Yes, two daughters. They're grown now. The oldest, that's Ellen, is married and has three children herself. The youngest, that's Kate, has a real streak of independence. She claims no man will ever tie her down."

"Like her mother, if I recall correctly," he said, imagining another redhead with a fiery temper and the strength of her convictions. Brandon wondered if meeting Lizzy's daughters would be like traveling back in time.

Lizzy laughed. "She'd never believe you, if she heard you say that. She says she's not a bit like me, that I'm old-fashioned."

"That's certainly not the way I remember you."

He heard her quiet sigh and wondered at the faint hint of regret it held.

"Brandon, we knew each other for such a short time. I suspect neither of us remembers those days with much accuracy."

"But you have thought of them?" he prodded, waving off Mrs. Farnsworth's second attempt to call him to dinner.

"Some, yes," Lizzy admitted. "I can't deny that."

"What do you remember?"

"That we were very young and very foolish."

"That's not the way I remember it at all," he said. "I remember that we were very much in love, that from the first instant I saw you I was enchanted."

"I think it's best if we don't talk about those days,

Brandon. A lifetime has passed since then.'' Her voice had cooled.

Brandon released a sigh. ''So you do regret it. I'm sorry, Lizzy. I don't regret one minute of that time we spent together. I can't.''

''Tell me about your family,'' she said in a sudden rush, as if she didn't dare allow his nostalgic note to linger. ''You have children?''

He thought of refusing to be turned from the past to the present, then decided there was nothing to be gained from pressing her to look back. Not yet, anyway.

''I have a son, Kevin. He's taking over Halloran Industries soon.''

''You're retiring?''

''I'm thinking of it.''

''Somehow I thought you'd never walk away from that company. You always loved it so, almost as much as flying. Do you still collect fabric samples the way some kids back then collected stamps?''

''I not only collect them, I improve on them.''

''Okay. Of course,'' she said, laughing. ''I'd forgotten how self-confident you are.''

''I suspect conceited is what you meant,'' he said, laughing with her. ''Oh, Lizzy, how I've missed that sharp wit of yours. You never let me get away with a thing.''

''It seems to me you got away with plenty,'' she said tartly.

The sly innuendo had Brandon chuckling again. That was the Lizzy of old, all right. She'd never been one to dance around the truth of things. He'd never known anyone else like her back then. Bold and sassy, she'd kept him constantly off balance, a rare occurrence for a man who even at eighteen had been pretty darned sure of himself.

"Lizzy, I want to see you again. I'll fly out tomorrow," he said, suddenly anxious to end a separation that never should have been. "We'll have ourselves a grand reunion. You can show me all the sights. Maybe we'll even go to Disneyland and pretend we're just a couple of kids again."

Silence greeted the suggestion, then, "No. Absolutely not. I'm sorry, Brandon."

"But, Lizzy, we owe it to ourselves. For old times' sake," he coaxed. "What's the harm?"

"No, Brandon," she said, her tone suddenly cold and forbidding in a way it never had been before. "It's best to leave the past where it belongs, in the past."

The phone clicked quietly, cutting him off. He called back immediately, only to get a busy signal. He tried again and again throughout the evening, but by midnight he knew she wasn't going to take his call.

"Well, I'll be damned," he muttered, staring at the phone. No little slip of a woman was going to thwart his dreams. Not a second time. Surely if Lizzy remembered him at all, she remembered that he liked nothing better than the challenge of a chase.

For what seemed like hours, Elizabeth sat staring at the phone, the receiver defiantly left off the hook. No, she corrected. It wasn't defiance. It was sheer terror. Brandon Halloran made her feel things—crazy, impossible things—she hadn't felt in years.

A day ago Elizabeth would have sworn that her life was complete. She would have laughed at the thought that a sixty-seven-year-old woman's pulse could flutter at the mere sound of a man's voice. Gracious, the last time her heart had pumped this fast, she'd been on a dance floor doing a pretty spirited tango with a man wearing a polyester suit and too much shaving cologne.

She tried to imagine Brandon Halloran in polyester and couldn't. Cashmere or the finest linen would be more his style. She could recall, all too vividly it seemed, the way his skin had felt beneath her nervous touch. She absentmindedly picked up a magazine and fanned herself, then realized what she was doing.

"Elizabeth, you're an old fool," she lectured herself aloud. "What do you think you're doing dredging up thoughts like that? Your daughters would be shocked."

Of course, the subconscious wasn't nearly as easily controlled as she might have liked. She deliberately walked away from the off-the-hook phone, hoping she could forget all about the long-buried memories Brandon had just stirred to life, memories she had done her very best to forget.

Some, admittedly, were sweet and filled with a rare tenderness. Some were wildly wicked, which certainly explained the way her pulse was thundering. And others, the ones she needed most to remember, were filled with hurt and anger and a deep sense of betrayal.

Nearly fifty years ago Brandon Halloran had roared into her life, swept her off her feet and then vanished, leaving her to suffer the consequences of a broken heart. He had no right to think he could do the same thing again, not at this late date. Not even one word of apology had crossed his lips. Instead, the conversation had been laced with persuasive teasing, riddled with nostalgia. She was no longer a naive seventeen-year-old. She wouldn't give in to the smooth and easy charm a second time.

Elizabeth felt the anger mount and clung to it gratefully. As long as she felt like this, she would be able to remain strong. She would be able to deny whatever pleas Brandon made. She could ignore his coaxing, as she should have done so long ago.

Still and all, she wondered just a little about how he'd changed. Was he still as handsome and dashing? Back then he'd had a smile that could charm the birds out of the trees. It had certainly worked its magic on her. He'd walked and talked with an air of bold confidence. He'd had unruly blond hair that had felt like the silk that was spun in his factory. His piercing eyes had been the color of the ocean at its deepest—blue and mysterious. When his eyes lit with laughter—or desire—she'd been sure that what they shared was rare and certainly forever.

Believing all that, Elizabeth had been tumbled back to reality with an abruptness that had shattered her. Only by the grace of God and through the love of her parents had she been able to pick up the pieces of her life and move on. David Newton had played a huge role in that as well.

Her senior by ten years, David had been a fine man, tolerant and sensitive. And he had loved her unconditionally and without restraint. She owed him her thanks for seeing to it that she finished college, that she was able to enter a profession that had been more fulfilling each year. More than that, she owed him for giving her the very best years of her life, while asking so little for himself in return. She'd been content with their bargain, happy with the life they'd shared. Maybe there had been no glorious highs, but there had never been the devastating lows she'd known with Brandon.

Unlike David, Brandon Halloran had demanded everything and had very nearly cheated her of any future at all.

The ringing of the doorbell interrupted her thoughts. Suddenly realizing that she'd been sitting here in the dark for hours, she snapped on a light on her way to the door. When she opened it, she found Kate, flanked by Ellen and the youngest of Ellen's girls, fifteen-year-old Penny.

"Goodness, what a surprise!" she said, delighted by the distraction their arrival promised.

"Surprise?" Kate repeated, sounding miffed. "Mother, your phone has been off the hook for the past three hours." She marched into the living room and hung it up. "We've been worried sick about you."

"Kate's been worried," Ellen corrected. "We just came along as moral support. She said it was us or the police."

Elizabeth managed an astonishingly casual air, hoping to forestall too many questions. "Well, as you can see, I am perfectly fine. The cat must have knocked the receiver off when she jumped on the table. It's not the first time that's happened," she said, because she was not about to tell them about Brandon's call and the way it had shaken her.

Ellen regarded her speculatively, as if she could almost read her mother's thoughts.

"Mother, are you sure you're all right?" her oldest asked quietly.

"Certainly. Why wouldn't I be?"

"It's just that you look, I don't know, a little flustered. I've never seen you look quite that way before."

Her granddaughter peered at her closely. ''Mom's right,'' Penny announced. ''Are you sure you don't have some man stashed away upstairs?''

''Penny!'' Ellen said sharply.

''Oh, Mom, don't act so shocked. Sex doesn't end just because you're over sixty.''

''And just where did you hear that?'' Elizabeth inquired, tucking an arm around her granddaughter's waist and steering her into the kitchen.

''It was in my health class. I could lend you the book, if you want.''

''Penny!'' Ellen exclaimed again with obvious dismay.

Elizabeth shot a grin at her daughter. ''Chill out, Ellen.'' She turned to Penny. ''That is the expression, isn't it?''

Ellen groaned. Kate looked from one to the other of them, her hands on her hips, her expression radiating indignation. ''Well, I'm delighted you all find this so amusing.''

Tension seemed to simmer in the air until Ellen gave her sister a hug. ''Oh, come on, Katie dearest. Chill out. As you can perfectly well see, Mother's just fine. You were worried over nothing. You should be relieved.''

''Why don't I fix us all some hot chocolate?'' Elizabeth suggested. ''The air's a bit damp tonight, don't you think?''

''Lace mine with brandy,'' Kate muttered, regarding the rest of them with a sour expression.

Elizabeth looked at her too-serious younger daughter and sighed. ''I'm sorry you were worried, dear. I really am.''

Some of the tension in Kate's shoulders eased. Finally she grinned. "Oh, what the hell. Let's go whole hog and order in a pizza, too. It's after nine and I just left the office. I missed dinner altogether."

"Now that's the spirit," Elizabeth said, noting that despite the long day Kate looked neat as a pin, every dark hair in place. What a contrast to Ellen's careless sandy hairstyle. "A large pizza with everything. I haven't eaten, either."

"Everything except anchovies," Penny countered.

"I happen to love anchovies, young lady. You can either learn to like them or pick them off."

Ellen and Kate shared an amused, conspiratorial glance at the familiar argument.

"You might as well give in kiddo," Ellen told her daughter. "Your grandmother will not budge on this."

By the time they'd finished the pizza, it was close to midnight. Elizabeth said good-night at the door and stood watching long after the taillights of their cars had disappeared.

She regretted worrying them earlier, but she was glad that it had brought them by, just when she needed a distraction the most. Now that they'd gone, the house felt empty and lifeless. It had never felt that way before. She'd never noticed the loneliness as she did tonight. Under the circumstances it was a dangerous state of mind.

For as long as Kate, Ellen and Penny were there, Elizabeth hadn't allowed a single thought of Brandon Halloran to creep in. Alone again, however, she knew that she had only delayed the inevitable. Brandon wasn't the type of man to be banished so easily from her thoughts.

To her dismay it seemed that that much at least hadn't changed over the past fifty years. He still had a way of capturing her attention and driving out all rational thought. She could only pray that some of that single-minded purpose with which he'd pursued her all those years ago had faded with age.

Chapter Two

Now that he'd found Lizzy, Brandon was not about to be thwarted in his campaign to arrange a reunion. What on earth could she find so threatening about a couple of old friends getting together to reminisce?

The next day he sent her two dozen pale pink roses, the day after that a huge basket of wildflowers. He followed up with rare orchids. The Beverly Hills florist was ecstatic over the lavish orders he phoned in daily. Brandon wasn't at all certain what Lizzy's reaction was likely to be. He figured it would be best not to call, to be patient and let her get used to the idea that he intended to become an important part of her life again.

It had been years since he'd courted a woman, but he knew the techniques couldn't have changed all that much. He would fill her whole damn house with flowers if he had to. Sooner or later she was bound to start chuckling at his extravagance. Then maybe she would experience a little twinge of purely feminine delight. By the time he exhausted the rare and exotic floral possibilities, he was hoping she'd cave in and track him down. Halloran Industries hadn't moved in nearly a century. She could find him anytime she wanted to.

Yet there were no calls, no letters as March gave way to April, so Brandon started sending extravagant boxes of candy. Lizzy had always had a sweet tooth. Half their dates had ended in a soda shop over hot-fudge sundaes. This time, though, a full week of chocolates produced no results. His patience started wearing thin.

Brandon was standing in front of a department store display of outrageously expensive French perfumes, totally at a loss, when Jason's wife sneaked up beside him.

"My, my, what are you up to?" Dana inquired, linking her arm through his.

He scowled at her. "How do you make heads or tails of all this?"

"Don't ask me. All those scents make me queasy."

He glanced at her swollen belly, which not even one of her boldly designed, loose-fitting sweaters could camouflage at this stage of her pregnancy. "Why aren't you and my great-grandbaby at home resting?"

"Because your great-grandbaby is coming in just a couple of months and I need to start buying things for the nursery."

"Nursery?" he said, readily dismissing the perfume as a purchase he could make later. "Let's go. I can help."

Dana stood stock-still. "Not until you tell me what

you're doing surrounded by the most expensive perfumes in the store."

"Just looking."

His granddaughter-in-law rolled her eyes. "Come on, Brandon. You can't kid a kidder. Who's the woman?"

"Young lady, mind your own business," he said, trying to sound stern, rather than flustered. He'd hoped to keep all this to himself. He could swear Dana to secrecy, but that seemed slightly absurd given the lack of anything much to talk about in the first place.

She grinned at him. "Talk about the pot calling the kettle black. If you ask me in this instance, turnabout is definitely fair play. You started meddling in my life on the first day we met and you haven't stopped yet."

"I think it's time we had another one of those talks about respecting your elders. Even that rapscallion brother of yours shows me more respect."

Dana didn't look the least bit intimidated. "Save the lecture for the baby," she told him. "Maybe you'll be able to convince your new great-grandchild to worship the ground you walk on. I'm just plain nosy, especially when my single grandfather-in-law is showing all the signs of courting some mysterious woman."

"Looking at perfume does *not* constitute courting. I could be buying the perfume for my secretary."

"Oh? Is it Harriet's birthday? Is she the one you've been lavishing all those flowers on?"

Brandon glared at her. "What do you know about any flowers?"

"Just that last month's florist bill nearly put Kevin back in the hospital with another heart attack. You really should pay cash, if you intend to keep these things secret from your nearest and dearest. Kevin reads the fine print on every one of those invoices, remember?''

''I remember,'' he grumbled. Unfortunately he hadn't considered that when he'd placed the orders. ''Are we going to look at baby things or not?''

''Sure,'' Dana said finally. ''That'll give me that much longer to try to pry some real information out of you.''

He waggled a finger under her nose. ''If I weren't afraid you would go out and buy little pink sissy things for my great-grandson, I'd let you go alone.''

''Your great-grand *daughter* may want little sissy things.''

''There hasn't been a girl born into the Halloran family as far back as I can remember.''

''Probably because nature knew what it would take to put up with the Halloran men. Now, come on. Let's look at wallpaper. I was thinking clowns. What do you think?''

''Clowns? Why not trains or boats?''

''How about little yellow ducks?''

''My great-grandson is not going to live with little yellow ducks,'' Brandon said indignantly. ''He'll quack before he talks.''

''Maybe we should look at cribs instead,'' Dana said. ''Or diapers? Do you have firm convictions about diapers? I was thinking cloth because of the environment.''

''Cloth is good,'' he conceded, then studied her worriedly. ''Are you sure you should be doing all this running around? Maybe you should go back home and rest. Leave the shopping up to Jason and me.''

''Not a chance. Now let's get moving. I have a list.''

Dana dragged him through the department store at a pace only slightly slower than a marathon runner's. She found at least a half-dozen more opportunities to slip in questions about his social life. Brandon had to be quick on his feet to keep up with her and even quicker to avoid the verbal traps she so neatly set.

When they'd finally put the bundles into the trunk of Dana's car, he shot her a triumphant look. "Thought you could wheedle it out of me, didn't you?"

She turned on her most innocent expression. "You mean the fact that this woman lives in California and her name is Elizabeth?" she asked as she slammed the car door.

Brandon stared at her in astonishment, then rapped on the window until she rolled it down. "How'd you know that?"

"Those invoices reveal a whole lot more than the cost of your flowers," she said smugly. "The word is out."

"If you knew all that, why'd you ask?"

"I wanted to watch you squirm," she admitted with a grin. "You've done it to us often enough."

Brandon couldn't stop the laugh that bubbled up despite his indignation at being caught. "I suppose you're feeling mighty proud of yourself?"

"As a matter of fact, yes."

"I wouldn't go getting too smug, young lady. There's still time for me to sneak my workmen into that nursery and paper the walls with itsy-bitsy footballs and baseballs."

"You do and your great-grandchild will be in college before you see her."

"You're mighty sassy," he observed with a

chuckle. He leaned down and kissed her forehead. ‘‘Come over some night and dig around in the attic. There just might be an old cradle up there you could use.’’

‘‘Was it Jason’s?’’ she asked with an immediate spark of enthusiasm in her eyes.

‘‘His and Kevin’s before him. Might even have been mine.’’

‘‘Oh, I’d love to have that. I’ll stop by.’’

‘‘Anytime you like. In the meantime, you take care of that baby.’’

‘‘Between you and Jason I don’t have a choice.’’ She backed the car out of the parking space, then called to him. ‘‘Whatever’s going on with you, I hope you’re having fun.’’

‘‘Not yet,’’ he admitted glumly, then brightened. ‘‘But I expect to be.’’

One week later Brandon packaged up a vintage recording of the song he and Lizzy had considered to be theirs—one of Glenn Miller’s best to Brandon’s way of thinking. He sent it overnight express. If that didn’t get to her, he didn’t know what would.

Sure enough, Elizabeth called that night just as he was getting ready to leave the office. ‘‘Brandon, this has to stop.’’

‘‘Why?’’

‘‘I don’t want all these gifts. Do you have any idea how overpowering all these flowers are in a five-room house? I feel like I’m sleeping in a garden.’’

‘‘Sounds romantic to me.’’

‘‘It might be, if I didn’t have allergies,’’ she grumbled, sneezing as if to prove the point.

Despite himself, Brandon chuckled. ‘‘Send the flowers to a hospital or a nursing home.’’

"Why are you doing this?"

"I told you. I want to see you. Why are you so reluctant?"

"I think it's wrong to try to go back."

It sounded to Brandon as if she'd wanted to say something else. The reluctance puzzled him. "We're talking dinner, maybe a little dancing. You always did like to dance, Lizzy. I remember the way you could waltz. I'll never forget the night we danced in that gazebo in the town square. I can still smell the honeysuckle. I loved holding you in my arms."

"No," she repeated, but there was less starch in her voice this time.

"You're weakening, aren't you? I'll be out tomorrow. Once I'm standing on your doorstep, you won't be able to resist."

"That's what I'm afraid of," she muttered.

Brandon waited as she drew in a deep breath. Finally, after yet another silence that seemed to last an eternity, she said, "I don't want you out here. I'll come there, Brandon. It's been a long time since I've been back to the East Coast."

"Tomorrow?" he said. "I'll call my travel agent and have her book you on the first available flight."

"You always were so impatient," she said on a breathless laugh. "Not tomorrow, but soon."

"Promise?"

"I promise. But I'll buy my own ticket, Brandon…when I'm ready."

He heard the determined note in her voice and knew she wouldn't budge. "I won't argue with you over the ticket," he said reluctantly. "But if you don't show up soon, I'll come after you, Lizzy. I swear I will."

That night, like so many others in recent months,

Brandon Halloran lay awake staring into the darkness. Unlike those other nights, though, this time he was filled with excitement, rather than loneliness. He felt as if nearly fifty years of his life had vanished in the blink of an eye and he was an impetuous, daring young man again.

There was nothing that eighteen-year-old Brandon Halloran loved more than flying. From the day he'd graduated from high school he'd wanted nothing more than to join the Air Force and do his part in World War II. His parents had been appalled when he'd gone and enlisted rather than pack his bags for the Ivy League college that had accepted him. Now with his training complete and his orders for overseas in his pocket, he had ten days to say goodbye.

Unfortunately, every time he tried to say the words, his mother burst into tears and left the room. His father, who'd come to the United States as an immigrant from England, understood only that he was in some way responsible for Brandon's decision. He and his uncles had told Brandon stories about England from the day he was born. Because of those stories, Brandon felt this compelling need to fight in a war that was endangering their homeland.

Besides, he looked damned good in his uniform. Everyone knew that soldiers and fly-boys had their pick of women caught up in the drama of sending young men off to war. He didn't delude himself that what he was doing was part idealism and part ego. He liked the image of himself as a hero, liked even more the idea of flirting with danger.

"I'd rather have my son alive," his mother said when Brandon tried one last time to explain. She slammed a plate onto the kitchen counter with such force it shattered. Then came the tears and she hurried away, refusing to meet his distraught gaze.

His father came in just then. "You've upset your mother again, haven't you?"

"Dad, I don't know what else I can say to her."

"She's afraid for you."

"I'm good, Dad. I'll come out of this okay."

In a rare display of emotion, his father gripped his hand. "I hope so, boy. For all our sakes. She'll never forgive me if you don't."

"You do understand why I need to go, though, don't you?"

His father nodded. "If I were a younger man, I'd be going with you."

It had been more of a blessing than Brandon had expected. "I think I'll hitch a ride up the coast with a friend of mine for a couple of days. Maybe that'll give Mom some time to adjust."

"I think that would be best. Make the most of these days, son. Once you ship out, it's hard telling when you'll have another chance to relax."

Jack Brice picked him up a few hours later and they headed north. Jack's family had a place overlooking the ocean on the coast of Maine. Brandon had agreed to come along as much to cushion the blow when Jack told his family about his overseas orders as he had to relax.

When Jack broke the news the following day at lunch, his parents and sisters were every bit as stunned and dismayed as Brandon's family had been. After a while Brandon left them alone and went for a walk along the cliff overlooking the sea.

Even in summer there was always a stiff, chilly

breeze blowing in hard from the north along there, but the sun beat down to counteract the cold. With his hands jammed in his pockets, he walked for the better part of an hour, thinking about the war taking place directly across the ocean that was splashing against the rocky coastline below.

He thought of the way the planes responded to his touch, the power he felt sitting at the controls defying gravity. And he thought of the reality of combat which up to now held no meaning for him. His mother, his father, the Brices, they were all right to be afraid. Hell, he'd be scared to death, too, if he allowed himself to ponder all the things that could go wrong on a mission. Fortunately he'd been blessed with an abundance of optimism. Hallorans made their own luck, and he intended to grab quite a handful.

Brandon was thinking about luck when he first saw the streak of white flashing past, a woman's bare feet kicking back, her hair streaming. The sunlight caught in the hair and turned it into fiery ribbons. He'd watched her run for no more than a heartbeat before the same compelling sense of fate that had drawn him to enlist sent him racing after her.

With his long, loping strides he could have caught up with her in no time, but he held back, enjoying the sight of her wide-flung arms, her bare legs, the way the white cotton dress clung to her curves.

He was so surprised when she suddenly whirled around and stopped stock-still that he almost ran into her. He drew up just in time to catch the bright spark of curiosity in her eyes, the faint sound of laughter on her lips. The run had pushed color into her cheeks and had her bosom rising and falling in a way that was all too provocative despite the demure style of the dress.

Brandon felt his breath go still as awareness slammed through him.

Hands on hips, an arrogant tilt to her chin, she demanded, "Who are you?"

"Brandon Halloran."

"You don't live around here."

He grinned at her certainty. "I suppose you know everyone?"

"Every handsome man, at any rate," she said boldly.

Brandon had a hunch her daring tone was one she never would have used under ordinary circumstances. She looked as if she were trying it out for the first time, a little hesitant, a little defiant.

"Who are *you?*"

"Elizabeth Forsythe, which you would have known if you lived around here," she said smugly.

"I suspect you have a reputation with all the men for being outrageous."

She grinned in obvious delight at that. "Why, of course."

"How old are you, outrageous Lizzy?"

"No one calls me Lizzy."

"I do," he said matter-of-factly, enjoying the notion of standing out in her memory. "How old are you?"

"Seventeen," she said. "And a half."

"That half certainly is important," he said solemnly, all the while thanking all the gods in heaven for making her old enough for him to court.

She regarded him intently. "You're teasing me, aren't you?"

"No more than you're teasing me."

She turned away from him then and started walking.

He fell into step beside her. "Tell me all about yourself, Lizzy Forsythe."

"Why?"

"Because I have a feeling we are going to be very important to each other and I want to know everything about you."

She glanced up at him with a look that was both shy and impish. "Now who's being outrageous?"

"We'll see about that," he said softly, wishing he dared to tangle his fingers in the silken threads of her hair, wishing he could see if her skin was nearly as soft as it looked.

"How long will you be here?"

"A week," he said. "Then I'm going to England."

"To fight?" she asked with a note of excitement threading unmistakably through her voice.

"Yes. Do you think a week is long enough for me to make you fall in love with me?"

She shook her head. "Not nearly long enough."

Brandon wondered how she could say that with such certainty, when he felt as if he'd been struck by lightning. There was no sense to the way he was feeling, no logic at all, just the gut-deep conviction that he'd finally met the woman with whom he would share the rest of his life.

He saw the strength in her and sensed that Elizabeth Forsythe could meet arrogance with confidence, passion with boldness. He knew intuitively that she was the sort of woman who could meet a man on his own terms. Making her fall in love with him might not be easy, but that would be more than half the fun of it.

Lying awake in the middle of the night nearly a half century later, Brandon sighed as he thought back to that time so long ago. How naive he'd been. And yet nothing that had happened in all the years since had changed the emotions that had filled his heart that day.

Brandon wondered if he would still feel that same sweet certainty when he saw Lizzy again. Maybe he was an old fool for wanting to tempt fate a second time, but he could hardly wait.

Chapter Three

Brandon waited impatiently for Lizzy to make good on her promise. There was a new spring in his step. He was actually humming an old tune—that Glenn Miller classic—in the office as he began planning in earnest for the retirement that had terrified him only a few weeks before. Kevin was back at work, his marriage on solid ground at last. Brandon finally felt he could leave Halloran Industries with his mind at ease. More importantly, he had something to look forward to.

Jason and Kevin clearly didn't know what to make of the change in Brandon's mood or the flurry of activity that accompanied putting his retirement plans into action. He caught their bemused expressions, the shake of their heads, more than once. It amused the hell out of him to keep them in the dark.

They probably thought he was getting senile—unless they'd added up the meaning of all those florist bills as cleverly as Dana had. Knowing Kevin, though, he'd probably only worried that there had been no line item in the corporate budget to justify the expense. Sooner or later he would grumble at his father for mixing his personal spending with the legitimate charges for Halloran Industries.

It was two long weeks before Lizzy's call finally came—enough time to plan, enough time to worry that she'd changed her mind, enough time to grow impatient.

When Brandon's housekeeper finally announced that a Mrs. Newton was on the phone, he was pacing the library like a caged lion, debating whether he ought to call her himself and put an end to this interminable waiting. Delighted he wouldn't have to make that decision, he grabbed the receiver before Mrs. Farns-worth had even left the room.

"Lizzy?"

"I'm here," she announced without preliminaries.

"Where?"

She named a hotel where they had once shared an intimate dinner. He wondered if she'd chosen it deliberately or merely because it was the only one she could recall when making her reservation. It pleased him to believe the former, rather than the latter, so he didn't ask.

"Alone?" he inquired with surprising hesitancy for a man who'd once been a daredevil fighter pilot and after that had commanded a large corporation and hundreds of employees for nearly fifty years.

Her sudden laughter seemed to float in the air between them. "You never did like to share, did you, Brandon?"

He knew she'd only meant to tease, but he answered the question seriously. "No, Lizzy, I never did. Not where you were concerned, anyway. You still haven't answered my question. Are you here alone?'

He feared more than he cared to admit that she would have packed up one of her daughters, maybe even the grandkids and brought them along as chaperons.

"Yes," she said, sounding satisfied that she'd taunted him into revealing a tiny hint of insecurity, "I'm alone."

"Then you'll come to the house for dinner," he said decisively. "I'll send a car at once. Can you be ready in ten minutes?"

Again she laughed, and he was transported back half a century to a time when life had been filled with possibilities and even minutes weren't to be squandered.

"Make it thirty minutes and I'll be waiting," she promised as she had then.

This time, Brandon thought, *nothing* was going to stand in their way.

Elizabeth stood in her hotel room for several minutes after hanging up the phone. It was just like Brandon to start making plans without giving her a second to think over her answer. Only just now had she realized how much she had missed that quick decisiveness, that rush of enthusiasm that spoke volumes about his feelings even when he couldn't say the words. A woman would always know where she stood with a man like Brandon.

If he'd had his way nearly fifty years ago, they'd have been married a week after they met. Truth be told, she'd wanted that as much as he had, but she'd been reared as a proper young lady and proper young ladies back then hadn't gone rushing off to get married on a whim, not when they'd barely turned seventeen and when the man was very nearly a stranger.

Brandon had coaxed. He'd wooed her with every bit of inventiveness at his command. He'd wanted to ask her father for her hand. She had believed in his love, but she was too cautious by far to give in, even to a handsome airman about to go off to war.

Even if she had been willing, her parents would have come between them. They had dreams for their only daughter and those dreams didn't include an impetuous marriage to a man heading straight into harm's way.

Nothing had stood in the way of her giving him her love, though. Right or wrong, Elizabeth had not wanted that regret weighing on her forever. There had been time enough later to consider that single, glorious night in his arms and all its implications in an era when nice girls definitely didn't go to bed with young men before marriage.

And she had paid for that night. Oh, how she had paid, but she hadn't been able to resent him for turning her into what her staid parents had called soiled goods. How quaint and unimportant that sounded in this day and age. At the time, though, it had seemed a calamity.

As she touched a bit of blusher to her cheeks and wondered what he would think when he saw her after all these years, she recalled the way he'd looked at her when she'd turned down his marriage proposal.

"You're saying no?" he'd said, his stunned expression reflecting the bemusement of a young man already used to getting his own way in everything that mattered. He'd counted on a splashy diamond ring to persuade her, but she'd refused to allow him to slip it on her finger. She was desperately afraid of being tempted to change her mind. It was difficult enough not to give in to the lure of an impulsive elopement.

"I'm saying no...for now," she'd told him gently, but firmly. "Our time will come when you're home again. I promise I'll wear the locket you gave me, every single day, and I'll be waiting."

She had meant it with all her heart.

But their time hadn't come. Brandon had gone off to England to fly daring missions that had terrified her more with each descriptive letter he sent. Those letters had reminded her how brave he was. Though he had thought her bold, she was weaker by far than he'd imagined. It would never have worked between them. Or so she tried to tell herself as the daily letters had slowly trickled down to one a week or less.

A few months later her family had left Maine and there had been no choice for Elizabeth but to go with them. They had made that clear, just as they had their feelings about Brandon. Brandon's letters had stopped altogether then. She'd been devastated, but not terribly surprised. Her parents told her over and over that he'd never loved her at all. She'd guessed he'd found someone else overseas, someone all too willing to make a commitment to a man with his money and charm and daring. Envisioning him with a war bride from England had hurt her more than she'd ever let on to anyone.

Resigned to never seeing him again, she had finally taken off the locket and relegated it to a box with other treasures. She made a safe, secure life for herself in California. She'd married and taught school. Widowed now, she had two beautiful daughters and three energetic grandchildren, two of whom were already older than she had been when she and Brandon had met.

Just this week it had been Ellen, her oldest daughter, who'd found the gold locket with Brandon's picture in it sitting in a crystal bowl on the coffee table. Elizabeth had placed it there after looking at the picture inside time and again, trying to make up her mind about the folly of taking this trip.

"I've never seen this before," Ellen said as the fragile gold chain sifted through her fingers. The heart-shaped locket had rested in her palm.

Elizabeth reached for it, flustered and uncertain, but she hadn't been able to prevent Ellen from looking inside.

Her daughter had studied the tiny photograph for several minutes before looking up and saying quietly, "He's very handsome. Who is he? It's not Father."

"No," Elizabeth admitted. "It's someone I knew long ago, before I met your father."

Ellen studied her face for what seemed an eternity, then said with obvious amazement, "You loved him very much, didn't you?"

Elizabeth shrugged nonchalantly, but her pulse scrambled. "I thought I did, but I was very young."

"What happened?"

"I'm not really sure. He went off to war and we lost touch." It was the simplest explanation she could think of for something that had seemed so terribly complicated at the time. She managed to keep any hint of bitterness out of her voice.

"Were you engaged?"

"Not officially, though he wanted very much to marry me before he left. I turned him down."

"But why, if you loved him?"

Elizabeth sighed. "You can't imagine how many times I asked myself that same question. In the end, though, it seems I made the right decision."

"Why do you have this out now?"

"I heard from him a few weeks ago."

Ellen's eyes lit up at once, clearly fascinated. "Really? He found you after all this time?"

"Yes," she said. Then because she was still amazed by it, she added, "He hired a detective of all things."

"Oh, Mother, that's so romantic."

Romantic. Yes, that definitely summed up Brandon. Romantic and, as it had turned out, irresponsible. Elizabeth took the locket from her daughter's hand and ran her fingers over the simple design engraved on the face of the heart. It felt warm from Ellen's touch.

"I don't know what to do," Elizabeth admitted.

"He wants to see you. Is that it?"

She nodded. "And I promised I'd go to Boston, but now I'm not so sure."

"Mother, you have to go. You promised, didn't you? He doesn't sound like the kind of man who'd let you go back on your promise. Besides, what's the worst that could happen?" her dreamy, romantic Ellen said with stars in her eyes. "He's gotten fat and bald?"

Even now that she'd made it as far as Boston, Elizabeth could think of a dozen worse things than that, that could go wrong with such an impetuous trip. None of them had she dared to share with Ellen.

There was no denying, though, that she wanted to be here, wanted to see Brandon again, if only to resolve all the old hurts that she'd so carefully banked in order to get on with her life. Maybe now, at last, she could truly put the past behind her.

It had surprised Elizabeth that Brandon had sounded almost as nostalgic about their brief romance as she felt. If the memories hadn't faded for him after all this time, why had he let her go so easily? Why had he abandoned her?

Her heart still ached when she thought about the way she'd watched the mail day after day, only to be disappointed again and again, until finally it had become too painful to watch. Now she would ask him why. She would satisfy herself that she'd gilded the memory, that Brandon Halloran wasn't the romantic hero she remembered at all.

And then she would run back to her full, satisfying life in California and live out her days in peace. One last piece of unresolved business would be finally put to rest. Until he'd called, she'd had no idea that it still mattered so much to her to know what had happened.

So here she was, back in Boston for the first time in decades, her stomach tied in knots, her fingers trembling. Even at seventeen she was certain she'd never felt this giddy sense of anticipation.

Elizabeth ran a brush through the short hair that she'd finally allowed to turn gray. Oh, how she wished it were the same rich auburn it had been way back then. Brandon had loved her hair, long and touched with fire, he used to say.

When they'd made love on that one incredible moonlit night, he'd allowed the strands to flow through his fingers like silken threads, fascinated with it. What would he think of this short cap of waves that her daughters said took ten years off her age, despite the gray?

She smoothed her pale blue suit over hips that were still slender and adjusted the flowered silk scarf at her throat. Beneath the scarf she could feel the locket pressing against her skin, its once-familiar touch oddly reassuring.

Still, she was filled with trepidation as she went with the driver Brandon had sent. Were either of them prepared for the changes? Could they possibly avoid disappointment?

When the car drove up the winding driveway of the same impressive brick Colonial family home that she recalled from one brief visit years before, for one instant she wanted to turn back. She wanted to flee before illusions were shattered—or confirmed.

She wasn't sure which she feared more, the answers he would give or the disappointed realization that things between them could never be the same. Maybe it would have been wisest, after all, to keep the past in the past, where memories could live on untarnished.

Then the door opened as if Brandon had been watching impatiently for her arrival from just inside. He stepped outside into the glow of the brass lamps on either side of the door. Elizabeth's breath snagged in her throat as she allowed herself the freedom to study him unobserved through the limousine's tinted windows.

He was older to be sure, but he was just as tall and handsome as she remembered him. Like hers, his hair had gone silver, but it only made him look more distinguished in his dark suit. Any woman would be proud to appear on his arm. She had envisioned him once exactly like this—lean, sophisticated, impressive—back in the days when she spent too many hours imagining the two of them growing old side by side.

The quick, once-familiar flutter of her pulse took her back nearly fifty years and she knew that, in this way at least, time had stood still.

Chapter Four

At the first sign of headlights turning into the driveway, Brandon felt his pulse begin to race. He had the front door open, his heart thudding with anticipation, before the limousine could brake to a stop. It took every last bit of restraint he possessed to keep from sprinting down the steps. Instead he waited impatiently for his driver to open the door, more impatiently yet for Elizabeth to emerge.

For no more than the space of a heartbeat he was taken aback by the short hairstyle, the unapologetic gray that had replaced the stunning auburn he'd remembered. Then he looked at her tanned face, the way the sassy style emphasized her unchanged, twinkling eyes and admitted that the short cut, even the gray, suited her.

He noted that her legs, as she swung them out of the car, were still slender, her figure still girlish in a sedate blue suit with a twist of something silky at her throat. By golly, she was still a looker all right.

Brandon thought back to the snapshot he'd carried off to war. It had shown off that figure. She'd worn white shorts and a skimpy top that tied behind her neck and at her waist. The provocative outfit had left her legs and back bare and gave the impression of height far taller than her actual five foot-two. She'd been glancing over her shoulder at the camera, Betty Grable pinup style.

He had pulled that picture out a dozen times a day, considering it his good luck talisman. Only after she'd stopped writing and vanished had he angrily torn it into shreds and thrown it away. The memory had lingered for far longer, along with regrets for his brash, ill-considered act.

He pushed the memories aside and went to meet her, holding out his hands. "Lizzy," he said, his gaze meeting hers, detecting the nervousness behind the brave smile. "It's wonderful to see you."

Her hands were like ice in his. She glanced at him far more shyly now than she had on the day they'd met, though her words were calmly gracious.

"Brandon. It's good to see you, too. You look well," she said.

"I'm better, now that you're here." He tucked her hand through his arm and led her inside. "I'm afraid I've rushed the housekeeper. She already has dinner on the table. Do you mind if we go straight in?"

"Of course not," she said, sounding surprisingly relieved.

He wondered if she'd feared the idle moments before the meal as he had, if she'd worried that conversation would lag, if she'd dreaded an endless evening begun in hope and ending in disappointment? How could a man who'd entertained politicians and celebrities in his time be so nervous about an evening with someone he'd once thought he knew even better than himself?

The elegant Queen Anne table in the formal dining room had been set for two with the finest Halloran china and crystal, brought over by his father from England at the beginning of the century. Candles glowed. A bottle of Brandon's best vintage wine was ready to be poured. White roses, opened just enough to scent the air, had been arranged dramatically in a crystal bowl in the center of the table. Even with such short notice, Mrs. Farnsworth had outdone herself. Although, she had told him with an indignant huff, no thanks to his agitated hovering.

Even with those exquisite touches, all Brandon noticed was the shine in Lizzy's eyes. She'd always had a twinkle in those eyes, a daring glimmer that belied her cautious nature.

Obviously, daring had overcome caution to bring her back to Boston, to bring her here tonight. He wondered why she'd been so reluctant in the first place. This wasn't some silly blind date she'd had cause to fear. But there'd been no mistaking the earlier reluctance, no ignoring the hesitation even now, a hesitation that he was certain went beyond simple nervousness.

Still he pushed curiosity aside and went through the motions of settling her in the chair next to his. He wasn't about to relegate her to the far end of a table big enough for Halloran family reunions.

Brandon's own meal cooled, untouched, while he listened to Elizabeth fill in the gaps they hadn't covered on the phone. More than the details, he heard the humor, the love, the fulfillment, and regretted more than he could say that he hadn't been the one to share them. How he wished that he'd been there to witness the shift from youthful impetuosity to mature strength, that he'd been the one to bring her laughter and contentment.

"Tell me about your husband," he said.

"He was a wonderful man, kind, thoughtful, generous. The girls adored him, especially Kate. She came along late, when we weren't sure we'd have another child. He doted on her. I wasn't sure what would happen to her when he died. For a long time she seemed almost lost without him."

"He made you happy, then?" Brandon asked, hiding the resentment that crept over him. It was foolish to be jealous of a man he'd never met, a man who'd been dead for five years. Yet knowing that didn't stop the pangs of regret.

"Very," she said.

Brandon regarded her speculatively, trying to interpret the note of determination in her voice, the defiant gleam in her eyes. "And love, Lizzy? Did he love you?"

"Perhaps more than I deserved," she said.

"What an odd way to put it."

"Don't you find that in relationships more often than not one partner cares more than the other, that one gives and the other takes? What about in your own marriage?"

Pained that she had hit upon something he had thought more than once about his relationship with Grace, he nodded. "I suppose that's so, about relationships, I mean."

"And your own?" she prodded, her gaze relentlessly searching his.

He felt it would be a betrayal of Grace to admit that she had loved more than he, yet he couldn't bring himself to lie. "I suppose we found a balance," he said finally, skirting the truth of it. There had been a balance of sorts. He didn't think his wife had ever felt cheated. He had cared deeply for her, honored their vows, and to his dying day he would be grateful for the life they had shared, the son she had borne him.

"Tell me more about your life in California," he said at last.

He sat back, then, and listened, watching the way laughter put such sparks in her eyes, the way her face became animated when she talked about her daughters and grandchildren. Then there was no mistaking the radiance of love, which proved he'd been right when he'd guessed she hadn't felt it nearly so deeply for her husband.

Finally, when she'd been talking nonstop for some time, Elizabeth lifted troubled eyes to his. "You've been awfully quiet, Brandon. It's not like you."

"I like listening to you. I've had too many quiet meals in this room over the past couple of years. It's wonderful to have some laughter in here again."

"Then why do you look so sad?"

"I suppose I was thinking about how much I missed."

She looked startled by the candid answer. "Don't try to make me believe you haven't had a good life," she chided. "You're not the sort of man to let life pass you by."

"No, I've had a wonderful life," he admitted. He told her about his business triumphs and his family, omitting the inexplicable emptiness that had nagged despite everything. He wouldn't have her thinking him ungrateful for all the genuine blessings in his life.

"The years since Grace died have been lonely, though. These past weeks I've been thinking how much I wished I had someone to share things with again."

"You're a handsome, successful man, Brandon. I'm sure there are dozens of women who'd be pleased by your attention."

It was odd, but he'd never really thought of that before. He supposed it was true enough. There had been invitations to dinners, the symphony, the ballet, charity affairs. He'd even accepted a few, but always in the back of his mind he must have been waiting for his search for Lizzy to be successful. He hadn't seriously considered any of those other women as candidates for his affection.

Brandon gazed solemnly into Elizabeth's eyes and took her hand. "I think fate has done it again, Lizzy. I think there was a reason for my finding you after all this time. Not a woman I know could hold a candle to you."

"And I think you've had too much wine to drink," she retorted, but there was a becoming blush of pink in her cheeks and she didn't withdraw her hand.

"Don't pretend you don't know exactly what I mean. You didn't come all this way just to say hello, did you?" he countered, watching the blush deepen.

"Of course not," she said hurriedly. "It's been years since I've seen Boston."

"Are you trying to say that I'm just one of the sights on your schedule?" he teased. "I'm old, Lizzy, but I'm not a monument."

"You still have a sizable ego, I see."

"You'd never want a man who wasn't sure of himself."

"And how would you know that?"

"No one changes that much, not even in a lifetime."

"Perhaps at my age I'm not even looking for a man," she said. "Did you consider that?"

"Then you're here for nothing more than a little talk about old times?"

"Yes," she said, but there was something wistful in her voice that touched his heart and told him the quick response wasn't quite the truth. She needed more than memories, the same way he did. Just thinking about proving that to her made his tired old blood pump a little faster.

"And maybe some answers," she added determinedly then, not quite meeting his gaze as she withdrew her hand from his. She folded her hands together as if to keep them from trembling. Her knuckles turned white and there was a sudden frost in her voice.

"Answers?" he asked warily, startled by the shift in her mood.

She looked up then, her gaze colliding with his. "What happened back then, Brandon?" she asked indignantly. "Did you meet someone else? Did you forget I was waiting? Explain it to me. I think you owe me that much."

Stunned by the sudden burst of anger over hurts a half century old, he simply stared at her. "Forget you? Never, Lizzy. Never!"

He hit the table with his fist and suddenly he was every bit as angry as she, drawing on emotions he'd thought dead and buried long ago. He shoved his chair back and stood, towering over her. She never even flinched, though her hands clenched even more tightly.

"How could you even ask something like that?" he demanded.

"Then why did the letters stop?"

"I could ask you the same thing," he shot back. "For weeks after I got your last letter, I kept on writing. Not a day passed that I didn't write some little note at least. Do you know what it's like being away from home, alone?" He held his fingers a scant inch apart. "This close to dying every single day, only to think that the woman you love more than life itself has forgotten all about you so quickly?"

"But *I* wrote," she swore just as vehemently. "It was *you.* I never got any letters, not after we moved."

Suddenly they stopped and stared at each other as the meaning of the furious words sank in. Brandon sank back into his chair as he realized that trust, as much as anything, was at stake. Either or both could have been lying.

To his regret, he saw that there was no way of proving what they said, not after all this time. There was no way of knowing for certain if the letters had simply been misdirected, lost in the chaos of war, destroyed by her parents—or never sent in the first place.

"We'll never know," she said finally, her voice filled with a sadness as deep as his own as she came to the same realization. "Will we?"

Brandon couldn't bear the uncertainty he saw in her eyes, heard in her voice. "You must believe me," he insisted. "I sent those letters. I swear I did. When I was injured and sent home, I moved heaven and earth to try to find you, but it was as if you'd vanished without a trace."

"You were injured?" she said, her eyes wide. "How seriously? What happened?"

"I'd only been there a few months when my plane went down. I got out with no more than some broken bones, but it was enough to get me sent home."

"So my letters could have gone astray?" she said slowly.

"Yes, as could mine."

He hoped she could see the truth in his eyes, could read the bitter agony of loss on his face. If only he'd hired a qualified detective back then, rather than counting on unreliable acquaintances in Maine and eventually in California. Leads had dwindled, then turned cold. By the time Grace had been introduced and encouraged as a suitable match, he had only discouraging answers. Grace had been there during the recuperation, not Lizzy. They had been, at the least, compatible. With no word on Lizzy, the choice had seemed clear.

"Only then did I give up," he swore. "That's the truth, Lizzy. You must believe me."

But rather than unqualified trust, all she said was, "I want to, Brandon. I want to believe you."

"We have another chance. Let's not let it go so easily this time," he urged. "Please, Lizzy. We're too old for more regrets. Say you'll stay and give me a chance to make it all up to you. We'll do all the things we never got to do back then."

For the longest time she looked indecisive, avoiding his eyes. Finally she said simply, "A few days, Brandon. I'll stay on for a few days."

There was an implied finality to the limit she set that nagged at him, but for the moment at least he would take what she was willing to give. He trusted in his own persuasiveness to see that a few days turned into weeks, then months and eventually a lifetime. He could explain his determination no more clearly now, than he could have decades ago. He only knew what he felt in his heart. It was there again, beating with the same strong certainty that had guided everything he did.

The phone in her hotel room was ringing when Elizabeth walked in, still shaken by the powerful emotions that had gripped her from the first instant she had seen Brandon again. It was after midnight, three hours earlier in California. She had no doubts at all that it was Ellen calling to see how this first meeting had gone.

Desperately needing the sense of grounding that a talk with her daughter would provide, Elizabeth kicked off her shoes as she reached for the phone.

''Hey, Grandma, how was the hot date?'' Penny asked. Obviously she'd pried the information about Brandon out of her mother and wanted details.

''We had a lovely dinner,'' she said primly.

''Boring,'' Penny pronounced. ''Where'd you go? Some real fancy restaurant?''

''His house.''

''Better,'' the teen decreed. ''Did he ask you to stay over?''

''I'm here, aren't I?''

''That doesn't mean he didn't ask.''

Elizabeth held back a chuckle as she heard a muffled discussion on the other end, then Penny's disgusted, ''Hold on, here's Mom. Don't tell her any of the juicy details. Save 'em for me.''

''There are no juicy details,'' Elizabeth said, wondering precisely when Penny had become so precocious. Maybe it was the result of being the youngest by nearly ten years, a delightful, much-loved surprise who, because she'd always had the company of those older than she, had grown up too fast by far.

"Okay, Mom," Ellen was saying, "let's cut to the chase. Is he bald?"

As Elizabeth settled herself on the bed, propped up by pillows, she thought of Brandon's thick silver hair. "Hardly."

"Fat?"

She recalled his trim body, which still did astonishing things for a custom-tailored suit. "Nope."

"Was that old zing still there?"

"For him or for me?"

"You're being evasive," Ellen accused. "That must mean it was there in spades."

"He is a very attractive man," Elizabeth conceded, regretting that she still felt that way about him despite everything. "Quite dashing, actually."

"And you're a gorgeous woman."

"A gorgeous *old* woman," Elizabeth corrected. "Stop talking foolishness. How's everything out there?"

"About the same as it was when you left here this morning," Ellen said dryly. "Don't try to change the subject. When are you seeing him again?"

"Tomorrow. We're going sight-seeing."

"And then?"

"And then I'm coming back to the hotel and going to bed."

"Oh, really?"

"Alone, Ellen. Alone," she said emphatically, but she couldn't help the feeling of anticipation that rushed through her as she considered the possibilities.

She really was an old fool, she thought as the heat of embarrassment climbed in her cheeks.

"Sweetie, I'm awfully tired. I'll call you in a few days."

"Mom, you sound funny," Ellen said, her tone suddenly serious. "Are you sure you're okay?"

"Just tired."

"And a little nostalgic?"

"A lot nostalgic," she admitted with a rueful chuckle. "I think I'd better sleep it off."

"Mom, if there's still something special with this man after all this time, go for it. Okay? Promise?"

"Good night, Ellen," she said deliberately and slid the phone back into the cradle. She wasn't ready yet to dissect all the feelings that had crowded in after seeing Brandon for the first time.

There was no denying that the thought of him moving heaven and earth to find her at this late date appealed to her sense of romance, just as it did to Ellen's and Penny's.

Kate—practical, down-to-earth Kate—would be appalled that Elizabeth had even spoken to a man who'd betrayed her, much less flown clear across the country to see him. Kate held on to hurt, too long by Elizabeth's standards. She'd never gotten over the awful man who'd thrown her over. Ellen was more like Elizabeth herself had been five decades ago, willing to throw caution to the wind, especially when it came to her heart.

What Elizabeth needed now was a good strong dose of Kate's tougher nature. Something told her if she didn't cling for dear life to rational thought, Brandon Halloran was going to sweep her off her feet all over again and that was the very last thing she could allow to happen. She'd meant to put the past to rest. Instead it seemed she'd merely stirred cold ashes back to flame.

Just a few days, she promised. She would indulge herself in some old dreams, allow herself the rare thrill of feeling desirable again. She deserved one last rollicking fling. Then she would don a shroud of common sense and go back to California with enough memories to carry her through the rest of her days.

Chapter Five

Brandon knew he should have expected the commotion that followed his call to the office in the morning, but he hadn't. Within minutes of telling his secretary that he wouldn't be in, first Kevin and then Jason called.

"Are you okay, Dad?" Kevin asked. "Harriet told me you called and said you weren't coming in today."

"Maybe I just thought you ought to get used to running things without me. I am retiring, remember?"

The comment was greeted with a heavy silence. Finally Kevin said carefully, "We haven't even talked about that. Are you sure you've given the idea enough thought? It seems to me you decided that all of a sudden."

"It was hardly sudden. You and Jason have been chomping at the bit to do things your own way for the past couple of years. I'd say it's past time for me to let you.''

''We're not trying to shove you out, Dad.''

''Hell, you think I don't know that? I just decided it was time to develop some new interests while I have time.''

''While you have time,'' Kevin repeated slowly. ''What's that supposed to mean? Dad, are you okay?''

''I think that's how this conversation started. I'm fine. I'm taking the day off because I have things to do. I can't recall the last time I took a long weekend.''

''Neither can I. That's why I'm worried.''

''Well, stop making such a fuss about it. I may even take the whole danged week off next week,'' he said irritably.

''Dad!''

Brandon ignored the note of alarm in Kevin's voice and hung up. Five minutes later he went through essentially the same conversation with Jason. At this rate he'd never finish his first cup of coffee, much less the once-fluffy scrambled eggs that had turned cold and hard while Kevin and Jason carried on about nothing. When a man got eggs only once a week, it was infuriating to see them ruined. He would never convince Mrs. Farnsworth he ought to have them again another morning. She was as rigid with his diet as any chef at some fancy health spa.

He regarded the eggs ruefully, muttered a curse and poured himself another cup of coffee. Decaf, but at least it was still hot.

He figured Kevin and Jason weren't done with their questions yet, but he rushed through the paper in an attempt to evade whatever meddling they were likely to do.

Unfortunately he wasn't fast enough. He was on his way out the front door when Dana's sporty little car screeched to a halt in front of him, kicking up gravel. She hauled her bulky form out. It was evident from the haphazardly chosen clothes, the lack of makeup and the mussed hair that she'd been roused from sleep and sent over here on the double to check up on him.

Hands on hips, Jason's wife looked him over from head to toe. "You don't look sick," she pronounced.

"Never said I was."

"But Jason—"

"Is an astonishing worrywart for someone his age. Maybe if he had a couple of babies to keep his mind occupied, he wouldn't carry on so about me."

Dana grinned at him and patted her belly. "I can't make this baby come a minute sooner just to keep my husband off your back," she said. "Where are you off to?"

"I'm going sight-seeing, not that it's any of your business."

"Sight-seeing? Is there any part of Boston you haven't seen a hundred times?"

"I'm taking an old friend on a trip down memory lane."

Clearly fascinated, Dana said, "I don't suppose you'd want company."

"You suppose right. Now get on about your business and tell that husband of yours next time he wants to check up on me, he should do it himself."

"And have you pitch a fit because he's away from his desk? Besides, I worry about you, too, you know."

Brandon squeezed her hand. "There's no need, girl. I'm better than I've been in a very long time."

She nodded. "I can see that. In fact, you look downright spiffy. I can't recall ever seeing you in anything but a suit on a weekday.'' She smoothed his blue cashmere pullover across his shoulders. ''Must be a woman involved. I don't suppose that mysterious Elizabeth from California has anything to do with your dapper attire?''

''Have I mentioned that you're a nosy little thing?''

''More than once,'' she said. ''Just giving you a taste of your own medicine.''

''I'll reform,'' he vowed.

''And pigs will fly,'' she retorted as she gave him a kiss on the cheek. ''Wherever you're off to, have fun.''

''I intend to.'' He waggled a finger under her nose. ''And don't you go sneaking around trying to see what I'm up to.''

''I wouldn't dream of it.''

Brandon eyed the sporty little convertible Jason had given her on their wedding day. Dana had adamantly refused a new car, so his grandson had given her his, then bought himself a new one. It was an interesting compromise. Brandon made note of the technique. It might come in handy with Lizzy.

''I don't suppose you'd like to trade cars for the day?'' he asked.

Dana's mouth dropped open. ''You're kidding?''

''Nope. I think a ride in a convertible on a beautiful spring day is just what I need to impress…'' He hesitated.

''Impress who?'' she taunted.

''Someone.''

''If you want my car, you're going to have to do better than that.''

''No wonder Jason thought you were one tough

cookie,'' he grumbled. ''Okay. You've got the name right. It's Elizabeth.''

''I already knew that much.''

''Take it or leave it.''

''I get the Mercedes for the day?''

''Yes.''

''I'll take it. It's getting harder and harder to squeeze myself behind the wheel of my car.'' She exchanged her keys for his and sauntered over to the luxury car his driver had brought around earlier. She ran her hand lovingly over the metallic gray finish, then shot him a look that had him thinking maybe the exchange had been made too hastily.

''Drive carefully,'' he said, suddenly recalling the way she tended to take curves as if she were on the Indy 500 course.

''I should be saying that to you. If you put even a tiny little scratch on that car Jason gave me, you'd better trade it in on a new model on the way home. He might have put the title in my name, but he still considers that car his baby.''

''As long as I don't catch sight of you in the rearview mirror, I'll be just fine,'' he warned.

''No problem,'' she promised.

''Let me see those fingers,'' he ordered. ''You got any of them crossed?''

''Nope,'' she said, laughing as she held out her hands for his inspection. ''I'm as good as my word.''

Brandon wasn't so sure her promise was worth spit, but she did take off and he didn't see any sign of his Mercedes as he drove into town to pick up Lizzy.

Lizzy was waiting for him in front of the hotel. She took one look at the flashy little car and a smile spread across her face. ''Don't tell me this is yours?''

"I borrowed it from Jason's wife. Do you mind the top down?"

"On a day like today? Absolutely not. One of the advantages to short hair is that I don't need to worry about a little wind. Where are we going?"

"I thought a leisurely drive so you could get your bearings, then maybe lunch at Faneuil Hall Marketplace. If you haven't been back to Boston in years, you probably haven't seen what they've done to it."

Lizzy sat up just a little straighter, her eyes alight with curiosity. With the trees budding new green leaves, the sky a soft shade of clear blue and just a handful of clouds scudding overhead, it was the perfect spring morning, one of Boston's finest.

Brandon felt rejuvenated at Elizabeth's exclamations of delight over everything she saw. It was as if he were seeing his beloved city through new eyes. Because she'd taught American history, Lizzy knew as much if not more than he did about the significance of many of the sights. She imbued the telling with a richness of detail and a liveliness that suggested what a magnificent teacher she must be.

"You've got to meet Jason's young brother-in-law while you're here," he told her. "He'd be fascinated by your stories. Sammy's not much for learning from books, but the boy has a lively mind. It came tragically close to being wasted."

"So many of them do," she said sadly. "It breaks my heart to see youngsters today graduating without the skills they need to make a go of it in today's world. There's no combatting crowded classrooms, the gangs and violence in so many cities. It's a wonder some of them get out alive, much less with any education."

"You're still teaching?"

"Substituting. In many ways that's the most frustrating of all. I go into a classroom not knowing the children. I see how they struggle. Maybe, if the teacher's out a week or more, I can see some tiny sign of progress and then it's over. I never know if they build on what I've been able to teach them, or if they simply go on muddling through."

"It sounds frustrating."

"It is. But I love being in the classroom so much that I wasn't prepared to give it up entirely."

A sudden thought struck him. "Why don't you found a school, Lizzy? A special one for the youngsters with disadvantages who could learn if only they were given the proper chance."

He could see the sparks in her eyes as her imagination caught fire.

"Oh, Brandon, wouldn't that be wonderful?" she said, then sighed. "But it's impossible."

"Why?"

"Money, for one thing."

"I have more than I could ever spend," he said, thinking of what such a school might have meant for a boy like Sammy. "I think a school might be the kind of legacy a man could be proud of. Lacey's looking for projects, too. She's talked Kevin and me into a Halloran Foundation. It's a grand idea. I can't imagine why I never thought of it myself. Come on, Lizzy. What do you say? You provide the brainpower and I'll provide the cash."

She reached over and patted his hand. "You are a dear for even thinking of such a generous offer, but no. It's impossible. You're being impulsive and I'm far too old to begin such a massive endeavor."

"No," he said fiercely. "The idea may be impulsive, but it's a sound one. And don't ever say you're too old, Lizzy. Thinking like that will make you old before your time. I've found that looking forward to a new challenge each and every day keeps a man alive. Promise me you'll think about it."

She hesitated, then said, "I suppose I could promise that much, at least."

He nodded in satisfaction as he found a parking space near the marketplace. "That's good. Now let's find some good old-fashioned junk food and indulge ourselves without a thought for cholesterol or fiber."

That lively spark was back in her eyes when she met his gaze. "Hot dogs with mustard and relish, French fries—"

"And a hot-fudge sundae for dessert," he said, completing the menu they'd shared more than once in those long-ago days. He'd wanted to eat his fill of those American favorites before being relegated to the dismal rations of wartime England. "Do you have any idea how I missed those things while I was gone?"

"I don't see how you could. It's a wonder you didn't make yourself sick, you ate so many hot dogs."

Brandon couldn't help chuckling at the memory. Lizzy was laughing right along with him, her lips parted, her eyes alight with shared amusement. Suddenly he couldn't resist leaning toward her and touching his lips to hers, catching the sound of her laughter. The kiss lasted no longer than the melting touch of a snowflake, but it stirred the embers of a fire that had once burned more brightly than anything either of them had ever known.

Shaken to discover that those old feelings could be rekindled so easily and with such a sense of inevitability, Brandon drew back slowly.

"Ah, Lizzy," he said softly. "You'll never know how happy I am that you decided to come to Boston."

Her voice just as quiet and serious as his, she said, "I think maybe I do."

The silence that fell then was alive with a new, exciting tension. Brandon wondered how he'd gone so long without such feelings. Had he simply forgotten what it was like to experience this edge-of-a-precipice sensation? Now that he'd rediscovered it, would he ever be able to go back to the dull loneliness he'd almost fooled himself into thinking was bearable?

Since such questions couldn't be answered in the blink of an eye, he finally broke the tension by catching Lizzy's hand in his. "Come on, gal. Let's go see how much trouble we can get ourselves into."

Aside from their culinary indulgences, though, they left the marketplace by mid-afternoon with no more than a handful of souvenirs for Elizabeth to take back to her family in California. There'd been a dozen things he'd been tempted to buy for her, but she'd firmly declined each and every one.

"It's far too soon to call it quits for the day," Brandon said when they got back to the car. "How do you feel about visiting the public gardens? If I remember correctly, the swan boats are back in the water."

"Oh, what fun!" she said.

The ride aboard the paddleboats was over far too quickly for either of them, so they took a second ride and then a third until the boat's captain began regarding them with amusement.

When they finally left the boat, he winked at Brandon. "Now you folks have a nice afternoon."

"We already have," Lizzy told him. "This has been a wonderful chance to put our feet up."

"And I thought it was holding my hand you enjoyed most," Brandon said, bringing a blush into Lizzy's cheeks.

As they walked away, she said to Brandon, "What must that man think of us?"

"That we're very lucky," he told her as they walked lazily along the paths. "And we are lucky, Lizzy. We're more fortunate than most people. We've found each other, not once, but twice. Now how shall we spend our evening?"

"I intend to spend mine with my feet propped up and a cup of tea from room service. I haven't walked so much in ages."

"What a waste of time that would be. I know a wonderful neighborhood Italian restaurant with red-checked tablecloths and candles stuck in old Chianti bottles. The owner makes an absolutely decadent lasagna."

"Another time," she said firmly.

He could see that there would be no swaying her on this. He hid his disappointment and said only, "If you promise that you'll give me time enough to show you all my favorite places, I won't press about tonight." He grinned. "You know how persuasive I can be when I set my mind to it."

"Oh, yes," she said. "I do know that."

"Then you promise?"

"I promise to think about it," she agreed.

Content that that was the best he could manage, he drove back to her hotel and helped her inside with all of her packages.

"It was a splendid day," Elizabeth said, squeezing Brandon's hands as they stood in the lobby. "I really can't remember when I've had such fun."

"Are you sure you don't want a cocktail at least?"

"Absolutely. You've worn me out. I'm just going to pick up my messages and go upstairs and get out of these shoes."

"You should have let me buy you those high-top sneakers we saw," he teased.

"If I went home with high-top, hot-pink sneakers, my daughters would have me committed."

"Wouldn't hurt to shake them up once in a while. That's what I've found with Kevin and my grandson. Whenever they get to thinking I'm stodgy, I do something outrageous. I want you to meet them while you're here."

"Am I the outrageousness you mean to stir them up with this time?"

"I suppose they might see it that way. Seriously, Lizzy, shall I plan a family dinner?"

Elizabeth tried to imagine such a scene. One part of her wanted desperately to meet his son and the lovely daughter-in-law Brandon had described so clearly. She felt an inexplicable bond with his zany granddaughter-in-law. And she suspected Jason would be a heart-breaking reminder of the way Brandon had looked when they had met. Could she possibly meet them all and not regret the past that had made them another woman's family, instead of her own?

"I think not," she said a little sadly.

Brandon's gaze narrowed as he studied her. "Why? What's wrong, Lizzy?"

"Nothing's wrong, Brandon. I just don't see any point to it."

"Does there have to be a point to having dinner with an old friend's family?"

"Are you saying this would be no more than a casual get-together?"

"Did you want it to be more?"

With his gaze burning into her, she shook her head and put a decisive note into her voice. "No. I made my intentions clear, Brandon. There's no going back for us."

Finally he shrugged. "Whatever you like. We'll discuss it again tomorrow. What time shall I pick you up? Or would you rather come to the house for breakfast? I could send the car."

The idea of sitting across a breakfast table from Brandon held a provocative appeal she couldn't resist. "I would love to come for breakfast."

"Wonderful. I'll have Mrs. Farnsworth make her famous apple pancakes."

"A bowl of cereal and some fruit would do. She needn't go to any trouble for me."

"Apple pancakes are her specialty. She would be disappointed if you didn't try them. Besides, she never makes them just for me and I love them."

"Then, by all means, the apple pancakes. About eight-thirty?"

"I'll send the car at eight," he said.

Secretly delighted by his impatience, she repeated firmly, "Eight-thirty. You have to remember I'm still on California time. That's practically the middle of the night for me."

"I seem to recall nights when we sat up until dawn."

"And I seem to recall that at that age we never required eight hours of sleep. We could run on pure adrenaline."

"Don't you go trying to make yourself sound old.

I saw the way your foot tapped when we heard that music earlier at the marketplace. I'm taking you dancing one of these nights."

She chuckled at the feigned ferocity in his expression. "Is that an invitation or a threat, Brandon Halloran?"

"Whichever works," he said, reaching out with surprisingly unsteady fingers to trace the curve of her cheek. He brushed gently at the wisps of hair that feathered around her face. "I can't get over the way you look with your hair like this. I couldn't imagine you ever being more beautiful than you were when we met, but you are, Lizzy. Like a rare wine, you've aged with dignity."

"And you're a sentimental old fool," she said gently, but she couldn't deny the sweet rush of pleasure that sped through her. She placed her hand over his and before she could think about it, brought his hand to her lips and pressed a kiss to his knuckles. "Good night, Brandon."

He leaned forward and touched his lips to her forehead. "Night, Lizzy. I can't wait till morning."

He turned then and strolled away, his step jaunty, his shoulders squared. She couldn't be sure, but it sounded as if he might be whistling the chorus of that old Glenn Miller song they'd called their own.

Chapter Six

When he'd encouraged Elizabeth to come for breakfast, Brandon hadn't stopped to consider that the next day was Saturday. On Saturdays he could never count on not having the morning interrupted. More often than not, Jason and Dana dropped by with Sammy in tow. Occasionally even Kevin and Lacey turned up, lured by Mrs. Farnsworth's delectable apple pancakes.

Perhaps, subliminally, he had hoped the whole clan would drop in, taking matters out of his hands. It would give him a chance to introduce Elizabeth despite her uncertainty about the wisdom of such a meeting. He might have mixed feelings about subjecting her to their scrutiny, but his desire to hasten a relationship between them far outweighed any reservations he might have.

Sure enough, no sooner had he seated Lizzy at the dining room table and served her a cup of coffee than the front door banged open and Dana's brother came barreling in.

"Hey, Grandpa Brandon, are you up yet?" Sammy yelled loudly enough to wake the dead.

"If I weren't, I would be now," he observed mildly as Sammy rounded the corner into the dining room.

Looking nonplussed, the teenager screeched to a halt at the sight of Brandon's company.

Elizabeth looked equally startled by the sight of the lanky young man with his hair moussed into spikes, his jeans frayed and a T-shirt that was emblazoned with the perfectly horrid bloodred design of some new music group. Actually it was one of his more reserved outfits.

"Sorry," Sammy said, his gaze shifting from Elizabeth to Brandon and back again. A knowing grin spread across his face. "I guess we should have called, huh?"

"It wouldn't hurt to observe the amenities," Brandon confirmed.

Sammy regarded him blankly. "The what?"

"You should have called. How'd you get here?" he asked suspiciously, expecting the worst.

His answer came in the form of the front door opening again. "Hey, Granddad," Jason called from the foyer. "We just came by to drop off your car and see how you're..." His voice trailed off as he reached the dining room and spotted Brandon's guest. "I guess you're doing fine."

"I *was*," Brandon said with an air of resignation. Suddenly he wished he'd relied more on caution, than impatience. "Lizzy, my grandson Jason. And our first intruder with the lousy manners is his young brother-in-law, Sammy Roberts. This is Elizabeth Newton."

"Hey," Sammy said, already seated at the table. "Jason, you were right. Mrs. Farnsworth is making those funny pancakes."

Brandon glanced at Lizzy's frozen expression and sighed. "I don't suppose you're in a hurry?" he inquired of the interlopers. The broad hint fell on deaf ears.

"Nope," Jason confirmed entirely too cheerfully. "We have all morning. Right, Sammy?"

"Yep. All morning."

"How lovely," Brandon said dryly. "Before you sit down, stick your head into the kitchen and tell Mrs. Farnsworth there will be four of us for breakfast, unless of course Dana is planning to wander in at any moment, as well."

"Nope. I think you can safely count her out. She's home practicing her breathing," Jason said.

"I thought you were supposed to help with that."

"She says I make her nervous."

"Probably because you hyperventilate," Brandon said critically. "I told you I'd be happy to assist. I have much more experience at remaining calm under trying circumstances." He purposely neglected to add that this morning was rapidly turning into a perfect example.

"Granddad, as much as I adore you, you are *not* going to take my place in the delivery room," Jason said patiently.

"You and me can pace the halls together," Sammy offered as a consolation. "You gotta bring the cigars, though. Dana says if she catches me with one, she'll tan my hide."

Brandon glanced over to see if Elizabeth was beginning to take all this with the sort of aplomb she'd been capable of years ago. Given her protest the day before when he'd suggested a family dinner, he thought she was doing rather well. He couldn't quite identify her expression, though. Astonishment and dismay seemed to have given way to fascination. In fact her gaze was fastened on Jason as if just looking at him carried her back in time.

"Lizzy?" Brandon said softly.

She blinked and turned to him. "The resemblance is remarkable," she murmured. Then as if she thought she'd said too much, she added quickly, "Do you really want to be in the delivery room?"

Jason, apparently oblivious to the meaning of her first remark, seized the second and grinned at her astonishment. "He's afraid the rest of us will botch it."

Brandon considered offering a rebuttal, but decided that Jason was pretty close to the truth. He wanted nothing to go wrong with the birth of his first great-grandchild. He hated trusting anything so critical to other people.

Of course, he hadn't been anywhere near the delivery room when Kevin was born. Even if the hospital had allowed it back then, Grace would never have permitted it. She would have thought it unseemly for him to witness her in the throes of labor. He was downright envious of all these young husbands today who got to share in one of God's own miracles.

"So, how do you and Granddad know each other?" Jason asked Elizabeth.

Jason's tone might be all innocent curiosity, Brandon thought worriedly, but that gleam in his eye was pure mischief. He had a hunch Dana had encouraged this visit by providing a few details about their encounter the previous morning. Elizabeth must not have caught that spark of devilment or she'd have been more cautious with her answer.

"We're old friends," she said, opening the door to a Pandora's box of speculation.

"You live here in Boston?"

"No, California."

"Ah, I see," Jason murmured, looking infinitely pleased.

"What are you grinning at?" Brandon grumbled.

"The flowers," Jason said.

"What flowers?" Sammy asked.

"Grandpa Brandon has been sending a lot of flowers to California lately."

"Why?" Sammy glanced at Elizabeth. "Oh, yeah, I get it. I guess that's why there are roses on the table, too, huh? There never have been before."

Sammy looked as if he were on the verge of making some even more outlandish remark. Brandon grasped at the first conversational gambit he could think of to deter him. "Sammy, if you're finished with breakfast, perhaps you'd like to go play some of those infernal video games you insisted I buy."

"Nah, I think I'll stick around for another pancake. Besides, it sounds like this could get interesting."

"I assure you it will not get to be anything close to interesting by your standards," Brandon commented. "Go play video games. Mrs. Farnsworth will be happy to bring your pancake to you in the library."

Sammy had no sooner shoved his chair back and departed than Jason said cheerfully, "So, Mrs. Newton, what exactly brings you to Boston?"

Color suddenly flooded Lizzy's cheeks as she realized how neatly Jason was backing her into the proverbial corner. Brandon tried to rescue her. "She's just here to do a little sight-seeing."

"That's right," she confirmed hurriedly. "It's been ages since I've seen all the sights in Boston."

"And how long has it been since you two last saw each other?"

She glanced desperately toward Brandon, then said, "Nearly fifty years."

"My goodness," Jason said, looking a little taken aback himself. "You've kept in touch, though, right?"

"No."

"Jason!" Brandon said with a soft warning note in his voice. "You're being impertinent."

His grandson ignored him. A grin slowly broke across his face. "This gets better and better, like one of those newspaper features you see on Valentine's day. Are you saying you'd lost touch? How'd you find each other again?"

Brandon watched as Elizabeth grew increasingly flustered. Finally he snapped, "Jason! This is none of your business."

His blasted grandson laughed at that.

"I know," he said delightedly.

"Jason Halloran, I am warning you," Brandon blustered. "If you don't behave, I'll..." Words failed him.

"You'll what, Granddad? Cut me out of the will?" He turned to Elizabeth. "I apologize if I've made you uncomfortable, but Granddad has this habit of meddling in our lives. He thinks it's his God-given right."

Apparently no longer caught off guard, the take-any-dare Lizzy of old suddenly emerged and seized the opportunity Jason had just handed her. She grinned, a genuine spark of devilment flaring in her eyes. Brandon didn't trust that spark one little bit.

''I can see how that would be taxing,'' she said. ''Perhaps it would help if I offered a little ammunition. I gather he hasn't mentioned how he tracked me down?''

Brandon regarded her indignantly. *''Et tu, Brute?''*

She smiled and delivered the knockout punch without so much as an instant's caution. ''He hired a detective. Isn't that like something right out of a movie?''

''Oh, Lord,'' Brandon moaned. ''I will never, ever hear the end of this.''

''No,'' Jason said, ''you won't. I'm just sorry I didn't know about Mrs. Newton sooner. I might have hired that detective myself and brought her here to surprise you. I do love surprises, don't you, Mrs. Newton?''

''Absolutely,'' she said.

''If the two of you are going to be in cahoots,'' Brandon grumbled, ''I might as well go play those video games with Sammy.''

''Go ahead, Granddad. I'm sure Mrs. Newton and I could find plenty to talk about.''

''Yes,'' she agreed. ''I suspect we could. You'd probably find a talk about old times fascinating. My youngest granddaughter surely does.''

Brandon regarded the two of them irritably. ''On second thought, I guess I'll sit right here and watch out for my interests. I might remind you, though, Jason, that if it weren't for my meddling, you and Dana would probably not be married.''

Jason instantly sobered. ''You're right. I do owe you one for that.''

''I should say so,'' Brandon said.

"Perhaps now would be the time to return the favor," Jason said slyly.

Brandon's gaze narrowed. "You could find yourself peddling pencils on street corners, if you're not careful," he warned grimly. "Now could we please talk about something else? Or perhaps you and Sammy would like to run along so Lizzy and I can get started on another day of sight-seeing."

"Where did you go yesterday?" Jason asked.

"The public gardens," Elizabeth said.

"Rode in one of the swan boats, I suppose?"

"Of course," she said, giving Jason a conspiratorial wink. "Three times. Your grandfather's quite the romantic, especially on these summer-like days. That's when we met, you know. The summer of 1942. He was about to ship out for England. He swept me off my feet."

"Oh, really," Jason said, shooting his grandfather a speculative look.

Brandon glared at both of them. "Lizzy, if I'd known what trouble you were going to give me, I would have insisted on coming to California. You just wait. I'll get even when I meet up with those daughters of yours. You won't know a moment's peace when I'm through."

Instantly her amusement vanished. The change was so subtle that at first Brandon thought maybe he'd imagined it, but when she remained too silent for too long, he shot her a look of genuine concern.

"Lizzy?" he said softly. "You okay?"

"Fine, Brandon."

She'd said the words, but there was no spunk behind them. Even Jason seemed puzzled by the change that had come over her.

"I'd better get Sammy and go," he said. "Dana will be wondering what happened to us. We told her we were going out for juice."

"And then you sneaked over here to spy on me," Brandon said. "Now that's one I can hold over you."

"Don't get your hopes up, Granddad. I suspect Sammy will spill the beans before you ever get a chance to." He turned to Elizabeth and clasped her hand in his. "It was nice meeting you, Mrs. Newton. I hope you'll be around for a while."

Lizzy's smile was genuine. "Meeting you and Sammy was my pleasure."

Jason leaned close and whispered something that made her laugh. Only after his grandson had gone did Brandon ask, "What was that he said to you?"

"He suggested I give you a run for your money."

"I like the sound of that," he said. "Lizzy, why did you go so quiet a few minutes ago? When I mentioned California, you clammed right up. You did the same thing the first time we talked on the phone."

He could tell how flustered she was by the way she was twisting her napkin and by the way her gaze evaded his. He'd never known the Lizzy of old to be at a loss for words. One of these days he'd have to accept that there were bound to be some changes over all this time, but at the moment he found this change particularly puzzling.

"I just can't see you being comfortable in my world," she said finally in a desperate tone that had him guessing that she was improvising.

"I never heard such a crazy idea," he protested, startled that she could even think such a thing. "You and I were comfortable from the first minute we met. Nothing's changed, Lizzy. Nothing. Why, when you stepped out of my car night before last, I felt all those years just slip away. I could be comfortable anywhere with you.''

''You're wrong if you think there haven't been changes,'' she said adamantly. ''A lot of time's gone by since then. We aren't the same people.''

''We are in all the ways that count,'' he insisted just as stubbornly.

''Don't press, Brandon. Not on this.''

Troubled by the expression of genuine dismay on her face, he reluctantly nodded his agreement. Then he spent the rest of the day wondering if he'd made a terrible mistake not forcing her to explain why she was more skittish around him now than when she'd been an innocent young virgin.

Elizabeth couldn't get to sleep, despite another long day of visiting Brandon's favorite haunts all over Boston. She was still deeply troubled by the conversation they'd had that morning.

Brandon had seen right through her. He'd guessed that she didn't want him in California, which was why she had to go back before he could get any notions about coming with her. Unfortunately he already seemed to have some pretty strong ideas about the future—crazy ideas that a man his age shouldn't be thinking. Even if she could entirely forget old hurts, too many things stood in their way. Things she could never explain. She had to put his crazy ideas out of his mind.

Because she didn't want to get caught up in the same fantasy, Elizabeth tried reading a paperback she'd picked up at the airport, but it was no better now than it had been when she'd tried to read it on the plane. She used the remote to switch on the television, skipped through the channels and couldn't find even an old movie to hold her interest.

"Face it, Elizabeth," she muttered under her breath, "you're not going to sleep until you deal with what's going on between you and Brandon."

He seemed to have this ridiculous notion that they could pick up right where they'd left off, as if they were a couple of kids. Why couldn't he see that the years had shaped them into very different people?

He was a business tycoon, for heaven's sake. She was a semiretired school teacher. He had traveled all over the world. Since moving to California, she'd rarely left—except for one incredible trip to Hawaii that the kids had given to her and David for their anniversary the year before he'd died. Brandon had a custom-tailored wardrobe, a six-bedroom mansion, a housekeeper and a chauffeur. Her clothes were off the rack, she owned a five-room house and did all of her own cooking, cleaning and driving. Years ago maybe none of that would have mattered. Today it seemed insurmountable.

It wasn't that she was insecure. Far from it, in fact. She knew her own worth, but she could take a realistic measure of that and see that it didn't stack up to be the right woman for a confident, sophisticated man like Brandon Halloran.

Of course, those were only excuses, she admitted reluctantly. There were far more pressing reasons why they couldn't have a future together, but she couldn't even bring herself to think about those.

Elizabeth was questioning whether it was even wise to remain in Boston for the duration of her promised visit, when the phone rang. It was nearly 1:00 a.m., but just before 10:00 p.m. in California.

Almost glad of the late-hour interruption, she grabbed the phone on the second ring, only to be greeted by Kate's exasperated "Mother!"

"Hello, darling. I see you've tracked me down."

"I wouldn't have had to do any tracking, if you'd seen fit to tell me you were going away," she declared, clearly annoyed.

"Sweetheart, you've been away on business for the past two weeks. How was I supposed to tell you?"

"The office would have told you how to find me."

"And if it had been an emergency, I might have called," she said reasonably. "I saw no reason to do so just because I was flying to Boston for a few days."

"Why on earth would you go to Boston after all this time? You haven't been back there in years."

"Decades, actually."

"So, why did you decide to go on the spur of the moment?"

Since Ellen had obviously reported the trip to Kate, Elizabeth wished her older daughter had also given Kate all the explanations. Maybe then Elizabeth would be feeling less defensive.

"An old friend called and invited me."

Kate paused at that. "I didn't know you kept in touch with anyone back there."

"Dear, you haven't exactly kept tabs on my correspondence, have you? Nor do you tell me about all of your trips and contracts," she pointed out.

"Then you have been in touch with this person?"

"Kate, darling, I really think you're making much too much of this. I'll be home in a few days and I'll tell you all about it. In the meantime, why don't you tell me how your business trip went? Did you win that divorce case for your client in Palm Springs?''

Momentarily distracted just as Elizabeth had hoped she would be, Kate said, ''We're still haggling over the settlement. The man has become a multimillionaire, thanks to his wife's investment savvy. He wants to hold her to a prenuptial agreement written in the dark ages.''

''I really do wish you'd gotten into some other aspect of law,'' Elizabeth told her. ''I think you've developed a very jaded view of marriage by handling all these high-profile, nasty divorce cases.''

''Mother, I do not care to discuss my views on marriage and romance. We both know that I think they're highly overrated.''

Elizabeth sighed wearily. ''I can't imagine how you could come to that view after growing up around your father and me.''

''Believe me, you were the exceptions, not the rule. Don't blame yourself. You set a wonderful example. I've just seen too many of my friends and my clients get royally screwed once the romance dies.''

''I think you'd change your mind, if you ever met the right young man,'' Elizabeth countered. ''How is that attractive new partner in your firm? Lance Hopkins, wasn't it? I believe you mentioned he's single.''

''You and Ellen,'' Kate grumbled. ''You're both far too romantic for your own good. I never mentioned that Lance Hopkins is single and you know it. Ellen concocted some excuse to pry the information out of my secretary. Now stop trying to change the subject. I want to know whom you're visiting and when you expect to be back home.''

"I'll be back in a few days. We'll talk about it then," she replied firmly.

"Mother, are you there with some man?" Kate asked suspiciously.

"If I were, it would be none of your business. You worry about your social life, young lady, and let me take care of my own."

"Mother," Kate protested, but Elizabeth was already lowering the phone back into its cradle.

Okay, maybe hanging up was the cowardly way out. But it was one thing to sit in this hotel room so far from home wondering if she was crazy for coming to Boston, crazier yet for not running away as fast as she could. It would be quite another to have her level-headed daughter confirm it.

Chapter Seven

Brandon was up at the crack of dawn, anxious to get the day under way, more optimistic than he had been in years. Since Mrs. Farnsworth was off on Sundays, he made his own coffee, then glanced through the first section of the paper. Not one paragraph, not even one headline he read registered. He turned the pages mechanically, thinking only of how light his heart had become since Lizzy had come back into his life.

Unfortunately the cursory study of the newspaper didn't waste nearly enough time. It was barely seven. He read the business section, then the sports section, and killed another half hour. He glanced at his watch impatiently, muttered a curse and picked up the phone.

Elizabeth's sleepy greeting set his blood to racing. How many times had he dreamed of waking beside her and hearing just such an innocently seductive purr in her voice? A half-dozen times in the past few weeks alone. Multiply that by years, when the memory of her crept in when he least expected it.

"Good morning," he said briskly. "I'm sorry if I woke you."

"You don't sound sorry," she said, laughter lacing through her voice. "What are you doing calling so early?"

"I didn't want to waste a minute of this beautiful day. How about coming to church with me, then going for a drive to see all the spring flowers in bloom? I know a wonderful old inn that would be the perfect place for lunch. If I play my cards right, I might even be able to borrow Dana's car again."

"It sounds lovely."

"Can you be ready in an hour? The service I had in mind is at nine."

"I'll be ready," she promised.

Brandon tried not to feel guilty as he rushed through his shower and dressed in a dark blue suit, a pale blue shirt and a silk tie—all made of Halloran fabrics. Maybe he should have mentioned that Lacey and Kevin were likely to be at the services.

Then again, he consoled himself, he wasn't absolutely certain they would be. They might even be out on Cape Cod, where they were spending more and more time since Kevin's last heart attack. No need getting Elizabeth all worked up over nothing. She'd handled the impromptu meeting with Jason and Sammy blithely enough. In the long run maybe it was better to spring things on her, so she didn't have time to fret and find a dozen excuses for saying no.

An hour later, with Lizzy by his side, he was pulling into the church parking lot.

"What a beautiful old church," Elizabeth said of

the plain white structure with its intricately designed stained glass windows and towering steeple.

"Wait until you see it inside," he told her, imagining it through her eyes. "The light filters through all that glass and creates a rainbow of colors."

Just then the bell began to chime, its resonance pure and strong as it filled the air.

"Let's get inside before the processional starts," he said.

He led the way to a pew halfway up the wide, carpeted aisle just as the first hymn began. He found the song in the hymnal and offered it to Elizabeth, but she was already singing in her clear soprano. Even so, in a gesture he remembered vividly from another long-ago Sunday, she placed her hand next to his so they could share.

As he stood next to her, fingers barely touching, and listened to the verses of the hymn, he realized that he had never felt so blessed or so joyous. Unexpected contentment stole through him. Finding his precious Elizabeth again must have been God's work.

She glanced up then and smiled, her face radiant. "You're not singing," she whispered.

He looked down, reminding himself of the familiar words, and then he too sang along with the congregation, his bass joining her sweet voice to soar above all the rest.

Brandon was oblivious to the rest of the service. Though he normally found the minister's sermons to be lively and meaningful, today he was far too conscious of the woman seated next to him. He couldn't stop himself from thinking that if all had gone the way he'd wanted years ago, she would have walked down this very aisle to become his bride.

As the service ended, he took Elizabeth's elbow and steered her through the crowd, murmuring greetings to friends, many of whom he'd known his whole life. He liked the continuity of that, just as he liked thinking that a relationship he'd once cherished was just as strong decades later.

But only for him, he conceded reluctantly. He knew deep down he had yet to win Lizzy over to that way of thinking.

Outside they lingered to chat with the minister. Elizabeth praised the sermon, but Brandon was forced to mutter some innocuous statement because he couldn't recall the topic, much less anything his old friend had said.

He was just about to beat a hasty retreat, when he heard Kevin's voice behind him.

"Dad, I didn't see you earlier. You must have been late."

"We got here just before the processional," he said, turning to face his son and Lacey. He kissed his daughter-in-law. "Good morning, you two. I thought maybe you'd be out at the Cape this weekend."

"Thought or hoped?" Lacey asked, with a pointed glance at Elizabeth. "I understand you have company. Hello, I'm Lacey Halloran and this is Kevin."

"This is Elizabeth Newton," Brandon said, watching Lizzy's face for some indication of her reaction to this chance meeting with his son and daughter-in-law. Judging from the glance she shot his way, he was going to hear about this encounter later. She might forgive one meeting as chance, but two in a row were bound to look suspicious in her eyes.

"It's a pleasure to meet you both," she said graciously. "Brandon has told me quite a lot about you."

Kevin scowled. ''Funny, he hasn't told us a thing about you. Have you been keeping secrets, Dad?''

His tone was teasing, but there was an underlying thread of dismay that Brandon caught even if no one else did. Fortunately Lacey had a knack for putting people at ease and she was already chatting a mile a minute with Lizzy, asking about California, her family, her teaching.

''That reminds me,'' Brandon said. ''Lizzy and I were talking about the need for a school that could cater to youngsters like Sammy, children who are bright enough, but need an extra boost if they're to succeed. You two should talk about it.''

''What a wonderful idea!'' Lacey exclaimed and began asking Lizzy questions in a voice filled with enthusiasm.

Brandon listened to them in satisfaction. Two of a kind, he thought complacently, just as Kevin pulled him aside.

''Who is this woman?'' his son demanded.

Brandon stared at him, startled by his thoroughly disgruntled tone. ''You say that as if she's got a big scarlet A pinned to her dress. What on earth's the matter with you?''

''I don't like it, Dad. You're quite a catch for any woman. I don't want to see you taken advantage of. Jason mentioned you hadn't seen this woman for almost fifty years. Out of the blue, she turns up again, now that Mother's dead. Quite a coincidence, wouldn't you say?''

Brandon felt his temper starting to boil. ''Son, that is enough! Elizabeth is a fine woman. If you'd done a little checking instead of flinging around slanderous opinions, you would have known that I went after her, not the other way around.''

The visible tension in Kevin's shoulders eased some at that explanation. ''Okay, maybe I misunderstood, but a man in your position needs to be careful, Dad. You're vulnerable with Mother gone. It would be easy enough for some gold digger to come along and take advantage of you. There are a dozen women right here in town, women you've known forever, who would be happy to share your life with you, if you feel the need for companionship.''

''You make it sound about as simple as choosing a puppy and training it to fetch my slippers,'' Brandon grumbled. ''I suppose I should have expected this. It's more retaliation for all my meddling over the years. Kevin, don't you think I have sense enough to spot a devious, conniving woman?''

''Frankly, no. You always did have a romantic streak. You'd imagine you were in love, no matter what the circumstances were.''

''You let me worry about my imagination. Unfortunately, I suspect what you're really worried about is your inheritance,'' he said with an undeniable edge of sarcasm.

Kevin couldn't have looked more shocked if Brandon had accused him of embezzling. ''Dad, you know that's not true.''

Brandon sighed heavily. ''I'm sorry. You're right. I know you're just thinking of me, but believe me, son, I know what I'm doing.''

''Is this relationship serious?''

''At the moment, let's just say it's a serious flirtation. I don't think Lizzy would stand for anything more.'' He glanced at her and his expression softened.

"I do believe, though, that I will do anything in my power to change that."

"Just go slowly, Dad. Promise me that."

"Son, at my age, there's not time enough left to go slow. I plan to grab whatever happiness I can. Don't begrudge me that." He moved back to Lizzy's side. "You ready for that drive in the country?"

"Indeed, I am," she said, smiling up at him.

"Have a good time, you two," Lacey said.

"We intend to," Brandon replied, hoping that Lizzy hadn't noticed Kevin's failure to join in Lacey's best wishes.

When they were alone in the car, though, she turned a troubled gaze toward him. "Kevin's unhappy about my being here, isn't he?"

"I wouldn't say unhappy."

"What would you say?"

"Concerned."

She sighed. "Isn't it amazing that we can live an entire lifetime, raise families, hold jobs, suffer devastating losses, and our kids still think we haven't got the brains the good Lord gave a duck?"

He chuckled. "You've been getting the third degree, too?"

"Only from my youngest. She called last night to fuss at me for not notifying her that I planned this trip. I tried to point out that she almost never tells me when or where she's going on a business trip, but she didn't quite get the similarity."

"Are you sure it's the same thing?" he asked. "Or did you make a point of *not* telling her, because you knew she wouldn't approve?"

"I could ask you the same thing. Seems to me like I was a big surprise to everyone in your family."

''Touché,'' he said. He glanced over at her. ''Let's make a pact that we will not allow family interference to get in the way of you and me having the time of our lives.''

''If we had a little champagne, I'd drink a toast to that,'' she agreed, reaching for his hand. ''Sometimes it seems you know exactly what's on my mind.''

''Because we're more alike than you want to admit. Now let's forget all our cares and take in this beautiful scenery. I'm sorry Dana wasn't at church so we could borrow her car, but spring's putting on a show for us just the same. And I, for one, don't want to miss it.''

Elizabeth released his hand and looked out the window at the budding trees about to burst forth with dogwood blossoms. Bright yellow forsythia spilled over split-rail fences. Purple and white lilac scented the air.

''I'd forgotten how beautiful it is here in the spring. We have a change of seasons in California, but it's not nearly as dramatic. Everything is bright and bold there, almost the whole year around. Here you go from dreary grays and stark browns to pastels. I guess it's sort of like comparing the soft colors chosen by Monet to the brilliant palette of Van Gogh or Gauguin.''

''With that kind of poetry in your soul, you'll love the place we're going for lunch.''

''Tell me,'' she urged, her voice laced with curiosity. She'd always wished for the time to discover romantic hideaways. David had been content with bland, ordinary restaurants and hotel chains.

''I'm not spoiling the surprise. You'll have to see what I mean when we get there.''

They reached the inn a half hour later, a huge old clapboard house painted white and trimmed with black shutters. A weather vane on the roof twirled in the breeze. Though it was lovely, it wasn't until they were inside that Elizabeth could see what Brandon had meant.

The entire back of the house had been redone with French doors that were glass from floor to ceiling. Beyond the doors was a patio that had not yet been opened. It was edged with honeysuckle tumbling over a white picket fence. The scent was sweeter than any air she'd breathed in years.

Beyond the inn's yard, the hillside spilled into a valley that was brilliant with thousands of tulips, daffodils and the bright green of new grass. If they'd taken a patch of the Netherlands in springtime and transported it to this site, it could not have been more beautiful.

Elizabeth drew in a deep breath of the air coming through the open doors and smiled in delight. She looked over and caught Brandon's gaze pinned on her.

"You like it?" he asked anxiously.

"I've never been anywhere like it. Thank you for bringing me."

"I didn't bring you just because of the picturesque view. The food is marvelous here, too."

Everyone seemed to know Brandon well, from the hostess to the waitress to the owner, who stopped by to ensure that everything was to their liking.

"You must come here often," she said, realizing as she said it that she sounded oddly miffed.

"Once or twice a year," he said.

"Then you must tip very generously to warrant all the attention."

He grinned so broadly that she felt color flooding into her cheeks.

"Jealous, Lizzy?"

"No, I am not jealous," she snapped. Then because her tone made it sound more like a confirmation than a denial, she added, "It's certainly none of my business what you've done."

"That doesn't keep you from being a mite curious. Am I right?"

"Absolutely not!" she said with as much conviction as she could muster.

"I should let you go on trying to squirm off the hook, but I'll have mercy on you," he teased. "The owner is a client. Halloran provides all the custom fabrics for the place—from the draperies to the tablecloths to the seat cushions. Notice how they pick up the colors from outdoors and bring them inside."

"Oh, my," she said with delight as she caught the similarity. "Brandon, you amaze me. I should have guessed it was something like that."

"Instead of the wild, clandestine rendezvous you were imagining? Made me feel young again, just to know you thought me capable of such carrying on."

She gazed boldly into his eyes. "I don't know why I let you agitate me so. You always did love to tease me."

"Do you know why?"

Her breath seemed to go still. "Why?"

"Because you blushed so prettily. You still do, Lizzy."

He reached across the table and took her hand in his. She told herself she ought to draw away, but she couldn't bring herself to do it. His hand was warm and strong, a hand that could comfort or excite. She recalled that all too vividly despite the time that had passed. Foolish notions, she chided herself.

"Lizzy, do you know that not once in all the times

I've been here did I bring another woman with me. Not even Grace.''

''Why?''

''Because from the first time I saw it, it made me think of you.''

Emotions crowded into her throat and tears stung her eyes. ''Oh, Brandon, even if they're lies, you do say the most romantic things.''

''It's not a lie,'' he said softly.

Whether it was or it wasn't, Elizabeth knew she didn't dare allow herself to fall for the tender web he was trying to spin around her heart.

It worried Brandon that Lizzy didn't trust him, especially when he knew he had only a short time to convince her of his sincerity. He wined and dined her. He wooed her with flowers. They shared quiet evenings at home and passionate arguments after movies. He tried to convince her to move into one of his guest rooms, but she was adamant about staying on at the hotel. He guessed that had as much to do with caution as it did with her sense of propriety.

In between, there were frantic calls from Kevin, who'd managed to dream up more questions about the running of Halloran Industries than he'd asked during the entire decade they'd worked together.

''Dad, can't you come in tomorrow? I think we should meet on the new contracts.''

''You've been negotiating those contracts on your own for the past five years. You know I don't like to mess with that sort of detail. I was delighted to have you take it off my hands. Why should I want to change that now? Besides, Lizzy and I have plans.''

''What plans?''

"None of your business," he said, because he was thinking of taking her to Maine for a nostalgic visit to the place they'd met. He intended to ask her tonight. "Kevin, I trust you to run Halloran Industries. I really do."

Kevin merely sighed in defeat and hung up.

That night Brandon took Lizzy dancing, though he stopped short of trying some of those fancy new steps that looked more suited to a bedroom than a public dance floor. In his day a man could have gotten his face slapped for some of those maneuvers. Damn, but they looked like fun, though.

Back at his place, he turned on the stereo and shot a glance at Lizzy, who'd ended the evening with her hair mussed and her cheeks flushed. He held out his arms.

"What do you say? Want to try one of those newfangled dances we saw tonight?"

"Get out of here, Brandon Halloran. We're too old."

Despite the protest, he saw the hint of curiosity in her eyes. "Not me. I'm feeling chipper as the day we met. Come on, Lizzy."

Breathless and laughing, they tried to imitate the intricate steps they'd seen earlier. As their bodies fit together intimately, the laughter suddenly died. Lizzy's startled gaze met his and years fell away.

Brandon touched his lips to hers with surprising caution, almost as if he feared a ladylike slap in response to a daring kiss. There was tenderness and longing in the tentative, velvet-soft kiss and the first breath of a passion that both had thought long over.

The flowery scent of Lizzy's perfume took Brandon back to the first time he'd dared to steal a kiss.

They had been in the garden behind the Halloran mansion, surrounded by the scent of spring and the gentle whisper of a breeze. He'd wanted Lizzy to meet his family, to see his home back then, too, but she'd been afraid. A little awestruck by the size of the house, she had come no farther than the garden before being overcome by second thoughts.

"They'll love you," he'd vowed, ignoring his own uncertainty to quiet hers.

"You can't just spring me on them days before you leave. They'll be certain you've taken leave of your senses."

"Do you love me?" he'd asked her quietly.

"Oh, yes." Her blue eyes sparkled like sapphires when she said it.

"Then that's all that matters." His mouth had covered hers, stilling her trembling lips.

There had been so much hope, so much sweet temptation in that kiss, he thought now. Was it any wonder she'd remained in his heart?

Brandon felt the stir of those same fragile emotions now, an echo that reverberated through him. They gave him the courage to speak his mind.

"Marry me, Lizzy," he said impulsively. "Don't let's make the same mistake twice."

Before the words were out of his mouth, he knew he should have waited, knew he should have settled for asking her to go back to Maine with him. There was no mistaking the flare of panic in her eyes, the way she trembled in his arms.

It was the sort of careless error that a man new to making deals might make, misjudging the opposition. Brandon cursed the arrogance that had misled him into thinking her misgivings were of no importance. Only a man totally blinded by love would not have seen that Lizzy wasn't ready to consider marriage.

Even so, he couldn't bring himself to withdraw the proposal, because more than anything he wanted her to say yes to it. But once the words were spoken, he could see that he'd made a terrible mistake. He'd underestimated her fears and exaggerated his claim on her heart.

Brandon's breath caught in his throat as he waited to see how much damage his impetuous proposal had done.

Chapter Eight

Elizabeth was caught off guard by Brandon's proposal now, just as she had been all those years back. For one crazy split second, she imagined saying yes. The word was on her lips as she thought how wonderful it would be to know that this strong, exciting man would spend the rest of his life at her side. She indulged herself in the fantasy that they would have a second chance at all the happiness they had lost.

As she struggled against her powerful desires, she was vibrantly aware of the ticking of an old grandfather clock, the whisper of branches against the library's glass doors. Everything seemed sharper and somehow dangerous as she flirted with Brandon's tempting offer.

There was no denying that it was romantic notions like that that had pulled her back to Boston in the first place. Yearnings, aroused by this compelling man, had kept her here beyond the scheduled end of the trip, but marriage? She had never really considered that an option because she knew it could never be. Never. Far too much was at risk. Once again she realized she would have to disappoint him—and, perhaps even more, herself.

She touched her fingers to his cheek. His skin was tanned and smooth with fine lines fanning out from the corners of his clear blue eyes. She recalled as vividly as if it had been only yesterday the first time she had dared to touch him intimately, the first time she had felt the sandpaper rasp of his unshaven face after they had lain in each other's arms for nearly an entire night of daring, blissful pleasure before parting discreetly before dawn. Then, as now, there had been as much sorrow as joy in her heart, knowing that their time together was drawing to a close.

"Oh, Brandon," she whispered now with a sigh as she tried to find the right words to make her refusal less painful for both of them. "You are such a dear, sweet man to ask. You almost sound as if you mean it."

"I *do* mean it," he said, radiating indignation. "I've never meant anything more. We're still good together, Lizzy. You can't deny that."

She tried to counter passionate impulsiveness with clear, cool reason. "No, I can't deny it. But you have your life here, and I have mine in California. This has been a wonderful time for us, but we can't go shaking things up so drastically. Not overnight like this. What would our families think?"

"That we've waited entirely too long," he said flatly.

How could he not see, she wondered, that what he

said was only partly true? ''Jason, perhaps. He's young and newly in love himself. Kevin is another story. Even you must recognize that. He sees me as an intruder, I'm sure.''

''He'd see any woman who stepped into his mama's place that way. He'll come to terms with it. Besides, what does it matter what he thinks? If his attitude upsets you, I'll have another talk with him, explain the way it is with us. I won't allow him to make you feel uncomfortable.''

Elizabeth laughed at his conviction that he could mold people's thoughts and deeds so easily. ''Brandon, you might be able to force him into polite acceptance, but you can't very well change the way he feels. And isn't that what really counts?''

For an instant Brandon looked defeated, then his expression brightened. ''I'll just remind him of how foolishly I behaved when I refused to recognize how important Lacey was to him. That'll make him see things more clearly.''

''And what should I tell Kate? She'd be no happier to learn of our relationship than Kevin.''

''Tell her that you love me,'' he said simply.

''I'm afraid she thinks that love is an illusion. At our age, she'd probably consider it insanity.''

''Then we'll just have to show her otherwise. Lizzy, we can't let our children dictate our lives, any more than they allow us to interfere in theirs.''

Elizabeth couldn't deny she was tempted, but she knew that part of the temptation for her—and for Brandon, whether he wanted to admit it or not—was based on memories that had managed to intertwine with the present. Those memories had given each moment of the past few days a bittersweet poignancy, had heightened every thrilling sensation. The tenderness, the laughter, the joy, how could they possibly be sure any of that was real?

Besides, she had meant what she'd said about their having separate lives. It was hard to get much farther apart than Boston and California. She couldn't bear the thought of not seeing her grandchildren.

And for all his stubborn denial, Brandon wouldn't like being separated from his family, either. Not that that was even a possibility. She would never have him in Los Angeles. The strain of it would kill her, though she couldn't tell him that. He'd guess in a minute the secret she was determined to keep to her death, no matter the cost to her personal happiness.

"What's the real reason, Lizzy?" he said as if he could see that she was dissembling. "You afraid to take a chance on a man my age?"

She scoffed at the ridiculous notion. "Brandon, you have more energy than men half your age. You'd still be running me ragged when we both turn eighty."

"I know that," he said with a twinkle in his eyes. "I just wondered if you did."

She raised her concerns about life-style and distance. But he shot each down promising to charter a jet if he had to to take her back and forth to California.

"So, you've assumed we'll settle here," she countered. "There you go again, making plans without a thought to what I might want."

"No, indeed. The only thing I care about is what you want. I'm just not sure you recognize what that is."

"Brandon, I do believe I know my own mind."

"Then say something that makes sense," he snapped impatiently.

His tone set her teeth on edge. "Just because you don't want to hear what I'm saying doesn't mean it doesn't make sense. Don't you think deciding where to live is critical for a couple our age?"

"I don't aim on settling anywhere. I'm thinking of seeing the world, getting myself out of Jason and Kevin's hair. Think about it, Lizzy. Have you been to Rome? Paris? Tahiti?"

Naturally Brandon would hit on an almost irresistible lure, she thought irritably. Just the sound of all those fascinating places thrilled her. They were rich with culture she'd only read about in books. She'd promised herself that one day she would see them all. Time was running out, but this wasn't the answer. They couldn't roam the world as if they were rootless, when the very opposite was true.

"Tahiti?" she inquired quizzically. "Isn't that a little exotic for the likes of us?"

"Why? I'll bet you still cut a fine figure in a bathing suit." His mood obviously improved, he winked when he said it, then sobered and added more seriously, "Besides, there are a lot of books I've been wanting to read. A month or two on the beach would help me to catch up." The twinkle came back. "Unless you'd prefer to lure me off to our room and have your way with me."

"Brandon!" Despite the stern disapproval in her tone, she couldn't banish the devilish quickening of her pulse. Brandon did have a way of saying the most outrageous things to shock her. Was she going to let silly fears and practicality stand in the way of happiness again? Perhaps a compromise was possible, a way to snag a few weeks or even months of pleasure.

"I've always wanted to run away to a tropical isle

with a handsome stranger,'' she admitted, not even trying to hide the wistfulness.

Brandon's big, gentle hands cupped her cheeks. ''We're hardly strangers, Lizzy. We've known each other our whole lives.''

''But we've only been together less than a month, counting these past few days. Isn't that part of the appeal? We've never had time to recognize all the little idiosyncrasies that might drive us crazy.''

''Is there anything important about me you don't know?''

''No,'' she had to admit. But there were things he didn't know about her, could never know. She could have a few more weeks, though. Just a few weeks of stolen happiness. They deserved that much.

''Let's just run away, Brandon,'' she coaxed. ''There's no need for a ceremony. We needn't worry about shocking anyone in this day and age.''

His hands fell away from her face. His eyes turned serious. ''Do you think our children would be happier to see us having an affair than they would be seeing us married? I doubt it. Besides, I can't bear the thought of waking up some morning to discover you've vanished during the night. I want a real commitment this time, Lizzy. I won't settle for less.''

''I can't give you that. I was never as brave or as strong as you, Brandon. I don't take risks.''

''But there's no risk involved. Can't you see that? After all these years our feelings haven't changed. That should tell you how right they are. We've cherished them in our hearts. Not that either of us short-changed the people we married.'' He tapped his chest. ''But here, where it counts, we've never forgotten.''

"Our feelings aren't the only ones that count anymore. We have families to consider."

"Dammit, Lizzy, you're thinking up excuses, not reasons."

"No," she said gently. "Your family is every bit as important to you as mine is to me. Neither of us could ever knowingly do something that would bring them unhappiness or pain."

"Lizzy, you're not making sense. How could our happiness cause them pain?"

She couldn't explain, no matter how badly she wanted to erase the confusion and hurt in his eyes.

"I'm sorry, Brandon," she whispered, fighting to hide the tears that threatened as she finalized the decision she should have made days earlier. "I'm going home in the morning. Alone."

He backed away from her then, and his expression turned colder than she'd ever seen it before. "I won't chase after you again, Lizzy."

She felt his anguish as deeply as her own. "I know," she said in a voice filled with regret. "Perhaps you should call a taxi to take me back to the hotel. We'll say our goodbyes here, just as we did the first time."

"No. I brought you here. I'll take you back," he said with stiff politeness.

"Really, it's not necessary."

"Yes," he said firmly. "It is."

The drive to the hotel was made in silence. It was colder by far in the car than it was outdoors. Elizabeth felt as if her heart had frozen inside her. She was certain she would never feel anything as magnificent as Brandon's caring again. She was trading love for peace of mind, and at the moment it seemed to be a lopsided exchange all the way around.

Brandon wondered how the devil things had gone so wrong again. Day after day, he'd seen the way Lizzy looked at him. He'd felt her pulse quicken at his touch, felt her flesh warm. Whatever the real explanation for her withdrawal, he knew he hadn't heard it yet. Not that she was lying. But she definitely wasn't telling him the whole truth.

He was a proud man, though. He wouldn't chase after her like some lovesick adolescent. If she couldn't be honest, if she couldn't trust him with the truth, then perhaps he'd been wrong all along about the depth of her feelings.

Perhaps it was just as well to discover now that there was no trust between them. They'd lost it over those damned letters decades back and nothing that had happened in the past few days had helped them to recapture it.

Maybe he'd fooled himself that what they'd once shared had been deeper and more meaningful than any-thing he'd experienced before or since. Maybe he'd simply been making a desperate, last grab for what had turned out to be no more than an illusion. Maybe love and marriage weren't even possible at his age. Perhaps he should be willing to settle for the fleeting companionship Lizzy offered. There were so damn many maybes, and so few solid answers.

Despite Lizzy's objections, Brandon turned the car over to the valet at the hotel and followed her inside. In front of the elevator he studied her and tried to convince himself that he'd been wrong about everything, but his heart ached with a real sense of loss. He might have tracked her down on impulse, but he'd kept her in Boston because she'd engaged his heart as no other woman ever had. He couldn't explain it, it just *was*—like the rising of the sun or the pull of the tides.

He brushed a wisp of hair back from her cheek and felt her tremble. His gaze caught hers and held them spellbound. Her lips parted on a soft sigh that could have been either pleasure or regret.

"I've spent the whole drive over here trying to convince myself that I'm wrong about us," he said finally, his knuckles grazing her soft cheek. "But I'd be a liar if I told you I believed it. There's a bond between us, Lizzy, one I can't deny. Can you?"

Her hand reached up and covered his. "No," she said. "I can't deny that."

"Then why won't you marry me?"

"I can't," she said with stubborn finality, slipping away from his touch.

"I won't make it easy for you to walk away," he warned, just before he pulled her into his arms and brought his mouth down to cover hers.

Oblivious to everything except the woman melting in his embrace, Brandon plundered. It wasn't a kiss meant just to remind. It was meant to brand. It was a hot, hungry claiming of a kind he'd nearly forgotten until Lizzy had come back into his life.

Her scent, like that of spring rain and sweetest flowers, surrounded them. Her skin was petal soft, her lips moist and inviting after that first shocked instant when his tongue had invaded.

Despite its urgency, the kiss should have been the end of it, but it brought too many provocative memories, too many seductive images of another time, another place. His pulse bucked like a young man's, as it had on that single splendid night he and Lizzy had shared.

"Let me come to your room," he whispered in a voice husky with desire. "If nothing else, let me hold you through this one last night." The words were an echo of a long-ago plea and he waited just as anxiously for her response. "Don't deny us that," he coaxed.

"Sometimes I wonder how I ever denied you anything," she said ruefully. She slid her hand into his. "One night, Brandon. I suppose there's no harm in grabbing that much happiness."

The elevator ride was the longest he'd ever taken. He couldn't stop looking at Lizzy, with her cheeks flushed with color and her eyes bright with anticipation. She looked every bit as beautiful tonight as she had as a girl, and he wanted her in his arms with the same aching urgency. Since Grace had died, he'd thought he would never again experience this fire in his blood, but it pulsed now with a demanding roar.

In Lizzy's room, the maid had turned down the expensive covers on the queen-size bed. A foil-wrapped candy was on each pillow. Light from the hall spilled in, until Brandon slowly shut the door behind them, leaving them in shadows.

He reached for the light, but Lizzy stayed his hand. "No," she whispered. "I want you to remember me the way I was, not the way I am now."

He touched her cheek in a gesture meant to reassure. "You will always be beautiful in my eyes. Time could never change that."

"Spoken like a true romantic," she said with a nervous laugh. "But I'd rather not take any chances."

"We don't have to go through with this," he said, cursing the sense of honor that demanded he offer to stop right now.

He heard her intake of breath and felt his own go still as he waited for her decision.

"I want you to hold me again," she said finally and his breath eased out in a soft sigh of relief.

A lifetime of marriage hadn't taught him enough patience to go as slowly as he knew he needed to tonight. He sensed that any moment Lizzy would panic and change her mind, unless he claimed her with only the tenderest of touches, the gentlest of words.

In the shadowy darkness Brandon pulled Lizzy into his arms and touched his lips to hers again. This time he allowed himself the delight of savoring, the slow exploration of tastes and textures. His senses exploded with a clash of sweet, poignant memory and glorious reality. As slowly and inevitably as the passage of time, he felt her hesitancy become bold desire.

And still he moved cautiously, allowing the weight of her breast to fill his hand, allowing his fingers to skim lightly over the sensitive nipple that had peaked despite layers of fabric. She moaned at the teasing, eyes closed as she gave herself up to his caresses.

"You're so responsive," he murmured. "Sometimes I ached to experience that again and I envied the man who'd replaced me in your life."

"I never expected to feel like this again," she admitted, meeting his gaze. "Thank you for that."

"No," he whispered. "Don't thank me. Just love me as you did that night."

Each touch after that became an echo of one that had gone before. Their bodies responded in harmony, as if they'd been made to fit together. Brandon didn't feel old in Lizzy's embrace. He felt rejuvenated, more passionate than ever before, more determined than ever not to sacrifice what they had found.

He did everything he could to see that she felt the same. The woman who came apart in his arms, the woman whose tears spilled onto his burning flesh was as spirited and as passionate as the one he'd held decades earlier.

Experience and time had taught them to be bolder, more demanding lovers. Love had taught them to give as much as they received.

As they lay in each other's arms, exhausted, sated, Brandon thought he had never known such joy or peace of mind. His fingers skimmed across her flesh, then halted at the locket that lay between her breasts. He heard her breath catch as he traced the shape and realized then that she was wearing the one piece of jewelry she had accepted from him years before.

"Why would you still have this, if you didn't care?" he murmured.

"I never said I didn't care."

"Have you always worn it?"

"No."

"But you did save it," he said in what sounded like an accusation. "Is my picture still inside?"

"Yes."

"Doesn't that tell you something, Lizzy? You can't mean to walk away from this," he said finally. "You can't."

He felt another hot tear spill onto his chest, and he propped himself up on one elbow to gaze down at the woman in his arms. "Why are you crying?" he asked, wiping away the tears.

“Because you’re wrong,” she whispered in a voice that broke. “I must walk away.”

Though she seemed to choking back a sob, there was no mistaking the stubborn finality in her eyes. Brandon felt his heart grow cold. “You mean that, don’t you?”

She nodded, not looking at him. Then she lifted her gaze to his and said, “But it will break my heart.”

Chapter Nine

There were times over the next few days when Brandon wondered how he'd ever gotten home from Lizzy's hotel that night. He'd risked everything on the hope that once they had made love again she would never walk away.

He should have known better. If she hadn't consented to marry him when they'd been wildly in love in their teens and she'd been an innocent virgin, she would never give in so easily now.

She had always been far stronger than he'd realized, perhaps even than she herself realized. Whatever was driving her back to California was not something he knew how to combat. She'd allowed him a peek inside her heart, but he knew nothing of her soul. She'd kept that part of herself private—a secret she wouldn't share, even with him. He'd left her room feeling a depth of sorrow and regret that matched the grieving he'd done for Grace and had hoped never to experience again.

Despite that, he called in the morning, intending one last-ditch attempt to persuade her to stay or, at the very least, to wrench a truthful explanation from her. But she had left already, without a note, without a goodbye.

Brandon thought back to another time when Lizzy had refused him in much the same way. Perhaps he'd been naive to expect a seventeen-year-old girl to make a lifetime commitment to a man she'd known only days. Yet he'd known in a matter of minutes that she had brought an inexplicable, heart-stopping excitement into his life.

Because he hadn't considered himself a man prone to sentiment at that time, he'd been stunned to learn that he was capable of such deep emotions. The discovery was especially unsettling since only moments before, he'd been anticipating the hero's welcome that would await him after the war and wondering how many women it might allow him to charm into his bed. In the blink of an eye an encounter with a dazzling, barefooted girl had changed all that. He'd been able to imagine no one in his life except Lizzy.

Up until the moment when she'd turned down his proposal on the eve of his departure for England, he'd been convinced she'd felt the same rare magic. Nothing she'd said back then had made a bit of sense, either. That's when he'd first realized that Lizzy had a stubbornness that matched his own. It had made her all the more appealing.

But that was then and this was now. All he felt now was anger and betrayal. Brandon swore he would never give her the chance to hurt him again. There would be no flood of flowers, no Belgian chocolates, no pleas, no coaxing. She had made her choice, for whatever reason, and he would honor it. He'd grown far too weary of challenges.

Instead Brandon ranted and raved at everyone else, making their lives a living hell. He dropped his plans to retire, offering no explanation. He filled up the lonely hours of each and every evening with work, littering Kevin's desk and Jason's with the memos he spent the night writing. When Sammy came around, eager to learn more about Halloran textiles, Brandon even chased him off with his foul temper.

The next day at the plant he overheard Sammy telling Dana about the encounter.

''Something's wrong with Grandpa Brandon,'' Sammy said, clearly worried. ''He wouldn't even talk about that new silk stuff when I asked him. You think maybe he's sick?''

Just out of sight, Brandon listened in dismay, knowing he owed the boy an apology. Aside from Dana, Sammy hadn't had a lot of people in his life he could count on. Brandon considered himself lucky to be one of them. Now, because of his own bleak outlook, he was letting Sammy down, and Dana was put in the awkward position of trying to make excuses for him.

''I'm sure he didn't mean to cut you off,'' she said. ''I have a pretty good idea what's troubling him, and it doesn't have anything to do with you. This moping around has gone on long enough, though. I intend to talk to him.''

Guilty over having eavesdropped, and guiltier yet over the way he'd yelled at Sammy to leave him be, Brandon went back to his office and tried to figure out how the devil he was going to get his life in order before everyone around him formed a lynch mob.

He was prowling around his office when Dana sashayed in. She looked as if she were just itching for a fight. She ignored his forbidding scowl and settled into the chair opposite his desk. It was obvious she had no intention of being scared off, but that didn't stop him from trying.

"What do you want?" he grumbled in a tone meant to intimidate. He stood towering over her as he asked.

"The truth," she said without blanching the way he'd have liked.

"About what?"

"Whatever's bugging you."

"Who says anything is bugging me?"

"Are you suggesting old age has suddenly made you crotchety?"

"Could be," he said, though he was suddenly fighting an unexpected grin. She was a tough one, all right. Just like Lizzy, he thought before he could stop himself. He moved to the window and stared out at the dreary April day that mirrored his mood.

"You weren't acting old when I saw you dancing a couple of weeks back," she commented idly. "I believe that was the lambada you and Elizabeth were trying."

Surprise and dismay left Brandon openmouthed. He turned to glower at her. "You were spying on me?"

"I was not," she retorted emphatically. "I stopped over to pick up that baby cradle you told me was in the attic. Mrs. Farnsworth let me in and said you'd gone out for the evening. I didn't even know you'd come home until I was on my way out. I started to say hello and then I realized you weren't alone."

"So you spied," he repeated.

She grinned. "Call it whatever you want. It was pretty interesting stuff. I didn't stick around for the finale, though. I left when things started heating up."

"Thank goodness for small favors."

"You still haven't said—is she the reason you've been in this funk? Has Elizabeth gone back to California?"

He considered lying to protect his privacy, then didn't see the use of it. Dana was too smart to buy a small fib, and he had too much integrity to offer a blatant lie. She'd obviously figured it out, anyway.

"Yes," he muttered finally.

"When do you plan to visit her?"

"I don't."

"Why on earth not?"

"She won't have it."

"Why?" she asked, sounding every bit as astonished and confused as he felt.

Relieved to have someone to talk to, someone who wasn't likely to laugh in his face or to make judgments, he cleared a spot on the sofa, tumbling bolts of fabric onto the floor, and sat down. Then he told Dana the whole sad story—at least as much as he understood of it.

"She said no," he concluded. "Again."

"And you're just giving up," she retorted in a tone that was part disbelief, part accusation. "Again."

"No," he said, but further denial died on his lips. "I can't go chasing all over the countryside for her."

"I don't see why not. You were planning to chase all over the world with her. Why not start in California?"

"I won't settle for less than marriage this time and she won't hear of that."

"Then I guess you'll just have to be more persuasive. Lord knows, you didn't give up on Jason and me or on Lacey and Kevin," she said. "You know what your trouble is? You're too used to getting your own way without a fight. Maybe this Lizzy of yours is smarter than you think. Maybe she sees that it'll do you good to have to work for something for a change. Maybe she needs to know she's worth fighting for this time."

Recognizing the wisdom and clinging to the tiny shred of hope in what she'd said, Brandon stood and scooped his granddaughter-in-law up in a bear hug.

"Damn, I did right by Jason when I picked you," he said with satisfaction. "My grandson is one very lucky man. I hope he knows that."

"I remind him all the time."

"I think I'll just stop by his office and tell him myself. At the same time I'll tell Kevin that I'm leaving the two of them in charge. I'm officially retiring as of today. Tonight I'll pack my bags, and in the morning I'll take the first flight to California. Don't you dare have that baby while I'm gone," he warned.

"I wouldn't dream of it. I promise," she said.

The next morning Brandon dug the detective's report out of his desk at home and made note of all the pertinent addresses and phone numbers—Lizzy's and those of her daughters. Then, his step lighter than it had been in days, he left for the airport. He refused to even consider the possibility that Lizzy wouldn't see him when he got there.

"Mother, what are you doing here?" Ellen asked when she walked into her own kitchen and found Elizabeth sitting there, staring out the window at the rain, a pile of socks on the table in front of her.

Elizabeth avoided her daughter's gaze.

"Not that I'm not glad to see you," Ellen added hurriedly as she plunked her bag of groceries onto the counter and dropped a kiss on her mother's cheek. She shrugged out of her raincoat, then ran her fingers through her short sandy hair. The damp strands fell back into enviable waves.

Finally she sat down across from Elizabeth, her expression worried. "Are you okay?"

"Of course I'm okay. I'm just darning Jake's socks," Elizabeth said defensively, picking up another pair of her son-in-law's heavy athletic socks from the stack of laundry. She reached for needle and thread.

"Why on earth would you be doing that?"

"It needs to be done."

Ellen plucked the socks from Elizabeth's hands and tossed them into the garbage. "It does not need to be done. You're bored, Mother. You've been restless ever since you got back from Boston and you haven't said a word about Brandon Halloran. I haven't wanted to press before, but enough is enough. Did something go wrong between you two? I thought you stayed on because you were having such a wonderful time."

"It was okay," she said, feeling heat climb into her cheeks at the memory of that last night. That was the second time in her life she'd made a dreadful mistake with Brandon. It had taken her decades to get over the first time. She didn't have decades left this time.

"Just okay?" Ellen asked, reaching for the teapot Elizabeth had filled and set in the middle of the table. She poured them both a cup of tea.

Elizabeth met her daughter's intense gaze and sighed heavily. "No," she admitted reluctantly. "It was more than okay."

"And?"

"And what?" she snapped, sitting her cup down so hard that tea sloshed onto the table. She ignored the mess and reached for another sock. "Why are you so interested, anyway?"

"Because when you left for Boston, there was a sparkle in your eyes and a spring in your step. When we talked on the phone, you sounded excited, alive. Now you look as though you've lost your best friend, and you sound perfectly miserable. To top it off, you're darning socks, something no one in this family has done since I was a child. Even then you only did it when you were angry or distraught," Ellen said bluntly. "Now if that man did something to upset you, I want to know about it."

Elizabeth hesitated, then finally blurted, "He asked me to marry him."

She dared a glance at her daughter. Ellen's mouth dropped open. The next instant she was on her feet, enveloping her mother in a hug. Elizabeth endured the embrace stiffly.

"He asked you to marry him?" Ellen said, barely containing her exuberance. Her blue-green eyes sparkled. "Mother, why didn't you say something sooner? That's wonderful. When's the wedding? Does Kate know? Penny will go nuts. She said you were probably…well, never mind what Penny said. I should have washed her mouth out with soap."

"Penny is entirely too precocious. Besides, I turned him down."

Looking stunned, Ellen sat back down and simply

stared at her. "Why would you do that? Weren't the sparks still there, after all? They must have been for him if he wants to get married. I could have sworn they were there for you; as well."

"Oh, yes," she admitted reluctantly. "The sparks were there."

"Then what happened? Why did you say no?"

"It was a little frightening," she explained. "Brandon can be a bit overpowering when he sets his mind to something."

"Which is what you always said you wanted. Dad let you run the show."

"Don't criticize you father, Ellen," she said sharply. "He was a good man."

"Oh, for heaven's sake Mother, I never said he wasn't. But you know what I said is true. He gave in to you on everything. I always thought you would have been better off with a man who would stand up to you. Now what's the real reason you said no to Brandon Halloran? You weren't worried about our reaction, were you?"

Elizabeth picked up her cup of tea, then set it back down. She wished more than anything that she could have this same conversation with Kate, so she could say everything that was on her mind. But, ironically, Kate was the one who wouldn't understand and the only one she could tell.

"Not exactly, but I couldn't go off and leave all of you," she said eventually, giving the truth a wide berth.

Ellen moved her chair closer to Elizabeth and took her hand. "Mom, are you sure that's not just an excuse? How often do you see us, anyway? I know we're all in the same city, but the only times we get together as a whole family are holidays. We could still manage that."

"But now I know you're just a phone call away."

Ellen grinned at her. "There are airplanes. We still would be a phone call away."

"I couldn't just drop in like this."

"Which you haven't done in months. You're usually too busy. You've spent more time here moping around since you got back, than you did in the entire six months before you left."

"I guess that's true."

Ellen's expression grew puzzled. "Mother, don't you want to marry him?"

Elizabeth took a deep breath, then met her daughter's gaze evenly. "More than anything," she said before she could stop herself.

"Then I say go for it."

"But there are things you don't know," she began, her voice trailing off helplessly. Things she could never tell her.

"What things?"

She shook her head, knowing she'd already said far too much. "Never mind. I'm just prattling on. I made my decision. I'll just have to learn to accept it."

"Mother, you're not making a bit of sense."

"Nobody ever said love made sense," she observed.

They both jumped at the sudden pounding on the front door. It was interspersed with the impatient ringing of the doorbell.

"What on earth?" Ellen muttered as she went to get it. "I suppose Penny must have forgotten her key."

But it wasn't Penny. Even from the kitchen Elizabeth could hear enough to send panic racing through her. There was no mistaking the gruff timbre of Brandon's voice.

"Oh my Lord," she whispered, wishing she could flee out the back door. He'd come. He'd actually come all the way to California for her, even though he'd sworn he wouldn't.

And he'd met Ellen, she realized with sudden, heart-stopping fear. My God, he'd met her daughter. She could practically feel the color drain from her cheeks as she stood up, uncertain whether to run to him or hide.

"Elizabeth," he said softly from the doorway, his voice a low command.

Just hearing him did astonishing things to her insides. Drawing on all her reserves of strength, she faced him sternly, wanting him gone, out of the house before he ruined everything. Even so, she couldn't help noting his haggard face, the glint of determination in his eyes—both were equally worrisome.

"Why have you come? You know I don't want you here," she said, her voice trembling with anger and frustration.

"I don't believe you. For just an instant, before you caught yourself, I could see the expression in your eyes. It wasn't dismay, Lizzy. It was longing."

"That's ego and imagination talking," she said, dismissing them. "Please, Brandon. Leave now. I meant what I said in Boston. It would never work between us."

"I'm not leaving without you," he said stubbornly. "I've made up my mind. You just might as well accept it."

She was as certain that he meant that as she was of

the next sunset. Knowing that and desperate to have him out of Ellen's house, she snatched up her bag.

"Have it your way, then," she said grudgingly and marched through the house. "Dear, we'll be going now," she told her daughter.

"It was a pleasure meeting you, Mr. Halloran," Ellen said at the door. "I hope we'll see more of you while you're in town."

"Believe me, I would love to get to know you, as well," he said. "I've heard a lot about you from your mother."

Elizabeth brushed past the two of them and hurried down the sidewalk to her car. Brandon's fancy rental car was parked right behind the small economy car she'd owned for five years. She turned back just once and saw that Ellen was watching them go with an expression of satisfaction on her face.

If only she knew, Elizabeth thought. If only they both knew.

But they couldn't and that was that, she thought with a sigh of resignation. She would not destroy her daughter's life, not even for a few years of happiness for herself. The secret she'd kept all these years was so explosive it might destroy that prospect for happiness, as well.

Without another word, Brandon climbed into his own car and followed Elizabeth home. For one wild instant she wished she had the evasive skills of some TV criminal, who could skid around corners and lose the police car following. The effort would be wasted, any-way. If Brandon had tracked her to Ellen's house, then surely he could find her own.

As she drove up in front of the small stucco house with its red-tiled roof and pink bougainvillea climbing up the sides, she tried visualizing it through Brandon's eyes. It came up wanting, especially when stacked against that lovely, roomy old mansion he owned in Boston.

Once inside, he stalked through her house so possessively, she wondered if she'd ever be able to forget his presence here. He paused in front of a credenza on which there were pictures of both her daughters and all the grandchildren. The photo he lingered over, though, was the one of her on her wedding day.

"I always imagined you just this way," he said regretfully. His gaze met hers. "You were a beautiful bride, Lizzy. David Newton was a lucky man."

"I was the lucky one," she said staunchly.

He went back to studying the pictures one by one, picking them up and gazing at them, his expression sad. He put the one of Ellen back last and turned to face her.

"I've made up my mind to something, Lizzy. You might as well know it up front."

"What?" she said nervously.

"I won't leave California without you," he said.

"I suppose I owe this visit to that detective, too."

"He did supply the addresses, if that's what you mean."

For the first time, she viewed the detective's invasion of her privacy as something less than romantic. "What else did he tell you?" she asked, a note of alarm in her voice.

"That was the gist of it," Brandon said, regarding her with an expression of puzzlement. "Why?"

To cover her anxiety she injected an edge of sarcasm into her tone. "I just wondered if he'd bothered to include the color of my wallpaper and made a note of the salon where I get my hair done.''

''No, Lizzy,'' Brandon said impatiently. ''Now stop trying to change the subject. Are you going with me or am I staying here?''

Her heart thumped harder with a beat that was surely as much anticipation as panic. She couldn't afford the eagerness. ''You have to leave, Brandon. Alone. This is pure craziness. I can't just pick up and go traveling at the drop of a hat.'' She ignored the implied marriage proposal entirely.

''I don't see why not.''

''Because I have responsibilities, a family.''

''You're making up excuses, Lizzy. I wonder why? What are you so afraid of? Are you worried you will fall in love with me again, and then I'll disappear like before? I can promise you that won't happen. What I want for us means taking a risk, I know, but isn't that better than leading a lonely, solitary existence? Surely you feel something for me, enough to make a commitment, enough to build on.''

Of course she did, she thought miserably. But that changed nothing for her. She had to deny her heart in favor of cool logic. ''Brandon, what makes you so sure you know what I feel? No matter what you want to believe, I'm not the same silly girl you once knew.''

He regarded her with an intensity that made her blood race. ''Maybe not,'' he conceded. ''But that daughter of yours didn't throw me out. In fact, she acted downright glad to see me. That must mean you've spoken of me favorably. I'll take that as a promising start.''

The man had always had the perceptiveness of a

clairvoyant, she thought dully. How could she convince him to go, when he read her so easily?

She weighed her options, then drew in a deep breath. "I told you before, Brandon. I'm willing to compromise. I'll travel with you, if you wish. I'll visit you in Boston as often as you like. But I won't marry you and I don't want you here." She recited the conditions as if they'd been etched in her mind, then waited for the explosion of impatience.

Instead he nodded slowly. "Okay," he said, his agreement coming far too readily. "I can see we're going to have to do this your way. We'll go to New Mexico to start with. There's a place there I've been wanting to visit. Pack your bags, woman. I'll call the airlines."

Despite herself, Elizabeth felt the dull pain in her chest begin to ease. A few days, she thought all too eagerly. She would have a few more days with Brandon before she did what had to be done and let him go.

Chapter Ten

Brandon hadn't expected to win quite so easily. On the flight from Boston to Los Angeles, he'd come up with an entire arsenal of arguments to convince Lizzy to marry him or at the least to take off on an adventure with him. That she herself had again suggested they go away together delighted him. It didn't, however, erase his confusion over what the devil made her tick.

Now, more than ever before, he was puzzled by her almost panicky determination to keep him away from California. He had the sense she would have agreed to follow him to Timbuktu, if it had meant catching an earlier flight away from her home.

Brandon waited until they'd reached Albuquerque, settled into very proper, separate rooms in a hotel and found a lovely restaurant that served fiery Mexican food before he dared to broach the subject. Even then he took a circuitous route.

As he sipped a glass of fruity sangria, he studied the woman seated across from him, her blue eyes luminous in the candlelight, her gray hair softly feathering around her face.

"Having fun so far?" he asked.

Elizabeth smiled at him, clearly amused by his obvious impatience and his need for reassurance. "Brandon, we've only been gone a few hours. What do you expect me to say? The flight was smooth. The hotel seems quiet and clean. This salsa is the best I've ever eaten. Unless you want me to praise your tipping technique, I don't know what more I can say about the trip so far."

He chuckled. "Okay, make fun of me, but I'm damned proud of my tipping technique," he said. "I can calculate the proper percentage in no time. I can manage it in at least a half dozen foreign currencies as well."

"Then I assure you I'll praise your technique lavishly the next time the matter comes up, along with any of the other experiences we share."

He reached across the wooden table and rested his hand on top of hers. Gazing deep into her eyes, he tried to read her thoughts. He couldn't. "Seriously, Lizzy," he said then, "are you looking forward to all of this or have I simply pressured you into it by turning up on your doorstep?"

"You've done your share of pressuring and you know it, so don't look for absolution from me," she accused.

To his relief she didn't really sound angry about it. If anything, there was a teasing note in her voice.

"Even so," she admitted, "It's a heady thing at my age to have a man sweep into town and carry me off to a place I've never seen before. It's the stuff romance novels are made of."

"And do you frequently indulge in romance novels?"

"They do remind me of a certain time in my life," she said with that now familiar wistful note in her voice.

"Dare I ask if that was the time you and I first spent together?"

"I suspect you'd dare just about anything. Don't fish for compliments, Brandon. You know I remember those days just as vividly as you do." A nostalgic note crept into her voice. "There is nothing in a woman's life quite like falling in love for the first time. If you'd asked me a few months ago if I would ever have the chance to recapture those feelings, even in some small measure, I'd have told you no."

"Do you regret my finding you, Lizzy? Has it been..." He searched for the right word, the one that captured the impression he had of her nervousness. "Has it been difficult for you?"

Her gaze rose and collided with his. "Why would you ask that?"

More than the question itself, the tone of her response bordered on panic, it seemed to him, confirming what he'd guessed. "I asked because it's been obvious from the start that you don't want me around your family. Is that because you never told them about me?"

At first she looked at a loss for an answer. Finally she said, "It's not easy admitting to your children that you might have feet of clay."

"Then you think of that time in your life as a mistake?" he prodded.

"Not a mistake exactly, but it was certainly an indiscretion. Neither of us were thinking clearly. We didn't have a bit of regard for the consequences."

"No. We were thinking more of life and death, more of love, than we were of the repercussions. I can't deny that. We might have been too impetuous, but our actions were rooted in love, Lizzy. Nothing less." He paused. "At least for me."

She sighed. "You're so sure of that, Brandon. Have you never doubted what we felt? Have you never once thought that maybe we were just caught up in all the drama of your leaving to fight overseas? We wouldn't have been the only couple to rush headlong into romance, thinking that there might be no tomorrow. Maybe it was nothing more than infatuation."

"No," he said with absolute certainty. "I think the fact that we are here together now proves the point. We have always held a place for each other in our hearts, even when we thought our paths might never cross again." He regarded her intently. "Or am I presuming too much?"

"No," she said softly and with a trace of reluctance. "I suppose I could deny it, but what would be the point? You may take far too many things for granted, but that's not one of them."

"You aren't feeling guilty because of that, are you?"

"Guilty? What on earth would I have to feel guilty about?" Elizabeth asked.

The denial was adamant, her tone clipped. Even more telling was the fact that her gaze slid away from his in a way that confirmed the very point he was making, despite her contradictory words.

Brandon deliberately shrugged with casual indifference, though he was filled with questions. "From my point of view, you've done nothing to feel guilty about. I'm not so sure, though, that you don't feel that you shortchanged David Newton in some essential way."

Again the response was lightning quick—too quick to Brandon's way of thinking.

"He never felt that way," she said.

He scooped up her hand and held it tight. Again, as they always were when she was most nervous, her fingers were like ice as they laced through his. Still he pressed her, ignoring the increasingly anxious expression in her eyes. He had this feeling that they were finally getting close to the truth. He sensed if he could just find the right question, he would unlock this mysterious attitude of hers that taunted him.

"I'm not talking about how David Newton felt, Lizzy. How did you feel? Are you feeling the weight of his blame even now for being here with me? Who are you cheating by being here tonight, sharing a full moon and a glass of sangria on this terrace, rather than being home alone?"

"No one," she said emphatically, but she withdrew her hand and covered the nervous gesture by quickly picking up her glass. "It's not as though we're doing anything immoral, for goodness' sake. I never thought of it that way even back then. It felt right to be with you from the very beginning."

"And now?"

"I'm not so sure I can describe the way it feels now."

"But not quite so right?" he said a little sadly. "Why not, Lizzy? What's changed? Now we have all the time in the world to get to know each other, to share adventures. No one will begrudge us that. Our children are grown. They don't need us anymore, despite what we may tell ourselves to feel useful. We've had full, satisfying careers. These are our precious golden years. It's time to live every minute to the fullest. Why can't you just relax at last and enjoy every experience?''

''I can't explain it,'' she evaded again, her gaze skittering away from his.

''Can't or won't,'' he pressed. ''Is there something you're hiding from me, Lizzy? Something you fear I'll discover if we spend too much time together?''

''No, of course not,'' she said in a rush of words that came out sounding far more nervous than convincing. She snatched up her purse and scooted from the booth as if she couldn't wait to escape. ''I believe I'll visit the powder room before they bring our dinner. Will you excuse me, Brandon?''

He wanted to tell her no. He wanted to force Lizzy to sit right where she was and tell him what had her so worried. But the genuine panic in her eyes wouldn't allow it.

''Of course,'' he said, standing while she hurried away from the table.

Away from answers.

Away from him.

While she was gone, he reluctantly resolved to probe no more that night. Whatever she was worried about would come out in due time, if he was patient. He sighed heavily. Lizzy always had asked things of him that taxed him. Patience was just one more thing to add to the list. Holding back alone ought to prove to her just how much he cared.

When she returned to the table, Brandon determinedly changed the subject and saw relief wash across her face. Her eyes brightened, and in no time at all they were laughing together as they once had, laughing as if they had not a care in the world. Whatever dark undercurrents he'd felt earlier seemed no more than a distant memory.

They walked back to the hotel, hand in hand like a couple of kids. The sky was filled with stars, diamonds on black velvet with a showy full moon. The temperature had fallen, bringing a chill to the air. Even with a delicate, lacy shawl of pale pink wool tossed around her shoulders, Lizzy shivered. Brandon shrugged out of his jacket and draped it over her shoulders, allowing his arm to linger in a casual embrace once he was done.

"Have you ever seen such a sky, Lizzy?" he asked, looking up at the cover of brilliant stars.

"Certainly not in Los Angeles," she said dryly. "With our smog, I'm lucky to get a decent view of the moon."

"Then I'm going to make a proposal."

"Oh?" she said, sounding cautious.

He smiled at her. "Come on, Lizzy. What I'm proposing is not indecent."

"That remains to be seen."

"Quiet, woman. Let me get it out. I propose that you and I spend the next few weeks auditioning the skies in all the corners of the globe until we find one that's perfect. What do you say?"

"It sounds romantic," she said with an undeniable eagerness, which gave way at once to sober reflection. "And impractical."

"Forget impractical. We can do anything we want, remember?" he asked, turning her until she faced him.

He could read the wistfulness in her eyes, then the hesitation. ''Come on, Lizzy. Say yes.''

Seconds turned into minutes as their gazes clashed.

''Lizzy?''

''Okay, yes,'' she said, a trifle breathlessly. She drew in a deep breath, squared her shoulders and met his gaze evenly, adding more firmly, ''Yes, Brandon. I think we should.''

''That's a verbal contract now,'' he teased. ''I'll hold you to it.''

''Brandon, tell me something,'' she teased right back. ''Do you always get your own way?''

''Almost always, at least until I met you.''

''Then perhaps it's good that I say no once in a while.''

''It probably is,'' he agreed. ''Just don't make a practice of it, Lizzy. I might get discouraged.''

''Something tells me a challenge never discourages you. It only draws out your competitive spirit. Just look at the way you turned up in L.A., after vowing never to chase after me.''

Brandon touched a finger to her chin and tilted her head up so he could look directly into her eyes. ''Don't you try telling me that was a test, Elizabeth Newton. I won't believe it.''

''Whether it was or it wasn't, the result's the same. We're here together now. What puzzles me is why I can't seem to resist you, no matter how hard I try. My daughters would tell you that I'm stubborn as a mule, unshakable in my convictions and a stick-in-the-mud of the first order.''

''Funny,'' he observed. ''I hadn't noticed your inability to resist me. Does that mean if I were to try to kiss you now, you wouldn't slap me?''

Rather than waiting for her response, he lowered his head until his lips were no more than a hairbreadth from hers. He could feel the soft whisper of her breath on his face as he heard it quicken.

"Ah, Lizzy," he said with a sigh, right before he slanted his mouth over hers, capturing either protest or acquiescence.

Elizabeth felt as if the world had suddenly tilted and the ground had fallen away. Brandon's kiss stole her breath and left her dizzy. If she'd experienced the same symptoms anywhere other than in his embrace, she thought wryly, she'd have taken herself straight off to a doctor. It had been a long time since she'd known the head-spinning whirl of a man's passionate kiss. Since being reunited with Brandon, it was becoming a habit.

A wonderful, frightening, exciting, dangerous habit! How was she supposed to resist a man who considered it his duty to turn her world topsy-turvy? What possible defenses could she mount against a man who thought nothing of whisking her off to the far corners of the earth just to compare the brightness of the stars? There was clearly nothing tentative or halfway about the way Brandon intended to pursue her. She would have to struggle to keep her wits about her. She'd done that once and lost to his more persuasive determination.

She would fight harder this time, she thought, just as soon as she knew every nuance of this kiss. When she tired of the way his lips coaxed, when she grew bored with the way his tongue invaded, when she no longer felt this dark, delicious swirl of temptation, then she would fend off his advances. However at the moment, with her pulse scrambling and her insides melting, that seemed eons away.

Elizabeth was shaky when Brandon finally released her, as shaky as she had been the very first time he stole a kiss. Back then, though she'd acted bold, she'd been new to a woman's lures, newer yet to a man's commanding, overpowering sensuality. From that first instant she had known that she belonged with Brandon in an inevitable way she had never belonged with another man. She felt complete in his embrace, radiant beneath his gaze, sensual beneath his touch.

Once he'd vanished from her life, she had convinced herself that what she'd felt was no more than the product of a child's romantic fantasies. She'd given up any expectation of feeling that way again. She had settled for what she knew now had been second best. That didn't make her marriage to David Newton a bad bargain. Perhaps just a misguided one. She hoped he'd never, ever known that.

Discovering, back in Boston, that she could recapture these incredible, spilling-through-the-sky feelings had both delighted and dismayed her. While it proved, as Penny's health book contested, that age was no barrier to sexuality, it also indicated that Brandon was the one partner who was expert at stirring her senses.

Perhaps she had fled California to protect a lifetime of secrets, but the action very definitely had a positive side. For as long as it lasted, she would know the wonder of Brandon's love again. As long as he didn't press her for any more than this, she would be content, ecstatic in fact.

She was still under the spell of his kiss when they reached the hotel. Outside her room, he took her key and opened the door in a charmingly old-fashioned gesture of gallantry, then stepped carefully aside to let her enter. Her blood raced with anticipation as she met his gaze and saw that familiar spark of desire in his eyes. She had newer, far more recent memories of all the promises that look implied.

He held out his hand and after an instant she took it, then started at the press of cold metal against her palm.

"Your key," he said, grinning smugly at her astonishment. "Good night, Lizzy."

Before she could recover from the shock, before the stir of disappointment could begin, he had strolled away, whistling under his breath. When Brandon had been a jaunty, self-confident young airman, that whistling had pleased her. Now it began to grate on her nerves.

She was tempted to march down the hall after him, then tried to envision herself demanding to know why the man had no intention of sleeping with her. Worse yet, she tried to imagine someone overhearing. It was too ludicrous and humiliating to contemplate.

Wide-awake and all stirred up, she slammed the door to her room with a moderately satisfying thud. Her only regret was that she hadn't caught some part of that sneaky man's anatomy between the door and the jamb.

She turned the television on full blast, soaked herself in a hot tub filled with the fragrant bath salts supplied by the hotel, then ordered a brandy sent up from the bar. She was still muttering about Brandon's low-down tactics and getting pleasantly drowsy, when the phone rang.

"Yes," she snapped, knowing instinctively it was him.

"Having trouble sleeping?" Brandon inquired lightly.

"What makes you ask a thing like that?"

"I was having a nightcap in the bar when I heard your order come in. Then I heard the TV when I passed by on my way back to my room. I can't be sure, but it also sounded as if you might be cussing a blue streak in there."

"Listen to me, you cantankerous old man," she began, then caught herself. Two could play at his game. Her tone was sweet as honey, when she added, "I've just spent a relaxing hour in a bubble bath. Didn't you mention that honeysuckle is one of your favorite scents?"

He cleared his throat suspiciously. "Okay, Lizzy, what are you up to?"

"Me?" she inquired innocently. "I'm just enjoying the luxury of this big queen-size bed. The sheets are so nice and cool against my skin."

She couldn't be absolutely certain, but it sounded as if he'd groaned. "I feel absolutely decadent, lying here naked," she added for good measure. "Good night, Brandon."

This time she was certain that he groaned as she quietly hung the phone up. There were a few benefits to getting old, she decided. At the top of the list was the ability to give as good as you got. She switched off the light and snuggled beneath the covers. Minutes later she was sound asleep.

And minutes after that, her dreams turned downright steamy.

Chapter Eleven

When the phone in his room rang, Brandon was shaving and thinking of the sly way Lizzy had gotten even with him the night before. Anticipating her on the phone, he was unprepared for Kevin's voice.

"Dad, what the devil are you doing in New Mexico?" he asked, sounding thoroughly miffed. "I heard you went to California. Even that I got secondhand."

"Good morning to you, too, son," Brandon said, keeping a tight rein on his own temper. He didn't want to get in some shouting match with a man who'd been warned to avoid stress. He especially didn't want to risk alienating the son from whom he'd already been estranged once. His tone mild, he added, "You'd have got it from the horse's mouth if you'd been in your office when I looked for you on the day I left."

"So it's my fault that I have to find out from my

son that my father is chasing around the country after some woman?''

''I'm on vacation,'' Brandon corrected. ''Besides, what does it matter to you which state I'm in? I'm retired. You and Jason are in charge.''

''Pardon me if I don't take your name off the letterhead just yet. You have a way of changing your mind.''

''I'm entitled,'' he grumbled. ''Now was there a reason for this call? I have places to go.''

''What places?''

''I'm in Albuquerque. Get a guidebook and figure it out.''

''Dad, you are straining my patience.''

''I know the feeling.''

''Is that woman with you?''

''*That woman* has a name.''

He heard Kevin suck in his breath before he finally said more calmly, ''Is Mrs. Newton with you?''

''As a matter of fact, yes.''

Kevin groaned. ''I knew it. I just knew it. Dad, she's trying to get her hooks into you.''

''You've got that backward and we've already had this discussion once. I don't expect to have it again,'' he snapped, then reminded himself that Kevin's concern quite likely stemmed from having his mother replaced in Brandon's affections.

''Son, my being here with Lizzy isn't some sort of slap at your mother,'' he said more calmly. ''I cared very deeply for your mother, but she's gone now. Nobody's sorrier about that than I am, but I don't want to spend the rest of my days all alone. Your mother wouldn't want that for me, either. If you'd give Lizzy a chance, I'm sure you'd come to love her.''

"Love her?" Kevin echoed dully. "Does that mean you're planning on her becoming an important part of your life?"

"For a man who deals in bottom lines, you sure have a way of dancing around the real question on your mind. I would be very proud to have her marry me. So far, though, she's not so inclined. Now, if you don't mind, I'm going to hang up. This conversation is making me cranky."

"Me, too," Kevin said as he thumped the receiver back on the hook.

Brandon wondered idly if it was possible to disown his son at this late date. He glanced in the mirror and caught the scowl on his face and forced a smile. "Just getting a taste of your own medicine," he said ruefully to his reflection. It seemed all the Halloran men were genetically inclined to meddle.

In the long run, Kevin would come around, he decided. Lacey and Jason were far more understanding. Dana was downright tickled to be a coconspirator. They all could probably make Kevin see reason eventually. And if he didn't, so be it. Brandon figured he had enough on his mind trying to win Lizzy over without worrying about his son, too.

The thought of Lizzy had him rushing to get ready. He hadn't been this anxious to start a day since she'd left Boston weeks earlier.

Unfortunately before he left the room he made the mistake of answering the phone again.

"Dad?"

Lord, give me patience, he thought. "What is it now, Kevin?"

"I know you said you didn't want to discuss this again, but I have to ask you one thing. You hired a detective to find this Mrs. Newton for you, didn't you?''

''Yes. What's your point?''

''Did you have him look into the sort of life she's been leading since you last saw her?''

''What the devil kind of question is that to be asking? Are you implying that there's something shady about Lizzy? If you are, you couldn't be more off base. She's a fine woman. Now, I've had about all I can take of your innuendos and slurs. Maybe it's just my comeuppance for putting in my two cents worth about Lacey, but I was wrong then and *you* are wrong now. Am I making myself clear?'' he said, angrier than he'd ever been with his son.

Apparently Kevin sensed his wrath. He sighed heavily. ''I'm sorry, Dad. You're right. It's none of my business.''

''Thank you.''

''You will stay in touch, though?''

''I'm in New Mexico, not some primitive backwoods in the Amazon. They've got phones here. I'll use 'em. Now stop worrying before Lacey comes after me for ruining your recuperation. Goodbye.''

''Goodbye, Dad.'' There was a hesitation, then, ''I do love you, you know.''

Brandon felt the sting of unexpected tears. ''I love you, too, Kevin. Give my love to Lacey and Jason. And tell Dana she is not to have that baby until I get back.''

''She says you already warned her. She also says if you want her to delay things one second longer than nine months, then you can come back here and lumber around in her place.''

Brandon was chuckling when he hung up. ''I guess

I'd better hurry Lizzy along, if I want to be back in Boston for the birth of that great-grandbaby,'' he said as he closed the door to his room behind him.

In many ways, she and Brandon were perfectly suited traveling companions, Elizabeth thought as they took a midday break for lunch several days into the trip. In fact, she could already see that traveling with Brandon would be more torment than fulfillment, precisely because she was starting to recognize just how much she was destined to give up.

How would she explain walking away when it was obvious to anyone how compatible they were? She had a natural curiosity about everything, and Brandon seemed to have an unlimited store of knowledge and the patience to share it.

Even more important, they had similar views about the pace of their days. They lingered and explored. They enjoyed a stop for a glass of wine and idle conversation every bit as much as they did a visit to some must-see historical sight. Maybe they'd go home having missed a few places, but they'd have pleasurable impressions of everywhere they had been.

Impressions and snapshots, she corrected with a trace of amusement. She'd never seen a man so taken with a camera. He'd shot a dozen rolls of film already, most of it of her.

''What will you do with all those pictures?'' she'd asked, laughing as he urged her to pose yet again.

''Carry 'em in my wallet. Now just climb up on that boulder,'' he'd insisted, pointing out a rocky ledge. ''A little higher. Yes, that's perfect,'' he said as she teetered on the edge with a straight drop into a dried-up creek bed behind her. ''This one will be a dandy.''

He'd been so positive of that, he had rushed the entire roll of film to a same-day photo shop and waited impatiently while they'd been developed. When the pictures were finally spread on the counter for his inspection, he zeroed in on his favorite, a long-distance shot with wildflowers spread at her feet. He nodded in satisfaction.

''That one,'' he told the clerk. ''Make me an eleven-by-fourteen print. In fact, make me four of them.''

Lizzy stared at him. ''What on earth for?''

''One each for your daughters, one for my den and one for my bedside until the day I can talk you into marrying me.''

She was stunned into silence by the sweet gesture.

''What are you thinking?'' he demanded.

''I thought you always knew.''

''Not always. Spill it. What put that look on your face?''

''I was just thinking what a remarkable man you are.''

He nodded in satisfaction. ''Good, then. We're making progress.''

Some days he marked the advancement of their relationship in tiny, intangible measures. On other occasions, he anticipated giant leaps. Elizabeth liked the quiet, leisurely, undemanding days the best. They'd courted once under terrible time constraints. There was something tantalizing about setting an undemanding pace, especially with a man used to grabbing what he wanted without a second's thought or effort.

''I'm surprised with the kind of life you lead, that

you don't want to rush through everything,'' she told him as they lingered over a ridiculously large lunch that began with a spicy corn chowder and ended with light-as-air sopaipillas dusted with cinnamon and drizzled with honey.

''I've spent my whole life rushing. I deserve to slow down and savor things,'' he said, his glance fixed on her mouth in a way that left no doubts at all about just what he'd like to be savoring. She caught herself licking her lips self-consciously as he added, ''I'd rather see one thing in a day and enjoy it, than visit a dozen places and wind up remembering none of them.''

''Have you been to New Mexico before?''

''No, but it was at the top of my list. I read an article sometime back about a small town called Chimayo between Santa Fe and Taos. We'll go there one of these days.''

''Is one of the Indian pueblos there?''

''No, but there's a family of weavers there that goes back seven generations to the early 1800s. I can't wait to see how they work. A friend discovered them and sent me one of their small rugs.''

She regarded him with amusement. ''Somehow I don't think you're nearly as committed to this idea of retirement as you say you are.''

''Kevin said much the same thing the other day.''

She regarded him curiously. ''He called? When?''

''Tuesday. Wednesday. I'm not sure.''

''Why didn't you mention it earlier?''

''I suppose because I didn't want to get into the reason for his call.''

''Us,'' she said bluntly. ''He doesn't approve of us traveling together.''

''Something like that.''

He reached across the table and brushed a strand of hair back from her face with a gentleness that had her heart constricting in her chest. There was so much affection in his touch, so much yearning in his eyes.

"I'm sorry his call upset you," Lizzy said quietly.

"It didn't upset me," he said, though to her ears it didn't sound as if there was much conviction behind the denial.

"Then why do you look so sad?"

Brandon smiled at her then. "I didn't realize I did. Especially since being with you makes me very happy."

"How long can that go on, though, if your son doesn't approve?"

"Dammit, Lizzy, he'll come around. Besides, we're not a couple of teenagers who need permission to get married, much less to see each other."

Though there was a glint of determination in his eyes and an unyielding strength behind his tough words, Lizzy couldn't help but think Brandon was deluding himself. Kevin's opinion mattered to him, just as Kate's and Ellen's mattered to her. She and Brandon were the kind of people who had always centered their lives around family. They couldn't very well start denying the strength of the ties at this late date.

In the long run, though, what did it really matter? she thought with an air of resignation. She had no intention of ever marrying Brandon, so his relationship with his son would never be tested. It might get bruised a little perhaps, but it would never be irrevocably broken.

Determined to banish all dark thoughts for the remainder of whatever time they did have together, Elizabeth deliberately changed the subject. ''Where are we going next?''

''I thought an art gallery,'' he said eagerly.

''Perfect.''

At the gallery, though, she noted he seemed far more interested in a close inspection of the attire worn by the Indians in the spectacular Western paintings, than he did in each artist's skill with a brush.

That, added to the comments he'd made earlier about the town they would visit in a few days, gave her the leverage she knew she would need when the time came to send him back to Boston and for her to return to California alone.

Elizabeth thought of her argument often over the next few days, turning the precise words over and over in her head, preparing herself for the separation she knew was inevitable. In so doing, she knew she was robbing herself of the precious time they did have. The internal torment cast a pall over everything they did.

Instead of being grateful that Brandon continued to insist on being a perfect gentleman, retreating nightly to his own room, Elizabeth grew increasingly frustrated. She didn't want her last memories of him to be of their increasingly strained conversations, their fleeting, innocuous touches. She tried her darnedest to recall the precise techniques of seduction practiced by some of the more skilled heroines in the books she read. Then she moaned aloud at the absurdity of her imitating them.

''The next thing you know, you'll be calling up your granddaughter and asking to borrow her health class textbook,'' she grumbled to herself as she tossed and turned through another night. ''Silly, old woman,'' she added for good measure, but she didn't feel silly and she didn't feel old. She felt like a woman who was falling in love all over again and the roller-coaster thrill of it was nearly irresistible.

The curtains in her room billowed as the dry, desert air stirred and sent its chill across the room and through her heart. Bleak thoughts of long, empty days tormented her.

"Lizzy, is something wrong?" Brandon inquired the next morning over his spartan breakfast of black coffee and the half grapefruit she'd insisted he add to his menu. "You have shadows under your eyes. Haven't you been sleeping well?"

There was genuine concern in his voice, and for once his expression wasn't smug.

Elizabeth toyed with her own grapefruit sections. "I'm fine," she said without much spunk.

"We aren't moving around too fast, are we? We could settle in one place for a few weeks, if you'd rather. Maybe Taos. We could be there this afternoon."

"Are you sure you've seen everything you wanted to see in Santa Fe?"

"I've seen enough," he said, which wasn't really an answer to her question. "Now let me tell you more about Chimayo. We'll stop there on the way to Taos."

As they veered off the highway between Sante Fe and Taos, he began describing the small town, which was no more than a dot on the map, with an intimacy that suggested he'd been there often.

"Brandon, how many guidebooks did you read before you came to California?" she teased. "Is that all you did with your days after I left Boston?"

"No. I had no way of knowing we'd end up in New Mexico. This was just a spur-of-the-moment decision when I realized my being in California made you uncomfortable. I figured it was as good a place to run to as any.''

''Then how do you know so much about Chimayo?''

''Like I told you the other day, when you love textiles as much as I do, you stumble across other people who feel the same way. The Ortegas in Chimayo are like that from all I've read about them.''

She smiled faintly at his exuberance. ''So this is a busman's holiday, after all, despite those staunch denials you made the other day. I suppose you'll want to adapt what you see and work it into the Halloran line for next year.''

''Maybe so. I admit to having an insatiable curiosity when it comes to this kind of thing. I think southwestern style is very popular these days. Wouldn't hurt to tap into that market.''

In the showrooms, Brandon headed straight for the bright room to one side where a young man worked at his craft on a hand loom that was primitive by comparison to the modern machinery in Brandon's Boston plant. Threads of darkest brown and indigo slowly formed a pattern in the beige rug he was creating.

Elizabeth found herself grinning as Brandon edged closer and closer to study the weaver's technique. He asked one question, nodded at the response and fingered the yarns being used. That one question opened the floodgate to more.

Sensing that Brandon would be engaged for hours, Elizabeth explored the attached showroom and a second one next door. She picked up souvenirs for Ellen and Kate, books about the Southwest for her grandchildren and a small rug that would fit perfectly in her foyer for herself. Satisfied with her purchases, she lingered outdoors, taking in the unspoiled scenery.

When she finally went back inside, Brandon was still engrossed, this time with the woven jackets and vests on display. Elizabeth seized the evidence of his absorption and determined that the time was rapidly coming when she would have to use it as her only weapon to cut the ties between them.

Hours later, alone in a new hotel room, she stared silently out the window and prayed for the strength to do what had to be done, before she lost the will to do it at all.

The phone rang and she grabbed it, hoping that just this once Brandon's iron will had weakened and he would come share the night with her. To her disappointment, it was Ellen's voice that greeted her.

"Hi, Mom. I got your message, but I must say I'm surprised to catch you in this early."

"Brandon and I are both morning people. We usually get started at dawn."

"I hope I'm not interrupting anything," Ellen said, her voice thick with teasing innuendo.

"No, my darling daughter. Now, tell me, what's happening in Los Angeles."

"Nothing new here. I must say, though, that I've been wondering how things are going out there. You slipped out of town practically in the dead of night. Were you afraid Kate and I would talk you out of going?"

"Not you. You're the sort who'd hold the ladder if someone wanted to climb up and carry me off to elope."

"Kate, then?"

"Ellen, we both know how Kate reacts to anything

she considers a betrayal of your father. Add that to her general view of romance and she's probably not very happy with me now.''

''No, she isn't,'' Ellen admitted. ''That's why I'm calling. I barely prevented her from getting on a plane and flying off to rescue you.''

''It will probably make her feel better to know that I expect to be back in Los Angeles in a day or two.''

''Is Mr. Halloran coming with you?''

''No, dear. I think not.''

''But why?'' she asked, her disappointment evident.

''I just think it's best that way.''

''Okay, Mother, what's going on? Did you two have a spat?''

''No. I just think it's wiser if we don't turn our lives upside down at this late date.''

''What on earth is that supposed to mean? Surely you don't think you're too old to fall in love, especially with a man who's obviously head over heels for you? As for getting married at your age, why not? I know some couples don't because it affects their Social Security payments or something, but somehow I doubt that's an issue with a man like Brandon Halloran. He looks as if he has buckets of money.''

''More likely barrels,'' she said dryly. ''I'm not saying we'll lose touch entirely again, just that there's no reason to commit to anything drastic.''

''Since when did you think of marriage as a drastic measure? That sounds like Kate talking, not you.''

''Dear, your sister may be foolish with regard to her own social life, but she does occasionally have a valid point.''

''Not about this,'' Ellen argued. ''Mother, if you're having fun, don't run away from it. Surely you don't think you could be happy with one of those old geezers in polyester at the community center?''

''No. Maybe not,'' she said wearily. ''Darling, I'm very tired. It's been a long day. We'll discuss this more when I get home. Right now I'd like to get some sleep.''

''Okay,'' Ellen agreed with obvious reluctance. ''I love you.''

''I love you, too.'' She just hoped that Ellen never discovered the lengths to which she was going to prove that.

Brandon was wakened from a sound sleep by the ringing of the phone. He fumbled for it, then said hello in a voice husky with sleep.

''Mr. Halloran?''

''Yes,'' he said, his heart suddenly hammering at the unfamiliar voice. Kevin? Jason? Had something happened to one of them?

''This is Ellen Hayden, Elizabeth Newton's daughter.''

What on earth? He struggled upright in the bed and clutched the receiver even tighter. ''Yes, Ellen. What can I do for you?''

''I thought there was something you ought to know,'' she said after a slight hesitation.

He heard a soft moan, then a mumbled comment that sounded something like, ''Mother is going to kill me for this.''

He had a feeling she hadn't meant him to hear the last remark. He swallowed a chuckle. ''What do you think I should know?''

''Mother seems to have some crazy idea about packing up and coming home.''

Brandon felt as if the wind had been knocked out of him. "What? How do you know that? She hasn't said anything like that to me. We've just begun to see all the places we've talked about going to."

"That may be, but I just got off the phone with her and she told me she'd be back here in a day or so. When I asked why, she said some things that made absolutely no sense. I thought you ought to be prepared."

His heart thudded dully. "Prepared how? I can't very well hog-tie her and make her stay here with me, if she doesn't want to."

"But that's exactly what I think you should do," Ellen said with conviction. "I don't mean hog-tie her exactly. Oh, you know what I mean. Just don't take her words at face value. I'm convinced she's in love with you, but she's finding all kinds of excuses not to be. You do love her, don't you? I probably should have asked that straight off."

"I love her," he said, his voice tight. "And thank you for the warning. Elizabeth won't slip away from me, not without the fight of her life."

"I'm glad," Ellen said. "Good night, Mr. Halloran."

"Good night," he said softly. He had a hunch that Ellen was very much her mother's daughter and that they both spent a lot of time with stars in their eyes. All he had to do was figure out why his precious Lizzy was so damned determined to deny that.

Chapter Twelve

Brandon woke up at dawn with an oppressive sense of foreboding. It took him less than a minute to recall why. Ellen's late-night warning, he thought with dismay. He was grateful that she'd told him, but now that he knew, what was he supposed to do about it?

How the devil was he supposed to talk Lizzy out of going home? If he hadn't convinced her by now of the strength and endurance of their love, how could he expect to do it in the space of a single conversation or even a single act of passion? That one tender, memorable night they'd shared in Boston weeks ago certainly hadn't gotten through to her. She'd dashed off first thing the next morning as if all the hounds of hell were after her.

Tricks were out. So was hog-tying, despite its appeal to his take-charge nature. Persuasive words hadn't worked. What the dickens was left? Hell, he'd inundated her with flowers once, only to have her grumble about her allergies. He'd tried candy. He'd tried sentiment. He'd dusted off just about every last thing in his courtship repertoire. He was getting too damned old for all this mincing around. Maybe he ought to fly her to Las Vegas, stand her in front of a minister and dare her to say anything short of "I do."

Before he could come up with a plan, his phone rang.

"Mr. Halloran?"

"Yes?"

"This is John Vecchio."

His heart seemed to constrict at the unexpected sound of the detective's voice. "How did you track me down?" he inquired testily.

"Finding people is what I'm best at," the man reminded him.

"But why would you even be looking for me?"

"Actually I was doing a job for someone else and something came up I thought you had a right to know about since it fits in with the investigation I was doing for you."

"Who hired you?" Brandon asked with deadly calm. He suspected he already knew the answer, and if he was right, there was going to be hell to pay back in Boston.

"That's confidential," the detective replied glibly.

"If the person who hired you is confidential, then it seems to me whatever you learned ought to be, too. Am I right?"

The man had the grace to sputter a bit at that. "Well, yes, I suppose. Although in this instance, it was made quite clear that you were to get the report."

Brandon lost it at that. Whatever curiosity he might

normally have felt was overshadowed by fury. ''Well, you tell your client, whoever the hell he might be, that he can take his damned report and... Well, never mind. He'll get the picture.''

''But, sir, I think he's right. You'd definitely want to know this.''

''No,'' Brandon said adamantly, ''I wouldn't.''

He slammed the phone back into its cradle and stood staring at it as if it were a nasty rattler about to strike. Before he could think twice, he snatched it back up and punched in Kevin's office number. When his secretary, Harriet answered, he demanded to speak to his son.

''He's on another line,'' she said. She served all three Halloran men but she'd been with Brandon the longest and knew all of his moods. She tried to buy Kevin some time. ''Shall I have him call you back?''

''No, you'll get him off whatever damned call he's on and put me through. If he knows what's good for him, he'll get on this line before I completely lose my patience.''

''Yes, sir,'' Harriet said. ''Is everything all right, Mr. Halloran?''

''Do I sound as if everything's all right?''

''No, not really.''

''That's very perceptive of you, Harriet. Now get Kevin.''

''Yes, of course. I'm sorry, sir.''

If he could have paced the room with the phone in his hand, he'd have done it. Instead, the short cord kept him in place, which added to his foul temper.

''Dad?'' Kevin said finally. ''What's wrong?''

''You know damned good and well what's wrong. You hired that detective, didn't you? How did you know which one to go to? Did you have Mrs. Farnsworth go digging around in my desk for you?''

Kevin sighed. ''No, actually the bill happened to come in yesterday. I know you're probably upset, Dad. But it's better that you know this now, before you get in any deeper.''

''Kevin, I know everything I need to know about Elizabeth. I told you that before and I meant it. I refused to listen to a word that detective had to say. The only reason I'm calling you is to tell you once and for all that I have had enough of your ridiculous suspicions and your meddling. If you ever expect to see me again, if you ever expect to have a civil conversation with me, you will drop this now!''

''But, Dad—''

''Goodbye,'' Brandon said. He hung up and then called the hotel operator. ''I want no more calls put through to this room. None.''

Whatever the hell his son had found out or thought he'd discovered didn't matter. He took a deep, calming breath and shoved his hand through his hair. He couldn't be at his persuasive best with Lizzy if he was all worked up like this. He deliberately forced himself to empty his mind, to dismiss the past fifteen minutes as if they'd never happened.

He could hardly wait to leave the entire incident behind. As a result, when he stepped out of his room and walked over to Elizabeth's, he still didn't have a detailed plan in mind. He rapped on the door. She took so long coming, he wondered if she'd fled during the night, and he found that more worrisome by far than any slander Kevin had intended to spread.

The door opened and Brandon's gaze took in the cool linen slacks, the rose-colored blouse, the careful makeup that made her eyes seem brighter and more compelling than ever, but didn't hide the shadows beneath. His heart ached at the prospect of losing her, especially without ever understanding why.

"Morning, Lizzy," he said and before he even realized what he intended, he hauled her into his arms for a bruising kiss that left them both gasping for breath.

"What on earth?" she murmured, her expression bemused. Her hands clung to his shoulders. "Brandon, have you taken leave of your senses?"

"No, Lizzy. I don't believe so. I believe I've just come to my senses."

"What is that supposed to mean?"

"It's just fair warning, woman. You and I have some serious things to talk about today. I figure on having a hearty breakfast and some straight answers." He scowled when he said it, so she'd know he meant business.

"About what?" she asked warily.

"Whatever you're up to," he said, figuring the enigmatic answer could take whatever meaning she wanted it to.

She immediately looked guilty, and he knew then that Ellen's fears weren't unfounded. Lizzy intended to run from him.

And, despite the way his son felt about it, Brandon intended to do everything he could to prevent her going.

Brandon certainly was in an odd mood this morning, Elizabeth thought edgily as she tried to recover from that breath-stealing kiss and the knockout punch of his warning. It was a mood that told her she'd been right to pick now as the time to flee. She couldn't withstand many more kisses like that one, not if she wanted to keep a clear head. As for answers, she had plenty. Yet none of them were likely to be the ones he wanted.

They settled at a table on an outdoor terrace, surrounded by flowering cactus. Brandon was as good as his word. He ordered bacon, eggs, hash browns and blueberry muffins. Without sparing her a glance, he ordered the same for her. Apparently he figured on needing stamina for the conversation he intended to have.

Elizabeth looked at all that food, considered the implications and felt her stomach churn. She tried to will herself to say the words she'd rehearsed again and again during the night.

A simple goodbye should have come easily, especially since she knew all the reasons why it had to be said. After all, they had parted twice before. If nothing else, practice should have made the phrasing perfect. But this one made her heart ache because she knew it was irrevocable. Brandon had put pride, love and commitment on the line by chasing after her. He wouldn't take yet another rejection.

Elizabeth surreptitiously studied him and dreaded ruining the morning. Maybe she could wait until after breakfast, she decided, furious at the weakness that that implied, but grateful for the reprieve.

What was so terrible? she argued with herself. She was putting it off a half hour, an hour at most. Sitting across the breakfast table from Brandon had become one of the highlights of her day. There was an intimacy to sharing the first part of the day with him that she knew she'd never forget.

A sigh trembled on her lips. How she would miss the easy, companionable talks about the news, the thrill of studying his face as his expressions shifted from amusement to sorrow, from troubled to angry as he studied the headlines. Even more, she would miss the lazy planning of their day.

Capturing every last memory she could, she delayed telling him as long as possible. They were through breakfast and Brandon was on his second cup of coffee by the time she found the courage.

''Brandon, I've come to a decision,'' Lizzy blurted finally, seizing the initiative he had threatened to steal. She desperately needed whatever edge might be gained by saying her piece first.

''About what?'' he inquired, lowering the newspaper he'd been reading for the past ten minutes. His gaze locked with hers. His brow furrowed in a show of concern. ''What is it, Lizzy? You sound so serious.''

''I am serious. I'm going home.''

The paper slid from his grasp as an expression she judged to be incredulous spread across his face. Or was it astonishment, after all? she wondered after a moment's study. Her own gaze narrowed. Brandon looked as if he'd actually anticipated the announcement, but how could that be?

''Why?'' he inquired with no evidence of the fury she'd expected. Instead, he was all solicitous concern. ''Aren't you feeling well?''

''I feel just fine,'' she mumbled, trying to figure out where she'd missed the mark with her strategy. Not that she'd wanted him to fight her decision, but this absolute calm was definitely disconcerting.

''Are you homesick already? Do you miss your

family? I must say I'm rather glad mine's out from underfoot.''

''It's not that,'' she said, increasingly uncomfortable under his penetrating eyes. This was the part she'd hoped to avoid, this intense scrutiny of her motives. She didn't want to have to sugarcoat the truth. She was no good at it.

''What is it then?'' he asked.

She could explain part of it, but certainly not all. She drew in a deep breath and tried to tell him what was in her heart. ''I went against everything that was right and proper more than forty years ago. I can't do it again.''

Lizzy wasn't surprised that Brandon regarded her as if she'd lost her marbles. The sudden surge of propriety was rather belated.

''What the devil are you talking about?'' he asked.

''This,'' she said with a gesture that encompassed the terrace, the inn, maybe even all of New Mexico. ''We're sneaking around like a couple of adolescents.''

''There's one surefire way to fix that,'' he countered without missing a beat. ''Marry me.''

She was just as quick to respond. ''No,'' she said in a rush before she dared to consider the offer. The rest came more slowly, because she had to make it up as she went along, watching his reactions, altering the excuse as necessary. ''I can't leave my family and you can't leave your work. I saw that yesterday.''

''Saw what, for goodness' sake?'' he asked, his expression thoroughly puzzled.

He still wasn't angry, though. She found his lack of outrage just a little insulting. ''You,'' she said grumpily. ''At that weaving place. You'll never truly retire,

Brandon. You love it too much. You belong back in Boston with your business, your friends, your family.''

Once again he looked only slightly surprised. ''Just because I looked at some old rugs, you're ready to throw away everything?''

''I won't take you away from that.'' If she'd meant it to sound noble, she failed miserably. Even to her own ears, she sounded like a woman grasping at straws.

''You're not taking me away from a damn thing, woman. You're giving me a future.'' His gaze narrowed. ''Lizzy, what's really going on with you? I've never heard such a trumped-up batch of excuses from a woman in all my days. Even forty-nine years ago you were more inventive.''

''Think what you will,'' she said stubbornly. ''That's the way it has to be. You're not ready for retirement.''

Despite her best intentions, tears sprang to her eyes as she confronted the actuality of losing him. He was on his feet in a heartbeat then, gathering her into his arms. Suddenly all she wanted to do was weep and have him promise that everything was going to work out just fine. When a man like Brandon said such a thing, he had a way of making it happen. She wondered, though, if even he could perform miracles.

''Oh, Lizzy,'' he soothed. ''I'll never set foot in that company of mine again, if that's what you're worried about. It's time for Jason and Kevin to have their turn, anyway. Now tell me what's really behind all this. No man could love a woman more than I love you, more than I have loved you all these years. Surely you know that.''

"But why?" she said miserably. "Why do you love me?"

"That's like asking why the sky is blue, Lizzy. It just is. From the moment I saw you running barefoot through the grass all those years ago in Maine, something within me turned inside out. There was a look about you, such a joyous zest for living. I felt as if being around you would be like basking in sunshine my whole life."

"That was so long ago, though. You were about to go off to war. You knew you could be killed. It was natural to want to grab hold of life. But what about now?"

"Nothing's changed," he said gently. "I still see endless possibilities when I look into your eyes. I still hear bells ringing when I hear your voice. I still feel sunshine when I touch you."

The beautiful, tender words spilled over Lizzy like a cozy comforter, wrapping her in warmth. The only problem was they were based on a dreadful misperception.

Those words he'd suffused with so much love brought on a fresh bout of tears and decades worth of self-recriminations. How could he possibly love her, when she knew for a fact she was a liar and a cheat?

"You don't know me, Brandon. I've done terrible things," she blurted out, then almost died from the regret that ripped through her. She'd done it now. She had really done it. He would poke and prod until the truth came out. All of it.

"Shh, Lizzy. Hush that kind of talk," he whispered, rubbing her back.

Brandon scooped her up, then sat back down and settled her on his lap, oblivious to everything and everyone around them. She wanted with all her heart to rest her head on his shoulder and pretend that there were no problems, no reasons why they could never be married. She wanted to cling to the memory of the way the sun felt on her shoulders, the way his arms felt around her at this precise instant. Those were the memories she'd cherish for the rest of her life.

"What do you mean terrible?" he chastised. "You couldn't do a terrible thing if you tried."

She had to prove he was wrong about that and about her. There was only one way to do it, one way to put an end to this charade of a love affair once and for all.

"I've lied," she told him, slowly daring to lift her gaze to meet his. Tears streamed unchecked down her cheeks. There was no need to wipe them away, when more were certain to follow. "For nearly fifty years, I've lied."

"About what? What on earth would you need to lie about?" he said, and now there truly was astonishment on his face. "And even if you did, so what? Nothing could be as bad as you're making it out to be."

"You wouldn't say that if you knew," she said, finally taking the handkerchief he offered and blotting up the tears, only to have more spill down her cheeks.

"Then tell me," he said matter-of-factly in a tone that promised understanding and forgiveness that she doubted he would offer if he knew everything. "Whatever it is, we'll handle it together," he vowed.

Elizabeth supposed she must have known from the moment the conversation started—no, even before that, when they'd met again—that Brandon would have to know the truth eventually. It was not the sort of thing she could hide forever from the man she loved, even though she'd hidden it for decades from the daughter she adored.

Now that she'd admitted to keeping some deep, dark secret, it seemed there was no way to prevent revealing it at long last. Even if she tried, Brandon would hound her forever for an adequate explanation.

"It's Ellen," she began slowly. "I've lied to my daughter." She looked into his eyes, then away. "And to you," she said in no more than a whisper, filled with regret.

She couldn't be sure, but it seemed for an instant he might have already guessed. But he waited for her to go on. She clung to his hand, trying to draw on his strength, desperate for the forgiveness he'd promised.

"Finish," he said quietly, his gaze riveted to hers. In his eyes there was no mistaking the storm already brewing. It was as if he anticipated the rest even before she found enough courage to say it.

She knew now there was no turning back. She kept her chin up. It was a matter of pride that she also kept her voice steady. "Ellen is our daughter, Brandon. Yours and mine."

Chapter Thirteen

The tension on the bricked patio of Kevin and Lacey's Beacon Hill house was suddenly so thick it was difficult to breathe the lilac-scented air. Kevin had invited Jason, Dana and Sammy over for one last luncheon before he and Lacey officially moved their residence to Cape Cod. After the closing on the sale of this house in the morning, they would keep an apartment in the city for use during the week.

Some of the rooms were already empty. Walking through the nearly barren house hadn't affected Kevin nearly as much as he'd expected it to. He was looking forward to building a new life with his wife.

Lacey had never liked this house and Jason had lived in it only briefly. Kevin's son had always preferred the smaller house he'd grown up in, more than this one that Lacey referred to as a mausoleum. They'd kept the other house, renting it out, and several years ago Jason had bought it from them and was about to start filling up its rooms with his own family.

As a result, this day, which was winding down now with coffee and dessert on the patio, seemed more of a celebration than a bittersweet farewell. At least it had until Kevin shattered the festive mood with his bombshell.

"You did what!" three members of the Halloran family exclaimed in unison when he told them about hiring his father's detective to do a further check on Elizabeth Newton.

"Well, you don't have to act so horrified," he shot back defensively. "Dad's obviously not thinking straight or he never would have done something this foolish. Somebody had to look out for his interests."

"Darling, what is so foolish about your father wanting some companionship in his life?" Lacey asked.

"Lacey's right," Dana chimed in. "I think the whole story of how he and Elizabeth were separated and how he found her again is rather sweet. Downright romantic in fact."

"There are plenty of women right here in Boston. Women we know," Kevin argued, though he could see now that it was a useless protest. Obviously no one saw this the way he did. In fact, none of them knew what he'd discovered about Elizabeth Forsythe Newton. He was only just now beginning to absorb the implications himself. She had an illegitimate daughter, a daughter only slightly older than himself. Given ev-erything else he knew about his father's obsession with this woman, it was possible this daughter was his half sister.

"In other words, you figured you had the right to choose for him, just as he tried to choose for you before we got married,'' Lacey countered with quiet calm and a deadly accuracy that had Kevin wincing. ''Darling,'' she said, ''don't you see what you're doing?''

''I am trying to protect my father from a woman he obviously knows nothing about.'' Was it possible though, that his father did know, that he had kept such a secret from all of them?

''He knows he loves her,'' Jason said quietly. ''Dad, I really think we have to trust him. If he's happy, isn't that all that matters?''

Kevin tried one last time to make them see his point. ''But if he knew everything—''

''Maybe he does,'' Lacey said. ''And maybe it doesn't matter to him.''

''It *would* matter,'' Kevin said darkly. ''I think I know Dad better than any of you, and I'm telling you that it would matter.''

He picked up the detective's report that had thoroughly shaken him and offered it to them. ''Read it for yourselves. You'll see what I mean.''

But after exchanging glances, not one of them took him up on the offer. It appeared they were all as stubborn as his father. They'd rather avoid the truth than deal with it.

''You called Granddad about it, didn't you?'' Jason asked mildly.

''Yes.''

''Would he listen?''

''No,'' Kevin admitted in frustration. ''He hung up on me.''

''Darling, if Brandon didn't want to hear the report, then I think we should respect that,'' Lacey said.

"Frankly, if I were you, I'd burn the damn thing and try to forget you ever read it yourself."

"How the devil am I supposed to do that?" he demanded, then sighed deeply. "Okay, fine then. But I just hope it isn't too late when Dad finds this out. You think my telling him is a mistake, but when the information comes out eventually, I'm convinced he'll never recover from it."

"Maybe not," Lacey said gently, "but it's not up to you to deliver the blow. If your father finds out whatever it is some other way and is truly distressed by it, then it will be up to all of us to support him the same way he's been there for us anytime we've been in trouble."

"I suppose you're right," Kevin conceded reluctantly. But God help them all when the information finally was revealed. With the sort of moral code his father had always adhered to, with his absolute belief in honesty, Kevin was convinced that his father would be inconsolable when he learned the truth about Elizabeth Forsythe Newton and her illegitimate daughter.

Nothing in his life had prepared Brandon for the emotions that thundered through him at Lizzy's announcement. Shock was chased by rage, only to be replaced by a terrible, terrible sense of loss.

Brandon thought of the beautiful, gracious woman who'd greeted him back in California with a delighted twinkle in her blue eyes. Those eyes were alive like Lizzy's and the same color as his own. She had hair that caught the light in its burnished gold strands. Knowing what he knew now, he could see the Halloran genes at play.

He thought of the generous, caring woman who'd

risked her mother's wrath last night in an attempt to keep Lizzy from making a mistake she would regret the rest of her life. That action bore Lizzy's sense of daring and his own determination.

That lovely, strong woman was his daughter, the daughter he'd never known, never even dreamed existed.

At least he finally understood why Lizzy had been jumpy as a june bug whenever he mentioned going to California, why she'd been so determined to keep him away, why she'd turned so pale when he'd shown up at Ellen's. Lizzy had been right to be afraid. The aftershocks from this would keep their worlds trembling for a long time to come. If this was what Kevin had discovered, what must he think? No wonder he'd been so distraught.

Brandon needed to be alone for a minute. He needed to gather his thoughts. He didn't want to say something to Elizabeth in anger. He didn't want to hurl terrible accusations at this woman he'd loved so deeply for so long. He wanted to go someplace and search his soul for the right way out of this.

There was no denying the depth of hurt he felt at Lizzy's betrayal. My God, he had a daughter and grandchildren he could claim. A daughter he'd met only fleetingly. Grandchildren he'd never even seen.

''Does she know?'' he asked finally, his voice toneless, wondering if that explained the reason for last night's call. Had Ellen spent a lifetime yearning for a father she thought had abandoned her? Had she worried that this chance to have her parents reunited was slipping away? Starry-eyed and sentimental, had she envisioned a future as a family?

''No,'' Lizzy said, robbing him of the fantasy. Then

at his look of dismay, she added in a rush, "She can never know, Brandon. Never."

"Why the hell not?" he shot back.

Her eyes flashed at his tone, but her voice was even. "Because David Newton adopted Ellen when we got married. She was just a baby. I owed him for being willing to take on another man's child. I vowed to him that she would never know. He was the only father she ever knew, and he couldn't have loved her more if she'd been his own. He gave her stability. You can't want me to rob her of that."

Lizzy couldn't have hurt Brandon more if she'd taken a knife and cut out his heart. Another man had known his daughter's love. Another man had been there to care for her, to nurture her. He'd been robbed of all that. And even now Lizzy expected him to keep the secret, to protect her lie.

"What about the truth, Lizzy?" he said, as a bone-deep weariness stole through him. For the first time since Grace's death he felt every one of his sixty-eight years. "Didn't you think you owed her the truth? And what about me? All these years, all this time I've thought there was nothing left to connect us, but you knew differently." He regarded her angrily. "Just how hard did you try to find me back then? Or was it easier to find some poor, unselfish bastard and let him take my place?"

She looked as if he'd slapped her. For an instant he was filled with regret and then the rage began to build again until he was almost blinded by it.

"I don't deserve that," she said just as angrily. "I did the best I could. I was seventeen when you left, eigh-teen when Ellen was born. For all I knew you were dead."

He studied Elizabeth as if he'd never seen her before. The woman he'd fallen in love with would have been incapable of such lies, such deceit. The fact that she expected him to perpetuate it simply proved that she didn't know him at all, either. He felt as if all his dreams and illusions had been shattered with a single blow. Maybe that's what came of trying to recapture the past. It would never live up to the memory.

''I have to get away,'' he said. He dragged himself to his feet as if he had no energy left for anything.

''Brandon, please,'' she whispered, her face pale and panic in her eyes. ''I'm sorry. Whatever else you think, you must believe that I never meant to hurt you. Maybe it wasn't your fault, but you simply weren't there. I had to do something. Stay. Let's talk about it.''

''Not now, Lizzy,'' he said, unable to even meet her gaze. ''Dammit, not now.''

Elizabeth trembled as Brandon vanished from sight, leaving her at a table cluttered with dishes. There went her life, she thought with a cry of dismay, even as she also thought, how dare he make judgments? Though she had to let him go, had no choice really, she resented his accusations while accepting the blame for his despair. For the first time in her life, she felt defeated.

Her shoulders shook with silent sobs, which she barely managed to contain until she got back to her room. Then she flung herself onto the bed and cried for what seemed like hours, cried in a way she hadn't since she'd sent Brandon off to war. It was much, much later when she finally fell into an exhausted sleep, only to have troubled dreams that gave no peace.

It was hours before she woke to the sound of knocking on the door. She opened it to find Brandon looking haggard and defeated. She would have given anything to have the right to console him, but this morning had taken away all of her rights where he was concerned.

"Are you okay?" she asked, thinking that in her worst nightmares he had never taken the news like this. He'd been rocked, but never destroyed. What had she done to him? What had she done to all of them?

"I'm just shell-shocked, I think," he said. "May I come in?"

"Of course," she said, stepping aside.

When he was in the room, he finally met her gaze, then took in the reddened eyes, the rumpled clothes. "What about you? Are you okay?"

"I'm sad more than anything. Sad over what you've been deprived of. Sadder still that Ellen hasn't had the same chance to know you that I have."

He sat on the edge of the bed, his hands folded together, his shoulders slumped. "I need answers, Lizzy."

Her own hands clenched, she sat in the chair opposite him. "I'll tell you whatever I can."

"Will you tell me what she was like as a baby? Can you describe her first words, her first steps?" he demanded heatedly. "Was she a good student? Did she go to college? Is her marriage strong? What about my grandchildren? How can you possibly expect to tell me everything I want to know?"

She drew in a deep breath and decided she would dare one more risk. "If you come back to California with me for a few days, I'll show you her baby book. I'll bring out all the photo albums, the old movies. If it will help you, I will tell you every single thing I can remember.''

''A lifetime of memories in how long, Lizzy? A single afternoon? An evening?''

''In however long it takes.''

''But you won't let me spend time with her. You won't let me claim her. You'll expect me to get on a plane and go back to Boston and forget all about her. Is that it?''

Though his wistful expression came close to breaking her heart, she whispered, ''Yes. That's how it has to be.''

As if he were unable to bear her sad expression, he got up and crossed the room. Brandon stood at the window, gazing out at the last flames of an orange sunset. Elizabeth found she couldn't even appreciate the beauty of the splashy display. She doubted he could, either.

''Will you tell me one more thing?'' he asked finally. ''Why did you do it, Lizzy? Why did you keep on lying to me?'' He turned to face her, his expression bleak. ''When you came to Boston, why in God's name didn't you tell me everything then?''

''Brandon, I've had years to go over and over the decision I made when I married David Newton. No matter how I look at it, even now knowing that you're alive, that you still love me, I think what I did was what I had to do for Ellen's sake.''

''I can't argue with you about what you decided then,'' he conceded reluctantly. ''As much as I'd like to think I have a right to criticize your choice, I know that you did what you did out of love for your daughter. But what about now?''

He met her gaze steadily then, holding it until she trembled inside.

"What about now, Lizzy?" he demanded again. "David Newton wouldn't hold you to that promise now. If he was as fine a man as you've told me, he wouldn't deny a daughter the chance to know her natural father."

"You make it sound so simple," she said.

"It is."

"No!" she argued as if her life depended on it. "Don't you see? If the truth comes out now, she'll hate me. She'll never forgive me for lying to her all this time. I know you'll think it's selfish, but I don't think I could bear losing her. And I'm not so sure she could stand it, either. Kate was always her father's daughter, but Ellen, she was mine. Just as Kate mourned her father's death, I think Ellen would mourn the loss of her trust in me."

As she said it, she knew she was leaving the fate of her relationship with her daughter in Brandon's hands. If he chose to ignore her wishes, there was nothing she could do about it. She simply had to trust him to reach a conclusion they all could live with.

Funny, she thought, almost unable to bear the irony, it all came down to trust again. Years ago she hadn't trusted Brandon's love enough to wait for him despite the lack of letters. Now she had no choice but to place her trust in a man whom she'd betrayed in a way he might never be able to forgive.

"There's no point in talking about this anymore tonight. I think it's best if we sleep on it," Brandon told her finally.

Right now he wanted to argue with her, wanted to tell her that Ellen would understand, but how could he make that sort of promise when his own world was shaken as it had never been before? If he was having trouble with the truth, if he felt this horrible, aching sense of loss, what would Lizzy's Ellen feel? Did he dare to turn her world upside down?

"I don't know how long I'll be able to stand the uncertainty," Lizzy said, her expression imploring him to reach a final decision now.

"I'm sorry. I don't think we'll find any answers tonight. All I can promise is that I won't do anything rash. We'll take our time and decide together what's best."

If his promise wasn't enough to reassure her, that was unfortunate. It was the best he could do. He gathered from her miserable expression that it wasn't enough.

"Don't try running out on me, Lizzy," he warned. "That won't solve anything."

"Brandon, please. I think it's best if I go back to California first thing in the morning. There's no future for us. I owe that much to my daughter and, for that matter, to you. It would kill you to keep silent around her day in and day out knowing what you know."

"She is *our* daughter," he reminded her angrily, forgetting all about the resolve to let things be until morning when he'd be calmer, more rational. "Remember, I do know the truth now. Maybe it wouldn't be right to claim her, but I do intend to get to know her with or without your blessing. When you go back to California, I intend to be right by your side. You owe me that."

Her eyes widened in dismay. "You can't," she breathed. "Oh, Brandon, no. Please don't be that cruel."

"To whom, Lizzy? You or Ellen?"

"Both of us. How would I ever explain what you're doing there?"

"That's your problem," he said coldly. "I've told you that I will do nothing to hurt Ellen. That's the last thing I want. But I believe it's always better to know the truth than to try to protect lies."

Brandon left her then, because he was afraid to stay. He was afraid that the terrible pain he saw in her eyes would begin to touch him. He was terrified that the love he'd treasured for so long would force him to try to understand, to forgive—not the past, but the lies of the last few weeks.

He couldn't allow that to happen. Right now, his anger was the only thing sustaining him. Without it he wasn't sure how he'd survive the hurt.

Chapter Fourteen

Brandon's harsh words, which carried the weight of a threat, were still ringing in Elizabeth's ears as she returned alone to California first thing the next morning. Despite his warning, she hadn't been able to bear a single second more of the condemnation in Brandon's eyes.

Nor had she wanted to put him to the test. If he came with her, surely there would be hell to pay. The truth would be out and there would be nothing she could do to stop it. She might not be able to prevent him from following her, but she would not willingly set things up for him to destroy her daughter's life.

Not that having Brandon for a father would be so terrible. He was a wonderful, loving man. But he was not the father Ellen had known and loved. He was not the one who had taught her that honesty was a trait to be treasured and deceit something to be scorned. Ellen wouldn't blame Brandon for the lies, but she would blame Elizabeth.

Back home alone, though, she discovered no peace. Elizabeth wasn't sure how long she could weather the terrible strain of waiting for Brandon to make good on his threat. When he didn't come on the next flight to Los Angeles, she took heart. When he didn't appear the next day, she began to believe that he might not come at all. That didn't stop her from worrying.

With each hour that passed, each day, she anticipated the worst. Every time the phone rang she flinched. When Ellen's car turned into the driveway, she panicked, certain that her daughter was coming to denounce her for a lifetime of lies.

"Okay, Mother, I've had it. What's wrong?" Ellen asked when she arrived unexpectedly on a Saturday morning in early May.

Elizabeth had been home for nearly a week and was still as jumpy as she had been on her first day back in Los Angeles. "What do you mean?" she asked quietly, trying to calm her nerves.

"You haven't been the same since you went on that trip with Brandon Halloran. You look exhausted. You haven't been out of the house, even to visit us. You don't call. Kate's worried that you're ill."

She was ill, heartsick in fact, but not in any way she could explain to them.

"I'm fine," she said.

"You look as if you haven't been sleeping."

"Just a touch of insomnia. I'm sure it will pass. In fact, I'm feeling rather sleepy right now. If you don't mind, dear, I think as soon as you leave, I'll go upstairs and have a little nap."

Ellen regarded her intently, looked as if she wanted

to ask something more, then sighed. ''Go ahead, if you're tired,'' she said finally. ''I can let myself out.''

Elizabeth slowly climbed the stairs, leaving Ellen to stare after her, her brow furrowed.

Upstairs, Elizabeth stretched out on top of the bedspread, stared up at the ceiling and waited for the sound of the front door closing. Instead she heard Ellen's low murmurings, followed a short time later by the sound of a car arriving, not departing. It didn't require razor-sharp intelligence to guess that Kate had joined Ellen downstairs.

Obviously her daughters intended to gang up on her to get some answers. Given a choice Elizabeth would have pulled the covers over her head and hidden out until they both found pressing business elsewhere. Knowing that levelheaded Kate was stubborn enough to outwait her, she got up, applied a dash of blusher to her cheeks and went down to face the music.

''Hello, darling,'' she greeted Kate pleasantly, as if she'd expected to find her camped out on the living room sofa looking through old issues of a news magazine. ''I thought you'd be on a tennis court on such a beautiful afternoon.''

''That's exactly where I will be, if you own up to what's bugging you in the next ten minutes.''

''Dear, there's no reason to miss your game on my account. Are you playing with that nice young man from the law firm?''

Kate rolled her eyes. ''You'll never give up, will you? No, Mother, I am playing doubles with a married couple and one of their friends who is visiting from Boston.''

Elizabeth felt a dull ache in her chest. ''Boston?''

Ellen regarded her speculatively. ''Mother, look at

yourself. The mere mention of the city practically turns you green. What on earth happened between you and Brandon Halloran?''

Elizabeth forced a smile. ''Certainly nothing you need to worry yourselves about. Kate, tell me about this blind date.''

''It is *not* a blind date. Their friend is a woman. I think she's in the fashion business somehow.''

Fashions? Textiles? Was it possible she knew Brandon? Elizabeth wondered, then dismissed the possibility with a sigh. ''Well, I don't suppose it matters whom you're playing tennis with. You shouldn't stand them up. Just run along, darling. You really needn't worry about me. I'm feeling much better since my nap.''

''What nap? You haven't been upstairs more than a half hour. I'm not going anywhere without a few answers,'' Kate said firmly. ''Sit down, Mother. Stop fluttering around as if you can't wait to get away from me. Ellen, you go make a pot of tea.''

Ellen took the order more cheerfully than usual. ''Has anybody mentioned how bossy you are?'' she inquired as she exited.

''That's how I got to be a lawyer,'' Kate called after her. ''I absolutely love all that undivided attention I get in a courtroom. Hurry up with that tea. I want raspberry if there is any.''

''You know I always keep raspberry for you,'' Elizabeth said. ''I'll go fix it. Ellen will never find it.''

''Ellen is the best scavenger I know,'' Kate corrected. ''Sit, Mother. You're not sneaking off on me.''

''I can't imagine what you're so worked up over.''

''Then your imagination is getting senile, which I seriously doubt. What the devil happened on that trip to New Mexico? Ever since you got back I've had a hard time telling if you're in mourning or terrified."

She'd never judged Kate as being that perceptive, Elizabeth thought dully. What a terrible time to discover she'd been mistaken. "Kate, you're exaggerating," she said with feigned cheer. "Naturally seeing Brandon again stirred up some old memories. Nothing more."

Kate rolled her eyes. "*Nothing more?* Mother, you are not the kind of woman who engages in some casual fling."

"Who said it was casual?"

"Well, you just dismissed that entire trip as if it were of no more importance than a visit to the dentist."

"Which reminds me, dear. Have you made that appointment to have your teeth cleaned?"

"Mother!"

"Kate, when exactly did you get to be older than I am?"

Her daughter started to interrupt, but Elizabeth held up her hand. She had to stop this now. She could maintain this cheery facade for just so long.

"Let me finish," she insisted. "I appreciate all the love and concern you and your sister are showing, but when I want your advice or your interference, I'll ask for it."

Ellen came in just in time to hear her little speech and almost dropped the tray of hot tea. Kate was regarding Elizabeth indignantly.

"If you don't want our help—"

"I don't."

"But—"

"There are no buts about it. Ellen, set the tray over

here. I'll pour the tea.'' She might not be able to do much about some aspects of her life at the moment, but by golly, she was not going to relinquish control of the rest of it. She beamed at her two precious and meddlesome worrywarts. ''You will stay for tea, won't you?''

Ellen and Kate exchanged a rueful look. Kate finally sighed. ''Of course.''

''I wouldn't want you to be late for your tennis game, though,'' Elizabeth said.

''You wouldn't be trying to rush us out of here, would you Mother?'' Ellen inquired.

Elizabeth adopted her most innocent expression. ''Never, darling. You know how I love to have you drop by.''

For once, though, she would be very, very glad to see them go.

Brandon couldn't get the image of Ellen Hayden out of his mind. He was enchanted with the thought of having a daughter. He wanted to know what she thought, how she spent her days, what the man she'd married was like, whether she was happy.

And with every day that went by, he was more and more inclined to push his way into her life and damn the consequences.

Lizzy's departure from New Mexico by dawn's early light had infuriated him. He'd raced to the airport, intent on following her, but at the last second he'd reconsidered. There was no purpose in going to California until he'd taken the time to think this situation through rationally. He'd caught a flight to Boston instead.

He'd been back in Boston for nearly two weeks before anyone in the family found out about his return. He'd sent Mrs. Farnsworth on an extended holiday before leaving for California, so he'd had the house to himself all that time. Unable to bear the thought of seeing a soul, he'd been a virtual hermit from the moment he'd arrived.

This morning, though, he was drinking some of the lousiest coffee he'd ever tasted, when he heard a key turn in the front door. He peeked between the drawn drapes and saw Dana's car in the driveway. Walking toward the foyer, he saw her step inside. He waited until she'd turned around and spotted him before saying anything.

"You sneaking in here to steal the silver?" he inquired dryly.

She scowled at him, but he had to admit she didn't seem all that surprised to see him.

"Actually, I'm on a mission," she confessed readily.

"Oh?"

"Word has it around the office that you've vanished without a trace."

"If I'm missing, why are you here?"

"It seems to me that a man who's hurting might sneak home to lick his wounds."

He shot her a dark look. "Who says I'm hurting?"

"Your son the mathematician, who apparently adds two and two better than the rest of us."

"What the devil does that mean?"

"It means that Kevin has been trying to track you down for the past two weeks. When he couldn't find you in New Mexico or in California, he guessed what had happened."

"So why isn't he here? I would have thought he'd want to gloat."

"Actually, quite the contrary. He had the distinct impression you might not want to talk to him about this. So I was elected. Unfortunately I have no idea what *this* is. Care to clue me in?" she asked. "And do you mind if we sit down? It's getting harder and harder to stay on my feet. This great-grandbaby of yours weighs a ton."

"You ought to stop feeding it all those salty pickles and fattening brownies," he said as he led the way back into the dining room. "Lord knows what kind of eating disorders that poor child will have." He pulled out a chair for her. "You want some coffee? It's pretty terrible. I made it."

"Based on that recommendation, I think I'll pass. Could you dredge up any milk?"

"Absolutely," he said, glad of the chance to escape for a minute and decide just how much he was willing to reveal to Dana. The girl was compassionate, but he had no business burdening her with his problems, especially not a doozy like this one.

By the time he'd poured the milk and returned to the dining room, Dana had pulled the drapes aside and opened the French doors to let a breeze in.

"I hope you don't mind. It was pretty dreary in here," she said. "No wonder you're depressed. You're not getting any oxygen."

"My state doesn't have a thing to do with the lack of air circulating in this house."

"Then what is the problem? You look like hell, by the way. I never knew you even owned a pair of blue jeans, much less a shirt quite that color. What happened? Did you wash the whites and colors together?"

He scowled at her. "Thanks. It's so nice to have someone drop by to cheer me up."

"I can't cheer you up until you give me something to work with. What went wrong between you and Elizabeth?"

"Now you're going straight for the jugular."

"Did you want me to waltz around it instead?"

"Maybe just a quiet fox-trot around the edges would have done."

"Hey, I'm easy. We could discuss the weather, but we'll get back to this eventually, anyway."

Brandon sighed heavily and shoved his hand through his hair. "I suppose you're going to push and nag until I spill it, aren't you?"

She nodded cheerfully. "That's the plan."

"How much do you know?"

"Not a thing, except that you're upset and, if anything, Kevin's in a worse state."

"He didn't tell you why?"

"Only that he hired that detective and got a report that shook him up. He was convinced you'd be devastated by it."

"He's got that right."

Dana's expression immediately turned sympathetic and the teasing note vanished from her voice. "Did Elizabeth tell you whatever it is herself, or did you find out some other way?"

"No. She told me. She hadn't meant to, but I was pressing her to get married and telling her what a wonderful woman she was and suddenly it all came pouring out, like a dam had burst. I guess I'm the only one outside of her parents who knows the whole story. They're not alive to tell."

"The whole story is?" Dana prodded.

When he remained silent and indecisive, she picked up his hand and held it. "You know how much I owe you. If it weren't for you, Jason and I might not be together. I owe you, Brandon. More than that, I love you every bit as much as if you were my own grandfather. If I can help you in any way, I want to."

He felt the sting of tears in his eyes and turned away. He didn't want her seeing how emotional he was these days, how much it pleased him that she considered him family. Then he thought of all those other grandchildren he'd never even met and his heart began to ache all over again.

As much as he wanted someone to confide in, though, as much as he knew Dana wanted to help, he realized that he couldn't share this with her. He might be angry with Lizzy at the moment, he might even be tossing around the notion of going to California to claim his daughter, but until he'd resolved once and for all the best course of action, he couldn't involve other people. He was grateful that discretion had kept Kevin from doing otherwise, as well. One day soon he and his son would have to have a long talk. He could only pray Kevin would forgive him for the delay.

There was no doubt in his mind that the report Kevin had gotten contained the truth—or a goodly portion of it, quite enough to raise a ruckus. A good detective, one smart enough to have traced Lizzy in the first place, would surely have been able to discover the rest, even if it had been no more than the information that she'd had a child out of wedlock. Brandon might be the only one, other than Lizzy herself, who'd been able to fill in the remaining details.

He hoped Kevin hadn't guessed anymore than that.

If he had, he was likely to be every bit as tormented by the discovery he had a half sister as Brandon was to learn he had a daughter.

None of this was going to be resolved by him staying shut up in this house, though. The only way to deal with this was the same way he would deal with a business crisis, straight on.

And that meant going to California.

"Dana, why don't you get on the phone and call the travel agent, while I pack my bags?"

Her expression brightened. "You're going to California?"

"On the first available flight."

"Will you and Elizabeth try to work things out?"

"I'm not sure that's possible, child. But I do know that sitting around here struggling with things on my own hasn't accomplished a blessed thing."

Dana drove him to the airport and insisted on going inside to see him off. When his flight was called, she hugged him as tightly as she could, given the swollen state of her tummy.

"Do whatever it takes to be happy," she murmured. "Promise me that."

"I promise."

"Even if it means eating a little crow?"

Just the thought of trying to put all this behind him and mending fences with Lizzy seemed impossible at the moment, but Brandon looked at Dana's hopeful expression and knew he couldn't tell her that.

"We'll see," he said. It was the best he could do.

Chapter Fifteen

Despite what he'd implied to Dana, Brandon had absolutely no idea where he planned to go when he arrived in Los Angeles. He had an entire flight to think about it.

He decided finally—sometime between the awful meal and the even worse movie—that he had no choice but to see Lizzy first. There were things to be resolved between the two of them before he could begin to consider what to do about Ellen.

He realized something else on that long flight. This situation he and Lizzy found themselves in was just one more test. He'd faced an abundance of them throughout his life, and more than once he'd come up wanting.

Most had been relatively insignificant, until the one with Kevin had come along many years ago. When his son had refused to join Halloran Industries, when he'd chosen Lacey despite Brandon's objections, Brandon hadn't taken it well. He'd held himself aloof, unable to forgive what he saw as rejection, impatient with himself for his inability to sway his son's decisions.

It had taken him a long time to see that patience and forgiveness were more important than pride, that a relationship with his son at any cost was worth more than the satisfaction of seeing Kevin working at a job of his father's choosing or marrying a bride who was his father's choice.

Now, half a lifetime later, he was faced with another dilemma involving forgiveness. If he'd learned nothing else over these past lonely weeks locked away in his house, it was that he missed Lizzy desperately. Until the end in Taos, he'd experienced a rare contentment in his life again, and there was no question that she was responsible. More than passion, more than memories, she'd given him back his zest for living. The old magic had mellowed into vintage fulfillment.

And she had given him a daughter. She might have made mistakes in the delay in telling him the truth, but she'd made them out of love for her daughter, not out of any intent to hurt him.

He had a choice now. He could forgive her and struggle to grab whatever years of joy they might share. Or he could allow foolish pride and misguided anger to force him into a life of loneliness and regrets. Pride and anger wouldn't keep his bed warm at night. They surely wouldn't provide much companionship.

Brandon thought of the sadness in Lizzy's eyes the last time he'd seen her and regretted, more than he could say, his responsibility for it being there. Forgiveness might not come easily, but it was the only choice he had. He could only pray that she was as ready to forgive him for his hasty condemnation of her.

Almost as soon as the decision was made, he felt his heart lighten. The dull ache in his chest eased as if his choice had received some sort of divine benediction.

At the airport he considered calling, then worried that the warning would only make Lizzy panic. Instead he rented a car and drove on the crowded highway as if he were in an Indy 500 time trial.

Parked at last along the curb in front of her house, he drew in a deep breath, praying for the courage it would take to make all of this come out right. He saw the curtains separate, then fall back into place and envisioned her reaction to seeing him outside.

He walked slowly up the flagstone walk, then rang the bell. When Lizzy finally opened her front door, he felt his heart climb into his throat. She looked miserable and frightened. Her hand gripped the door as if she felt the need for something to steady her. And yet there was that familiar spark in her eyes, that hint of mother-hen protectiveness and daring.

''Brandon,'' she said after an endless hesitation. Then as if she couldn't manage any more, she fell silent, her gaze locked with his. Time ticked slowly past as each of them measured their reactions.

''Hello, Lizzy. We have to talk.''

She nodded and let him in, closing the door softly behind him.

''Would you like something? Coffee? Tea?''

''No. Nothing.''

She gestured toward a chair, then stood framed by

the archway into the dining room as if she wanted to be in a position to flee. Suddenly Brandon saw himself as an ogre and regretted more than he could say that it had come to this between them.

"Sit down, Lizzy. I'm not planning to take your head off."

"Why are you here?" she asked warily.

"I'm not sure entirely. I just knew that all the answers I needed were here, not in Boston. I had to come."

He finally dared to meet her gaze. "I missed you, Lizzy. It's odd, but the more I thought about this, the more I wanted someone to talk to. Not until today did I realize that that someone had to be you."

Her shoulders eased some, then, and she finally sat down. "Brandon, I never meant to hurt you like this. Never."

"I know. You said it before, but I don't think I really believed it until I did some soul-searching on the flight out here. I've never been much good at forgiveness, Lizzy. Maybe when you've grown up with power and self-confidence, you start thinking that things will always go your way, that you never need to bend. I learned differently with Kevin, when we were estranged for all those years, but apparently I forgot the lesson again until you came along to test me." He regarded her evenly. "Do you understand what I'm trying to say?"

"I'm not sure, Brandon."

"I think maybe you do but you want me to spell it out. I suppose that's only fair, since I suspect my actions have put you through hell these past couple of weeks." He drew in a deep breath. "I want you to know that I forgive you for keeping the truth from me.

It wasn't my place to criticize choices you made to protect your daughter and I apologize for that. And I'd like to ask your forgiveness for the way I bungled things when you told me.''

Lizzy's eyes filled with tears. ''Oh, Brandon, thank you. Does that mean you've changed your mind about keeping the secret? Will you go back to Boston and forget all about us?''

He shook his head. ''I'm afraid that's the one thing I can't do,'' he said. ''I can't force myself a second time to try to forget you. And the only way you and I can possibly have the future we deserve is to tell Ellen the truth.'' As soon as he said the words, he realized that it was what he'd known in his heart from the first.

''No,'' she said, her expression crumbling. ''Oh, Brandon, how can you say you love me and ask me to do that?''

''Because now that you know I'm alive, now that you know that I never stopped caring for you, you will never know a moment's peace if you try to go on living with the lie. That's not the kind of woman you are, Lizzy, any more than it's the kind of man I am. The only thing left to resolve is whether you'll tell your daughter everything alone or whether I will be there with you.''

''You make it sound so easy, but then what, Brandon?'' she demanded angrily. ''Who will pick up the pieces?''

''We'll do that together.''

''And what if I can't forgive you?''

''You will,'' he said confidently. ''In time.''

She closed her eyes, as if that would block out the

pain, but he could tell from the tears tracking down her cheeks that she was still desperately afraid.

"Lizzy, I will be with you in this," he reassured her. "Together don't you think we have the strength to weather just about anything?"

"There's no way I can make you change your mind, is there?" she asked slowly, her tone resigned.

"No."

"Then I will tell her, Brandon. Alone."

He nodded. "If that's the way you want it. Shall I wait for you here?"

"No. I think I'll ask her to come here so we can be sure of some privacy."

"Then I'll go for a drive. I won't come back until I see that her car is gone."

He crossed the room and hunkered down in front of her, despite the sharp pain that shot through his poor old arthritic knees when he did it. He tilted her chin up with the tip of his finger, forcing her to meet his gaze.

"It's the only way, Lizzy. Whether I go or stay, it's the only way you'll be able to live with yourself."

She clasped his hand then. After a full minute while his hand slowly warmed hers, she seemed to gather her strength.

"Please don't go far, Brandon. I have a feeling I'm going to need you more tonight than I've ever needed anyone before in my life."

It was good that Brandon had forced her hand, Elizabeth told herself over and over as she sat with the phone cradled in her lap, willing herself to have the courage to dial. Only the certain knowledge that Brandon would be back in an hour or two or three forced her hand.

''Ellen,'' she said when her daughter finally answered.

''Mother, what's wrong?'' Ellen asked at once. ''Are you okay? You sound as if you've been crying.''

''I'm fine, dear, but I would appreciate it if you could stop by.''

''When? Now?''

''Yes, if it isn't inconvenient.''

''I'll be right there,'' she said briskly, as if she'd guessed the urgency without her mother expressing it in words. Elizabeth made tea while she waited. A whole pot brimming with chamomile, which was supposed to calm the nerves. Then she couldn't even bring the cup to her lips, because her hands were shaking so badly.

It took Ellen barely fifteen minutes to get there, a miracle by L.A. standards.

''Mother, what's wrong?'' she was asking even before she was inside the door.

Elizabeth kept a tight rein on her panic. Forcing herself to remain calm for Ellen's sake was the only thing keeping her steady at all. She studied her beautiful daughter's anxious expression, her troubled blue eyes and wished that this moment were past, that the truth was behind them and they were starting to rebuild their relationship.

''Mother,'' Ellen said again. ''I'm starting to worry. Something must be terribly wrong.''

''Sit down, darling. We have to talk.'' She reached behind her neck and unclasped the locket she hadn't taken off for weeks now. She took Ellen's hand and allowed the delicate gold chain to pool in her palm.

"Why are you giving me this?"

"I want you to open it and take a good look at the man inside."

"But why? I already know it's Brandon Halloran."

"Look again, darling. Even if you had never met Brandon, wouldn't he look familiar?"

Ellen studied the tiny photograph, then looked up, her expression puzzled. "I don't understand."

"You should recognize the eyes, darling. They're just like yours."

Ellen's expression was thunderstruck as she looked from her mother to the locket and back again. "What are you saying?" she asked finally in a voice that was barely more than a horrified whisper.

Elizabeth thought of the strong, caring man who was waiting somewhere out in the night and wished for just a little of his courage, just a little of his conviction that he could make anything turn out right.

"Brandon Halloran is your father."

The locket slid through Ellen's fingers and fell to the floor. "No," she said, oblivious to it. "I don't believe you."

"It's true, darling. Your father—that is, David—and I decided that you should never know. Maybe we were wrong, but there seemed to be no point in dredging up ancient history, especially when it seemed unlikely that Brandon would ever turn up here."

"You mean Dad knew all along?"

Elizabeth nodded, worried by her daughter's pale complexion. "You were just a baby when we married," she explained. "He could never have loved you more if you had been his own flesh and blood. He was so proud of you, so proud of being your father. And he was, Ellen. He was your father in every way that counted.''

''But you lied to me, Mother. Both of you lied to me. Didn't you think I had a right to know? Maybe it would have helped me to understand why Kate and I are so different. Maybe it would have helped me to understand why she and Dad were always closer than he and I were.''

''That's not true,'' Elizabeth said, shocked. ''He loved you both.'' But even as she said it, she knew it wasn't true. He hadn't loved them equally. There had been a special bond between him and Kate, though he had done everything in his power to deny it. And her darling Ellen had recognized that bond and hurt for all these years because of it.

''Oh, darling, I'm sorry. I never knew how you felt. You never let on.'' She couldn't console her by explaining that Ellen was the child she had connected with—because she was the link to her lost lover.

''I suppose I never wanted to admit it out loud.'' She stood up then, picked up her purse and started for the door.

''Where are you going?'' Elizabeth asked anxiously. ''You must have questions.''

''I do, but I can't deal with them right now. I have to figure out who I am.'' She glanced back. ''Did Brandon Halloran know he was my father?''

''No. He never knew I was pregnant. Darling, none of this is his fault. Will you be back?'' Elizabeth said, following her down the walk to her car.

Ellen turned toward her briefly, the tears on her cheeks glistening in the glow of the streetlight. ''I don't know. It seems I don't know anything anymore.''

Then, with her heart breaking apart inside, Elizabeth watched as her precious daughter drove away.

Elizabeth was still standing there, her arms wrapped tightly around herself as if she were trying to hold herself together, when Brandon came back. He emerged from his car and walked slowly to where she stood. He slid his arms around her and pulled her against his chest, where she could hear the steady, reassuring beat of his heart.

And for one brief moment she tried to imagine that she was safe in a place where nothing would ever hurt her so deeply again.

Brandon had grown tired of waiting, tired of watching Elizabeth grow increasingly pale, increasingly anxious as her daughter continued to avoid her day after day. Though Kate called regularly, oblivious to the undercurrents that were tearing her family apart, it wasn't Kate whom Lizzy longed for. She needed to hear Ellen's voice. More, she needed Ellen's forgiveness.

"Lizzy, I think I'll go out for a while," he said a week after he'd arrived in Los Angeles.

She barely spared him a glance.

"Is there anything you'd like me to pick up from the store?"

"No, nothing."

He dropped a kiss on her forehead. "I'll see you soon then."

He climbed into his rental car and drove straight to Ellen's. She might slam the door in his face, but that would be better by a long shot than this silence that was destroying them all.

When Ellen opened the door and recognized him, her eyes widened in dismay. "Why are you here?"

"I think you know the answer to that," he said quietly. "May I come in?"

Too well-bred to deny him, she stepped aside, and he found himself once again in the house where he'd come for Lizzy just a few short weeks back. It seemed as if that had been a lifetime ago.

Ellen followed him into the living room and stood nervously by as he chose a seat on the sofa. She kept sneaking curious glances at him, as if she weren't quite willing for him to know how badly she wanted to reconcile the man she had met so recently with the abstract title of father that she had thought belonged to another man.

He tried to imagine how Kevin would feel if some woman appeared after all these years and stripped him of everything in which he'd believed. Kevin was having difficulty enough simply accepting that there was a woman in Brandon's life who meant as much to his father as Grace Halloran had, a woman who'd preceded Kevin's mother in Brandon's affections.

"I think I have some idea of what you must be feeling," Brandon told Ellen finally.

"Do you? Then you're better off than I am. All I feel is numb. I keep trying to fit all the pieces together, but it never comes together right. My father, the man I've always known as my father, no longer fits. In his place there's this stranger. Worse, my mother never told me, never even hinted at it."

"So you feel as though your whole life has been a lie?"

"I suppose."

"In a way that's very much what I'm feeling. You

see in my picture, there is a woman who looks nothing like your mother and there is a son. Later there's even a grandson. But there is no daughter. All of a sudden, I discover there is this beautiful woman who carries my blood in her veins. But try as I might, I can't make her fit in, either.''

He regarded her steadily then, until she met his gaze and held it. ''I want to, Ellen. I want more than anything to get to know my daughter, to become a part of her life. I don't expect that to happen overnight, but if we took it slowly, don't you think we might create a whole new family portrait?''

Her gaze slid away from his. Her lower lip trembled. ''My mother says she loved you very much,'' she said in a low voice that begged him to confirm it.

''And I loved her with all my heart. You are the blessing of that love, Ellen. Don't ever believe anything less.''

She blinked away fresh tears. ''All my life I was told there was no sin worse than lying. The two people who told me that carried out the biggest lie of all.''

''Why?'' he said. ''Why do you think they did that?''

She was silent for what seemed an eternity before she finally said, ''I want to believe they did it out of love, not fear.''

''Then believe that, because it's the truth.''

''I can't.''

''Why not?''

''Then I would have to forgive them,'' she said in a small voice, ''and it still hurts too much to do that.''

''Ah, Ellen,'' he said with a rueful sigh. ''Let me tell you something I've only recently discovered about forgiveness. It's when it's needed the most that it becomes the hardest to give. You will never be happy until you forgive your mother, your father, even me.''

''Why you?''

''Because I set it all in motion by searching for your mother. If I hadn't, you would never have known. Would that have been better?''

She hesitated, then finally admitted, ''No. I think, if I give it some time, it might turn out that I'm luckier than anyone to have had the love of two fathers.''

Brandon knew then that though it would take time for Ellen to accept him into her life, it would be all right. The healing really had begun. ''Do you think you could tell your mother that?''

''Now?''

He nodded. ''I think it's the only way I'll ever convince her to marry me.''

A smile crept over her lips. ''Better late than never, I always say,'' she said with more spirit. ''Just let me fix my face.''

''Your face is lovely just as it is.''

''Only a father would say that,'' she said, then caught herself. Her smile broadened. ''How about that? I can actually begin to laugh again. By the way, am I the only thing standing between the two of you?''

''Not the only thing,'' he conceded. ''Just the most important.''

''What else stands in the way? I knew weeks ago you loved each other.''

''Time. Too much water under the bridge. Stubbornness.''

''Yours or hers?'' she asked slyly.

Brandon could tell his daughter had Lizzy's spunk from the twinkle in her eyes. ''Maybe some of each.''

Before Ellen could offer any advice, the front door

slammed open and Lizzy stood there, her expression wary. ‘‘Brandon,’’ she said worriedly. ‘‘You didn’t say you were coming here.’’

‘‘Ellen and I were just getting to know each other,’’ he said.

Elizabeth cast an anxious glance at her daughter. ‘‘Is everything okay?’’

Ellen hesitated, her expression indecisive. Then, after a glance at Brandon, she moved slowly toward her mother and put her arms around her. ‘‘Not quite yet,’’ she said with the kind of honesty Brandon had come to respect. ‘‘But it will be. I’m sorry for shutting you out. I needed time to sort things out for myself.’’

‘‘You had a right to be angry.’’

‘‘Maybe. Maybe not.’’ She glanced at Brandon. ‘‘It was…it was Father who made me see the light.’’

Lizzy turned to him, tears glistening in her eyes. ‘‘Thank you,’’ she mouthed as she held her daughter.

Ellen gave her one last squeeze, then shot a pointed look at Brandon. ‘‘I think I’ll leave you two alone now,’’ she said. ‘‘There’s tea in the kitchen, if you want some, Mother.’’

When she had gone, Lizzy crossed the room to him. ‘‘You worked a miracle here this afternoon.’’

He shook his head. ‘‘No, Lizzy, the miracle is you and me. We’ve got our second chance. I don’t plan to let it pass us by. How about you?’’

A smile spread across her face and her eyes lit with sparks of pure mischief. ‘‘You knew all along you’d have your way this time, didn’t you?’’

‘‘Of course,’’ he said. ‘‘You never could resist a story with a happy ending, could you?’’

‘‘Brandon, how will I be able to thank you?’’

‘‘By marrying me, Lizzy. By letting me become a

part of your family, just as you'll become a part of mine.''

She squeezed his hand. ''I do love you, Brandon Halloran. I always have.''

''And I you, my love. And I you.''

''It won't be easy, you know. Kate and your family still have to be told.''

''I think Kevin already knows, at least some of it. He may have guessed the rest.''

''Then don't you think you should call him? He must have a thousand questions.''

''I can't call, not about something as important as this. I'll stay here until you've had time to make things right with both your daughters, then we'll go to Boston together. I figure we can manage a June wedding, don't you?''

''Brandon, June is just around the corner.''

He grinned at her stunned expression. ''Then I'd say you'd better get a move on, woman.''

Epilogue

"Ohmigosh," Dana murmured just as Brandon was about to cut the tiered wedding cake that was decorated with a frothy confection of white frosting and pink rosebuds.

"Sis?" Sammy said, an expression of alarm on his face as she clutched her belly.

Brandon heard the mix of anxiety and surprise in Dana's voice and immediately dropped the sterling silver cake knife. He shot her a look of pure delight. "Now?"

A grin split her face. "Now," she confirmed. "This great-grandchild of yours is definitely coming."

"By golly, I knew this was going to be a day to remember," Brandon said and started giving orders. "Jason, get the car. Kevin, you tell the guests they'll have to excuse us."

Dana looked him straight in the eye. ''Don't you dare ruin this reception on my account.''

''Ruin it! Hell, girl, this is the best thing that could have happened. Now I'll be able to leave on my honeymoon without worrying about missing the big event.''

Forgetting that he'd just given the assignment to Kevin, he grabbed the microphone from the bandleader in mid-song and called for silence. ''Well, folks, I guess you all know we wanted you with us on this special day because we care about you. It's a mighty big blessing to have so many friends and family around us on a day when we celebrate the true meaning of the wedding vows. There's been a little hitch in our schedule, though. I'm afraid you're going to have to excuse us. We've got a baby to deliver.''

As a murmur of excitement spread through the room, he again asked for quiet. ''While we get ourselves to the hospital, I hope you'll all stay here and enjoy yourselves and drink a toast to the newest Halloran, our fourth generation.''

At the hospital it was difficult to tell who was more impatient—Brandon, Kevin or Sammy. They paced the waiting room, while Elizabeth and Lacey exchanged looks of amusement. Ellen and Kate hovered nearby, still awkward around their new family but clearly wanting to be a part of this special moment.

''Why the devil don't they tell us something?'' Brandon grumbled.

''First babies generally take their own sweet time,'' Elizabeth reminded him. ''I'm sure they'll let us know when there's anything to tell us. Why don't we go have a nice cup of tea to settle your nerves?''

"A stiff scotch couldn't settle my nerves," he said. "I don't recall it taking this long for Kevin or Jason to come into this world."

"Probably because you were at work on both occasions," Kevin reminded him dryly. "Maybe you and Elizabeth should leave before you miss your plane."

"Not on your life." He stared down the corridor toward the delivery room. "Maybe I could get one of those gowns and just take a peek inside to see what's happening."

"Bad idea," Kevin said. "This is Jason's big day. There's no need for you to intrude."

"How would I be intruding? It's my great-grandbaby."

"Which puts you two generations away from the right to be in there," his son reminded him with a grin that had been a long time coming.

Though Kevin had taken the events of the past few weeks far better than Brandon had anticipated, it hadn't been easy. Once Kevin had been told the whole story, he'd swallowed any criticisms he might have had of his father or Elizabeth. He had not welcomed his new step mother as wholeheartedly as Brandon might have liked, but there had been no overt resentment. Brandon suspected he could thank Lacey and Dana for that, just as he owed them for making both Ellen and Kate feel welcome under difficult circumstances. He was proud of all of them for trying to put the past behind them.

It had been most difficult of all for Kate, he suspected. She alone had no blood ties to her new family. But she was strong and independent, and a damned sight too cynical about romance from what he'd seen.

Whatever hurts she'd suffered, it was time she let them go. She needed a new man in her life to spark things up. He might look around among the up-and-coming young men in Boston and see to that himself, once he and Lizzy got back from their honeymoon.

"Lizzy, have you seen the doctor?" he asked worriedly. "I didn't see him go in. Who ever heard of delivering a baby without a doctor?"

"The doctor probably slipped in the back way just to avoid you and all your last-minute instructions," Lacey teased.

Sammy sidled up to him. "Come on, Grandpa Brandon. Let's go get some cigars."

"I suppose we could," he said with a last grudging glance down the hall. He looked at Elizabeth. "You suppose there's time?"

"More than likely," she told him.

"What's that mean?"

"It means I can't guarantee it," she said.

"Then I'm not budging. What do you suppose they'll name him? Did they tell anybody?"

"Not me," Sammy said. "I've been bugging Dana for weeks, but she wouldn't say a word."

"You seem awfully certain it's going to be a boy," Elizabeth said. "Last I heard girls were a possibility as well."

Brandon shot Lizzy a pleased look, then gazed for a moment at his new daughter. "I guess they are at that," he said, just as a nurse came out of the delivery room and started toward them.

"You're all here with Dana and Jason Halloran?" she asked.

"Yes," Brandon said. "Everything's okay in there, isn't it?"

''Everything is just fine. If you'd like, you can come with me. Dana and Jason want you to see your new grandchild.''

Brandon was the first one down the hall. This great-grandbaby of his was going to have a fine life. He'd personally guarantee that. He fumbled with the ties on the gown he'd been given, then struggled with the mask. He seemed to be all thumbs. He felt Elizabeth's fingers nudging his aside, then her sure touch at the fastenings.

Then the nurse was opening the door to Dana's private room. Brandon stepped inside, his gaze going at once toward Dana and his grandson. Jason was holding a tiny bundle cradled in his arms.

As they stepped closer, he could see Dana's radiant face and felt as though his own heart would fill to bursting with sheer joy at having a new little Halloran born on this day that would always be special to all of them.

''Dad, Granddad, Mom, Elizabeth, and Sammy,'' Jason said slowly, beaming with pride. His glance included Ellen and Kate, though he didn't mention their names. ''I'd like you to meet our daughter.''

''Oh, my,'' Lacey said softly, taking Dana's hand and squeezing it. ''A girl. Darling, that's wonderful.''

Dana looked at each one of them, then said, ''If you don't mind, we'd like to name her Elizabeth Lacey Halloran... We'll call her Beth.''

Brandon watched as his new bride and his beloved daughter-in-law exchanged a misty-eyed look. Truth be told, his own eyes seemed to be stinging just a bit.

''I would be honored,'' Lizzy said.

''So would I,'' Lacey added.

Elizabeth Lacey Halloran, Brandon thought with a

sigh as he gazed into that tiny, precious face. A new generation, named for the old and made strong by their love.

Indeed, he thought, as he took Elizabeth's hand in his, the best was yet to come.

* * * * *

Come join Sherryl Woods as
she continues her popular

AND BABY MAKES THREE:
THE DELACOURTS OF TEXAS

miniseries this July in Silhouette Special Edition.
This time Jeb Delacourt has met his match in the
mysterious beauty Brianna O'Ryan.
For a sneak preview of

THE PINT-SIZED SECRET (SE #1333),

please turn the page.

Jeb was a big believer in the direct approach, especially when it came to his social life. There were plenty of people in Houston who thought of him as a scoundrel, nothing more than a rich playboy who thought he had a right to use women, but the truth was actually very different.

For all his carefree ways, he felt things deeply. Once he had wanted nothing more than to marry and have a family, but now he doubted he ever would. He wasn't sure that he'd ever trust a woman deeply enough to risk his heart. He'd made a decision to keep his relationships casual and his intentions direct. There would be no promises of happily ever after, not on his part anyway. He couldn't see himself getting past his now ingrained suspicions. Of course, Dylan and Trish had felt exactly the same way before they'd met their current matches. Given the family track record, it probably would be wise to never say never, but he knew himself well enough to say it with conviction.

In the meantime, there was Brianna. The very beautiful, very brilliant Brianna. There was no question of falling for her. He already had very valid reasons for distrusting her. Getting close to her would be a little like going into a foreign country with all the necessary inoculations very much up-to-date. That didn't mean he couldn't appreciate the journey.

After a restless night during which he considered, then again dismissed, his father's warning to steer clear of the geologist, Jeb concluded that the simplest way to discover just what kind of person Brianna was would be to ask her out, get to know her outside the office, see what her life-style was like and if there was any chance she might be spending income that outdistanced her Delacourt Oil salary.

He knew she was single. Divorced, according to the rumor mill, though no one seemed to know much about the circumstances. He also knew she'd turned down dates with half a dozen of their colleagues. Her social life—if she had one—was a mystery. He considered such discretion to be admirable, as well as wise. He also considered it a challenge.

And that was what brought him to the fourth floor at Delacourt Oil just after seven in the morning. Although he knew very little about Brianna's habits, he did know that she was an early riser. A morning person himself, on several occasions he'd spotted her car already in the parking lot when he arrived. Obviously neither of them had the sort of exciting night life that others probably thought they did.

As he walked toward her office, Jeb wasn't the least bit surprised to find Brianna's lights on and her head bent over a huge geological map spread across her desk. Her computer was booted up, and all sorts of mysterious calculations were on the screen.

Since she was totally absorbed, he took a moment simply to stand there and appreciate the auburn highlights in her no muss, no fuss short hair. If her hairstyle was almost boyish, the graceful curve of her neck was contrastingly feminine. She was wearing an outfit with simple lines, in natural fabrics—linen and silk.

''Find anything interesting?'' he asked eventually, trying to tame hormones that seemed inclined to run amok at the mere sight of her.

Her head shot up, and startled blue-green eyes stared at him guiltily...or so he thought. Was she trying to pinpoint a new site she could pass on to the competition? When she made no attempt to hide the map, he told himself he was being ridiculous. Any investigator worth the title should think more rationally and behave more objectively than he was at this moment. So far, he had suspicions and coincidence and not much else, yet he'd already all but tried and convicted her.

''You,'' she said as if he were a particularly annoying interruption, despite the fact that they probably hadn't exchanged more than a few dozen words since she'd been hired.

''Now is that any way to greet a man who's come bearing coffee and pastry?''

''No thanks,'' she said, pointedly going back to her study of the map.

Ignoring the blatant dismissal, Jeb crossed the room and perched on the corner of her desk, close enough to be impossible for her to ignore. He opened the bag he'd brought, removed two cups of coffee and two warm cheese danishes. He wafted first one,. Then the other, under her nose. Though she didn't look up, there was no mistaking her subtle sniff of the aroma.

"Tempting, aren't they?"

She heaved a resigned sigh, then sat back. "You're not going to go away, are you?"

Despite the exasperation in her tone, there was a faint hint of a smile on her lips.

He beamed at her. "Nope." He held out the coffee. She accepted it with exaggerated reluctance, then took a quick sip, then another slow, appreciative swallow.

"You didn't get this here," she said. "Not even the executive dining room makes coffee like this."

"Nope. I made a stop at a bakery."

She regarded him warily. "Why?"

"No special reason."

"Of course not," she said with blatant skepticism. "This is something you make a habit of doing for everyone around here. Sort of an executive welcome, a way to let the troops know that management cares. Today just happens to be my turn."

"Exactly."

Her unflinching gaze met his. "Bull, Mr. Delacourt."

Startled by the direct hit, he laughed. This was going to be more fun than he'd anticipated. "You don't mince words, do you, Mrs. O'Ryan?"

"Not enough time in the day as it is. Why waste it searching for polite phrases when the direct approach is quicker?"

"A woman after my own heart," Jeb concluded. "Okay, then, I'll be direct, too. I have a charity ball to attend on Friday. It's for a good cause. The food and wine promise to be excellent. How about going with me?"

"Thanks, but no thanks."

Vaguely insulted by the quick, unequivocal—if not unexpected—refusal, Jeb pulled out his trump card. "Max Coleman will be there," he said innocently, watching closely for a reaction. Other than a slight narrowing of her lips, there was nothing to give away the fact that the name meant anything at all to her. He pressed harder. "Might be interesting to see how he reacts to just how well you're doing at Delacourt Oil, don't you think?"

"Max Coleman is slime," she said at once. "I don't care what he thinks."

"Sure you do, sweetheart. It wouldn't be human not to want a little revenge against the man who fired you." He let his gaze travel slowly over her, waited until he saw the color rise in her cheeks before adding, "You look very human to me." He winked. "Pick you up at six-thirty."

He headed for the door, anticipating all the way that she might contradict him, might refuse even more emphatically, even though he knew he'd found her Achilles' heel.

Instead, she said softly, "Formal?"

He turned back, feigning confusion, "What was that?"

She frowned at him. "I asked if it was formal?"

"Definitely black tie," he said. "Wear something sexy. You'll bring him to his knees."

"Could be. I guess we'll just have to wait and see." To his sincere regret, in the last couple of minutes he'd discovered it was definitely possible. That alone should have been warning enough to induce him to abandon his investigation before it went wildly awry. Instead, it merely increased his anticipation.